THE ILLUSIONIST

By the same Author
BETHANY

THE ILLUSIONIST

a novel by

Anita Mason

HAMISH HAMILTON LONDON

The author gratefully acknowledges the
financial assistance of South West Arts.

Unless ye make the things of the right hand as those of the
left, and those of the left as those of the right, and those that
are above as those below, and those that are behind as those that
are before, ye shall not have knowledge of the kingdom.

The Acts of Peter

First published in Great Britain 1983
by Hamish Hamilton Ltd.
Garden House 57–59 Long Acre London WC2 9JZ
Copyright © 1983 by Anita Mason

British Library Cataloguing in Publication Data
Mason, Anita
   The illusionist.
   I. Title
   813'.54[F]   PS3563.A7874
ISBN 0-241-10973-6

Printed in Great Britain by
St Edmundsbury Press, Bury St Edmunds, Suffolk

I

THE SATYR

The man stood on a rooftop and faced the rising sun.

'First beginning of my beginning ...'

He spoke quietly, as if to himself.

'First source of my source, spirit's spirit, fire ...'

His linen sleeves fluttered lightly in the wind blowing in from the Great Sea.

'Perfect body of me, moulded by a hand incorruptible in a world devoid of light ...'

The crowd jostled and pointed in the street below. He was not aware of them. He was entirely focused in his will. His voice, no longer consciously directed by him, rose in a chant. He chanted to the hawk of the sun.

'May it be right that I, though mortal born of mortal womb, shall in this flesh ascend, through the strength of the immortal spirit in me, borne up by an almighty arm ...'

The will, as it drew tauter, passed beyond supplication. His voice rang out in challenge.

'For I am the Son, I surpass the limit of my souls, I am ...'

He paused. Into the pure drop of silence he pronounced the name of God.

He stepped forward and upward, like a man ascending a stair-case, but on air.

He flew.

In another age it would not be thought miraculous: all men could fly, but they did not know it. Meanwhile, he was the first.

He used his faculty only when it was necessary for purposes of demonstration, and never for personal enjoyment. This was for two reasons. Firstly, he knew that power was likely to be withdrawn if abused. Secondly, the mental preparation was very tiring and it was necessary to fast for twenty-four hours beforehand. Perhaps there was a third reason. Sometimes as he flew he was afraid that he might fall. This feeling was always associated with a certain face half-glimpsed among the spectators: a face which, turned upward like the rest, seemed to look not at him but at something beyond and above him, with a look of strange intent. On closer scrutiny this face had always vanished. He did not pursue the image. The face was curiously like his own.

He lay on his bed, too tired to move. The shouting crowd had long since been dispersed by the soldiers, and the house rested in the still afternoon heat. A few faint sounds disturbed the quietness: a distant clatter from the bazaar, the splash of the fountains in the public square, the yelp of a scavenging dog driven off with a stone. The man lying on the bed did not hear these sounds, or notice that the steady north-west wind that brought them also lifted, so that they rustled pleasantly, the silk wall-hangings in the room. He was listening to a sound in his head. It was intermittent, now rising, now falling, but never wholly absent. As soon as he thought it had stopped it began again. It was a roar, sometimes of many voices, sometimes of one. The roar was a single word, endlessly repeated. It was his name.

'Simon. Simon.'

He groaned in a wave of nausea and twisted his head into the pillow. The room lifted a little, as if stepping into space.

It would pass. It was always like this after he had made a great effort: he felt as if the blood had been drained out of him and his veins filled with some thin and poisonous substance, like stagnant water.

'Simon. Simon.'

The sun danced in his head, assuming strange forms.

Why was it always like this? The weakness was like a curse. When it came on him he could see no way back from the desolation. Sometimes he thought his powers were themselves a curse. Perhaps it was all an enormous joke he was not intended to understand.

It would pass. A drink of wine might help. With difficulty he raised himself on his elbow to call Demetrius, then remembered that the boy was out. He had ordered everyone, including the widow's servants, to leave the house for the afternoon so that he would be undisturbed. He fell back on his pillow. They need not have obeyed him so literally. He closed his eyes, and felt the room sway over the abyss again.

When he awoke the air had freshened, and the shadow of the plane tree in the courtyard had crept half-way across the mosaic floor. There was a clatter of carts in the street, and a muffled din of business from the bazaar. He lay and listened.

'Simon.'

He shuddered. Demetrius came forward and held his master's head in cool hands.

'Ah, it's you', said Simon. His relief turned to petulance. 'I wanted you earlier, but you were out.'

'You sent me out,' said Demetrius.

4

'You needn't have been gone so long.'

Demetrius waited.

'Bring me some wine', said Simon, and then, as the boy turned to go, 'No, not yet. Come here.'

Demetrius looked down at him with unfathomable eyes. Simon studied them for a moment. He would never know what the boy was thinking. Sometimes it did not matter.

'Lie down', he said softly.

Demetrius lay down. His skin was silky, his breath sweet from honey-cakes, and his hair smelt of incense.

Simon touched the curly hair.

'Where did you go?'

'To the temple,' said Demetrius.

Simon smiled. For a time he half-slept. He began to feel better.

In those days there was great uncertainty, and marvels were commonplace but seldom useful. No one knew what to believe, so some people believed everything and some nothing at all. It was a country whose history was its religion, and its history was becoming steadily more difficult to decipher. Meaning seemed attached exclusively to past and future, never present. For generations the present had been an ante-room for a future that never came.

Wars came instead. The people were killed, deported and enslaved. The temple was desecrated with miserable regularity. Eventually, when continual warfare was replaced by subjugation to a large and indifferent empire, many people were relieved. Not all. There were always a few proud spirits who could not forget their god's promises of universal dominion, and impatiently took up arms on behalf of a deity who inscrutably refused to defend himself. The risings were always suppressed by the imperial forces. It was a small country, but could not get used to the fact. Its mythical history and actual geography were ridiculously at variance. To a race less serious it might have been a matter for irony.

Being serious, they had no defence against their feeling of futility, of there having been an incomprehensible injustice. It soured their bread and darkened their thoughts. Introverts looked for reasons for the national calamity, and found them in their fathers' sins, or more rarely in their own. Most people looked for answers, and found them in the veiled and tantalising prophecies of their sacred writings. In these writings a Deliverer was promised. He would come on the clouds to avenge his people's wrongs. The sun would shine at midnight and the moon fill with blood to announce that the consummation of time was at hand.

Men scanned the heavens for a sign, and in the heavens they saw strange things.

From time to time rumours swept the country that the Deliverer had appeared, and hope flared like fire. In desert cells the holy men raised their heads from their books to listen for the thunder of the Lord's advance; in mountain caves the Zealots sharpened their swords. But as quickly as it had flared, hope guttered. The Deliverer was a fake. After a few miracles and fine speeches he failed to perform what was expected of him; he was discredited, his followers abandoned him and returned to their homes. He ended his life usually on a gibbet or in a skirmish with the Emperor's troops. The priests smiled and washed their hands. They were protected by the occupying power: they did not want trouble.

Perhaps the people were wrong to expect their god to honour his promises. Perhaps they had misunderstood him. Perhaps, indeed, the Deliverer had appeared and they had not noticed. In time a sect arose which claimed precisely that. The sect won few supporters in its native country: people pointed scornfully to the lamentable gulf between the prophesied glory and the ignominious fact. The sect replied that the people had been looking at the wrong prophecies. In the end, to everybody's surprise, the sect became a great success in a part of the Empire where none of these prophecies had ever been heard of.

Meanwhile people who were unable to believe that their god had lied to them continued to look for miracles. Where miracles are expected, they will occur. But if a miracle is anything at all, it is (by definition) not what it appears to be. This is why miracles are not to be trusted. However, if miracles are not believed in they do not occur. None of this was understood at the time, and as a result there were many miracles.

Simon of Gitta was a magician. Some said he was a god: his own pronouncements on the subject were obscure. Gitta was a village in Samaria. After he had become famous he preferred to dissociate himself from it, although he would not have been the first wonder-worker to be embarrassed by his origins. In time a title fittingly ambiguous, whose sombre magnificence had been degraded until no one any longer knew whether it meant a fire-priest of the ancient mysteries or a street-corner charlatan, came to be so regularly attributed to him that it became a kind of surname: he was known as Simon Magus.

He had been the guest of Philoxena for a month. It was three weeks too long, but the arrangement was too convenient to be terminated. Philoxena was rich, and did not stint her hospitality.

She owed her fortune to the untimely death of her husband, a government official who had succumbed to a fever on an irrelevant posting. She celebrated her freedom – or took her revenge – by spending his money on the arts, which he had despised. The house contained some of the finest statuary, bronzes and silverware Simon had ever seen. He turned his eyes from it with reluctance, and discoursed on the mutability of the world.

His conversation was his side of the bargain. In most circles he would pass for a learned man, although not all circles would approve of the uses to which he put his learning. In the small commercial town of Askalon he was a rare acquisition. He had been invited to stay for as long as he wished. All that was required of him was that he enliven the widow's evenings with his talk. He suspected that she also had designs on his nights, but he did not regard intimacies as part of the bargain: the cage was small enough already. He had told her that his magical powers depended on his remaining celibate. That rendered rather tricky the matter of Demetrius. So far she had not noticed.

All in all, it was clear that he could not stay in the house much longer.

Several days after her magician had astonished the townspeople by floating gently from the roof of a high building, Philoxena held a dinner party in his honour. Simon, glancing round the room as Demetrius removed his sandals, saw that the widow with unconscious inspiration had brought together one of the civic magistrates, a jovial bookseller called Flavius who a week earlier had bought from Simon a drug to procure abortion on the same magistrate's daughter, and a spice merchant whose eldest son was enamoured of his step-mother and had consulted Simon about his father's horoscope. The spice merchant was next to Simon on the couch. He smelt formidably of cinnamon.

Simon greeted his fellow-guests gravely and, as the appetisers were brought round, enquired of his neighbour the state of business.

'Terrible', said the spice merchant, with such vehemence that little crumbs of pastry showered out of his mouth onto the couch. He picked them up in plump fingers heavy with rings, and put them back in his mouth. 'The import duties are crippling. Hardly any profit on staple commodities, a little more on the high-class goods, but then if I lose a small consignment – which I'm all too likely to, with all these bandits on the roads – I make a loss. There's absolutely no incentive to expand.'

'Damned administration's wringing this country dry', growled Flavius.

The magistrate's face twitched.

'I was going to take my sons into the business', said the spice merchant. 'Good boys they are, though the eldest ... I don't know. Well, he'll shape up. Anyway, now I tell them they'd do better to study for a profession. Law, for instance. There's money in law.'

'And in banditry', remarked Simon absently. His attention had been caught by a table ornament which he had not seen in the house before. It was a small gold satyr, set with gems, supporting a sweetmeat tray. It was charming. If the gems were real, it was also extremely valuable.

He became aware that nine pairs of eyes were fixed on him.

'You surely don't approve of this current lawlessness', said the magistrate. Simon noticed with interest that he appeared to be able to speak without moving his facial muscles.

'Of course not', said Simon quickly. 'It's merely another sign that the problems of this country are still not taken seriously by those at the highest level of government.'

It was well judged. There was an approving murmur. Philoxena smiled at him tenderly, and Flavius, concealed from the magistrate's view by a large bowl of fruit, gave him a sly grin.

The conversation passed on to politics. Simon, who made it a rule to express no political views that could possibly be construed as controversial, drank his wine and listened. The company was divided over the action of the governor in quelling the latest riot in the capital.

'He over-reacted', declared a heavy-jowled man who had been introduced to Simon as a banker. 'People won't stand for it: they're a hotheaded lot up there at the best of times. Mark my words, there'll be bloodshed.'

'There has been bloodshed', objected Flavius. 'Twenty people killed by the troops and another fifty trampled to death in the panic. I'd call that bloodshed, wouldn't you?'

8

'I lost ten pounds of tragacanth in that riot', mourned the spice merchant.

'Well, it'll happen again as long as he's governor', said the banker. 'He doesn't understand this province.'

'Surely that's almost a prerequisite of holding office these days', remarked Flavius.

The magistrate compressed his lips and addressed himself to the banker.

'Are you suggesting he should have let them riot through the streets?' he enquired coldly.

'He provoked the trouble in the first place', said the banker.

'How, precisely?'

'By using their temple treasure to build his blasted aqueduct.'

'Oh, really!' The magistrate's mask-like features gave a convulsive twitch of impatience. 'That city has never had a proper water supply. They're forever having to build new cisterns. And have you ever been there at festival time?'

'Can't say I have', said the banker.

'Well I can tell you that it's complete chaos. A couple of hundred thousand pilgrims crowding into narrow little streets you can't even get a cart down, all taking their sheep to be sacrificed or whatever it is they do, and a water supply which is already stretched to the limit to cater for the existing population. Now that', said the magistrate, '*is* a dangerous situation.'

'It sounds quite frightful', said Philoxena. 'Isn't it terribly noisy, with all that bleating?'

'The noise', said the magistrate, 'is as nothing compared with the smell.'

'Well, I maintain', said the banker doggedly, 'that he should not have used the money from the temple. Everyone knows how touchy they are about these things.'

'I suppose,' said the spice merchant bitterly, 'he could have taken it out of the taxes.'

'There's nothing in that temple', remarked a young cavalry officer at the bottom of the table suddenly. 'My great-grandfather went into it, when he was on Pompey's staff. It's empty. No image, nothing. Just an empty space.'

'What?' There were murmurs of disbelief.

'I've heard that, too', said the banker. He turned to Simon. 'Our distinguished visitor can tell us. Is it true?'

'I am not of that religion', said Simon, studying his reflection in the purple wine, 'but I can tell you. Yes, it is true. The sanctuary is quite empty.'

His words were followed by a strange hush, as if the ancient intransigence of that religion they spoke of had come down for a moment from its mountain fastnesses and manifested its presence in the elegant room.

The widow broke the awkward silence, leaning close towards Simon so that he could see the white cleft between her breasts.

'Our distinguished visitor', she murmured, 'has been very reticent this evening. We know, of course, that modesty is the sign of true distinction, but surely we should hear some words from him. Our chatter must have bored him dreadfully: I'm sure he's used to a *much* loftier level of conversation.'

She bestowed on him an intimate smile plainly intended to convey to the rest of the company that she and Simon had many times engaged in such lofty converse.

'On the contrary, it has been most interesting', said Simon. 'I am always interested in people's opinions. *Humani nil a me alienum puto.*' He paused, and his eye dwelt for a moment on the gold satyr in the centre of the table. 'Nothing more concerns the philosopher', he resumed, 'than the study of human nature. Although properly speaking, of course, the highest object of philosophical contemplation is the nature of the soul.'

The company studied the food on their plates with serious expressions.

'Now Plato', pursued Simon, 'expressed his vision of the soul in an extremely beautiful metaphor, with which you may be familiar.' He expounded in some detail the famous image of the charioteer with the ill-matched steeds, and, warming to his theme, elaborated on it for the next hour. The wine circulated with increasing frequency. At the end of the hour the spice merchant and the banker were asleep and the young officer at the bottom of the table was having difficulty setting down his goblet at the required angle. Philoxena's eyes, as she gazed at Simon, appeared moist and slightly unfocused.

Simon refreshed himself with a fig and launched relentlessly into the doctrines of Pythagoras. He had been kept in this house like a pet monkey for the past month. Very well: he would perform.

He finished with Pythagoras, passed on, via the aphorisms of Heraclitus, to a cursory treatment of the Stoic school, to which he was averse, and was expounding the atomist theory of Lucretius

10

when the young officer pulled himself together, drained his wine and said malevolently, 'My tutor was a Stoic.'

'You are fortunate', said Simon smoothly.

'He was a good man. He knew m-more than you do.'

'No doubt.'

'You were making them out to be stupid. The Stoics. They're not stupid. They're quite right.'

'In what are they right?' enquired Simon.

The young man shook his head to clear it. 'Pleasure and pain. They're illusions. Meaningless. Nothing to be afraid of in dying. I believe that.'

'Illusions? Meaningless?'

The other guests had been roused to attention. It was late: the servants had lit the lamps some time ago. Simon tilted his head back and gazed at the ceiling. From it, roughly above the lower end of the table, hung a magnificent candelabrum of coloured glass, opalescent and glinting in the light.

'That is not what I believe', said Simon. 'And I do not think you do.'

He gazed at the candelabrum. Then for a moment he dropped his gaze to take in the little company of diners. All eyes were on him. He returned his gaze to the candelabrum.

'Look!' he said.

There was a lithe, shocking movement. Something glistened yellow in the lamplight. Something uncoiled itself with deadly sureness down between the little plates of coloured glass over the richly laden table, and extended its slit mouth and flickering tongue towards the young man's head.

The young man yelled and leapt from his couch. Philoxena screamed. The guests scrambled to their feet. Someone grabbed a heavy candlestick from the table and smashed it through the air.

Simon sat motionless. The confusion stilled as abruptly as it had begun. The guests stared in front of them stupidly. There was nothing there.

'What is the matter?' enquired Simon.

'It was a v-viper', stammered the young man. 'Didn't you see it?'

'But what were you afraid of?' said Simon. 'Pain is an illusion, and death is nothing to be feared.'

No one moved. There was a long silence. The young officer's face had turned from white to dark red, and the magistrate's

11

features were distorted with anger. Unexpectedly, the spice merchant chuckled.

'There is no viper', said Simon. 'I merely wanted to demonstrate that one must be very careful to distinguish between what is an illusion and what is not. And now, if you'll excuse me, I shall retire to my room. It has been a most entertaining evening.'

He bowed and left them. Half of them were still staring at the candelabrum. As he turned under the arch and began to go up the stairs to his room the spice merchant appeared at his elbow, looking happy for the first time that evening.

'I hope you don't mind me having a word with you', he said. 'To tell you the truth, I didn't quite follow all that stuff about Plato, but I liked the trick with the snake.'

'Thank you', said Simon. 'One tries to please everybody.'

'There's a little matter I'd like to discuss with you', said the spice merchant. 'Something rather delicate, if you take my meaning. I'll make it worth your while.'

'I take your meaning', said Simon.

'Can you dine with me the day after tomorrow?'

'It will be a pleasure', said Simon. 'You would be surprised how many delicate matters I am privy to.'

He walked thoughtfully up the marble staircase, his inner vision occupied by a small gold satyr. The stones were genuine, and one of them was an emerald. He had been looking for a good emerald for months: they were hard to come by, and none of the recommended substitutes was satisfactory.

'It's time we left this town', said Simon.

Demetrius frowned. 'Why?' he said.

Demetrius was beautiful when he frowned. It gave to his boyish features a totally deceptive cast of nobility.

'Because I'm bored', said Simon.

'But I like it here. I like going to the temple. The priest let me burn the incense last time.'

'I know. You stank of it. You're never so keen to burn incense for me.'

'That's different', said Demetrius.

It was not the first time they had had this conversation. It was implicit in their relationship as master and slave that what Demetrius did in his spare time was his own business. It was implicit in the fact that Demetrius shared Simon's bed that what he did in his

12

spare time was Simon's business. Simon attempted, when he thought of it, to strike a balance between the two spheres of obligation. In one respect he notably failed. He did not like Demetrius going to the temple of Isis.

'How can it be different', said Simon, 'when it's the same incense and the same goddess?'

'It feels different.'

'Of course it does. At the temple you can flirt with the priest.'

'I don't!'

Demetrius was on the verge of tears. Simon regarded him with exasperation.

'I don't understand you', he said. 'A lot of boys would give their ears to be my assistant. I am not, you know, just any magician. They talk about me as far afield as Antioch. You seem quite unaware what a great opportunity you have. If you showed a bit more interest I would give you your freedom and make you my apprentice. You have a natural aptitude for the work.'

'I hate spells', said Demetrius. 'They frighten me.'

Simon stared at him. The idea that the boy might be frightened by the things he was made to do had never occurred to him. He thought about it.

'The best magicians are afraid', he said. 'I am sometimes afraid myself. It is fatal to succumb to the fear, but necessary to feel it. It must be mastered. Once it is mastered, it can be used. It becomes part of your power.'

'But I don't like being frightened', said Demetrius.

'You must overcome it. You would make a good magician.'

'I don't want to be a magician', said Demetrius. 'I want to be a priest.'

'You what?' roared Simon. 'Spending your time singing hymns and trailing in processions with flowers round your neck?'

'There's more to it than that', said Demetrius with dignity. 'In a couple of years I shall be old enough to be initiated into the Mysteries.'

'*Mysteries*! You stupid boy! I know more mysteries than your priest can conceive of.'

Simon stood up and walked angrily round the room. 'Don't you understand that religion is a refuge for people who haven't the courage required for Magic? Magic is the true discipline, the true knowledge. The *nature* of things, that is what the magician knows, that is where the power is. Have I taught you nothing?'

13

Demetrius was silent. Or, if he said anything, it was obliterated by the cushions.

Simon picked up a small silver mirror and examined the face of a magician. It was a face not given to showing fear. The black eyes were piercing, the mouth full-lipped and arrogant, the nose hooked, dominant and uncompromising. It was a predatory face, but he was not aware of it. He was careful of his appearance. His beard was neatly trimmed: he stroked it with strong curved fingers.

He made a decision.

'Tonight', he said, 'I am dining with a man who believes, quite rightly, that his son is cuckolding him and will pay me a large sum of money to do something about it. That piece of business concluded, there is nothing to keep us in this town and we shall leave tomorrow. But when we leave we shall take something with us, and you will obtain it. It is the gold satyr which was on the table during that ridiculous dinner party two days ago. I want it. I am also owed it, in return for many evenings of excruciating boredom spent with our hostess. While I am out this evening you will find it and hide it somewhere, preferably outside the house, so that we can collect it tomorrow. Do not tell me that it is against your principles, because you have none. Do not tell me that it is against your religion, because I know more about your religion than you do. Do not tell me that it is against the law, because you and I, dear boy, break the law every day. And do not complain, because you are uncommonly well treated and there are prettier boys than you scrubbing floors in the barracks. Do you understand?'

'Yes', said Demetrius.

'Good', said Simon. His glance softened. 'We shall go to Joppa', he said. 'You'll like it there.'

He felt suddenly good-humoured. It was always exhilarating to leave a place. Joppa was a large city: there would be many opportunities. He might even stay there for a while, and settle down to some serious work.

His mood continued buoyant as he walked home from the spice merchant's house. Dusk had fallen but the pavements gleamed under a generous moon, and in its light Simon turned on his finger a turquoise ring which had lately adorned the merchant's hand. Turquoise: protector of chastity. Simon smiled.

He was still smiling as he rounded the last corner towards the

14

widow's house and saw lights in the street. There were men with weapons and torches, and in the middle of them, protesting loudly his innocence of everything conceivable, was Demetrius.

Simon slipped into the shadow, and was gone.

There was the crux of it, the bitter paradox. A man who could command his body to float weightless through the air could not command the necessities of life. He had astonished thousands by materialising objects out of nothing – a lion, a forest, a table of delicacies – but they returned to nothing, and he could not bid one loaf of bread appear that would fill his stomach. Instead he must sell his skill for money earned by ignorant hands. He felt it keenly.

His control over his body was in fact extraordinary. Not only could he rise and float in the air in defiance of all human experience, but he seemed to be able to change the very nature of his flesh at will. Once in a brothel a sailor had slashed at him with a knife: the knife had encountered strange resistance, a substance hard as cedar, and the man's face had jarred with shock. Many people had seen the Magus plunge his hands into a brazier of glowing coals and bring them out unscathed. His enemies said it was an illusion, but it was not. His body understood fire.

It was by means of fire that he did it. At least, so he believed. At the centre of him there was a slumbering fire. By certain practices –fasting, incantations, a special way of using the breath – he could arouse it and make it do his will. As its heat rose in him, consuming his flesh into a finer substance, turning his bones to parchment, his body became a glowing lamp out of which light streamed to meet the sun, and on this golden beam of light he ascended. That was the subtle fire.

The less subtle fire wrought outward transformations in his body. He could appear very old or very young, a dwarf or a giant, passing from one form to another in a moment. He could assume another man's features. The changes were transient, and his enemies said that they too were illusions.

The cold fire made his body dense and heavy, and he could not then be hurt.

The fires were like a horse: he rode them. He held them in check by his will. His will was his weapon, his armour. It stood between him and destruction by the fires.

He used his will to influence people's minds, and to that extent the charge that he was an illusionist was true. He wondered if the people who made the accusation knew what was involved in the creating of an illusion. For to do it he had to take by storm the minds of his audience and submit them to his own. To do it he had to prise the very atoms of the air apart and rearrange them to his fantasy.

He had learnt these arts in Egypt, where the greatest masters studied. In Egypt he had learnt the names of the gods and the choruses of the stars, the qualities of herbs and of transformations, and how to interpret the movements of animals and the flight of birds and the sounds made by stone. He had learnt, more important than all these, underlying and infusing them, the signs of sympathy.

Even after many years in which his art had been degraded into entertainment, the beauty of the system captivated his soul. Through all the created world and extending to the stars the invisible lines of sympathy ran. The universe was a shimmering web in which plant answered to planet, root to mineral, and animal to hour. Subtle, irresistible, complex beyond understanding, the network of correspondences extended itself, and he who had learned its symbols could play on it as on an instrument. Sound, indeed, was its strongest thread, and of all sounds the human voice was the most potent. The voice was the vehicle of the will, and the words it uttered gave form. The name summoned. The word created. God had created the earth by uttering his Name.

When he returned from Egypt Simon had possessed more of the occult science than almost any man alive. However, there were some things he did not know. He travelled the roads of Judaea and Samaria, and up the Syrian coast, looking for men who understood more of the great arcanum than he did. He found none. He spoke with philosophers who could not control their own tempers and astrologers who had been unable to predict their imprisonment. He practised his art, and in some places gained a great following.

He never stayed long in any town. People tired of marvels, and if they did not he tired of their demands. He was well aware, too, of something he would not have admitted: that he did not fully understand his art. There lay behind it a secret he could not penetrate. Finding that secret was his only constant purpose, and sometimes he thought that after fifteen years he was no nearer to it. He needed to be alone, to think and study. But he could not live without an audience; and he never had enough money.

*

16

The jurisdiction of the magistrates of Askalon extended to a few mud villages not far beyond the city's outskirts. Once he had passed the last of these, and left behind the barking dogs who followed him for a further half a mile, Simon felt himself safe from immediate arrest. He decided it would be foolish, even so, to invite questions by arriving at a roadside inn alone in the middle of the night. He trudged on until he came to a neglected orchard, in one corner of which stood a derelict stone shelter. There was a heap of damp straw against one wall. He slept there.

Waking at dawn, chilled, and with his cloak covered in cobwebs, he reviewed the situation. It was not promising. He had with him only the belongings he had taken to the spice merchant's house, although these included, fortunately, his three books of magic. Apart from those he had a few miscellaneous items of professional equipment, and twenty-four silver drachmas given him by the merchant. The asset on which he usually relied most heavily – his reputation – was in the circumstances his greatest danger. He would have to travel incognito.

Cold and breakfastless, he searched for olives in the orchard. There were none, of course: it was spring. He cursed the trees half-heartedly, and began to walk north along the road that skirted the coast.

In the early afternoon, approaching a small seaside town, he saw a straggle of tents and donkeys, and left the road to investigate. It was a travelling show: jugglers, acrobats and assorted freaks. Simon took in the scene with a practised eye, then asked if he could join them.

The manager's wife studied him suspiciously. 'What can you do?' she said.

'Anything', said Simon. A moment's reflection suggested that this might be an unwise claim. 'I don't do storms or raising the dead', he said.

'What name do you use?'

He cast about for a suitable pseudonym. 'Joshua', he said eventually, at the end of an obscure chain of associations.

'I thought you were dead.'

'Don't be ridiculous', said Simon.

'Can you walk on water?' she demanded.

'With the right equipment.'

There was a conference.

'The name won't do', said the manager. 'You'll have to think of something else. What about Moses?'

'No thank you', said Simon. 'But Aaron would be acceptable.'

'Can you do tricks with a rod?'

'Many', said Simon, 'but not for a family audience. I have a nice line in illusions, though.'

'Oh, no illusions, if you please. They always ask for their money back. Can you do oracles?'

'Yes', said Simon, 'I can do oracles.'

'Right. You're Aaron the Oracle. You can share a tent with the Gorgon.'

The Gorgon was a hermaphrodite with a squeaky voice and a turban full of snakes.

'I hope they're under control', said Simon.

'They're very sweet-natured', said the Gorgon venomously, 'but loud noises frighten them. So please keep your oracles quiet.'

Simon said he needed a boy assistant, and was given the juggler's boy on temporary loan. The juggler had dislocated his elbow and been drunk for two days. The boy looked like Demetrius. Ah, Demetrius. Simon's heart felt an uncustomary pang. Had they tortured the lad? It was too painful to contemplate. The juggler's boy was very pretty.

'What's your name?' he asked.

'Thomas, sir.'

'Do you know anything about oracles, Thomas?'

'No, sir.'

Simon told him about oracles, and hinted at other matters with which the boy did not seem to be acquainted. The hints were met with a look of blank incomprehension. Simon dropped the subject: it was no time to create a scandal. They partitioned off the tent, and then put up another curtain to create two small rooms.

'A brazier in the inner room', said Simon, 'and one lamp in the outer. Unfortunately we have no incense. I was obliged to leave without warning and brought nothing with me.'

He sent Thomas into the town to buy incense, salt, a special kind of wax, and a length of brass pipe.

'Aaron's rod,' he said, and winked. Thomas gazed at him.

'Oh, get on with it,' said Aaron.

By evening the tent of the oracle was ready, and they sat and waited for customers.

Magic was prohibited in those days, on the assumption that it worked. Some people said that it didn't, and that the gods it

18

invoked did not exist, and were driven to doubtful shifts to justify their condemnation of it. Some of these people were active in the eastern provinces of the empire at the same time as Simon.

Not all magic was illegal. It was an open-minded age, and a thing was judged largely on its intended effects. A spell to cast harm on a neighbour was punishable; a spell to take away toothache was not. If it had been, many doctors would have been seriously inconvenienced.

Magic was part of the fabric of life, and a great deal of it was not recognised as magic at all. It shaded imperceptibly into religion on the one hand and science on the other – inevitably, since it had begotten them. It was practised by a strange assortment of people, from conjurers whose skill resided wholly in hand and tongue to ascetic sages who could calm a storm at sea. Since the small fry of the magical world were limited by their capacities to catering for the baser needs of human nature – a love-potion, a curse, a spell to make a woman tell the truth – while those of greater aptitude could afford to exercise their gifts benignly, the shadowy distinction between permitted and forbidden magic tended regrettably to resolve itself into a class distinction, in which the artisans were nearly always on the wrong side of the law and the great masters were above it.

Greatest of all the masters were the so-called 'divine men'. The divine man (obviously, from its optimism, a Greek concept) was a magician who needed none of the paraphernalia of a magician. No spells, incantations and drugs for him: he performed his wonders by his word alone. He spoke, and it was done. He saw the future, not in the smoky flame of an enchanted fire, but with his inner eye. He was able to do these things because he possessed or had at his command the spirit of a god. Some said that Simon Magus was a man of this kind. Others said that Simon had, not the spirit of a god, but the spirit of a demon.

Since white magic was believed to be performed by gods and black or illegal magic by demons, this sort of assertion brought the argument about legality into an area where it could not be settled. For the supernatural agents who performed the magician's will did not normally identify themselves to the beholders. Thus a celebrated exorcist was several times accused of casting out devils by the power of Beelzebub.

Demons were in any case a very vexed question. They were numerous in all parts of the empire, but in Judaea, where God admitted no rival, they particularly thrived. Every field, every bush, every privy, every shadow, every pool of stagnant water, every twinge of headache, had its demon. There was disagreement as to what they were. A favoured theory was that God had created them on Sabbath-eve and the Sabbath had intervened before there was time to give them bodies. A more sophisticated school of thought said they were the fallen angels who had taught men the civilised arts. This brought black and white perilously close together, and further illuminated the ambiguity of angels. These were fiery, quarrelsome creatures whose attitude towards the human race was not to be depended on. They disliked spiritual ambition: they had tried to prevent Moses from receiving the Law, they would bar the mystic's ascent to heaven if they could. The Jews invoked them fearfully, and magicians of neighbouring races borrowed their beautiful, outlandish names.

Thus between legal and illegal, black and white, god and demon, the boundaries were hopelessly confused. Most people did not bother about this confusion: it did not appear to them to be a problem. To the magician, as to the prostitute, the occasional severity of the law was an occupational hazard. To Simon Magus, who saw very clearly that one man's harm is another man's blessing, and who operated in a world of forces where there is no good and evil but only power, the illogicalities of the law were the predictable outcome of a system in which men of little imagination made rules for their betters.

One idea which does not seem to have occurred to the lawmakers of the time was that magic should be anyone's property. It was simply there, as the air was there. The principle that the same act, performed with the same intent, should be licit or illicit depending on the identity of the magician, would have been found incomprehensible. It would, of course, have simplified the situation at a stroke. Perhaps they did not take magic very seriously in those days.

Three men stood in a group at the door of the tent, self-consciously holding palm fronds. The two older men were arguing.

'I don't like it', said the thin one. 'We shouldn't have come here. It's dangerous, messing about with demons.'

'If you hadn't been so stupid', said the fat one, 'it wouldn't be necessary. How else can we find out what he's done with it?'

The young man looked bored.

'The oracle will receive you', said Simon, who had been listening with interest through the wall of the tent. He was wearing a purple robe on which were sewn the signs of the planets, and a green turban, borrowed from the Gorgon, wound in fantastic fashion on his head. The talisman of Osiris hung on his chest and a strangely-fashioned ring shone on his finger. His black eyes glittered fiercely under heavy lids.

The thin man and the fat man backed away.

'Oh, come on', said the youngest.

They went in. It was dimly lit and heavy with incense. The magician ordered them to write down their enquiry on a scrap of parchment which he gave them. The fat man, after much thought, wrote.

'Fold it up,' said Simon, 'so that I cannot see what is written.'

The fat man folded it, then folded it again.

'I shall now burn it', said the magician. 'The smoke will carry your words to the god.'

They watched him walk to the brazier in the inner room and lay the folded parchment on the coals, where it curled, flared and vanished.

'He didn't look at it', hissed the thin man.

'No. He burnt it. We saw him.'

Simon came back, solemn, his eyes glittering. He turned up the lamp to give them more light. 'Shortly the god will appear to answer your question,' he said. 'You are to compose yourselves into a reverent frame of mind. I will begin the invocation, and prepare my assistant, through whom the oracle will speak. Please remain here until you are summoned. When I summon you, you must enter waving your offering of palm leaves.'

He struck a gong, and they jumped with fright. A pale, wide-eyed boy appeared and followed the magician into the inner room. The curtain was pulled across.

Simon fished a scrap of parchment out of his sleeve and read it. He frowned. 'That's three questions', he said. 'What do they think this is, a bazaar?'

He settled Demetrius – ah, no, Thomas – in a recumbent position on the cushions, placed pieces of the mingled salt and wax on the coals, and began to chant. He chanted scraps of Greek, Hebrew, Egyptian. Anything would do, and the less it meant the better. The last thing that was required in the circumstances was a genuine manifestation.

He began to breathe deeply. His voice rose, elongating the vowels, trailing off into an unearthly wail. The men on the other side of the curtain shivered.

'Come!' cried the magician. 'Enter into the presence of the god!'

They blundered in, into almost total blackness, and began hitting each other with their palm fronds. The fire blazed up with a loud crack into a leaping inferno of colours, and the thin man squealed, rushed for the entrance and became entangled in the curtain, from which he fought to free himself with mounting panic.

'Will you be quiet!' squeaked the Gorgon behind the partition.

'Oh great god Serapis', intoned Simon, 'that knowest all mysteries, we beseech thee that thou wilt answer the enquiry of thy servant, speaking through the mouth of this innocent child here.'

Thomas-Demetrius writhed convincingly on his cushions. Simon, a few feet away in the shadows, regarded him fondly. With training, he would do well. The boy moaned.

'I feel sick', he said.

'What did he say?' demanded the young man.

'His senses are overwhelmed by the presence of the god', said Simon.

The thin man sobbed.

Simon raised the end of the brass tube to his lips and whispered into it. The boy struggled feebly.

'The god speaks', said Simon.

'You're hurting my ear', said Thomas into the cushions.

'Now look here', said the young man, 'there's something funny going on. This is a fraud.'

He moved purposefully towards Simon, fell over his palm frond and crashed to the floor, throwing the fat man into the gong, which clanged deafeningly. Simon, searching for something suitable, raised his voice in the invocation to Bacchus. The Gorgon, snakes erect, tore aside the partition and stood before them in squeaking fury.

The thin man screamed.

The Gorgon lunged for Simon and pulled off his robe. One of the snakes, recognising home, transferred itself in a flash to Simon's turban and coiled its tail affectionately round his neck. The thin man gibbered, the fat man fought with the gong and the young man dived under the side of the tent and ran.

Simon was aware that he was rising: rising in every part. He struggled, but not laughter not concupiscence could be solely

22

blamed for the state in which he now appeared. He floated, Aaron, rod ascendant, a foot above the floor.

Thomas was sick.

Demetrius had not been tortured, but it was an imminent possibility.

He had tried to guard against it by telling the whole truth, suitably garnished, as soon as it became clear that Simon was not going to return and rescue him. Yes, he said, he had stolen the satyr on his master's orders, because he was afraid of what would happen to him if he disobeyed. His master was a cruel man and a great magician, and had threatened to turn him into a camel if he did not do as he was told. Demetrius added that he knew his master was able to turn him into a camel because he had seen him turn an old woman into a cockroach, and once ...

Struck in the mouth at this point by a guard, Demetrius returned to the satyr. Yes, he said indistinctly, he had wrapped it in a cloth and had been attempting to hide it in the cellar when he was discovered. He had been too frightened to take it outside, and had hoped that while in the cellar it would be found by the servants and returned to the widow, whom he, Demetrius, held in high esteem and had indeed reproached his master ...

A second blow, delivered casually to the stomach, winded him and he relapsed into silence.

The magistrate regarded him above folded hands.

'Where has your master gone?' he asked.

He seemed to speak without moving his facial muscles. It was like being addressed by a statue.

'I don't know, sir', whispered Demetrius.

'Take him to the cells', said the magistrate. And there, for a week, he remained.

He hoped and feared alternately that they had forgotten about him. It seemed likely. Days went by in which he saw no one. The grating in the door was unlocked at noon and a plateful of something unpleasant was pushed through. Sometimes footsteps halted outside the door and an eye peered through the grating. Demetrius smiled tentatively at it, but the eye did not respond.

From time to time a very large jailer, who might or might not be the owner of the eye, came into the cell and stood there. He said nothing. He simply stood with his hands on his hips and surveyed Demetrius, with the smile of a man who knows something that would be of great interest but will not divulge it. Demetrius smiled back. The two smiles did not quite connect. After a few minutes the jailer would go away.

On his third visit the jailer lifted Demetrius's arm and fingered the joints thoughtfully.

'What a pity', he said.

He ran his meaty hand over the biceps, and then with a quick movement caught the upper arm in an excruciating pressure between his thumb and middle finger. Demetrius yelled.

The jailer chuckled, and went away.

On the eighth day a very pale Demetrius was brought before the magistrate again. The magistrate was writing, and did not look up as they entered. After a while, still writing, he remarked, 'I could have you flogged.'

'Yes, sir,' agreed Demetrius. Flogging was better than torture: at least you knew what was going to happen next.

'Or,' pursued the magistrate, 'I could have you tortured.' He raised his eyes and briefly surveyed Demetrius's trembling frame. 'But I don't think you'd last long. Or' – he returned to his writing – 'I could simply keep you in prison until your teeth rot, your hair falls out and even your putative mother has forgotten you. I am not sure, in the circumstances, which is the most appropriate.'

'M-m-m-mercy', suggested Demetrius.

'Mercy? This is mercy, you stupid boy. I could send you to the governor, in which case, on a proven charge of theft, you would almost certainly be crucified.'

Demetrius had always thought of death as something that happened to other people. He now contemplated his own, and felt a cold sensation expanding from the pit of his stomach and spreading through his entire body until it reached his toes and fingers. He began to cry.

The magistrate waited, expressionless, for Demetrius to compose himself. When, after some time, Demetrius had not done so, the magistrate's rigid features convulsed in a spasm of impatience.

'Where is your master?' he barked.

Demetrius jumped. 'Please sir, I don't know', he snivelled.

'Well, where would he go? Who are his friends?'

'I don't know', wept Demetrius.

'Tcha!' The magistrate brought his fist down on the table with a crash. Demetrius collapsed in terror to his knees and was hauled up again by the guards.

'Simon of Gitta', said the magistrate, 'who prefers to be known as Simon the Magus. Miracle-monger, trickster and thief. Most people privileged to hold my office would be glad to get rid of him. They would be only too pleased that he'd gone to some other town to work his mischief. But I happen to have a larger sense of social responsibility than most people. I want him back. I want him for theft, fraud, sorcery, and incitement to civil unrest. I want him here, in my jail, in chains.'

'Incitement to what?' said Demetrius.

'What do you know of his political activities?' said the magistrate.

Demetrius was startled. He stopped snivelling. 'He doesn't have any political activities', he said. 'He just flies, and makes people see things that aren't there, and tells the future, and things.'

'I cannot make up my mind,' said the magistrate, 'whether you are very stupid or very clever. Perhaps I will have you tortured.'

A fresh flood of tears persuaded him that the process would be unproductive.

'Well', he said at last, 'the law will catch up with him. A man so convinced of his own importance will not be able to live in obscurity. In any case, there is a price on his head.'

'How much?' asked Demetrius, out of long habit.

'The usual price. Thirty shekels.'

'Thirty shekels', echoed Demetrius. He had never owned one-tenth of that sum.

The magistrate watched him through narrowed eyes.

'If you let me go', ventured Demetrius, 'I might be able to find him for you.'

'I thought you said you didn't know where he was.'

'I don't,' said Demetrius, 'but I might be able to find out.'

'How?'

Demetrius's head had cleared miraculously. 'I've been with him two years', he said. 'I've learnt certain things. Ways of finding out where people are, for instance.'

'Are you talking about sorcery?'

'No sir, of course not.'

The magistrate sighed. 'Very well,' he said. 'You could hardly be more of a nuisance at large than you are here. And I can see that flogging you would serve no useful purpose whatever.'

He nodded to the guards. 'Let him go.'

And free, penniless, red-eyed and hungry, Demetrius wandered into the town.

25

There appeared to be some kind of procession going on. To the sound of clashing cymbals and shrill tambourines, men in strange gaudy costumes were leaping and dancing through the street. At the head of the procession walked a donkey drawing a cart on which stood the tall, brightly-painted image of a woman, hung with flower garlands and the masks and skins of animals. Knots of people had gathered and were watching the display with amusement and some ribaldry.

Demetrius was interested to see that a number of men, also gaily costumed, were walking among the spectators with begging bowls. Coins clinked: it seemed the mockery was not entirely hostile. The men with begging bowls did not look hungry: in fact they were well-fleshed and had the smooth skin that betokened easy living. It deserved emulation, thought Demetrius. He followed a few paces behind one of the mendicants; having no bowl, he cupped his hands.

'Shocking', said someone. 'It shouldn't be allowed.'

But coins, a few small ones, fell into his hands.

At the end of the street the man he was following turned and looked at him. Demetrius at that moment realised what was odd about the costumes. His eye had been confused by their foreignness, but they were surely not men's clothes at all, but women's.

'Well well', said the man he had been following. 'You'd better come along with us.'

At about this time, and less than a hundred miles away, a sect which proclaimed that the end of the world was at hand and that only its members would survive was making itself rather unpopular. This was not surprising, since to its implacable message of doom it added a comprehensive attack on the social fabric of the community.

It seduced wives from their husbands, husbands from their wives and young people from their parents, and said that since the end of the world was at hand people had better things to do than get married in any case. It practised communal ownership of goods, which aroused the scorn of the merchant class and the unease of the rich, and said that the slave was the equal of his master, which, while plainly nonsense, was undesirable nonsense. It talked in vague but passionate terms of a kingdom, thus disquieting officials of the imperial government. It claimed that its founder, lately executed as a political nuisance, had been not only innocent but in some unexplained way above the Law, and had conferred a similar privilege on his followers; thus drawing down upon itself the execration of the priests who for centuries had been the guardians of the Law. The most exasperating of its characteristics was its refusal to do anything that could unequivocally be condemned. Its members paid their taxes, declined to defend themselves against physical assault, and went on talking.

Obviously the tensions created by the existence of such a group could not be contained indefinitely. A minor administrator of the sect who had gained a reputation for magical powers and was a persuasive speaker fell foul of a group of conservatively-minded citizens, and was brought before the religious authorities on a charge of blasphemy. His friends maintained that the charge was trumped-up, but at his trial the accused man substantiated it. At the end of a tedious harangue in which he reminded his hearers of their national history and the failings of their ancestors, he declared that the dead leader venerated by the sect was the Deliverer who had been promised to the nation, and claimed to see in a vision this executed law-breaker and failed revolutionary glorified in heaven beside the national deity.

Now, the rock of the nation's religion, and the pride of its people, was the Law – a judicial, moral and religious code of extraordinary complexity, dictated to them by their god, so the people believed, at the dawn of their history. For observing that Law in defiance of foreign masters, their forefathers had risked death and seen their children tortured. The suggestion that contempt of the Law might actually win divine *approval* was intolerable. The religious leaders really had no choice in the matter. The penalty for blasphemy was death by stoning. The guilty man was accordingly stoned, and everyone agreed that nothing else could have been done.

Demetrius was delighted with his new companions.

On the first night they shared their food with him and lent him a coarse blanket, smelling of goat, to keep him warm. Gazing up at the stars he thought of Simon, remembering an occasion when they had been ejected from an inhospitable town and had walked many miles on a dangerous road looking for an inn, and in the end had not found one, but slept in the shelter of a rock. Simon had been kind to him that night. Simon had often been kind, thought Demetrius: more often than he had realised. And even when Simon had not been kind, he had been there. But where was Simon now? Tears

27

of self-pity came to Demetrius's eyes as he contemplated the loneliness of his freedom. He fell asleep curled in a miserable ball.

In the course of the next few days he forgot Simon. His friends found a red cloak and a cap for him, like the ones they wore, and taught him to clash the cymbals. He learnt some of the dances of the goddess – strange, exhilarating, whirling dances that at first made him feel faint but after a while produced, he found, a peculiar concentrated stillness in his head, so that his mind became extraordinarily clear and detached while somewhere far below it his body spun like a top. He wanted to go on and on doing it, but they would not let him. It was dangerous, they said: he was a novice. But if he stayed with them they would teach him.

He clashed the cymbals and he danced as they passed through villages and towns. The inhabitants were mostly friendly, though once or twice stones were thrown. They kept to the coastal areas where Greek was spoken and the population was mixed: there was a lot of religious intolerance in the hill-country. They carried the image of the goddess in procession through the streets. She was the Mother, Demetrius was told. He asked if she was the same as his own goddess, and they explained to him that she was worshipped under many names, but her first name was Life. She gave, and she took away. They were carrying her in procession through the region, and before the moon had waned they would hold the yearly sacrifice and bathe her in the river.

Demetrius asked about the sacrifice, but was told that there were many mysteries and he was still a novice. If he stayed with them, they would teach him.

There were two young men in the group, not much older than he was. They were Greek, and seemed to be close friends. They had been devotees of the goddess for a year, they said, and they would be initiated very soon. They would not tell him anything about the initiation, except that it was a ceremony of purification and would dedicate them for ever to the service of the goddess. They said this with such quiet fervour that Demetrius was envious. He felt it would be very satisfying to dedicate himself to something. He asked if he could be initiated with them, but they smiled and said he was too young.

He clashed the cymbals and he danced, and his life with Simon seemed very far away. He felt secure with his friends: no

28

one was unkind to him, no law hunted him, no terrifying spirits lurked in fire and lamp and divination bowl to dog his footsteps down deserted roads and fill his sleep with monsters.

One day he saw something that amazed him. It was their last day on the coast: tomorrow they were turning inland, up to the hills and the forest. They had danced through a village and begged their food for the evening, but when they stopped for the night one of the men was still dancing. Curiously rigid, glistening with sweat, the pupils of his eyes turned abnormally upward, he danced slowly, rhythmically, with the dreadful endless energy of near-exhaustion, the tambourine thudding and trilling in his outstretched hand. He danced round and round the fire, weaving and retreating in a pattern which only his feet could read, weaving and retreating through the circle of watchers gathered round the fire. He danced into the fire, and stood there.

He stood there, barefoot, unflinching, and then danced out again.

Demetrius, after a while, said, 'I thought only my master could do that.'

'Pain is a secret', said the man next to him. 'It can be learnt.'

'Will you teach me', said Demetrius, 'not to feel pain?'

'If you stay with us, we will teach you.'

He stayed with them.

'I am not a necromancer', said Simon Magus.

'There's a lot of money in it', said the goldsmith.

'I am not interested in money', said Simon.

The goldsmith smiled. 'That ring', he said, touching the spice merchant's turquoise, 'cost a few drachmas.'

They had been sitting in the tavern for several hours, while the goldsmith ordered jug after jug of the sour local wine and Simon in return talked. Talking was one of the ways in which he earned his living. On this occasion, however, he had talked somewhat too much. He had strayed from philosophy into astrology and from astrology into magic, and under the goldsmith's questioning, whose pertinence he realised too late, he had been unable to resist displaying the extent of his knowledge. When the next jug of wine appeared a proposition was put to him. The goldsmith had a brother, whose wife's uncle ... It was a long and unedifying story, involving, among other elements, a lawsuit, a disputed will, and a squabble over land. Simon half-listened: he had heard it a dozen

29

times before. Stripped of polite circumlocutions, it was a matter of murder by sorcery. A magician saw humanity at its most abject: he was asked to do only those things which people dared not do for themselves.

'No', he said.

'You are a magician', said the goldsmith.

'I am not a necromancer', said Simon.

But it was true that the money would be welcome. He did not believe that interest in his whereabouts would have ceased when it was known that he had left Askalon. There might even be a reward for his capture. He would not feel safe until he was on the other side of the country. The coast roads were full of troops: he had come to Joppa with the intention of finding a ship, but he had barely enough money to buy his passage to the next port.

'I suspect that you would find the money very useful', said the goldsmith. He surveyed Simon's travel-stained clothing. 'But perhaps your skill is not equal to the job?'

'Of course I can do it', said Simon contemptuously, and relapsed into an irritable silence.

The goldsmith adopted a more relaxed approach.

'This is not necromancy', he said softly, with an eye on the serving girl, who seemed to be showing an interest in the conversation, or perhaps it was just an interest in Simon. 'This is the righting of a wrong.'

'By means of a curse.'

'No one is asking you actually to raise the spirit of a dead man.'

'Nonsense', snapped Simon. 'The spirit must be invoked whether it appears or not. It can't be done in any other way. And very dangerous it is.'

'Oh well, if you're afraid ...'

'Of course I'm not afraid. I know what I can do. It is a question of what I choose to do. Magic is a noble art. Sorcery is a contamination of it.'

The goldsmith stood up. 'It has been a pleasure making your acquaintance', he said, and with a nod walked away.

As he went out of the door two soldiers came in, short-haired, short-sworded and arrogant. They glanced round at the customers, a swift, efficient glance, the glance of the ruling race in a still insufficiently pacified country. The glance missed nothing: it lingered momentarily on Simon. He finished his wine and, as soon as the soldiers' backs were turned, left the tavern.

The goldsmith was at the end of the street. Simon caught up with him.

'You realise', he said, 'that just any ... ah, corpse won't do. It must be someone who has died a violent death.'

'That is not too difficult in these parts', said the goldsmith.

'Preferably an executed criminal. And preferably the skull.'

'A man was hanged two days ago', said the goldsmith. 'Most conveniently. The body is in the cemetery.'

'I shall have nothing to do with that part of it.'

'Of course not.'

'If your men are discovered in the cemetery, I shall deny all knowledge of the matter.'

'Naturally.'

'Fifty drachmas?'

'Fifty drachmas.'

'Half of it in advance.'

'Oh – if you insist.'

'Good', said Simon. He thought for a moment. 'I shall need it as soon as possible', he said. 'I'm staying at the inn we've just come from. The room above the stable. If you'd rather not give it to me in person, you can throw it in through the window.'

'All right', said the goldsmith.

Simon walked away quickly down a sidestreet. By the time the goldsmith had realised there was a question he should ask him, he has disappeared from sight.

Simon spent the afternoon at the gymnasium, where there was a boy who looked like Demetrius, and then went to the baths. By evening he felt rested and good-humoured. He would get his money. There was very little risk. A boat was sailing in three days for Caesarea. He allowed himself a good meal from the spice merchant's dwindling drachmas.

Back at the inn, he indulged himself in more wine and a flirtation with the serving girl. She was the innkeeper's daughter. Her father kept a close and rancorous eye upon her. Simon suspected that she not infrequently managed to evade it. It would not be difficult to evade: the man was as stupid as a bullock and drank heavily. Simon bought him a number of drinks.

He asked the girl casually about the soldiers, and was dismayed to hear that they were lodging at the inn. From her next remark, however, he realised that they would not be looking for him.

'They're bringing a prisoner to the assizes', she said. 'Don't know what he's done, but there's three of them guarding him, poor devil. My father was going to put two of them in your room, but I said I thought they'd rather be all together. So you're all on your own.' She eyed him frankly. 'That's nice, isn't it? Or perhaps you'd rather have company.'

'That depends,' said Simon, 'whose company it is.'

He saw the innkeeper blundering towards them and quickly waved her away. 'I asked for some better wine', he complained, 'but the girl tells me this is all you have.'

The innkeeper turned on her with a clumsy blow, which she avoided, and ordered her to the cellar to find the best vintage. He apologised profusely to Simon for his daughter's stupidity. It had been difficult bringing her up, he said: his wife had died. A vinous tear crept out of his eye.

'Your company, for instance', resumed Simon when the girl returned, 'would be welcome at any time.'

It was late when she came to his room: the innkeeper had retired, swaying, to his quarters two hours previously, and a drunken argument between the soldiers next door had long since declined into a contest of drunken snores.

In Simon's room a more melodic contest was played, and replayed, and played again, with many a pleasing variation, subtle harmony, and enraptured close. When the last strains of the last and most complicated development had spent themselves, Simon rested on his elbow and studied her with wonder. She was wasted in a town like this. In Caesarea, now . . .

'Why don't you come with me?' he said. 'I'm leaving in a few days. Caesarea, Tyre . . . We could go anywhere. You don't want to stay in this back-street inn, with that dreadful father of yours.'

'Rome,' she said dreamily, 'I've always wanted to go to Rome.'

Rome. The centre of the world. For some reason he had never wished to go there. He felt in fact a strong aversion to the idea. Could it be that he was afraid of finding in that great city a greater magician than he was? He was conscious for the first time of his provincialism, and felt ashamed.

'Rome', he repeated, in just short of an affirmation.

Why not? He would have the money. Rome was possible: everything was possible. The girl pressed her lips to him, teasing him for his seriousness, and he found to his surprise that indeed everything was possible. He was pursuing the limits of this discovery when there was a footstep in the street outside.

Something flew through the window and landed on the bed. It was not a bag of money.

A human head in which green and purple strove for dominance stared at them from eyes of melted jelly. Clods of earth still matted the hair.

Simon was dressed and out of the window by the time the girl drew breath for the third shattering scream.

They had been walking all day, and Demetrius was tired. If he had not been so tired he might have noticed an unusual thoughtfulness on the part of his companions. There was no dancing: they had skirted the edge of several villages without entering them. It was as if the company were saving its strength for a great effort.

The landscape had changed: the lush cornfields of the plain had given way to rough, broken country, scrub-covered and pocked with caves, interrupted at intervals by green terraces of olive groves in the neighbourhood of a village. The road wound east between clusters of pale rounded hills, allowing every now and then a dazzling glimpse of sea in the distance. To the east rose the long jagged cliff of the mountains, cleft by steep ravines. Once, as the group rested to drink at a well, an eagle wheeled over, black against the sky.

They stopped for the night in a sheltered valley a few miles from the forest. At the evening meal Demetrius sat next to the two young men who were to be initiated. They were quiet and did not want to talk. They seemed absorbed in their own thoughts. The initiation would take place the day after tomorrow, they said. Tomorrow everyone would rest.

The music began at midnight the following night. Cymbal and tambourine, and the high piping flute. The music had a new quality: a yearning, a lamentation. Demetrius felt it invade his heart like a memory of something infinitely precious, lost beyond recall. For some while he did not join the dancers, but sat gazing at the dark outlines of the mountain tops against the faint light of the sky, trying to remember what it was he had lost.

Then he began to dance, imitating the deliberate footsteps of the others as they circled round and round the fire. A slow, relentless rhythm. He waited for the rhythm to rise, as it always rose, but it remained constant, and it came to him that they were dancing the dance of eternity, of the unchanging return of all things, of the mingling of death with life and life with death. A sense of utter helplessness took possession of him as he danced the endless succession of night and day, season and season, birth and decay. There was no escape, there was no rest, from the circling planets and the circling seasons, and the circling dance round the unknown fire of the serpent biting its tail.

At dawn they began the last procession towards the forest. The scent of pines was fresh and heady in the damp air, and the sun rose behind mist like a shrouded ghost.

The divination required a boy, a lamp and a bowl. He had borrowed a lamp, and purchased a bowl from a coppersmith in the village. He lacked the boy.

Simon missed Demetrius on a number of counts, but his absence on this occasion was a positive nuisance. For divinations the boy was superb. He entered trance easily, and looked so terrified that it was impossible not to believe that spirits were conversing with him. Simon often wondered what Demetrius really saw in the shadowy depths of the bowl. He himself frequently saw nothing. Sometimes he saw something he wished he had not seen, which was one reason why he preferred not to do the divination himself.

This time he had no choice. He had left the coast, after his hasty departure from the inn at Joppa, and was making his way north through the hill-country, announcing himself as a wandering fortune teller, when a larger fish than he had bargained for had swum into his net. A Syrian merchant, visiting the district on family business, had been told of the soothsayer and had consulted him about an overdue shipment of silks. There was a great deal of money at stake: the merchant offered a substantial fee for a genuine divination.

It was unlikely in the circumstances that anything would manifest at all, but Simon had made his preparations with as much care as possible. The place he had chosen for the ritual was a dry cave in the hillside behind the village. In the mouth of the cave he had lit a small fire, and on it lumps of incense now fumed and crackled. The fire threw strange shadows on the walls of the cave, which seemed to dance. The merchant sat near the fire, his cloak wrapped round him, watching the shadows. He looked bored, but his fingers clutched the edge of his cloak with unnecessary tightness.

Simon set the lamp down so that it cast its light on the glistening film of oil floating in the copper bowl. Softly he began the invocation.

34

'Noble child that came forth from the lotus, Horus, lord of time ...'

As he chanted he felt the spell weaving him into it.

'Whose name is not known, nor his nature, nor his likeness. I know thy name, thy nature, thy likeness.'

Patterns of light drifted on the filmy mirror of liquid.

'Great god that diest not, that sittest in the flame, reveal thyself to me. Answer thou my questioning.'

A knob of spice flared up with ghostly brilliance, and spat out a blue streak of fire. The merchant shivered.

'For I am he that came forth in the east: let darkness depart. Great is my name.'

The glimmering patches on the surface of the oil had come together to form an unbroken sheet of light.

'I am Horus, son of Osiris, who enquires for his father.'

The light crazed. Along the hair-like cracks the darkness deepened and spread, the light retreating before it like broken ice. At last only a jagged rim of light remained. He was gazing into a pool of blackness. In its depths a darkness yet denser evolved, a purple blackness that was the shadow of intense light. It took form, and the form began to glow. It rose towards him with appalling distinctness. Eyes cold as stone above a curved beak. A face from nightmare, a face older than time.

Simon found he could not move or speak. The face still seemed to rise towards him. He held it back by his will. He groped for the words of the enquiry, but his mind was empty. He did not know for what purpose he had summoned this frightful apparition. In a flash of terror he became conscious of how utterly alone he was; and then suddenly into his mind came an image of Demetrius, hunched shivering over another bowl of demons in another place, another time. Without his volition, his lips formed the boy's name.

The enquiry came back to him: a cargo of silks. He spoke.

For a moment the face threatened to draw him into it. Then it creased and puckered like a parchment, and faded. He was looking at the wrinkled surface of a hillside. Stunted bushes, scattered trees, and in the background, its shadows lengthened by an evening sun, the green edge of a forest. Figures moved into the picture, gaily clothed, dancing to musical instruments. The dancers circled round and round a pine tree. Under the tree was a single figure, also dancing, but with jerky convulsive movements, and holding something in either hand. The figure was a boy. In his right hand he held some gleaming object, in his left ...

Creeping up from the lower edge of the picture was a red stain. It spread quickly. Just before it obliterated the figure of the boy Simon saw his face. Then the red tide rolled over the whole scene. He knelt before a bowl of blood.

The red darkened to black, on which returning flickers of silver danced. Slowly the patterns of light resumed their drifting.

Simon pronounced the dismissal.

He knelt for a time with his head in his hands. Then he stood up and, turning, remembered the merchant. The man had stood up also, and was impatient.

'Well, what did you see?'

'Your ship ...' said Simon, and closed his eyes. The hawk-face glared at him behind his eyelids.

'Yes?'

'Your ship is safe', said Simon. He was swaying slightly. 'It will be in port in three days.'

The merchant stared uncertainly at him, torn between relief, suspicion and unwilling respect.

'How do I know you're telling the truth?' he said. 'I didn't see it.'

'No, you did not', said Simon. 'Thank your gods that they do not show themselves to you.'

The merchant stared at him a moment longer, threw down some coins, and walked from the cave.

Simon counted the money and put it away. For a while he stood at the mouth of the cave and watched the sky lightening. Then he kicked out the fire, gathered his belongings into a small bundle and began to walk up the hillside towards the south-east.

Demetrius danced. He had gone beyond exhaustion. There was a cool, still space in his mind, and beyond it, seemingly far beyond it and yet ready to engulf him the moment he stopped dancing, was a jungle of confusion, colour and noise. He dared not stop dancing. He could not stop dancing. When he stopped dancing the world would end.

The music had changed several times. The endless circling, the dance of eternity they had danced in the dawn, had not been danced again: the serpent was placated. Instead they had danced, under the rising sun, a simple, playful dance of leaps and runs and childish gestures, which he had understood was the dance of birth.

36

Resting briefly during this dance he saw they had been joined by groups of people, mostly women, from the surrounding countryside. The women chanted, clapped, and some of them joined in the dancing.

Towards noon the music had become faster and more insistent: it was the dance of maturity, of the flesh in its pride and vigour, the sun in its strength. The sun beat down on the hillside, and the colours and the music pulsed and swam together in Demetrius's head. When the glare became intolerable he danced with his eyes shut, and saw the white sun behind his eyelids.

The sun began to dip towards the west, and the music became wilder. Demetrius danced. The music would not let him stop: it possessed him, it had become the blood that pulsed in his veins; when it stopped the blood would run out and he would die. The music danced him, on and on, towards its consummation.

And then, a change of pitch on the flutes, chill like an evening breeze, chill and pure. The rhythm changed. No longer wild, but measured, even stately, a tread of ageless dignity, a tread, his blood informed him, of sorrow. Demetrius had never known real sorrow: he knew it now. The tragedy of human endeavour unfolded itself before his inward-gazing eyes as his feet trod instinctively the dance of death. He saw again the prison of the eternal serpent and the futility of the tiny lives that it consumed. He saw the bravery of men and the beauty of women, and that both would end in dust. He saw the laughter of children and the smile of the torturer, and that both of them ended in dust. He saw with strange clarity the figure of his master, and saw that magicians were powerless against the silent return to the dust. And then he saw that, being helpless, a man still could do one thing. He could choose the manner and time of his dying; he could be the owner of his death. More, he could be the owner of himself, and give no hostages to the serpent: for he could choose to die without sowing seed.

The chill, pure music. The sun dipped. The rhythm had quickened slightly, there seemed a new urgency in it. But what urgency could there be, since all things were circling towards death? Demetrius danced, knowing it was his last dance. The music pierced him with longing, with an aching melancholy. The women were all dancing now, their faces rapt and turned to the setting sun. Demetrius danced.

The music was faster, and then faster. The dancers, the hillside, receded, and he was alone, far above them, his mind still, in a cool transparent region where quiet voices spoke to him of mysteries. He was flying over a wrinkled silver sea, and the voices spoke encouragement. He was on a journey, and had nearly reached its end; when he reached it he could rest, rest for ever in the pure stillness, for he would have done what was required.

To help him, something had been put into his hand. It was to do with the thing that was required. Looking down, many miles down from where he flew above the silver sea, he saw that his body, with which unhappily and inexplicably his mind seemed still connected, was as yet not purified. It was a small matter: in his mind he raised the knife, and his hand raised it.

Shouting came to him. It was offensive, and his hand paused. His hand was then grasped roughly by another hand. Demetrius did not want that. He did not want the heavy blows that yet another hand delivered to his face, although they did not hurt him. But the blows dislodged his mind from its airy floating, and he felt himself slipping down, back into the gross and sweating body, into tumult. Grotesque faces thronged round him, his waist was gripped by a powerful arm against which he struggled furiously and impotently. The ground – ah, God, the ground – was covered in blood and bloody mangled flesh. He swayed against the arm that held him, vomited, and collapsed.

There was icy water on his face and running down his neck. He shuddered. He was picked up, carried a short distance and set down near a fire. A cloak was put over him. Leaves were thrown on the fire. The smoke was sharp and aromatic. Demetrius sneezed violently. The sneeze made everything fly apart. Then it all flew back together again with a sort of silent crash. After that it stayed still.

'Good', said Simon.

A long time seemed to pass. Demetrius realised he had had a dream. He had never been away from Simon. It was not possible.

Simon said quietly, 'You little fool.'

Demetrius tried to think about this, but it was too difficult. Something seemed to be in the way. He tested his voice, and found that it worked. 'What happened?' he said.

'You were about to geld yourself', growled Simon. 'Not that it would have made much difference.'

Demetrius felt the ground lurch. Something cleared in his head, and he thought he heard music.

'Did you stop me?' he whispered.

'Well, you've still got it all, haven't you?'

He felt with his hand the warm, intact flesh. He was filled with a furious bitterness.

'You took me away!' he shouted. 'I wanted to purify myself!'

He broke into wild sobbing. Simon watched as he sobbed himself to sleep.

The morning was hard and bright, with no mist. Demetrius awoke with his head pillowed on Simon's arm. He lay and thought, and it seemed to him that the situation could be worse. After a while he decided that it could be a great deal worse. Further thought suggested that it also required explanation. He wriggled to see if Simon was awake.

'Don't wriggle,' said Simon.

'How did you get here?' said Demetrius. 'I mean, how did you know where I was?'

'Do you think I came looking for you, conceited boy?'

'Oh', said Demetrius.

Simon smiled at him. 'I divined you', he said.

'What?'

'I was looking for a cargo of silks, and I found you instead. A very poor bargain.'

Demetrius wriggled with contentment. He realised he had been getting very bored with processions. They lay and talked. Simon told him about the divination of Horus, and Demetrius shivered. Simon told him about the green and purple head, and Demetrius squealed. Simon told him about the Gorgon, and Demetrius howled with laughter.

'Now', said Simon, 'you can tell me how you came to fall in with those murderous Corybantes and decide to make a career as a eunuch. But first you can tell me what happened when you were captured. If they tortured you, you have made a remarkable recovery.'

Demetrius told him, with a few embellishments.

'So', said Simon, 'you were going to sell me for thirty pieces of silver?'

'Of course not', said Demetrius indignantly. 'It was a trick to make them let me go.'

'Ah, I see', said Simon. After a pause he said, 'Thirty shekels is an insult.' A little later he said, 'On the other hand ...' Then for a while he said nothing, but studied the sky.

39

'All right,' he said eventually. 'We'll go back there.'

'But you'll be captured!' cried Demetrius.

'Think of the money', said Simon. 'With thirty shekels we could go to Sebaste. You'd like it there.'

He watched as the boy's stare of amazement cleared into comprehension. He was a good boy. Simon ran his fingers over the bouncy curls and the nape of the clean young neck. The corners of Demetrius's mouth twitched – with amusement, or acquiescence, or even pleasure: Simon never knew.

He removed his arm from under the boy's head, turned him over and tenderly sodomised him. It had been a long time, and he always found his concentration greatly improved afterwards.

It was three days' journey back to Askalon by the longer route, avoiding the coast road. They arranged to meet at an inn five miles outside the town.

'If you aren't there,' said Simon, 'if you double-cross me, I shall seek you out again and I shall find you, and I shall do a number of unspeakable things to you and geld you last of all, and you will not have been dancing all day and therefore you will feel every bit of it. You know that, don't you, lion-hearted boy?'

Demetrius nodded humbly. He had already briefly entertained the idea and rejected it.

They walked casually through the gates and parted. Demetrius went to the magistrate's house. Simon strolled in the direction of the amphitheatre. It was early evening and the streets were busy.

Simon sat on the marble steps of the theatre and seemed to gaze at the ground. After an interval Demetrius, pointing, reappeared with a group of six soldiers. They came towards Simon, who continued to gaze at the ground.

'Simon of Gitta?' demanded the largest soldier.

Simon looked up. 'I am Simon the Magus', he said.

They seized him, surprised and mocking when he made no resistance. One of the soldiers, chuckling, threw Demetrius a bag of money. The boy made off, melting into the curious crowd.

The soldiers shoved Simon forward and waved the onlookers away. At the point where the street was crossed by a network of alleys and the crowds were thickest, Simon stopped.

'My sandal is broken', he said.

He half-stooped. The soldiers never knew what happened. One moment there was a solid, muscular body under their hands: the next there was not.

'It went like wax in a fire', one of them said afterwards, but they flogged him just the same.

Simon walked quickly through the crowds until he came to the gates. Then he ran.

He ran like the devil.

II

GODS

Sebaste was the new name for the ancient hilltop capital of Samaria, formerly and confusingly called Samaria. The name had been changed by Herod the Idumean, who liked clarity in his kingdom and later gained a very bad reputation for over-efficiency.

Herod also liked modern architecture, and endowed Sebaste with many fine buildings in the Greek style. This did little to endear him to his native subjects, who suspected, quite rightly, that Greek buildings would be followed by Greek manners, and watched with gloomy satisfaction as their sons threw off the modesty with which circumcision was traditionally cloaked to wrestle naked in the new gymnasium.

By that time, however, the original inhabitants of Samaria no longer formed a majority of the population. Indeed their Jewish neighbours maintained that there were no original Samaritans left. According to the Jews, all Samaritans were now of mixed blood if not downright heathen, being descended from the eastern races with whom Sargon of Assyria had populated the northern kingdom (having first depopulated it of Israelites) seven centuries before. The Samaritans indignantly asserted their membership of the chosen race, and explained their apparent deviations from Jewish doctrine by saying that it was not they who had deviated. It was a very old quarrel, and was never understood by anyone except the parties concerned.

Half a century after the Idumean's death, in circumstances which were in every respect disgusting (the terminal stage of disease being delayed long enough for the rotting monarch to burn alive a group of young religious protesters), Sebaste was one of the most cosmopolitan cities of the empire. Its population included a large community of Greeks and a scattering of Italians, north Africans and Asians, as well as the surviving stock of the Assyrian plantation. A dozen religions were practised there, earning it the title of an irreligious city. Standing on the site of the temple of Baal built by Ahab the Backslider, the pious Samaritan could lift his eyes to the holy mountain of Gerizim, on which (contrary to Jewish belief) Moses had received the Law, and to which in recent memory a prophet had led his followers to find the long-lost sacred vessels of the Sanctuary. (The vessels were never found, the pilgrims being massacred by order of the procurator Pilate.)

Providing one did not mix one's religion with politics, Sebaste was an accommodating, pleasant city, and after his tribulations in Judaea Simon Magus the Samaritan bent his steps towards it as towards home. He felt he would be safe there. In this he was mistaken.

He had not been in Sebaste for five years, but remembered it fondly as a place where he had made no little stir. Entering it, dusty, tired and irritable, with a donkey that tried to eat its baggage and Demetrius complaining of blisters, Simon felt a great sense of relief. He was sure to be quickly recognised. He hoped recognition would be delayed until he had had time to take a bath. Ideally he would prefer not to be recognised until he had found respectable lodgings and recovered from the journey. However, if he encountered a former acquaintance and was offered a room, it would not be unwelcome.

He trudged through the streets with Demetrius and the donkey, and was not recognised.

They found lodgings at an inn, run-down and none too clean, in a cheap quarter of the city. Simon glanced around him with distaste.

'What line of business might you be in?' enquired the innkeeper, eyeing him doubtfully.

Simon was enraged. He was tempted to reveal his identity: the magician who five years ago had turned the main square of Sebaste into a green forest and filled it with lions and tigers and leaping gazelles. He refrained. He would not be believed, which was worse than not being recognised.

'I am a merchant', he said stiffly, 'but I trade in a very rare commodity. The room will do.'

It would have to do, until he could arrange something better. He sank down on the bed and was overwhelmed by despondency. Town after town, and in every place he had to start again. Here, where he had expected to find friends, it was no different. No one remembered him.

Demetrius, picking his blisters, looked up with an expression that might almost have been interpreted as sympathy.

'It'll be all right in a few days', he said.

'You're an imbecile', said Simon.

Demetrius often knew what he was thinking. It was infuriating. He was better at reading minds than Simon was himself.

But Demetrius was right.

Two days after his arrival in Sebaste, a bath, a rest and a new cloak had restored Simon's spirits, and he strolled confidently through the mid-morning bustle of the streets. Sometimes he thought he saw a face he recognised, but his glance was returned blankly.

Well, they would know him soon enough.

He stopped in front of a man who was selling singing birds in small wooden cages. He pointed to a cage which contained a single bird.

'You have too many birds in that cage', he said. 'They'll fight each other.'

The man stared at him. 'What are you talking about? There's only one bird in there.'

'Nonsense', said Simon. 'There are five at least.'

'There's one, I tell you.'

'In fact,' said Simon, 'I can count ten.'

'You mad or something?'

A crowd was gathering.

'Ten, twenty, what does it matter?' said Simon. 'At any rate, some of them should clearly be removed.'

He lifted the latch of the cage door with his finger.

''Ere', said the bird seller. 'Hands off.'

'How much do you want', asked Simon, 'for the total number of birds in this cage?'

The bystanders murmured and tittered.

'Two sesterces, and that's for the cage as well. If you want it, take it and clear off.'

Simon dropped a coin into the outstretched palm and opened the cage door. The bird hopped to the edge of the cage and stood there for a moment, cheeping, frightened, testing freedom. Simon turned his head and swept the crowd with his gaze.

The bird fluttered and, with sudden sureness, opened its wings and darted into the sky. The second bird, fluttering behind it, hesitated only a moment before soaring skyward. Its place was immediately taken by a third bird, a fourth, a fifth, until it was no longer possible to count the tiny, bright-feathered bodies that spilled out of the cage and streamed over the heads of the gaping crowd.

Simon closed the little wooden door with a flick of his finger.

'Keep the cage', he said, and walked away.

The sect which maintained that the end of the world was at hand was experiencing the beginnings of internal dissension. It was nothing serious at first: a squabble between two groups over the distribution of food. One party complained that some of its members were being left out. Underlying the ill-feeling was an antipathy between two cultural groups, but the distinction embraced religious and political attitudes as well. The sect had been founded by men of narrow political outlook who thought of themselves as reformers within the national religion. It now found itself attracting members whose religion and politics had, as it were, been contaminated by contact with the sophisticated culture of the empire. The differences polarised in terms of language: the new members spoke Greek.

The trouble over the food was sorted out and an equitable distribution established. But it was a symptom of a deep-rooted problem which in time assumed alarming proportions for the leadership. Whom, ultimately, could they accept as members of their racially exclusive, class-biased, apocalyptic elect? They were simple men, and had not thought of the future: there was none. So they went fishing for minnows, and caught Leviathan.

Meanwhile there were other problems: inevitable perhaps, but distressing to a community which claimed to live in truth and harmony. All property was held in common by the members, and those with investments sold them and gave the money to the administrators, who divided it among the needy. Human nature eventually reasserted itself. A certain landowner sold some property, kept part of the proceeds, and gave the rest to the sect saying that it was the whole sum.

The leader of the sect at this time was a man who went by the nickname of Kepha. Of obscure origins, a man of faith and instinct rather than reason, he compelled respect by the simplicity of his life and by his reputation for miraculous powers. It was believed that he could read people's thoughts. He was known to have performed several astonishing feats of magic. He was approaching middle years, but maturity had done nothing to mellow his temper.

According to the only surviving record of the event, the luckless landowner brought his gift to Kepha, who instantly detected its dishonesty. 'You have lied to God!' he thundered. The landowner collapsed where he stood, and when picked up was found to be dead.

Not even its bitterest enemies ever accused the sect of frivolity. Among its enemies was a cultured young man of well-to-do family whose liberal education had in no way diluted his piety. He saw in these antisocial sectarians the most dangerous threat his people's religion had faced for centuries, and applied his considerable abilities to combating it. He began with a campaign of legal harassment.

It was a stroke of luck, or of brilliance: Simon inclined to think the latter. Within days the whole of Sebaste knew about the flock of eagles which had poured out of a tiny cage and blotted out the sun. He was greeted in the street by people he did not know, and invited to dinner by men he had never met before. For the time being, he declined. He did not, however, refuse the clients who turned up at the inn with strange requests. Money accumulated pleasingly in his purse, under the mattress, and in the innkeeper's strong box.

The innkeeper, put out of temper by a flow of visitors who did not stay to drink his wine, demanded to know the nature of the lucrative business transacted in Simon's room. Simon tipped him to enquire no further, and found a house to rent in the fashionable part of town.

The house was pleasant, airy, and had more than the average number of rooms. It was expensive, but he told himself he needed the space. He was planning some serious work. He required, in addition to his bedroom, a small study and a workroom in which to carry out experiments. He moved in, Demetrius labouring under books and cases of equipment which Simon had purchased in a rush of enthusiasm at the bazaar.

To celebrate his change in circumstances, he accepted an invitation to dinner.

'I have never found any difficulty in curing epilepsy', pronounced the doctor. 'Goat's flesh, roasted on a funeral pyre, is an infallible remedy.'

'Infallible?' murmured Simon. He was concentrating on removing the bones from the smallest fish he had ever seen. He had found out, after accepting the invitation, that Morphus's dinners were renowned for their stinginess.

'Ah.' The doctor wagged a fat finger at him. 'The gall of the animal must not be allowed to touch the ground. It's my belief that in every case in which the remedy has failed, this simple precaution has been omitted.'

'How interesting', said Morphus. 'Why must it not be allowed to touch the ground?'

49

'The humours of the gall', began the physician, 'being hot and moist ...'

'The thumb of a virgin', remarked Simon, 'being cool and dry ...'

'Sorcery!' snapped the doctor.

'No, no', said Simon. 'I was speaking not of a severed thumb, but of one still attached to its owner.'

'Epilepsy can be cured by the touch of a virgin's thumb?' marvelled Morphus.

'Certainly. The right thumb, of course.'

Thrasyllus, the young fop who had arrived late and been yawning ever since, drawled, 'Are there any virgins in Sebaste?'

The fourth guest was the tribune who had recently been posted to the town. He was responsible for public order. Morphus hoped to make a friend of him, but had started badly. The tribune was scowling. He had been scowling for the past half-hour, which was the length of time in which his wine-goblet had remained unfilled.

'I thought in this part of the world', said the tribune coldly, 'epilepsy was caused by demons. Along with nearly everything else.'

'Oh yes', put in Morphus eagerly. 'My cousin had a servant whose daughter was possessed by a demon. She was quite violent, they had to lock her in a cupboard, sometimes she was there for weeks. She was very strong, nearly broke the door down. Amazing, really.'

'Stuff and nonsense', said the doctor.

'That demons can possess people?' asked Simon.

'Of course not. They can and do. But they do not cause epilepsy.'

'How do you know?' objected Simon. 'If a demon takes possession of someone it might as well amuse itself in causing epilepsy as in any other way.'

'A totally unscientific view. Epilepsy is caused by an accession of heat to the brain, which, being naturally cold and lacking blood, is thrown into disorder –'

'That there is no blood in the brain', interrupted the tribune, 'can be disproved by any soldier who has ever seen a man's head split open.'

There was silence for a while. The servants brought in a very small portion of a very small roasted lamb. The tribune peered at it in disbelief.

Thrasyllus said lazily, 'Talking of devils, one of my servants ran into a chap the other day who was exorcising them. Fellow from Judaea.'

'Oh, these wretched Jewish exorcists', grumbled the doctor. 'They cause more trouble than they cure.'

'My cousin's servant's daughter's demon', said Morphus, 'was driven out by a travelling exorcist. It shrieked horribly, and came out in a puff of black smoke. It was quite terrifying, my cousin said.'

'What happened to the girl?' asked Simon.

'Oh, she was all right for a time, but then she got another one and was worse than ever. Some people attract them, I think.'

'That is exactly what I mean', said the doctor. 'Get rid of one and before you know where you are there are ten in its place.'

'Seven', corrected Simon absently.

'Leave well alone, I say. Better the demon you know –'

'Ah, but if you know it', said Simon, 'you can cast it out. The first principle of exorcism is to learn the demon's name.'

'I believe', said the tribune with a straight look at Simon, 'that it is also the first principle of sorcery.'

'All things may be put to bad uses,' said Simon smoothly. 'I know nothing of sorcery myself.'

'They say you can fly', said the tribune.

'Indeed I can. But I call on no demons and make no nocturnal sacrifices. It is a power given by the gods.'

'I'll believe it when I see it', growled the doctor.

'You shall see it quite soon', smiled Simon.

The doctor glared. 'As a man of science I can categorically assure you –'

'What else can you do?' demanded the tribune.

'A number of things', replied Simon, 'but they require a sympathetic audience.'

'I'm sure everyone here –' began Morphus.

'This chap from Judaea', said Thrasyllus, 'cures lepers. By just touching them.'

'Rubbish!' cried the doctor. 'Leprosy is caused by an excessive coldness and dryness of the –'

'Doubtless', said Simon. He turned to Thrasyllus. 'What is he called, this miracle-worker of yours?'

'Oh, I didn't bother to ask. He didn't sound very amusing. One of these religious fanatics – wants everybody to repent.'

'How tiresome', said Simon.

51

'Though actually from my servant's account he sounded a bit odd', continued Thrasyllus. 'I mean, you know what the Jews are like – only one God and all the rest of it. Well, this man wasn't invoking the Jewish god, but somebody quite different.'

'Oh?' Simon became attentive. 'Then he can't have been a Jew.'

'But he was.'

'Which god was he invoking?'

'Well, according to my servant, he was calling on the spirit of some chap who'd been executed a few years back.'

'*What*?' said Simon and the tribune in unison.

There was a startled silence. Simon leaned back and picked his teeth clean of the lamb: there seemed to be as much between his teeth as had gone into his stomach.

'Well well', he said. 'A necromancer. Quite open about it, too. I give him a month before the authorities catch up with him.'

He caught the tribune's eye. He and the tribune smiled at each other like cats.

Simon felt all at once very pleased with life.

'It is sometimes vouchsafed to me', he said, 'to turn water into wine, and I feel that in the circumstances it might be a useful contribution. Would you like me to try?'

He got up and walked to where a meagre fountain played in the adjoining courtyard. The trick was only safely performed when the company had drunk well already, but it was amazing what need could do to the palate. He looked upward: the night sky was brilliant with stars. Orion and Cassiopeia, Alpha and Omega, the unending web of mystery. Gods of the night, gods of the spaces, accept me as your own. Tonight he could do anything.

Half Sebaste, it seemed, had gathered in the square. Even the villagers had left their fields and come into town to watch. The magician had promised to create a grand illusion.

Simon stood at one side of the square on a dais draped with purple cloth. To his left was an empty space which had been cordoned off from the crowd.

He extended his hands to them in salutation.

'My friends', he cried, 'you have come for entertainment, but I give you instruction. I shall tell you a story. It is the oldest story in the world.'

The air seemed to freshen. In the roped-off area of the square there appeared a drifting green mist. Within it eddies of denser

52

green developed and took bulky form; the forms sharpened, emerging from the mist, which sank and settled on the ground around them, and became grass. It was a garden, lush with plants and creepers, and bright with darting birds.

'Look up', said Simon.

The air had darkened, as if in a gigantic shadow. Looking up, they saw huge leafy boughs waving above the square. A majestic tree, tall as a Lebanon cedar, its lower branches hung with glistening globular fruit.

Simon focused their attention on what was happening just in front of the tree.

A woman stood there, with her back to them, apparently gazing at the trunk. Then she moved away, and they saw that coiled around the tree trunk was a fat yellow serpent.

The serpent moved the upper part of its body in an ingratiating dance, stopping every now and then to indicate, by the position of its head, a fruit on the lowest branch of the tree.

The woman shook her head vigorously. The snake resumed its dancing. The silent dialogue was repeated several times. Then slowly the woman walked back to the tree. Slowly she reached for the fruit, picked it, and raised it to her lips.

The crowd sighed.

In another part of the garden appeared a man, carrying on his shoulder a basket of grapes. He came towards the woman, who offered him the fruit in her hand. He stopped in his tracks and made a gesture as if to push her away. She smiled, offering the fruit. He came forward, and took it.

There was a crack of thunder and the two figures reeled backwards. It was suddenly dark. Then in front of the tree there appeared a dazzling light.

Out of the light stepped a tall and shining figure, snowy-haired, with a face like fire. The letters of the Holy Name burned on his breast. In his hand he held a sword that was like a streak of flame. He turned it towards the man and the woman, who fled, writhing under its bite, into the darkness.

Gradually the darkness lifted. The fiery figure had gone.

The colours of the tree began to fade, as if bleached out by the sun, and the outline of the trunk wavered as in a heat-mist. Patches of sky interrupted the massive boughs, which shrank and crumbled until at last only patches of green hung like worn fabric on the sky.

He held the vision a moment longer, then let it go.

53

There was silence for about the time it takes to understand that a thing was a dream. Then a low, involuntary murmur began. It swelled until it was a roar in a thousand throats.

'Simon! Simon! Simon!'

He stood on the dais, his ears ringing with the sound, his mind curiously empty. He smiled at them, feeling a kind of remote pity.

'Simon! Simon! Simon Magus!'

The buildings around the square caught the chant and flung it back, until the air itself seemed to rock. Among the stray shouts that pierced the chanting he heard a voice cry 'Hail to the god Simon!'

Other voices took up the cry. Some of the women began to tear off their jewellery and throw it at his feet. Several people were prostrating themselves.

He could not allow it. He raised his arms in a gesture of authority, and as the chanting briefly died away he bowed slightly and stepped down from the dais. The people parted before him like the Red Sea waters.

It was no blasphemy to most ears, in those days, to call a man a god. The line between humanity and divinity was vaguely drawn, and had been crossed by a regular procession of pharaohs, kings, heroes and emperors. The qualifications did not have anything to do with morality. The only distinction between men and gods was one of power.

Inevitably, in such a culture, a man who performed acts of magic was thought to be a kind of god. It would be a remarkable wonder-worker who did not, at least occasionally, believe himself to be what he was thought to be. His problem was to maintain his peculiar status without being elevated by his admirers to a level at which failure would be both inescapable and disastrous. None of this was understood at the time, since there was no knowledge of psychology and demonology was used instead.

The expectations of their public placed a heavy burden on the shoulders of miracle-workers. Some of them undoubtedly succumbed to the pressure and went insane. Numerous rituals were developed to enable the magician to increase his power. The most dramatic were designed to effect a union between the magician and a supernatural being. They were, in intent, rites of self-deification. Most of them involved a period of fasting, a purification, and, at the culmination of the rite, the descent of a bird.

54

It seems likely, however, that the performance of such a rite, if it appeared to have been successful, can only have made the magician's problem worse.

Simon flew.

It was a warm spring morning, clear and windless. The muted murmur of the crowd reached him as he stood on the roof of the law courts, his palms extended to the sun. Glancing down, he saw the tribune, standing apart with a group of officials. For a moment he thought he glimpsed another face, obscurely disquieting. When he looked again it had gone. He dismissed it. Omens had no power today.

He chanted his love to Horus, sublime source of his strength. And Horus answered.

A shock of fire. Fire burning through his face, hands and unsandalled feet, burning down through the soles of his feet and striking up again, burning in the space between the roof and the soles of his feet, which lifted as he rose, incandescent, and glided, light as ash, on air.

Over the crowd he floated, over buildings, gardens, a silver stream. In the immense silence he heard distinctly the tinkling of the water over pebbles. He saw the little huddled houses of the outskirts, the sun-basking dogs, a donkey dozing in a courtyard. He saw, beyond the houses, the endless hills.

Imperceptibly the air thinned. He was being drawn downward, but with such gentleness it seemed he had a lifetime left in which to prepare. Ahead of him a cool green garden opened like a friend's smile, and he let himself be drawn to it, and sank slowly, or it rose to greet him, and he was standing, firm earth under feet, his toes kissed by grass.

He heard, like a distant sea, the crowd's thunder.

There was one part of the empire where the line between humanity and divinity was not only firmly drawn, it was unapproachable. The intransigence of the Hebrews on this point was respected by their rulers, who exempted them – a privilege granted to no other race – from worship of the emperor. This was merely enlightened common sense. The last ruler who had attempted to impose alien worship on the province had precipitated a revolt which went on for twenty years and lost his successors control of the country.

But the mystical imagination is not to be contained by law, even divine law. The seers and sages of the Hebrews sometimes found themselves, at the end of their soaring speculations, on the wrong side of the forbidden line. To the intuition the leap was but a step. The fiery ascent of Elijah, the strange disappearance of Enoch, what were they but hints of a not-to-be-spoken-of apotheosis? From such hints Jews of a desperate generation, far from averting their eyes, wove the stuff of apocalyptic dreams. The Samaritans, who set no store by Elijah, elaborated their theology to accommodate the imminent return to earth, and by implication the divinity, of Moses.

The *Ta'eb* was the Deliverer awaited by the Samaritans, and that he would be a second incarnation of the great deliverer from captivity seemed obvious. He would unite the long-divided kingdoms of Israel and lead them to a final, crushing victory over their oppressors. He would restore the true worship on Mount Gerizim and inaugurate the Second Kingdom, which after a period of a hundred years would end in the destruction of the world by fire and a general resurrection.

These violent fantasies were not favoured by the imperial power, and were mostly indulged in private.

It was dangerous wine the crowd offered Simon. He declined to drink it. But despite his judgement, he could not resist sipping it a little. It made his head buzz, and the aftertaste was bitter.

He knew, of course, that he was not a god. He slept, rose, ate, defecated, suffered from toothache and was sometimes afraid, like all other men. He wanted things he could not have and did not know as much as he would like to know. His mother had been a vine-dresser's daughter and his father, having enjoyed her among the vines, had never been seen again. Gods are not of such stock.

He did not know what he was.

Sensibly, he arranged his time in such a way that he did not have leisure to think about it. In the morning he received clients. Three hours in the afternoon he set aside for his own private work. He did not allow this period to be intruded on: if he was required to give a public demonstration he would do it in the morning. The evenings, at first, he spent at the theatre and in dining out, but as the weeks went by he found himself spending more and more evenings at home. His house had become the meeting place for a circle of young men, mostly drawn from the upper ranks of local society, who had come at first out of curiosity, and now came for the conversation.

Most of the conversation was provided by Simon. He discoursed with erudition and wit on whatever subject they cared to raise, but mostly on matters of philosophy. He enjoyed an audience. They treated him with deference and brought him gifts. Most of them were rather stupid, but it was agreeable to have disciples.

He wished sometimes that they would not come. Having organised his time, he began to find he did not have enough of it. He was planning something that needed careful preparation. He had wanted to attempt it for years, but this was the first time he had been in one place long enough to make the necessary arrangements.

The 'obot were as old as the earth, and dwelt in its depths. Their voices, squeaking and gibbering from fissures in the ground, could be heard at night in lonely places, at crossroads, and in the vicinity of tombs. The Israelites had turned secretly to their worship throughout the generations, braving the rantings of the prophets and the thunder of Jahweh. The 'obot knew the secrets of the future, and could be used for divination. Under priestly law the penalty for consulting them was death. There was risk of another penalty as well. The 'ob, once evoked, might try to enter the body of the enchanter. If it succeeded, it would drive him into the wilderness and possess him. Many cases had been known.

Simon had made a profession of dangers, and he knew that many dangers were not as great as they appeared. The laws of magic were precise. When procedures were correctly observed, results followed. Nothing could diminish the power of the words to bind and loose. Magic was a chain of causes and effects. The weak link was the magician. He must be free from any imperfection of body, any frailty of mind, on which the demon could fasten. His will must be a weapon that could not be deflected.

Simon studied his books, fasted, meditated, and abstained from sexual acts.

He took a further precaution. He believed that one of the reasons why the spirit-raising so often ended in disaster was that the experimenters had failed to consider the demon's over-riding need to take possession of matter, and had also not realised that a spirit which dwelt in ugly places would have a great susceptibility to beauty. With this in mind he had commissioned a small marble statue: it should, he said, express the ideal harmony and grace of the human form. When it was ready he was astonished at how well the sculptor had caught his intention. It was beautiful. It showed a boy, naked in the Greek style, in the act of raising a flute to his lips. The head, covered in short curls, was bent slightly forward in concentration, and a half-smile seemed to hover on the features.

Simon carried it home, wrapped it in silk and placed it in his bedroom. Into these veins of virgin marble he would entice, threaten and conjure his demon, and there he would bind it. It would be his to command.

The risk was great but measurable. The prize was beyond measure. The 'obot knew secrets that were denied to men.

The disciples lounged in a circle, drinking a good vintage and eating green olives. They spat the stones into a bronze bowl in the centre. The bowl was embossed with a frieze of Zeus and Ganymede. It rang pleasantly as the stones shot into it.

Morphus spat. The bowl did not ring. He had missed again. He always missed. He was a positive hazard when urinating.

'Try again', said Simon.

He was speaking, not to Morphus, but to Thrasyllus, who sprawled elegantly on a couch and toyed with his bracelets as he strove to formulate a thought. It was unlikely to be a profound thought, although he had been gingerly approaching it for several minutes.

'Well, I don't see how the earth can be a god', he said at last. 'If it was, it wouldn't let people cut canals in it.'

They had been discussing the *Timaeus*. That is to say, Simon had been discussing it and the disciples had been attempting to follow.

'Why did Plato say the earth was a god?' asked the thin poet nervously. He did not often speak, and Simon could never remember his name.

'Because it is beautiful, eternal, and has the perfect shape of a sphere', said Simon for the third time that evening.

Morphus thought. 'Does that mean', he said, 'that the gods are spherical?'

'Not quite', said Simon.

Eli the Samaritan convulsed himself with laughter, and Simon grinned at him. Eli was his best pupil. The trouble was that he was religious.

Eli had reached that delicate stage where a man has half-abandoned the religion of his childhood with his intellect but it retains its hold on his heart. Eli's heart and mind were engaged in a constant warfare from which he sought relief in politics. He had the tact not to bring his politics to Simon's house, but he brought his conflicts. He was looking for a guide, a teacher; but in Simon he had made an uncomfortable choice. Simon teased him. He told himself that Simon did not always mean what he said. This was true, but it was usually not true when Eli thought it was.

'The Greeks', Eli now observed, 'will deify anything.'

'And why not?' asked Simon. 'Why should divinity not reside everywhere?'

'Because if it does,' said Eli, 'it resides in things which are subject to change and decay, and that is contrary to reason and offends the moral sense.'

'Splendid', said Simon. 'At least someone's been listening.'

'However, that's not the point', said Eli. 'The point surely is that it's nonsense to call something a god when we have power over it – as Thrasyllus says. God is that over which we have no power.'

'Many people would not agree with you.'

'Of course not. They worship gods that don't exist.'

'Ah,' said Simon. 'Only Eli's God exists. A belief impossible to justify, which will not prevent him from holding it.'

Eli said nothing. He was not to be drawn this evening.

'What about your own beliefs?' ventured the thin poet. 'Can you justify them?'

'I don't hold beliefs in the sense you're speaking of', answered Simon. 'As a magician, I am a scientist, and therefore I don't *believe* things, I either know them or regard them as doubtful.'

'But you believe, for instance, in the god Horus', objected the poet.

'No. I have seen manifestations of a certain power and experienced its effects. I call this power Horus. That's all.'

'You've *seen* Horus?' said Thrasyllus, wide-eyed.

'Yes, in divinations and dreams.'

'What does he look like?'

'He usually appears as a hawk.'

'But have you ever seen him in his true form standing in front of you?' the poet persisted.

'No, and I hope not to.'

'In that case', put in Eli, 'how do you know he exists? What you see might just be a demon.'

'True', said Simon, 'but how do you know your God exists? You can't see Him at all: you aren't allowed to.'

Eli scowled.

The thin poet said, 'There's a man from Judaea who casts out demons.'

'Good heavens', said Simon, 'haven't they caught him yet?'

'My cousin –' began Morphus.

'Morphus', said Simon, 'would you be so kind as to bring us some more wine from the kitchen? My slave-boy is out for the evening.'

'Again?' said Eli.

'It's his evening off', explained Simon.

'I thought tomorrow was his evening off.'

'Well he's out tonight instead, because I shall need him tomorrow.' Simon felt suddenly irritated. Since he had had disciples he had had no privacy. 'I shall be very busy for the next few days', he said. 'I'd rather you didn't come round for a while.'

Eli looked both surprised and hurt.

Morphus brought the wine, and poured it. Quite a lot of it went on the floor.

The day was calm and without wind: a good omen. Simon spent most of it in meditation. He ate nothing, and drank only water. In the evening he and Demetrius bathed, and put on clean clothes. Then they waited.

They set off at sunset. The conjuration was to be performed at the hour of Saturn. Simon carried the statue, carefully wrapped: Demetrius carried the book and other equipment. The place was a disused cemetery just outside the town. As they walked, Simon noticed with a frown that small clouds were scudding across the moon. A wind had risen. It could not be helped.

They reached the place and Demetrius helped him draw the circle with the tip of his sword: a double circle, reinforced at the cardinal points with the names of God. Outside the circle they placed the statue on a small plinth, and near it kindled a charcoal fire. In the centre of the circle they fixed a lighted torch. Simon then dismissed Demetrius. He would have liked his assistance, but the risk was too great. He waited until the boy was well beyond the area before unveiling the statue and placing the incense on the fire. He re-entered and closed the circle, and began the invocation.

For a long time nothing happened. Then behind him he heard a faint, squeaky gibbering. The hair prickled on his neck. He repeated the invocation, commanding the spirit to show itself in a harmless form. Again the faint, non-human gibbering. He swung to face it, but it had moved; now it was to his right, now behind him again. For a few moments he spun stupidly in one direction and another, until the realisation of his peril brought him to himself. Lifting the sword in his right hand and grasping the book in his left, he turned in a slow circle, cleaving the darkness to north, east, south and west, driving the demon before the sword's edge.

'I conjure thee and command thee that thou come instantly before me, without noise, deformity or monstrous appearance. I conjure thee with strength and violence by the names Shaddai, Elohim, Sabaoth, Adonai. I conjure thee by the Day of Judgement and by the Crystal Sea, and by the eyes of the Watchers and the wheels of the Ofanim, and by the fire of the countenance of the Most High.'

The tremendous words rolled and thundered among the rocks. As they died away there came a faint, mocking twitter behind him.

'I conjure thee anew, by the most holy name of God, Adonai Melekh, that Joshua invoked and stayed the course of the sun; I conjure thee by the name Elohim, that Moses invoked, and having struck the waters, they parted; I conjure thee by the name Agla, that David invoked, and smote Goliath.'

Silence. A long, watching silence.

Simon, the sweat standing on his face, raised his hands towards the sky.

'I constrain and command thee, by the Name of four letters that may not be spoken, the most holy and terrible Name –'

Something moved, just out of vision. He fought the impulse to turn his head, and fixed his gaze instead on the smoke that streamed from the fire, tossed in stray directions by snatches of wind. He sent out his will and commanded the spirit to make for itself a form in the smoke.

Suddenly he felt it. His mind was caught and held by a force as strong as his own; but not, he realised, as directed. It was playful, capricious: it had engaged him in fun. He tightened his grasp, willing it to submit. It bucked and twisted, trying to throw him, and he felt strength draining out of him and a racking pain in his entrails. He could not hold the force. It flung him off. It had flung him physically to the ground: he found himself on his knees, only a hand's breadth away from the edge of the circle. He had dropped the book. Groping, he searched in the torchlight for the passage he needed, and could not find it. He was shaking.

He stood up, grasping the sword and his talisman, and began to recite the conjuration from memory. But something had happened to his tongue: it stumbled over the words, and he realised in panic that he did not know what came next. He stopped abruptly, before he made a fatal mistake. Behind him he heard a quick, delighted twittering.

He became conscious that his body was unnaturally cold. He was in terrible danger. He must banish the spirit while he still had the power to do so. By a great effort of concentration he summoned the words to his mind. Before he could speak them a wild gust of wind swept between the rocks, fanning the fire from red to leaping gold, and throwing the smoke like a scarf across the circle. Simon, momentarily blinded, opened his eyes in time to see the statue sway on its perch, lean and topple. The wind dropped instantly. For a space everything was still. Then there formed fleetingly in the now vertically-rising smoke a bulbous, legged shape of such grotesqueness that he involuntarily stepped back and raised his talisman against it.

Then there was nothing. The smoke rose clean. The demon had gone. Lest it had not quite gone, he pronounced loudly, not once but three times, the formula of the licence to depart.

It is a commonplace that beliefs thrive on persecution, but it happens to be untrue. For every belief that has so thrived, ten have been extinguished, and are unearthed by historians at a time when reasons for their non-viability can with hindsight be easily adduced.

It is likewise not difficult, with hindsight, to adduce reasons why a belief survived. The sect who thought that the end of the world was at hand subsequently attributed their survival, some time after the world had failed to end, to the protecting hand of God. Others attributed it to an emperor's dream on the eve of a battle, and yet others to the constellation of Pisces, into whose sphere of influence the planet was moving at the time.

It might with equal likelihood be attributed to an event which took place on a desert road and was witnessed by a handful of people, only one of whom claimed to understand its meaning. It appears to have been in the nature of a vision. Its recipient was the devout young Jew who had made it his mission to root out the apocalyptic sectarians from the earth.

He had more or less succeeded in extirpating them from Jerusalem, where they had their headquarters. Most of those who had

62

not been locked up had fled to the country districts, and the leaders had gone into hiding. Searching for fresh fields of activity, their persecutor obtained permission to extend his harrying tactics to a city in a neighbouring province where the sect had a few adherents. He set out on his journey robust, arrogant, fanatical, the scourge of God. He arrived at his destination frightened, bewildered, emotionally shattered, and blind.

The nature of the experience which had done this to him is tersely recorded. While on the road he saw a brilliant light flash from the sky. He fell to the ground, and heard a voice address him by name. It was the voice of a dead man, the sect's founder, and it reproached him for his cruelty. It told him to proceed to the city and wait for instructions. When he stood up he was unable to see.

His companions led him the remaining few miles to the city, where after three days he was visited by a member of the community he had come to destroy and instructed in its beliefs. He accepted the new teachings, recovered his sight forthwith, and set about preaching the doctrines of the sect as vigorously as he had condemned them.

His dramatic conversion, naturally, did not at once convince all those he had previously persecuted. Nevertheless he made enough enemies among his former friends to have to leave the city in great haste and under cover of darkness.

The transforming effect of his strange experience cannot be disputed. To signal the start of his new life he changed his name. He had been called after a king of his tribe. For his new name he chose a word which was not even native to his people: it was an everyday adjective in one of the common languages of the empire. The act was significant, but, like most of the things he did, its significance was not realised for a long time.

'Can you calm storms?' asked Demetrius one morning.
'No,' said Simon, 'and neither can anyone else.'
'Oh', said Demetrius.
There was a pause.
'Can you raise the dead?' said Demetrius.
Simon hit him.
Demetrius had been behaving oddly for some time. He had an abstracted air. When he did attend to what Simon was saying, he seemed to listen in a critical way, as if privately balancing the words against something else. Private: that was it. Demetrius had

become private. He kept himself to himself, even at those moments when it was least appropriate.

'Are you in love?' demanded Simon one day, studying the boy's slender and unwelcoming flanks.

Demetrius looked up in astonishment.

'Well, what *is* the matter with you?'

'Nothing', said Demetrius sulkily, and got up.

If it wasn't sex, ruminated Simon, it was, even more regrettably, likely to be politics. Demetrius was just the sort to get mixed up with some clandestine group, and in a city like this there were doubtless several from which he could choose. The boy had learnt no discrimination, and since his escapade with the eunuchs had seemed peculiarly restless. Heaven knew where he went, what people he associated with, when he left the house in the evenings.

Simon felt he should pursue the matter, but postponed it. It had taken him a week to recover his strength after the attempt to capture the *'ob*; he had suffered from a feeling of lassitude and from painful cramps in his stomach. He consoled himself with the thought that the experiment had not been a complete failure and that the statue had not been damaged by its fall – he had inspected it carefully before replacing it in his bedroom. Nevertheless, it was time wasted. He was pursuing studies and experiments in a number of directions now, and he could not afford to waste time. He certainly could not afford to waste it thinking about Demetrius.

'The world', said Simon Magus aloud to an empty room, 'was, is, and ever shall be, fire, with measures of it kindling, and measures going out.'

'All things', said Simon, 'are an exchange for fire.'

'Fire lives the death of air', said Simon. 'Air lives the death of fire. The way up and the way down are one and the same.'

He re-wound the scroll and put it aside. Justly was Heraclitus called 'the Obscure'. Was it obscurity? Or was it the darkness which came on eyes that had just seen a brilliant light?

'The world is fire', he said, as though repetition would make it easier to understand. Perpetual exchange, nothing but the birth and dying that were the same, all things and their opposites the same. Fire and air, air and fire.

He was at the edge of an enormous discovery. He almost grasped it. He paced the room, as though by movement he could come nearer to it. It receded, but he felt its presence, always to the side of his thoughts.

'All things are one. Nature loves to hide.' Indeed she did. She hid so well that no one had ever found her.

Fire and air, air and fire.

He sat down again before his books.

After a time he rose and went into the room which he had set aside for experiments.

There lay behind his art a secret he could not penetrate.

He knew it, because his powers were strictly limited in scope. He had no power over nature, no power over matter except that of his own body. The things he brought out of the air did not exist. He could not create one fly out of nothing, or turn one pebble into bread. He could not call down rain, or raise the dead. He could not even – the inability distressed him out of all proportion – read people's minds.

Perhaps these things could not be done. There were the stories of Moses and the magicians of Pharaoh, but perhaps that had been a contest of illusions; and in any case Moses had seen, with his own eyes, the fire of God, and lived.

Simon believed that such feats could be done; that in the past they had been done, by men possessed of some extraordinary power. The question that tormented him was how such a power would operate. There could not be a power that did not obey the laws he knew. There could not be a name greater than the names he knew. He possessed the hidden names of Osiris, who had conquered death, of Isis, who had outwitted the god of heaven, and of Thoth, who knew the secrets of the universe. He possessed the name of Hermes, who trod the paths of the underworld. He possessed the greatest name of all, the name which the Jews were afraid to utter and called their god The Holy One instead. Nothing could be added to these names: they contained the world.

Yet there was a way, if he could find it.

He speculated about the nature of his fire. Did it participate in the fire of the sun and stars? Was if of the same nature as the fire which Moses saw, that burned without consuming? Was it the fire which the Greeks taught was the seed of things? He spun many theories, but none of them satisfied him. He wondered if the fire he possessed slept in everyone. Surely it must, or the correspondences would not hold. All men were gods, if he was. The power was to know it.

As he meditated on the hidden web of sympathies that bound things seen to things unseen and linked all life together, he sensed that he was at the edge of the mystery he sought. That mystery was the source of the mysteries he knew, and showed them forth like shadows. If they were subtle, their laws known only to the initiate who could read their symbols, how much more fine, transparent and pervading was the Mystery itself. Yet it was the real fabric of the world, and the world he saw and touched was an illusion. If he could grasp its nature …

But it was a thing of air and light. He could not capture it. It was …

He did not know. He dug his fingers into the sockets of his useless eyes, and groaned.

He had to know. It was the key to matter. If he could penetrate that veil he could rend the forms apart with his mind and re-create them. Nothing could resist him. It was the supreme power.

It was more than that. He knew, as he groped clumsily towards the elusive synthesis, that it was not power he wanted. What he wanted was to *know*.

Over the years he pursued various paths towards his objective. He fasted, kept long vigils, and contemplated the names of God. He prayed. He studied his books intently, in case there was something hidden in them which he had not seen. He sought the aid of spirits. He used his knowledge of herbs and roots to make potions that affected the mind and senses. He lashed the god of secrets with the violence of his invocation.

He had strange dreams. He saw visions. He was sometimes ill. He did not find the key.

'The religion of the Jews', observed Simon, 'should really be regarded as a form of art. It's the equivalent of a Greek tragedy. It opens grandly, has a chorus of moralising old men, involves a large number of corpses, and contains the seeds of its own downfall.'

'That is clever', said Eli, 'and cheap.'

'It is clever', said Simon, 'and true.'

There was a small gathering this evening: Morphus, Thrasyllus and Eli. Simon had initiated a debate on monotheism. The debate, so far, had been between himself and Eli. Morphus had confined himself to studying the floor with a worried expression, and Thrasyllus, who was rumoured to be having an illicit affair and had been looking tired lately, had gone to sleep.

'In what way', demanded Eli, 'does it contain the seeds of its downfall?'

'Logically. It appeals for its proof to the Writings, and the Writings disprove it. Most people are not aware of the fact because they haven't the patience, or the literacy, to wade through them. To anyone who does, it must immediately occur that God is not the only god.'

'Oh?'

'For one thing, if he has no rivals, why is he so tyrannically jealous?'

'He knew people would invent other gods and worship them.'

'Then what did he mean by "Let us make man in our image"?'

'If he is God', said Eli, 'why should he not refer to himself in the plural?'

'In that case, how do you explain "Among the gods there is not one like thee, Lord"? The book of Psalms. And "The gods who did not make heaven and earth shall perish"? Jeremiah. There are many more in the same vein.'

'Figures of speech', said Eli.

'The trouble with monotheists', said Simon, 'is that they have absolutely no intellectual integrity.'

Eli bit crossly into an olive and jarred his teeth. Simon smiled at him. People who lived by the Book never realised how easily they could be refuted by the Book. There were more blasphemies in that Book than could be counted.

He would pursue the game a little further.

'Is he omniscient,' he teased, 'this God of yours?'

'Of course. What use is a God who isn't?'

'Then he makes a very poor showing. Doesn't know that Adam and Eve are going to eat the apple, has to go down to Sodom to find out what's going on there, regrets making the human race, which obviously implies that he did not foresee the outcome ... And then there are the characteristics he is fondest of claiming – his justice, his mercy, his general fatherly concern. For obeying an order of David's – which, incidentally, he had prompted David to give in the first place – he kills more people than the Assyrian army on the rampage. Two children are rude to a prophet and get eaten by bears. Somebody else was swallowed up by the earth for not performing a sacrifice correctly. Even Moses was within an inch of his life on one occasion, for no reason I have ever been able to discern. And look at poor old Job! He wasn't doing anything at all when his herds were carried off and the house fell down on his children and he came out in boils all over. All you have to do to be blasted into the ground by this loving father is step outside your door on a clear day when he can see you.'

Eli, who had been scowling for the first part of this speech, gave up, and grinned feebly.

'Well ...', he said.

'It isn't good enough, is it?' continued Simon. 'Believe, if you must, that this appalling God is all the things he says he is. You may even be right. But if you are, you'll need better arguments than the Writings provide.'

'Fortunately,' noted Eli primly, 'a truth remains true irrespective of what arguments are used to support it.'

'Yes. But you're mistaken if you think a belief needs no intellectual buttress.'

Eli chewed his lip.

'If no good arguments can be found, then almost certainly the belief is false', said Simon. 'A true belief will always produce its own justification. And it will produce it in the terms that are required. Times and circumstances have changed since the Books were written, and the terms required have changed. You do your belief no service by supplying it with proofs which in the circumstances can be seen to be spurious.'

He was making it difficult, but Eli was listening intently.

'To put it more plainly', said Simon, 'what was good enough for our fathers is not good enough for us, and if we're to retain the belief of our fathers we have to find a new interpretation of it that doesn't compromise our thinking.'

'A new interpretation?' Eli tested the words. 'What kind of interpretation?'

Simon shrugged. In fact he had no idea. The issue was purely theoretical and not worth pursuing. He tried to push the question aside, but became aware that Eli was staring at him as if trying to penetrate behind the words to a concealed meaning.

'You yourself', said Eli, 'were brought up in the faith.'

'Yes. I found it insufficient.'

'But you speak of "we". "We" have to find a new interpretation.'

'I spoke rhetorically.'

'Did you?' said Eli. It did not sound like a question. He studied the floor as if it contained a message. '*Can* you find a new interpretation?' he asked suddenly.

68

Simon started to smile, but the smile froze as he encountered, again, a peculiar intensity in the young man's gaze.

'This is not an easy matter', he said. 'We'll talk about it later, if you like.'

Eli nodded. The evasion seemed, inexplicably, to please him.

In the ensuing pause Morphus stirred out of his torpor.

'If there's only one God', he said, 'then the emperor can't be a god, can he?'

'You don't really believe that nonsense?' scoffed Eli.

Morphus looked hurt.

'It is sometimes politic not to enquire too deeply', murmured Simon. 'After all, what does it hurt to burn a little incense? And in any case, perhaps we are all gods.'

'What?' said Morphus, thunderstruck.

'Just a thought', said Simon.

Thrasyllus had woken up. 'People call you a god, don't they?' he yawned.

Simon laughed. 'People call me a lot of things.'

He realised that they were waiting for him to say something more. He did not.

'Well ... I mean ... are you?' mumbled Morphus.

It was ridiculous, but touching. Eli was gazing at him again. He could not read what was in the dark, serious eyes.

'Look ...' began Simon, and stopped. It was too complicated, and he did not want to talk about it. However, it might be amusing to turn the question back to them.

'Who do you think I am?' he asked.

There was a silence which seemed to go on for a long time. It was Eli, of course, who broke it. Simon, long accustomed to surprises from his moody pet disciple, was shocked by the reply.

'I think you are the *Ta'eb*', said Eli.

Fire, cooling, became air. Air, cooling, became water. Water, cooling and solidifying, became earth. This much was known. Theoretically it should be possible to transmute one element into another and create solid matter where it had not previously existed.

Simon had had a small furnace constructed in a corner of his workroom. Over it he had placed a complicated arrangement of copper vessels linked by pipes. The containers, specially made, could be sealed so that air could not escape. He was experimenting, first, with the union of air and fire. Air, heated, became larger. He was curious to know whether, in the heating process, the coolness of the air flowed into the heat of the fire and reduced it, making the fire, as it were, become smaller. Thus, in an observable way, would air 'live the death' of fire. How to observe the principle which Heraclitus called 'an exchange for fire' was a problem he had not yet been able to solve, but he had sketched out a series of preliminary experiments.

He applied himself to the task with enthusiasm. The main difficulty was maintaining a constant temperature with the charcoal fire. Demetrius, commanded to operate the bellows, was terrified of the whole contraption and begged not to have anything to do with it. Simon cuffed him into submission. The work was proceeding well and he had made some promising discoveries when Eli produced his astonishing and catastrophic declaration of faith.

It was the most dangerous thing that could have been said. If it came to the ears of the authorities, he would stand no chance of clearing himself. One whisper, set against the background of his public acclaim in Sebaste, would be enough.

He swore the three disciples to secrecy, but for a long time was consumed with anxiety that one of them would let slip a careless word. They were all imbeciles, and he was the greatest fool of all for not seeing what was in Eli's mind and forestalling it.

For the next few weeks Simon made himself as inconspicuous as possible. He declined invitations, forbade the disciples to come to the house, and looked over his shoulder in the street. Except when it was essential to go out, he stayed at home and occupied himself with his experiments.

To his irritation the work, now that he had more time to devote to it, no longer went well. He obtained puzzling and contradictory results, and sometimes nothing that could be called a result at all. He began to be confused about what he was doing, and abandoned the experiments for a time so that he could reorganise his thoughts.

He was finding it difficult to concentrate, however. His mind skipped about, he could not hold it to a subject. Sometimes, sitting in his study, he would look up from his books with the conviction that he was being watched; but there was no one there. Once or twice, out of the corner of his eye, he thought he saw something move on the other side of the room. But when he looked again there was nothing.

As day after day passed with nothing achieved, he sank into a depression broken by irrational fits of temper. He vented his rage on Demetrius, who was increasingly silent and withdrawn. He took a sudden dislike to the statue, and moved it out of his bedroom into a corner of the study. He did not like having it there, either, and in the end moved it back to his bedroom again. It offended him wherever he saw it. It reminded him of failure.

He told himself that he was overtired. He had been working hard for months, and had not rested properly after the levitation. He must use his enforced retreat from the public eye to rest now.

He tried to rest, and found his thoughts spinning like dust in a sunbeam. He took to dosing himself with herbs, and they plunged him every night into a bottomless well of sleep from which he awoke with his head clouded and his body heavy and sweating. He wondered if he was getting ill. For days at a time he suffered from painful cramps in the stomach.

Eli came to see him. He had come six times and had been refused admittance by Demetrius, on Simon's orders. On the seventh occasion Demetrius was out on one of his evening excursions, and Simon opened the door.

'You are an irresponsible young fool', stormed Simon, 'and you could have got me into a great deal of trouble.'

'I'm sorry', said Eli.

'What on earth possessed you?'

'I don't know. It just came to me', said Eli.

'Well, next time something like that comes to you, keep it to yourself.'

'Yes', said Eli.

'I'm not well', said Simon. 'However, since you're here, you might as well stay for a while.

No, he was not ill. But something was happening to him.

His state of mind fluctuated violently. For days at a stretch he would work feverishly in his study, covering sheets of paper with notes and drawings for future experiments. At such times he was filled with enormous confidence and an excitement he could barely contain: his heart pounded as he noted down thought after thought, the pen struggling to keep pace with the flood of ideas that tumbled into his brain. Intoxicated by lack of sleep, driven by an extraordinary urgency, he would work for days and

71

nights, snatching food, rising from his chair only to pace the room and then return to the table and write again.

These periods of almost superhuman activity were succeeded by long periods of lassitude and depression which could not be accounted for solely by fatigue. Looking again at the notes he had scribbled in his frenzy of creation, he could make no sense of them. It was not that they were incoherent, but he could not understand what they were about. The light which had illumined them at the time of writing had faded, leaving only the shreds of a vision of which he had forgotten the form.

It was as if they had been written by someone else.

'What's the news in town?' enquired Simon.

'Nothing much', said Eli. 'What do you want, politics or gossip?'

'Gossip.'

'Thrasyllus was found in bed with the tribune's wife, and has gone to the country for a few months.'

Simon chuckled. 'Poor old Thrasyllus. I hope it was worth it.'

'Oh, I imagine so. Haven't you met the tribune's wife?'

'I don't think I have.'

'She's very pretty. Husband's a swine.'

'I know. I met him at a dinner party at Morphus's house.'

'Oh, Morphus lost some money at the races.'

'Morphus is always losing money at the races. He's worked out a system by which he can treble his investment over a six month period with no risk, and so far it's cost him three hundred drachmas', said Simon.

Eli laughed.

Simon found his spirits lighter in the young man's company. Perhaps he was making a mistake in shutting himself away for weeks on end.

'Do they talk about me?' he asked. 'In town?'

Eli looked embarrassed. 'Well, you know how it is', he said, 'when someone isn't around for a long time.'

'I see', said Simon.

'In fact', said Eli, 'I did hear a couple of people talking about you in the bazaar. One of them said you'd left Sebaste, and the other one said no, you hadn't left, you were in prison.'

Simon compressed his lips.

'Why don't you come back?' pleaded Eli.

'And perform a few more tricks for them, just to show that I'm still alive?'

Eli looked at him in surprise.

'I don't feel like it', said Simon. His elation had evaporated. 'I have more serious things to occupy me.'

'What exactly', asked Eli with some hesitation, 'are you doing?'

'Something very important. Something' – Simon stood up and walked to his table, littered with incomprehensible writings – 'something which, when it is finished, will change the world.'

But the change was in him.

Beginning with fluctuations of mood and concentration, the change penetrated deeper, producing ever wilder aberrations until it touched the core of him.

Sitting before his books one day, unable to focus his thoughts, he saw one of the scrolls rolling of its own volition towards the edge of the table. It was a heavy parchment, and there was no draught. The scroll reached the edge and fell off. He watched transfixed as, one by one, all his books progressed across the surface of the table and landed on the floor.

He had often been able to play tricks with objects, but he had always known when he was doing it.

A few days later, running an appreciative thumb over the raised figurework of his bronze bowl, he saw a strange reflection in the polished metal. He picked up a mirror and found himself staring at a beaked and feathered face whose monstrous features slowly, as he gazed, dissolved into his own.

It was unthinkable, it was hideous.

It was not impossible. There had been cases of possession by the god.

He paced the room and tried to think calmly. He told himself that as long as his thoughts remained clear he was safe: his mind was unviolated. The possessed, surely, did not know they were possessed.

But how did he know that his mind was *his* mind? And what use was a mind that could not tell him who he was?

Words echoed in his head. 'I am Horus, the son of Osiris ...' Mask of the hawk-face, mirrored sun. A mirrored sun could burn.

Fire, light, and fire.

'I am the Son', he muttered. 'I surpass ...'

The words whirled in his head.

He remembered that he had never known his father.

At times he felt his power enormously increased. He would pass from a sensation of weakness to unbounded confidence in a few moments. From these high peaks of confidence he would survey the intervening valleys, and the shallow plains on which he observed all other people to live, with godlike serenity.

He knew, at such moments, that he was able to do anything. But he did not do it. He had no need to transform the world: it did not touch him. In so far as he touched it, it would lessen him. To create, transform, unmake, would be a kind of blasphemy. He refrained, lest by action he violate the purity of his detachment.

The descent came without warning. The mountain-top on which he stood would in a second invert itself into a precipice. He was in some deep place cut off from light and warmth, not able even to understand the sounds that reached him. There was no sense in anything he saw: the patterns had disintegrated.

Often he began to pray, and stopped, dreading the answering hawk-flash of fire, the irreversible advent.

'Well, what have you come for this time?' demanded Simon.

Eli looked startled. 'I ... er ... just came to see how you were.'

'To see how I was? Have I been ill?'

'Well, no ... I just ...'

'Do they say I'm ill? In the town?'

'No, they don't.'

'What do they say about me?'

'Well, they don't actually ... I mean ... Nothing', said Eli.

'So that's it', said Simon. 'They're waiting.'

'Waiting?'

'Yes, waiting. To see what happens. Well, they'll see.'

Eli said, 'Simon, I can't make sense of anything you're saying.'

'Oh, go away', said Simon wearily. He picked up a mirror and studied his reflection. 'You can't help me', he said.

Was it an advent, or a valediction? It was as if he were being tested. But for what purpose? Into what state were these dizzying ascents, these paralysing falls, an initiation?

74

Was it an initiation, or a punishment? How had he offended? It was as if something were being fought out within him: some wild see-sawing of contraries that would find its balance only in his extinction.

At times he thought he must be dying. Then the god transported him again to the mountain-top, and he knew he alone, in his ecstasy, was alive.

He wept with anguish when he left the mountain. He cursed himself, his god, his life. He cursed, one bitter night, Eli the Samaritan, whose words now seemed to mark the moment when his life had changed. In retribution he cursed Eli, for surely Eli had cursed him. Eli had laid on him the curse of his dreadful God, the God of Simon's childhood, the God who rejoiced in chastising his own.

A cold finger touched Simon's neck.

Curse or blessing?

He stood up abruptly and walked round the room, touching familiar objects as if they could impart to him their solidity. Curse or blessing: were they not the same, the attentions of that terrible Deity who had tricked David and forsaken Saul and in arbitrary anger tried to murder Moses; who had created men to drown them and given Esau's birthright to his lying brother and handed his servant Job over to the torments of the Adversary? The Jewish storytellers said that when the Holy One was angry the angels hid the chosen race beneath the Throne of Glory so that He could not see them. They were indivisible, the favour and the fury of the God of Abraham, who had been told to sacrifice his son, and Moses, whom God had wished to kill. Moses, the great magician, who had not known his father.

A jealous God, a God who dwelt in air and fire. A God so contemptuous of human expectation that he chose a shepherd boy to be a king, and commanded his prophet to marry a whore, and vented his spleen on the righteous. A God whose spirit was a bird. A God who had said, 'I will raise up another prophet for them, after Moses.'

A God who delighted in perversity. When such a God fulfilled his promises, whom would He choose as His instrument but a man who for twenty years had taken His name in vain?

The valediction of Horus. The advent of Adonai.

Simon fell to his knees. For hours he prayed, weeping, in fear and desperate confusion, that the mantle of Moses should not fall to him and that he should be strong enough to bear it.

*

75

Demetrius had made some strange friends. They were not outwardly remarkable – in fact they were very ordinary people – but that was partly what was strange about them. He had never before met people who were poor and apparently content to be so. They seemed in fact to regard their poverty as a kind of privilege, and pity those who were denied it. He could not understand it.

Their leader was a man called Philip. Here Demetrius thought himself on familiar ground. For Philip was a miracle-worker.

He could not, Demetrius noted with loyal satisfaction, fly, or fashion things out of the air, or hold fire in his hand. Or if he could, he did not. He did, however, do something rather more practical: he healed people. Demetrius had seen him do it: a man, bedridden for years, had, at a touch of Philip's hand, got up from his litter and walked away. Simon could heal people too, of course, but with spells, not by touching. Simon did not on the whole like touching people much, except boys. He said it was bad for him. They said Philip could heal lepers. When Simon saw a leper he walked quickly in the opposite direction. Demetrius thought this only sensible, although it did sometimes occur to him that it must be very unpleasant to be a leper.

Philip did not look like a magician. He looked quite ordinary, and took no money for his services. They said he could cast out demons. Simon did not cast out demons. He knew how to invoke them, though, which came to the same thing.

Philip did not wear the robe of a magician, but he did use spells. Demetrius had heard him mutter invocations to his god. Demetrius enquired, out of professional interest, about the spells, but to his surprise was told they were not spells. He let this pass, but remarked that the name invoked, although it was not familiar to him, must be that of a very powerful god. He was told to be quiet, that was blasphemy. He relapsed into a puzzled silence.

Thinking about it, he realised he did not understand a word they said. Nevertheless he liked them: they were friendly people, and did not treat him like a slave. They could not, of course, help treating him as different from themselves. He briefly entertained the idea of having his foreskin cut so he could join them, but after his experience with the priests of Cybele he was sensitive about his organ.

They seemed to believe that the end of the world was coming, although they had a peculiar way of putting it. Well, that at least made sense. Half the Jews you met were hoping for the end of the world. Even Simon had started talking about it.

Demetrius stared absently in front of him. Simon was behaving in a very odd manner these days.

Fire and air, light and fire.

His laboratory was a shrine, his furnace the altar on which Elijah had called down fire on the priests of Baal, the burning bush of Moses.

He stood before the altar, Moses, robed in white, and called down fire.

He no longer knew himself. He had abandoned the struggle to defend the fortress of his identity against the assaults of an over-mastering God. Let God then come to him, let Him show the sign of His election, let Him possess.

He called down the purifying fire.

He transcended himself. His body was consumed by its inner heat into a thin and porous shell, and through its apertures his spirit streamed like light, and like light expanding from a little source filled every space, the spaces unfolding endlessly before it until it filled the world. He contained all things. All joys, all sorrows, all thoughts and their denials, all seas and mountains, all that might and might not be. His head touched heaven. The seven spheres revolved by impulse of his thought. The moon was a ring upon his finger.

He rested. He was complete. He did not know how long he rested, because time was a part of him. But allowing his conscious-ness to pass into the sphere of time which he contained, he became aware of thought. The thought told him that he was finite.

He felt distress. Beyond him there was Other. He yearned towards it.

It came to him.

Eli, wrenching open the heavy door a few seconds after the explosion, thought he stood in the pit of hell. Then the smoke cleared in the draught from the open door, and the blazing cur-tains, fanned by the same draught, flared into extinction, and he saw.

He ran to Simon and pulled off the charred and smouldering robe. The face and hands were blackened. Steam still hissed from the upturned copper vessels scattered on the floor, but mercifully there seemed to be no scalding on the body. He listened for a heart beat.

He shouted for Demetrius, who came, trembling. Together they carried Simon into his bedroom and laid him on the bed. The red scorch-marks were darkening on his chest.

Simon moved his head. He spoke with great effort.

'I ... am ...', he said.

It was a chasm in the earth. The walls were rock, black and wet with a slimy substance. There was no sky. The walls gleamed faintly. The light came from the fire at the far end of the ravine. The fire seemed to come out of the earth. It filled the entire space between the ground and the walls of the chasm and where the sky should have been.

He was part of a procession. The others were shadowy figures. They jostled and sometimes seemed to merge into each other. Each figure had the same vacant face. They moved in silence. They were being herded from behind. There was a noise from behind, like a hundred rats squeaking. It came from the creatures who were herding them forward. They were being herded towards the fire.

Simon's breast heaved in a cry but no sound came out. He tried to turn and make his way out of the procession, but it was like turning against a tide of sand. Slowly, very slowly, pressing with all his weight against the mass of sand, he began to turn. The sand pushed him back into the river of shadows that moved towards the fire. He fought, pressing inch by inch through the tiny spaces between the grains of sand, clawing and dragging his body through each grain of space.

He reached the edge.

The black walls rose in front of him. They were slippery with slime, but there were footholds. He began to climb. He climbed for a long time, and at last found the walls inclining outwards into a steep slope. There was a grey light in the air. Ahead of him he saw the beginning of a path.

Something was behind him. He sensed it and did not look back. He heard it twitter. It had many legs and could climb faster than he could. He scrambled desperately up the slope. But the rock was becoming soft, like flesh. His feet and hands sank into it. He thrust himself upwards and plunged deeper into the yielding rock. The thing was very close. He had nearly reached the path: he clutched at the ground with his hands, trying to drag himself forward, but the ground broke away in soft lumps and he fell himself sinking through it. Something landed on his back and twittered in his ear. He screamed.

The sickness, if that was what it was, lasted for three weeks. Gradually the nightmares became less frequent and the master's strength returned. His progress, however, was erratic. Some days his eyes were clear and he could take food easily. Then, when Eli and Demetrius were telling each other that the worst was past, he would relapse into a state in which he did not seem to recognise them, or to know where he was, or even who he was. His eyes would fix on something they could not see, and he would stare at it with loathing. Once, waking from a dream, he shouted at them to take the statue away and smash it. They did not, of course. It had cost a lot of money. Afterwards he seemed to forget about it.

He refused a physician, and instructed Demetrius to make up infusions of herbs for him. Sometimes the herbs he asked for were unobtainable, and he would rage at the trembling Demetrius until the boy cried. Eli was usually able to calm him, but his attitude to Eli had become strangely ambivalent. Often he welcomed the disciple with pleasure, made him sit close to the bedside, pressed him with questions about what he had been doing and what was happening in the city, and made Eli read to him. At other times Eli would catch the master looking at him coldly, with suspicion, as if he were a stranger.

'Are you the tempter?' Simon demanded of him once.

Eli stared. 'I don't know what you mean', he said.

Simon smiled, a weary, knowing smile of infinite bitterness.

'You know what I mean', he said.

But afterwards he seemed to forget about it.

The way back to the light was very long.

He bore his punishment with fortitude. Only sometimes did he groan under it. That was when the demon, which had now insolently taken up residence in the corner, no longer content with its early tricks of making the statue contort its features at him and walk at night around the room, came too close. It did not touch him. But it came close, bulbous head swaying above the sideways-stepping legs, so that he could see the fine hairs on it and the small intimate beak. At such moments he turned his head away and prayed. Afterwards it would not be there for a while. He did not attempt to exorcise it. God knew it was there: He would send it away when He wanted to.

The days passed. Sometimes the disciples came to see him. They seemed awkward and embarrassed and did not stay long. They did not know how to regard a teacher who had been smitten by his god. Eli came ever day. Simon watched him carefully. He knew that Eli played an important role in his destiny but he could not decide what it was. Was he the friend, the trusted one; or was he the trap against which Simon must be ever on his guard? He prayed for guidance, but none was given. It was a test. He must be patient.

It was difficult, so intense was his suffering at first, to hold on to his faith. He reminded himself constantly that his punishment was just. He had presumed. He had challenged the Transcendent for a sign. He had received a sign. It was merciful: his life was spared.

Merciful? Simon's eyes strayed towards the corner of the room, and moved away quickly before they saw what was there. What mockery, to send him, who had aspired to heaven, this foul thing from under the earth to be his companion. But it was just, very just: had he not once invoked its aid?

Perhaps as a reward for his patience, his physical state improved. At first he was racked by a heat and cold which divided his body into two separate zones of agony. His skin burned with an incessant fire, while the core of him lay clenched in ice. Between the zones there was a space in which he did not exist. The space gradually diminished. The fire on his skin cooled little by little, until he no longer fancied he saw it glow at night. It turned its warmth inward, and he felt the icy fingers start to loosen. He began tentatively to explore the returning kingdom of his flesh.

Demetrius said one day, 'I know a man called Philip.'

At least, that was what Simon thought he said. It did not seem to make much sense. It was a day when he was not sure of words. Sometimes they did not mean what they pretended to mean: you could open them up like a nut and there was something quite different inside. Something possibly dangerous. The demon swayed towards him.

'What did you say?' asked Simon.

'A man called Philip. He heals people.'

"Philip"? What might "Philip" mean?

'I could bring him to see you.'

The words formed and re-formed in various patterns. None of the patterns had any meaning. The demon stole all meanings away.

'You must speak louder', said Simon wearily. 'It's twittering again'.

Demetrius backed away from the bedside: he must have seen it. Simon closed his eyes. Patience.

On the eighteenth day he knew it had gone. There was a freshness in the room when he awoke. He looked at the statue. It returned his gaze serenely: still and empty marble.

He called Demetrius and asked for food: a proper meal, he said, not slops. When it arrived he attacked it hungrily, and ate four mouthfuls before his stomach closed like a fist. He pushed the plate away. He was still weak: he must wait until his strength came back. He lay back on the pillows and let his thoughts drift. He lay there for some time, enjoying the morning sunlight, before the question 'wait to do what?' formed with unkind clarity in his mind.

When his strength came back, what was he going to do? He had still not received the unequivocal call. He might not receive it for months or even years. Until it came, how was he to occupy himself?

He could not, of course, resume his life as a magician. It was unthinkable. He would have to find some other means of livelihood. It should not be difficult, for a man of his resource. He cast about for possibilities. Few presented themselves that were not somehow connected with the art he was forbidden to practise. He wondered if he would make a good schoolmaster. The idea depressed him so profoundly that he pushed the whole question out of his mind before it made him ill again.

He turned his thoughts instead to the matter of how he should prepare himself for the call. He must pray, of course; but it must be prayer of a different sort from the kind he was accustomed to making. He must not ask for anything. He must seek to ascertain the divine will for him, and attune himself to it. He must desire to be no more than an instrument. The only thing he might permit himself to ask for was guidance. He must be humble and patient. He must wait.

Simon picked restlessly at the bright threads of his coverlet. It did not sound very interesting.

Well, he could also prepare himself by study. He should study the Writings. He had studied them before, but with the cold eye of an enemy, seeking their errors and absurdities. He would study them now with the eye of one who sought their truth. He would study, particularly, the accounts of Moses. It would give him some idea of the task that lay before him.

81

The task. He had never clearly thought about it. In his exalta-
tion, details had seemed unimportant: his identity was all that
mattered. In his suffering he had not dared. Now, at last, he was
free to think about it. Reverently, joyfully, he turned his mind to
contemplation of his treasure. And he felt the chill of the sephulcre
fall upon his soul.

There was nothing there.

He grasped in bewilderment for the words that would bring it
back.

'*Ta'eb*.'

An empty suit of clothes.

'*Elohim*.'

Insubstantial as wind.

'*Shaddai*.'

Brittle as glass.

He lay still, unable to grasp what had happened.

The sanctuary was empty. It had all been mockery. There would
be no call.

Eli came to visit him.

'Go', said Simon quietly. 'Don't come back. Never come near me
again.'

Eli, miserable and baffled, left.

Simon turned his head into the pillow and wept.

In time the tide of his despair receded. It left behind a numbness,
as if he had been washed clean of emotion. He lay and thought
about his state, and found in it nothing even pitiable. It was simply
futile. Life stretched before him featureless and unremarkable. He
wondered where he would find the energy to traverse it.

He got up, finally, out of boredom, and went to his study. His
head swam at first and his legs were weak, but the very act of
movement made him feel a little better. He read Plato for an hour
before going back to bed, and found his appetite for reading beginning to return. The next day he spent the afternoon reading at his
table. The day following, he got up after breakfast and told Demetrius he had recovered.

He spent the greater part of each day reading. Mostly he read
philosophy, but from time to time he would take a book of poetry, a
historical work or one of his treatises on magic from the shelf. He
read with a kind of restless concentration, re-reading certain passages a dozen times, skipping over sections entirely, turning from

one author to another to pursue a theme. He was looking for something.

He knew, at the end of a week, that he was not going to find it. There was nothing in the books but words.

He returned them to the shelf and went to the window. It was early evening. A cool breeze disturbed the dust of the day and brought the distant ring of a coppersmith's hammer. From a few streets away came the sound of a lusty argument between two carters. A bird chirruped on a neighbouring roof.

Simon called to Demetrius that he was going for a walk, and left the house.

He walked down to the theatre – a silly comedy, revived at public demand – strolled through the crowds in the bazaar, and was turning homeward when, passing a street that led to one of the poorer districts, he saw a cluster of people. On impulse he walked towards them. Perhaps it was a juggler or an acrobatic show; perhaps even – a twinge of jealousy surprised him – another magician.

It was an ordinary-looking man of slight build, simply dressed, standing in the midst of the circle created by the crowd. In front of him was a woman, bent almost double, her face contorted in a habitual grimace of pain. Her right arm twitched uncontrollably. Simon had seen her in the market place: she had been like it since birth.

He climbed on to an olive crate in order to see better.

The man stretched out his hand and laid it on the woman's shoulder. He said something. There was a deep quiet among the crowd.

It was like the stirring of a parched plant after rain. Something flowed through the humped form, loosening, straightening, stilling.

She stood upright. There was wholeness.

'*Mirabile*', breathed Simon.

The woman flung herself at the healer's feet. He raised her up. Over the heads of the crowd his eyes found, and held, Simon's.

III

THE KINGDOM

'I was out in the fields,' said sister Rebecca excitedly, 'gathering sticks for the fire, and I was thinking about how many sticks I would need and I must get enough to keep some kindling for tomorrow, and would there be enough sticks in the field for tomorrow's fire or would I have to go somewhere else to look for them, and I was getting quite worried about it, and then it suddenly came to me. I had a sort of – it just came to me. "Don't worry about tomorrow." And I realised. *It's all right. There'll always be enough sticks.*'

She paused, and laid a hand on Simon's knee.

'Do you understand that?' she asked.

'Oh yes', said Simon numbly.

'And even if there aren't,' continued sister Rebecca, '*it doesn't matter*. Every day we're given what we need, and we don't have to think about it. And I thought, *that's what it means*. And I felt – I really felt so happy.'

She cast a radiant smile at the small group of people gathered round Joseph's fire. They smiled too: at her, at each other, at the sharing of a discovery.

The fire was going out.

'It really means,' expounded sister Miriam, 'that we don't have to worry about anything. That's what it really means.'

'That's right', agreed sister Rebecca. 'Because God knows everything.'

'Yes. It makes you feel – really safe, doesn't it?'

'Yes, it makes you feel really wonderful.'

'I feel very sorry', mused sister Miriam, 'for people who don't know what we know.'

A comfortable silence settled over the little group, as each person communed with an inner peace.

Simon looked at Philip. He was sitting in the corner, taking no part in the conversation, but apparently listening. There was a smile on his face. Simon studied the smile. It contained not the slightest hint of irony.

'How do you work your miracles?' asked Simon.

'Through the power of God', said Philip.

'But you invoke another name as well', said Simon.

'Yes,' said Philip, 'the name of Joshua.'

'The man you keep talking about?'

'Yes.'

'You invoke his spirit?'

'Yes.'

Simon pounced. 'He was executed as a criminal.'

'Yes, but he was not a criminal.'

Simon laughed. 'Well, who was he, then?'

'He was the Deliverer', said Philip.

Simon turned on his heel and walked away.

Later he tried again.

'This Joshua, was he a god?'

'Of course not', said Philip. 'You should know better than that. There is only one God.'

'So when you invoke his name, it's as a miracle-worker? Like Moses?'

'He was greater than Moses.'

Simon's eyebrows lifted.

'What miracles did he perform?'

'A great many miracles of healing.'

'Natural remission accounts for a lot of it', said Simon.

'He turned water into wine.'

'Elementary.'

'He walked on the sea.'

'I can walk on the air', said Simon.

'He turned a few leaves and fishes into a meal for five thousand people.'

'I can turn nothing at all into a meal for five thousand people', said Simon.

Philip's eyebrows lifted.

'He raised the dead', said Philip.

'Oh, come on', said Simon.

He tried once more.

'You say you never met Joshua, and so you never saw him do any of the things he's said to have done. How do you know it's true?' he asked.

'The proof', said Philip, 'is that with his name I work miracles.'

'I work miracles too', said Simon, 'without it.'

'Your miracles are a fraud', said Philip.

Simon stared at him. After a moment he laughed.

'What on earth do you mean?' he said. 'How can they be a fraud?'

'How can they be genuine', said Philip, 'when there is only one God?'

There was no point in talking to such people. Yet Simon went back. He came away each evening baffled, angry and contemptuous, and next morning went back again.

It was Philip's miracles, and Philip's air of authority, which drew him. Simon had recognised at once that he was in the presence of a man who possessed unusual power. But whenever he tried to question Philip on the subject of his power, Philip evaded the issue. He talked instead about his beliefs.

These were so bizarre that Simon listened at first out of sheer incredulity. The sect had been founded by a wandering preacher-magician who had believed himself to be the Deliverer of the Jews. This in itself was not remarkable; what was extraordinary was that the belief still survived nearly ten years after he had been crucified for inciting revolt. His followers explained his dramatic failure to deliver anybody by saying that he had risen from the dead, was now in Heaven, and would shortly return, clothed in the glory of his true identity, to fulfil the programme laid down for him.

After several hours of this, Simon's patience wore thin.

'Who saw him when he came back from the dead?' he interrupted finally, when Philip was labouring to explain to him for the third time the significance of this miracle.

'Kepha and the others', answered Philip.

Kepha was the head of the sect.

'His friends?' said Simon. 'He only showed himself to his friends?'

'Well, yes. What of it?'

'If he'd wanted people to believe he'd risen from the dead, there would have been more point in showing himself to his enemies.'

Philip looked surprised, then smiled faintly, and dismissed the remark with a shrug. In much the same way he dismissed all Simon's objections. He was simply not interested, Simon realised, in rational discussion.

That, presumably, was what enabled him to put up with his flock. They were, of course, uneducated people, artisans and peasants, but even so they displayed in their daily lives and the conversations he had with them a degree of childishness which took Simon's breath away. They made no attempt to think or plan, but trusted in the benevolence of a God whom they believed to have a special interest in them. That the benevolence of this God was historically highly suspect they did not seem to know, for when he questioned them they said that God was love.

They believed that they possessed a truth denied to the rest of mankind. The arrogance of this claim shocked him, but they did not appear conscious of it. He asked them what this truth was, but they had difficulty in articulating it. It was something to do with love.

Love was their philosophy, their religion. Love abolished the necessity for thought. All knowledge, all speculation, all endeavour, were reduced to this children's milk. Love your enemies. Love God. Love one another.

They smiled a great deal. It was part of loving. They talked in platitudes, and shared their food, and smiled. Their smiles weighed on Simon like iron.

He fought, in that stifling banality, to clear a space around him with his mind. And he found that against the massive simplicity of their faith his mental armoury was impotent. His syllogisms closed on nothing, his logic sliced air. Every analysis disintegrated, every argument crumbled, in an atmosphere in which thought simply did not count. The only thing that counted was love.

If he had been less sure of his superiority he might have found it threatening.

'Did Joshua think he was going to be killed?' he asked Philip one morning. He was trying to form a mental picture of the man behind the legends. It was difficult.

'He knew it', said Philip. 'He said as much to Kepha.'

'Then couldn't he have done something to avoid it? Leave the country, go into hiding ...?'

'He could have, but he chose not to', said Philip. 'He sacrificed himself for us.'

The patience in Philip's voice reminded Simon that he had been told this before.

'It is his death that makes possible our entry to the Kingdom' said Philip.

The Kingdom, ah yes. Like so many others, they dreamed of Kingdom; and, as was always the case, thought it would be only for them. They believed it was imminent. They prayed for the end of the world, in a prayer they said Joshua had left them.

'We could never, on our own merits, deserve the Kingdom

90

explained Philip. 'We are all sinful people. If it were left to our own merits, the Judgement would destroy us.'

Simon picked his teeth. The part of his heritage he was most thankful to have jettisoned was the national obsession with sin. Sin was the breaking of the Law; but since no one had ever been able to count all the minute and finicking precepts which the Law contained, it was hardly possible that any human being could avoid breaking them. Thus the Law made sin inescapable; and at the same time employed a huge native industry of experts in finding loopholes in its mesh. The employment it provided was, so far as Simon could see, its only purpose.

'So', continued Philip, 'he died instead of us. He submitted to a punishment for something he hadn't done in order that we might not be punished for what we have done. It is an atonement. That idea must be familiar to you.'

'Oh yes', said Simon. The blood-offerings and the self-abasement; yes, it was familiar. He loathed it.

'Joshua called it a ransom', said Philip. 'Do you see?'

Simon studied a fig-seed he had extracted from between his incisors. He saw; he saw a great deal.

'Ransomed', he murmured, 'from the terrible justice of God?'

'Exactly.' Philip looked pleased. 'It was the only way it could be done.'

'I thought you said', remarked Simon, 'that God was love?'

'Yes.'

'And that in fact all we needed to know about God was that God was love?'

'Yes.'

'How many different Gods are you talking about?' enquired Simon blandly.

'Don't misinterpret me –'

'How do you wish to be interpreted? If God is just, he cannot abrogate punishment of an infinite number of sins in return for one man's death. If God is love, and if he is able to abrogate punishment at all, he can surely do it without being bribed to it by an agonising death on the part of his prophet. And speaking of the manner of death, you are presumably aware that according to the Law a man executed in that manner is to be regarded as accursed? Yet we are expected to believe that this man was the instrument of God! It amounts to saying that the Law is nonsense. I personally have always regarded it as nonsense, but *he* can hardly have done so, given who he believed he was. How can he possibly have gone voluntarily to a death of that kind? And how did he reconcile that death to the fact that it is in total contradiction to the prophecies, convenient portions of which you are so fond of quoting?' Simon paused for breath. 'If you ask me', he said, 'someone made an absolutely dreadful mistake. I have never in my life heard such a striking case of rationalisation *post factum.*'

And yet ...

A stranger stopped one evening in front of Joseph's house where they were sitting in the shade of the fig tree. He looked as if he had travelled a long way: his clothes were dusty and threadbare and as he walked he glanced about him with a kind of hopelessness. He shifted his bundle from his shoulders and sat down under the tree.

'Mind if I have some water?' he said.

Rebecca brought him some, and some bread and olives. He thanked her, and ate hungrily.

After a while he said, 'Any work here?'

'I'm afraid not', said Joseph. 'The harvest is late. There won't be any work for a month.'

The man grunted. His eyes were restless, scanning the narrow streets, the square, the men coming back from the fields.

'Best be going', he said when he had finished. 'Thank you.'

Philip said suddenly, 'Your son isn't here. I'm sorry.'

The stranger's face froze. He searched Philip's eyes for a moment, then looked away quickly.

'Thank you', he said.

He walked away in the silence.

Simon turned to Philip. 'How did you do that?' he demanded.

'What?'

'Read his mind.'

'I don't know', said Philip.

'Can you often do it?'

'Sometimes', said Philip.

'I wish you'd teach me to do it.'

Philip laughed, not unkindly, but for no reason that Simon could see.

'You must have some idea how it's done', persisted Simon.

'I don't think the answer would mean much to you', said Philip.

92

'What is it?'

'Love', said Philip.

He should have expected it, of course.

He thought he might discover more by asking about Joshua's miracles. Even on this point Philip was infuriatingly unhelpful.

'The miracles', said Philip, 'are not important.'

'*Not important?*'

'They were merely a sign.'

'A sign of what?'

'That he was the Deliverer.'

'Oh', said Simon.

'In fact', continued Philip, 'he promised his followers that any of them could work miracles too, if they believed.'

'Believed what?'

'That he was the Deliverer.'

'Oh', said Simon.

He kicked irritably at the tip of a stone protruding through the dust. The stone did not move: it was bigger than it looked.

He sighed. 'All right', he said. 'We'll come back to that. What sort of miracles did he say his followers would be able to perform?'

'It's not *important*.'

'What sort of miracles?'

'Oh, very well, if you insist. He said we would be able to do everything he'd done, and more.'

'What?' Simon was startled. 'Are you telling me', he said, 'that all anyone has to do in order to calm storms and raise the dead and come back from the grave is believe that this man was the Deliverer?'

'Yes', said Philip.

Simon considered. He began to smile. In a moment he was laughing loudly.

'It's a fair bargain', he said. 'I mean, who in his right senses *could* believe it?'

Yet Philip believed it, and Philip was not a stupid man. He merely refused to use his mind for its proper purpose.

Simon realised that if he was to find the secret of Philip's power he would have to learn more about Joshua.

'What kind of man was he?' he asked.

'Well, of course, I never knew him', said Philip. 'Those who did, say he had the most extraordinary quality of –'

93

'No, no', said Simon. 'What *kind* of man was he? Where was he educated? What was his background? Had he read the philosophers?'

'If he had I'm not aware of it', said Philip. 'Does it matter?'

'Did he know Greek at all? Where did he study magic?'

'*Magic*? Good heavens, he never studied magic.'

'To calm storms and raise the dead –' said Simon.

'Not only did he not study magic, but I doubt if he studied anything', said Philip. 'He was a poor man. If he went to the village school that's certainly the only education he ever had.'

'A poor man?'

'I've told you that before. Why don't you listen? He was poor, and he chose his disciples from among the poor.'

'Uneducated people?'

'If you like.'

'But why? If he wanted them to spread his teachings, why didn't he choose people who could –'

'He chose them *because* they were poor. Simple, ordinary people.'

'That's the silliest answer I ever heard', retorted Simon in an upsurge of irritation.

'The Kingdom belongs to the simple', said Philip.

'So I've noticed', snapped Simon.

He took a grip on his temper. He would learn nothing this way.

'He was poor and uneducated, you say? He never studied? He was never in Egypt?'

'Egypt? What would he be doing in Egypt?'

'If he was the kind of person you describe, I can't understand how he was able to attract the following he obviously did attract. There must be something else.'

'There was', said Philip. 'He was the Deliverer.'

It was utterly frustrating. It was like drawing patterns in water: as soon as you thought you had established something, it dissolved. Questions were met with evasive answers, or with answers that meant nothing. Assertions were made without regard to logic or to their implications. The possession of power was attributed solely to belief in a claim both grotesque and absurd. In a word, the cult was nonsense. Only one thing could make sense of it.

'Is there a secret teaching?' asked Simon.

It was the first time he had seen Philip look offended.

'Certainly not', said Philip. 'We have no secrets.'

'All other religions have secrets', said Simon.

'All other religions are false', said Philip.

Simon turned away, but Philip laid a hand on his shoulder.

'The Way is the same for everyone', said Philip, 'and although it sounds easy, it is quite difficult enough without there being secrets.'

'What is it, then?'

'Love', said Philip.

Simon ground his teeth.

'You haven't listened, have you?' said Philip. 'You ask for the secret teaching and you haven't taken in a word of the teaching I've been giving you.'

'Listen?' roared Simon. 'I've done nothing but listen since the first day I came here, and I've heard not a single word that makes sense.'

He stumped away angrily. He went home and opened his books, but found he could not concentrate. He shouted at Demetrius for an hour, and then went to the theatre, where he saw an irritating play, badly performed, and left early. He sat in a tavern for a while and listened to the conversation. Its stupidity disgusted him.

In the morning he went back to Philip.

'Perhaps I haven't listened as well as I might', he said. 'Perhaps you ought to tell me again.'

It was true that he had not listened. He listened now, and something began to happen to him. It was as if little chinks of light were appearing in a hitherto blank wall. There were many of these chinks. Some of them let in a light which in the first instant dazzled him.

'Be careful what you value. It will lock up your heart.'

'The sons of the earth shall inherit the earth.'

'Forgive, and be forgiven. Judge, and be judged.'

'The truth will free you.'

Free? His heart leapt, as if somewhere a door had opened. But, looking, he could not find the door, nor did he understand how he could be freer than he was.

He listened again, and he grew puzzled.

'I do not bring peace, I bring a sword.'

'The last first. The first last.'

'More is given to those who have. Everything is taken from those who have not.'

'I have come to give sight to the blind, and to blind those who can see.'

95

He shook his head. 'I don't understand', he said. Philip smiled at him. Simon went home to think.

The teaching, he began to realise, was not consistent. That was why it was hard to grasp. If you understood one part of it you would not necessarily understand what came next. It was full of paradoxes. It was elusive, ever-changing. And yet, in some way he dimly discerned, it was a whole. Behind the scattered, brilliant sayings there danced a luminous harmony.

It fascinated him.

'Have you decided to join us?' asked brother Joseph. He was a small, wrinkled man with kind eyes and a bad limp. One of his legs was shorter than the other. Philip had not been able to cure it.

'I haven't quite made up my mind', said Simon. 'I'm thinking about it.'

Joseph nodded. He was content with little.

His wife was not.

'Well, you'd better hurry up', said sister Rebecca. 'There isn't much time, you know.'

She gave a last slap of encouragement to the three loaves of dough she had been kneading, and set them in the sun to prove. She fetched a handful of herbs, chopped them and threw them into the large pot which steamed over the clay stove. She brought a basketful of beans from a corner and sat down in the sun to pod them.

'There really isn't any time to waste,' said sister Rebecca.

Simon mused. He knew, of course, what she was referring to. But on this blue and golden morning, with a light breeze cooling the air, it was very difficult to believe that the world was going to end.

'I think I have a little longer', he said comfortably.

'Don't be too sure', said sister Rebecca. She ran her thumb expertly down a row of nestling beans and ejected them into the bowl before her. 'Nobody knows when the Kingdom is going to arrive. One moment it won't be here, the next it will. Like a ... thief in the night.'

'I thought you said', observed Simon mildly, 'that it would be preceded by earthquakes, floods, fire, universal warfare and the opening of graves.'

'Oh well, it will, of course. Well, it'll all happen at once, I suppose. I don't know. Anyway it doesn't matter. It'll come.'

'It will come, and that's all that concerns us', said Joseph.

96

'It's a mystery, you see', explained sister Rebecca.

'A mystery?'

'We aren't supposed to ask about it.'

'Oh, I see', said Simon.

'All the same,' said sister Rebecca, 'you can't help wondering about it, can you? What it's going to be like.'

Her thumb paused half-way down a bean-row. Her eyes sought her husband.

'Will there be thrones for us, Joseph?'

'No, no', said Joseph. 'The thrones are for the leaders. What would the likes of us be doing on thrones?'

'But I thought Philip said we were going to sit on thrones and judge the angels.'

'*Angels*? What would we want to judge angels for?'

'I don't know, but that's what he said, I'm sure it was.'

'I think you must have misunderstood him', said brother Joseph.

'Oh.'

The reprieved beans shot with a clatter into the bowl.

'Well anyway', said sister Rebecca, 'it's going to be everything we ever wanted. Palaces, and feasts, and we shall never get old, or die, and everybody who's ever been unkind to us will be punished.'

'How satisfying', said Simon.

'Yes. That old Hedekiah who wouldn't let us rent his orchard – and it was worth nothing, all overgrown with weeds – he'll get what's coming to him, the old misery.'

'That is not the right way to think', reproved Joseph. 'We have to love those who have wronged us.'

'Oh I do love him. I do really. I just think he ought to be punished.'

For a while no one spoke. The bowl in front of sister Rebecca filled steadily with plump, tawny beans, and to her right the little heap of empty pods grew.

'This kingdom', said Simon at last. 'Where will it be?'

'Here', said Joseph.

'In Heaven', said Rebecca.

'I see', said Simon.

There was a pause.

'No, we haven't got the right way of thinking about it', said Joseph. 'We aren't educated people.' He smiled at Simon apologetically. 'We get things a bit mixed up. You should ask Philip questions like that. He puts everything very clearly, so that you understand it.'

'But if it was clear at the time', asked Simon, 'how can you come to have such different ideas about it afterwards?'

'Joseph doesn't listen', said sister Rebecca into the beans.

'I do listen, my dear, and I do my best to understand. But some things are too deep for me, and I'm not ashamed to admit it.'

Sister Rebecca stood up and brushed a few clinging bean-pods from her skirt.

'It seems perfectly clear to me', she said. 'I don't know why everybody makes such a mystery about it. When things have got so bad that they can't get any worse, then Joshua will come back and rescue us. The world will catch fire, and we shall go and live with him in Heaven. And all our enemies, and all his enemies, and all the people who don't believe in him, will be burnt up.'

She gathered up an armful of bean-pods and threw them into the fire. They crackled, spat, and began to blacken.

'A persuasive argument', said Simon.

His irony was gentle. He felt, for the moment, disinclined to distress these people by a show of logic. He found their company refreshing, as one is sometimes refreshed by the conversation of the very young. Too much, of course, and it would become intolerable.

But as yet he made no movement to leave. The breeze caressed his face. In the distance, the children were chanting an old riddle-song he had known in his childhood. He looked over the rooftops at the rippling hills: they dozed white in the sun, their flanks dotted with scrub, like sleeping leopards. It was peaceful here. Very peaceful.

'You said there wasn't a secret doctrine,' said Simon, 'and I'm sorry but I don't believe you. This is not a teaching that can be fully grasped by simple people. It contains paradoxes.'

'Yes,' said Philip, 'it does.'

'How do you explain that?'

'I don't explain it', said Philip. 'It's a fact. I repeat what I've been told by those who heard the teachings at first hand.'

'But don't you want to understand it?'

'I accept my limitations.'

'Tcha!' said Simon.

Philip smiled.

'Look,' said Simon, 'there are some things which cry out for explanation. Like that strange story about the dishonest steward. What does it mean? Is it in praise of dishonesty?'

'I don't know what it means', said Philip, 'but someone will one day, and who am I to change it?'

Simon stared at him.

'Why did he talk in stories at all,' demanded Simon, 'if the message was as simple as you say? The point of a story is surely to make something clearer. But Joshua's stories very often didn't make things clearer. After he'd told his stories to the crowds he had to explain them to his disciples. Goodness knows, the disciples seem to have been dim-witted enough, so the crowds must have been even dimmer. And the crowds didn't get the benefit of the interpretation. Why not? And you're telling me there isn't one version for the masses and another for the initiates?'

Philip's gaze roved over the distant hilltops. He said nothing.

'Altogether', pursued Simon, 'what you're asking me to believe amounts to a series of improbabilities, impossibilities and blatant contradictions.'

'I'm not asking you to believe anything', said Philip. 'You don't have to come here. Why don't you go home and get on with your magic, and let me get on with my work?'

Simon stopped drawing circles in the dust and sat up, wide-eyed.

'Every one of these people', said Philip, indicating with his hand the cluster of small earth-roofed dwellings where most of the followers lived, 'is just as important as you. They never ask me for anything, unless their children are sick or they need advice. They would never dream of taking up my time the way you do. What makes you think you have the right?'

Simon's cheeks flamed. He stood up and was about to leave, but Philip laid a detaining hand on his arm.

'You complain of impossibilities and things that don't make sense', said Philip. 'You mutter about paradoxes and secrets. It never seems to occur to you that there might be a fault in your own understanding.'

'I have more intelligence –' exploded Simon.

'There's nothing wrong with your intelligence. You just don't know how to use it. You pick away at details and miss what's in front of your nose. The truth in *simple*. That is why *they*' – he jabbed his finger in the direction of a woman, followed by a tribe of children, carrying a pitcher of water to her house – 'understand it and you don't.'

'Understand? They understand nothing!' raged Simon. 'Just listen to them talk. They babble on about the Kingdom, *their*

99

Kingdom, specially prepared for them, and they don't even know what it is. Everything they say about it is contradictory.'

'Of course they don't know what it is', said Philip. 'That's why they can go to it.'

'I have had enough of this nonsense!' shouted Simon. The passers-by turned to look at him curiously. He regained control of his temper with an effort. 'Your beliefs', he said coldly to Philip, 'seem to consist entirely in turning common sense upside-down.'

'Joshua would agree with you', said Philip. ' "The last first. The first last." '

Simon blinked.

'That's presumably why he decided to end his career as a failure', he snapped. 'At least his death is consistent with his teaching.'

'Yes, it is', said Philip. 'I'm glad you see that. Not many people do.'

It was suddenly quiet. The things Simon had meant to say appeared all at once to be not worth saying. He felt confused. Something was tugging at his mind and he did not want to listen to it.

He said angrily, 'I don't believe this master of yours ever existed. He's the most unlikely character I've ever heard of. A man of no education, who said things so clever that nobody could understand them, and sent out a bunch of peasants to repeat them to other people who wouldn't understand them either. A man who in fact did not want to be understood, since he promised the Kingdom to whoever didn't understand what it was. Provided, of course, they also believed that he fulfilled in his own person prophecies about a national saviour whose career his own life in no way resembled. Just to make sure there was no mistake about it, he got himself executed on a charge of which he was guiltless before there was any danger of his becoming a success.'

Philip smiled at him.

'It is a mockery of reason!' howled Simon.

'Quite so', said Philip. 'That is what I have been trying to tell you.'

Simon stared at him, and felt a chill run down his back.

'It is not only reason that's mocked', said Philip. 'Think of it. We are talking about a man who respected nothing. A man from nowhere, who rejected his family, begged his food, slept rough, ate with prostitutes and drank with men who took bribes, worked on the Day of Rest, didn't bother to wash his hands, and told the entire spiritual and legal hierarchy they were hypocrites. Everything he said, everything he did, mocked everything they were and

100

everything they thought. All they could see was the mockery. They killed him for it.'

Simon was silent.

'They did not understand', said Philip, 'that he was the man they had been waiting for.'

Understand? Who could possibly understand it? It was the most fantastic paradox of all. It was monstrous.

It was a paradox only God could have thought of.

'I believe it', said Simon, 'because it is ridiculous.'

Brother Joseph said, 'I sold that bit of land behind the vineyard today.'

'Joseph!' squeaked sister Rebecca in excitement. 'How much did you get for it?'

'Quite a good sum', said brother Joseph.

'But how much? Where's the money?'

'I gave it away', said brother Joseph contentedly.

Sister Rebecca went stiff with shock.

'You *gave it away*?'

'Yes', said brother Joseph, 'to the poor.'

'But we *are* the poor!' cried sister Rebecca.

'No we're not', said brother Joseph. 'We have enough.'

Sister Rebecca opened her mouth to say something, did not say it, and applied herself with unnecessary noise to the cooking. The little group of people around the fire smiled vaguely, though not at each other.

Philip said, 'Joseph did right. By giving his money away, he has bought something much more precious.'

'The Kingdom', explained sister Miriam helpfully.

Simon said with a smile, 'The Kingdom can be bought?'

'Yes, in a manner of speaking', said Philip. 'Everything has to be paid for.'

Simon, reflecting, realised he was right. It was indeed a kind of commercial transaction. Pay what you have now, and receive ten-fold later. Much later, probably. But the sons of the earth shall inherit it if they wait long enough.

Philip's voice cut into his thoughts. 'When are you going to pay?' he asked, laughing.

Simon blushed. He had been meaning to do it for weeks. But it was somehow not very easy to give one's money away.

'Tomorrow', he said.

Yes, he would give his money away. It was the least he could do. He had, indeed, discovered a kingdom.

He had left his past behind, and started again. That was the only way to describe what had happened to him as he emerged, gasping, from the cold water of his baptism.

Life presented itself afresh each morning, untrammelled, unencumbered by a weight of obligations. He did not have to be or do anything. He did not have to worry about his abilities, because he did not need them, or about his limitations, because they did not limit anything he wanted. He did not have to worry about his reputation, because he had relinquished it. He did not have to worry about who he was, because he had started again and he could be who he wanted to be. He did not have to think about tomorrow. Indeed he did not have to think at all; but he did so, out of habit.

Philip called it a new life. Simon was pleased by the doctrine of the new life: it was intellectually satisfying. Joshua had died and returned from the dead. His followers, ritually baptised with his name, participated in a dual sense in his death and resurrection.

They 'died', firstly, in the sense that they shed their past life and with it their sins. Simon did not attach a great deal of importance to this, since sin had never been a problem to him. It was, however, reassuring to feel that the risk of accountability was now removed.

More important was the literal sense in which those who put their faith in Joshua's return from the grave would themselves survive death. Those who were alive when the Kingdom came would not die but be caught up to Heaven; those who had died would rise from their tombs and embark, with them, on an everlasting and blissful existence. The master's own return had been the first, isolated note in the great music of that general resurrection.

Simon remarked that it had indeed been isolated and the rest was long in following. Philip replied with asperity that God's music did not observe human intervals. Simon laughed, and did not pursue it.

He enjoyed his conversations with Philip much more now that he did not feel constrained to attack everything that Philip said. It was another aspect of his freedom, he reflected. He was, in fact, free to do almost anything he liked: free to accompany Philip when he

102

went to heal, and to speculate on how it was done; free to spend his time, or not, with the believers, in whose company nothing was required of him except that he smile. Free, surprisingly, of what he had feared would be heavy moral demands, for the ethical teaching of the sect boiled down quite simply to 'Do to no one what you would not want done to yourself' – the principle all good Samaritans were brought up on, and not difficult to observe when he did very little but sit in the shade of the fig tree listening to Philip. One day, when he was ready, Philip would tell him the mystery of the Kingdom.

It was just as well that he enjoyed his conversations with Philip, because, come to think of it, there was really no one else to talk to.

'Relax, can't you?' said Simon. Demetrius's normally accommodating orifice had contracted like a vice.

'We shouldn't be doing this', muttered Demetrius.

'Nonsense. I'm not doing to you anything I wouldn't let you do to me.'

'I don't feel like it', said Demetrius.

'Well, make up your mind.'

Simon finished, a little quicker than he had intended to, and began to drift in a pleasant lethargy.

Demetrius sat up, tidied his curls with his fingers, and said, 'When are you going to give your money away?'

Simon had converted most of his possessions into cash. The money had been sitting in a small leather bag in his bedroom for three weeks.

'When are you going to be circumcised?' enquired Simon.

'Oh well ...' said Demetrius, and fidgeted.

'Does it hurt?' he asked after a while.

'Terribly', said Simon.

'Oh', said Demetrius.

There was a long pause.

'They don't ever ... make mistakes, do they?'

'Well, I did hear of a nasty case once ... but people make a lot of fuss', said Simon.

'I'll tell you what', offered Demetrius, 'I'll be circumcised when you give your money away.'

'You're an impertinent boy', said Simon. 'We will both do it tomorrow.'

But when tomorrow came, something so much more important was happening that they both forgot.

103

'Kepha is coming here', announced Philip with excitement. 'He's coming to meet you all, and to give you the baptism of the Spirit.'

'Really?' Simon brightened. 'When will he be here?'

'In a few days.'

'Wonderful!' exclaimed Simon. Kepha, the leader. Kepha, who had been with Joshua when he uttered his enigmatic sayings and went to his strange death. Kepha, who must know many things that Philip did not.

Simon realised that he had been rather bored of late.

Dark, deep eyes. A full mouth, half-hidden in an untidy bush of beard. A nose like a rudder. The skin as seamed and weatherbeaten as rock. A face which, when it was unsmiling, you thought could never smile: but then suddenly it would lighten like a child's. Simon studied it, and thought that he had seen it somewhere before.

'So this is the great magician', said Kepha. His eyes probed Simon's, then gleamed with friendship. 'We are glad to have you with us.'

'My pleasure', said Simon awkwardly.

They ate. Kepha had a good appetite. He talked between mouthfuls, wiping his mouth with the back of his hand. He talked to Philip about events in Jerusalem and somebody called Saul. He talked to brother Joseph about the cultivation of vines, the state of the soil and the price of sheep, and complimented sister Rebecca on her cooking. He drank his wine with evident enjoyment, belched, and laid his hand lightly on the heads of children as they passed him.

To Simon he said, 'We heard of you in Judaea. A man who could fly, and make caverns open up in the sides of mountains, and all the rest of it. I believe you had quite a following.'

'Yes,' said Simon.

'Illusions, of course', said Kepha.

Simon said carefully, 'I did perform illusions, yes.'

'Well, never mind', said Kepha. 'We're all sinners.'

Simon gazed at his food, and found he did not want it.

'Not everything I did was an illusion', he said.

Kepha glanced at him sharply. 'The flying?'

'I really did fly.' He paused. 'I can fly.'

'Demons', said Kepha. 'Done by demons.'

'Do you think so?'

'How else?' Kepha reached for more bread and wiped his plate with it. He ate the bread and wiped his mouth with the back of his hand.

After a while Simon said, 'Can you walk on water?'

'I tried once', said Kepha, 'but I sank like a stone. That's how I got my name.'

'Why couldn't you do it?' asked Simon.

'Lack of faith. If you believe, you can do anything.'

'I believe I can fly.'

'Demons', said Kepha. 'They carried you through the air. That was before your baptism.'

His face lit with a boyish grin. 'I bet you can't fly now', he said.

Kepha preached.

'The world', he cried, 'has run out of time. There have been signs and portents, and they have not been heeded. People make plans for tomorrow, for next year, for their grandchildren's inheritance. Friends, it will never happen. There will be no world for their grandchildren to inherit. There is no time left. There is only *now*.'

His gaze passed over the silent crowd.

'God sent us a prophet, a man marked out by His special favour, greater than the prophets of old, a man of whom those prophets had spoken. God gave many signs, by miracles, by healing and the casting-out of demons, that this man was specially chosen by Him. Thousands were fed with a basketful of loaves; the unclean were cleansed, the lame danced, the blind saw, the storm was stilled. The dead were raised from their sleep and gave thanks to God. And the people rejoiced.

'But the priests and the lawyers, and those who make it their business to know everything, shook their heads and said, "Who is this man?" And he did not answer them. Instead, he pointed to what he had done. And they said, "By what right do you do these things? Why have you not asked our permission?" And he did not answer.'

'And they grew angry, because he would not answer them, and because he called them hypocrites. And they became afraid, because the people loved him. And they went to their lords and masters and said, "Help us to get rid of this man." And so they plotted against him. And they killed him. He, who had never harmed anyone; he, who had given all he had: they strung him up like a thief and left him to die in the sun.'

Kepha paused.

'He was my friend', he said.

His voice cracked. He lowered his head for a moment. When he raised it again his eyes were shining. Simon could not tell whether it was with joy or tears.

'Great is God!' cried Kepha. 'For there happened then the most wonderful thing that had ever happened since the world was made. God himself raised this man from the dead. He brought him back to us from beyond the grave. Alive, to walk and talk among us. *We saw him.*'

A sigh like an autumn wind rippled through the square.

'Do you understand what that means?' thundered Kepha, and his eyes burned into the crowd. Then he smiled. 'No,' he said quietly, 'which of us can understand it? I only know what it means to me. It means that my master and my friend, the man I knew and broke bread with, is alive and in Heaven, in a form as radiant as an angel's, the form in which in his earthly life I was once privileged to see him, and that in that form, so greatly has God blessed him, he has been given power over the end of all things, the end to which they are hastening, and power to judge the souls of men.'

His voice rang out again, exultant. 'And it is right that he should judge, for he alone has been judged worthy. And it is right that he should judge, for he first came to save. This, friends, is my Deliverer. Accept him in your hearts, I beg you, as yours.'

He fell silent, and bent his head in prayer. Some of the crowd were weeping.

'And now', said Kepha, 'I give you the greatest gift it is in my power to give you. I give you his spirit.'

He came down from the steps and began to move among the crowd, laying his hands for a moment on the head of each person who knelt before him. He passed through the crowd, smiling, blessing, touching. Behind him he left a stillness like the moment before Creation: a stillness so full that it must break.

It gathered, and broke.

People screamed, wept, howled. They tore their hair and shuddered, and flung themselves about with flailing hands. They moaned, laughed, embraced each other and shouted incomprehensible things. The square was filled with a tumult of voices raised in ecstatic and meaningless speech. Simon stared about him, shocked and incredulous. They were possessed.

He had barely the presence of mind to kneel as Kepha

106

approached him. The hands rested for a long moment on his head. Their weight, it seemed to him, was the shadow of a weight so immense it could not be borne. The hands rested, and moved on.

He was in a cool well of peace. But no sooner had he drunk than he was rising out of it, rising up to meet the tumult, which bore him up and up on waves of sound until he thought he must be flying. He felt a stab of panic, and then began to laugh, because it would be a joke too good for God to miss. He laughed and laughed, tears coursing down his cheeks, laughing for joy at his unimaginable freedom and his total helplessness, the fool of God, God's toy, possession.

'How did you do it?' asked Simon.

'Do what?' said Kepha. 'Have an olive, they're very good.'

'Call down a spirit on a hundred people', said Simon. 'I've never seen anything like it.'

'No, I don't suppose you have', said Kepha. He munched. After a while he said, 'You'll never find it.'

'Find what?' said Simon, surprised.

'Peace. You'll taste it and it'll go away again, because you drive it away. Always asking questions. Philip told me. You stopped for a time, but now you're doing it again. How do I call down the Spirit? I don't know how I do it. I was promised that I would be able to do it, and I can. I invoke it, and it comes. That's all.'

He added the olive stone to the little pile of olive stones in front of him, and smiled. In the distance the children played.

Simon said, 'This gift you have of inducing possession by the spirit, can you bestow it on others?'

'I can', said Kepha.

'Will you bestow it on me?'

It was the first time he had heard the man laugh. It was a great booming laugh. It scattered the sparrows and stopped the children in their tracks. Kepha laughed and laughed.

'No', he said eventually, and wiped his eyes.

Simon flushed.

'Ah, I shouldn't have laughed at you', said Kepha. 'But you really don't understand at all. You still think like a magician. What you saw yesterday wasn't a magical trick, you know.'

'The invocation of a spirit is never a trick', said Simon stiffly.

'I beg your pardon. I don't really know much about magic.'

'But your master was a magician', objected Simon.

107

'Of course he wasn't.'

'Is turning water into wine not magic? It's almost the first thing in the textbooks.'

'It was a miracle', said Kepha.

'What's the difference?'

'Miracles are performed by the power of God. Magic is performed with the aid of demons.'

'The same act can be performed by the power of God or the power of a demon?'

'Certainly. Demons are very good at counterfeiting.'

'So when you see such an act performed, how do you know whether it is a miracle or magic?'

'Quite easily', said Kepha. 'If the man who does it is one of us, then he is invoking the power of God and it is a miracle. If he is not one of us, then he is being aided by demons and it is magic.'

'You aren't serious', said Simon.

'I am very serious', said Kepha. 'It's a serious matter. Demons love to deceive. Many people are taken in by so-called miracles which in fact are just magic, and an insult to God.'

'I see', said Simon. They sat in silence for a while. There seemed little left to say.

In the end Simon ventured, 'There isn't a secret teaching, I suppose?'

'No, no', said Kepha. 'Oh, no, no. Nothing like that.'

'I see', said Simon. They sat a little longer. 'Well,' said Simon finally, 'thank you.' He stood up. Turning to leave, he then remembered the thing he had originally meant to ask Kepha. In the circumstances he doubted whether the answer would be worth anything; however, it would be a pity not to try.

'May I ask you one more question?'

'Certainly', said Kepha.

'When Joshua predicted his death, what did he say about it?'

'He said he must be given up to be killed', said Kepha, frowning at the memory.

'How did he know? What prompted him to say it?'

Kepha gave a short laugh. 'He didn't usually wait to be prompted. However, I suppose ...'

He gazed ahead, apparently absorbed in some inner vision.

'Yes?' said Simon.

'I suppose it was to correct any mistaken ideas we might have.

We had just realised, you see, who he was. It was the very first time anyone had said it.'

Simon went rigid.

'Who said it?' he whispered.

'Oh, I did', said Kepha modestly.

Simon reflected. The cult he had joined was unlike any other he had ever met. It made grandiose promises and sought its adherents among the lowest classes of society, while enjoining them to remain humble. It relied for the validation of its central myth on prophecies which contradicted it. It claimed the sole right to work magic, denied that it *was* magic, appealed to its success in working magic as proof of its beliefs, and said magic was unimportant. It revered a founder whose teaching it made no attempt to understand and whose death it had probably caused. It preached love, and said that anyone who did not join it would be burnt alive.

But for two things, it was not worth a thinking man's consideration. The first thing was the sayings and stories left by Joshua. They were rich, deceptively simple: they teased the mind. They contained the core of a philosophy which had yet to be extracted from them.

The second thing was that the leaders, while choosing to deny it, were magicians of a high order. The question was how they had obtained their power. Neither Philip nor Kepha had studied the art. Kepha probably could not even read. The secret of Joshua's power was as mysterious as everything else about him. What seemed certain, though, was that that secret had been passed on to Kepha, and indirectly to Philip.

Again and again he came back to it. There was a secret. Everyone denied it: everything pointed to it. It was the only hypothesis which explained all the puzzling features. Kepha knew something he would not tell, and would not admit he knew it.

But the believers knew. They knew Kepha was in possession of something extraordinarily precious, and interpreted it in their own way. They said it was a key which he wore under his tunic. When the Kingdom came, Kepha with that key would unlock the gate. It was as heavy as the Temple cornerstone, they whispered, and when he was tired the angels helped him carry it. Philip had heard them whispering, and been angry.

Simple people. Since the cult found its members among the simple, and kept them by saying that it was to the simple that the

Kingdom belonged, presumably it could not then tell the simple that they were not good enough for the Secret.

Simon sat and thought. How to breach the barrier of silence which surrounded the subject? He had joined the cult; he had professed the belief; he had been baptised and been possessed by the spirit. What else did he have to do, to make them talk to him?

But of course. It was so elementary that he laughed. He picked up the bag of money and went to see Kepha.

'I should have done this before', said Simon. 'I didn't realise it was so important. It's amazing how obtuse one can be. However, here it is.'

He placed the bag of money on the table.

'What are you talking about?' asked Kepha.

'Call it my payment', said Simon. 'This is all the money I have. It's an earnest of good faith. I suppose you didn't think I was serious. Well, that was understandable. I hope now you will accept that I am. And now, perhaps we can talk.'

'Talk about what?' said Kepha.

Simon sighed.

'Look, I know you're in a difficult position', he said. 'There are all these people who think there's nothing else to it but what you've told them. But I *know*. You can't go on like this, concealing the truth even from people who are entitled to hear it. I want to be one of you. I feel I am fitted to be one of you. If I'm wrong, if there's something else I need to do, please tell me and I will try to do it. Meanwhile I've done the only other thing I can think of.' He indicated the bag of coins.

'I do not think', said Kepha, 'I understand a word you're saying. You talk of concealing the truth. I devote myself night and day to nothing but telling people the truth. You talk of being one of us. You are one of us, and the fact seems if anything to embarrass you rather than give you pleasure. You talk of entitlement. There is no entitlement. God is not bound by obligations. And what' – he tapped the bag of money with his finger – 'has this to do with it?'

'I'm sorry, I have not expressed myself clearly.' Simon chewed his lip. The interview was not proceeding well. 'When I said I wanted to be one of you, I meant that I want to be one of the inner circle. You understand what I mean.'

'You want to be an apostle? You want to preach, and tramp the roads in all weathers, and be flogged and thrown into prison, and flee for your life?'

110

'Oh really? Has that happened to you? I had to flee once, and it was most uncomfortable. No, what I really meant', said Simon, 'was that I want to share your knowledge. Your power, if you like.'

Kepha sat very still. 'Knowledge', he said. 'Power.'

'Yes. I have powers of my own, of course, but they can't compare with yours.' Flattery was out of place, but it was too late. 'I suppose you will accuse me again of thinking like a magician, but I'm afraid I can't shed a lifetime's training overnight. And after all, it's a technicality, isn't it? We both know that. You and I have a great deal in common.'

A muscle in Kepha's cheek twitched.

'I think I could be quite an asset to you', continued Simon, although it was difficult in face of the frozen silence, 'if you'd give me a chance. But you must *give* me a chance. How can I learn if you won't teach me?'

'Teach you what?' said Kepha. He spat out each word like a small stone.

'What you know', said Simon desperately. 'The invocation of the spirit, for one thing.'

'The gift of the holy Spirit,' said Kepha. His voice trembled slightly. He prodded the bag of coins with his finger. 'And this?'

'Money', said Simon, 'as I explained. It's all I have ...'

Kepha stood up. His eyes blazed. His voice shook the rafters.

'Money? *Money?* You think you can *buy* the gift of God? Why, you insolent piece of Satan! Fit to be one of us? You aren't fit to clean our privies. Leave this place and stay away, Simon of Gitta. As long as you live, stay away from my people. Feed on your own poison and perversity, not on the children's bread. Take your money. Take it to damnation with you.'

As Simon went through the doorway the bag of money swished through the air and landed at his feet. He picked it up and walked away.

'Go into the market place', said Simon, 'and tell everyone you meet to assemble in the square tomorrow at noon. Tell them they will witness the greatest feat of magic that has ever been performed. When you've been to the market place you can go to the temple precincts, and after that you can go to the public baths. Tell everyone.'

'But –' said Demetrius.

'Go!' roared Simon. Demetrius went.

The boy did his work well, or perhaps it was just that the citizens of Sebaste were eager to see their magician again after so long an absence. By noon on the following day the sides of the square were jammed with people, with others crowding the balconies and sitting on the rooftops.

Simon raised his hands for silence.

'Friends', he cried, 'I have been away from you a long time. You will have heard many rumours about me. I ask you not to believe them. I have been unwell – a mysterious sickness which certain people who wish me harm have sought to take advantage of. They have not succeeded. I come before you restored, and ready to show you marvels the like of which you have never seen.' He paused. 'I show you, here in this square, the palace of King Herod.'

With a flourish of his arm he focused their attention on the large roped-off space. With his mind he began to fashion the palace: colonnade, courtyard, fountains, the great white building beyond. He intensified his concentration, and the air seemed to shiver and fragment into blocks of light. As the blocks solidified, he brought trees into the courtyard, willed water from the fountains, carved capitals upon the columns which rose in front of the ...

But it had gone. There was no building. It had dislimned into the air. He strove frantically to bring it back and felt the whole creation slipping, piece by piece, away from him, the green of the trees fading, the columns warping and disintegrating, the paved courtyard fissured with the dust of the square. He made a supreme effort, and the air glowed bright for a moment with a fractured memory, and then was dull and empty in the heat of an ordinary afternoon.

The crowd began to mutter.

'I didn't see anything, did you?'

'I don't think this is Simon at all.'

'Where's the palace, then?'

'Cheat!'

The muttering became a shout. 'Show us the palace! Show us the palace!'

Simon gave a hunted glance around him, then hurried from the rostrum. Hands clutched at him, but he shook them off and darted into a back street. Laughter and derisive shouts pursued him.

He walked quickly, with a strange lightness in his head, to his house. There, in the study, Demetrius found him, his eyes vacant, his arms clutched about his knees, shivering.

His power had gone.

IV

THE KEY

Click, click, click. Pause.

Clatter.

'Double on the three.'

Chink.

Click, click, click.

Clatter.

'Well, Lady Venus.'

Their patience, he reflected, although of a different kind, was as great as his. In a sense it was greater, since they did not know what they were waiting for. Their hopelessness touched him, and, catching the eye of one of them, he smiled. His smile was returned by an even stare, the sort of look a man might exchange with an animal.

There would be a time for the setting straight of records. That was not the right way to think about it. He shifted on his straw, and felt the iron bite into his wrist. The time was long in coming. He might not live to see it. Jacob bar Zabdai had not. They had severed his neck.

'Do you want to share what is in store for me? You shall share it.'

Strange, he had never thought at the time that the words might refer to a future years distant. It had not been possible at the time to think beyond the next day. He had thought – they had all thought – that they were all expected to die together. He was prepared to die, then, should it be necessary, although he could not understand why it should be necessary. But then there had been so many things he did not understand that the thought that they might have to die had been almost welcome, it had seemed to make everything much clearer. More important, too.

Not that he had ever doubted the importance, the seriousness, of what they were doing; but he had always been faintly surprised when the rest of the world took it seriously. If the world required them to die for it, then undoubtedly it was serious.

But of course he had not. Died. He rested his head against the uneven stone. It had not been required. That much had, at the last moment, been made clear. At first they had misunderstood the terms on which they were spared. That, too, was now clear. One of them was dead. It was proof that the interpretation they had arrived at with so much difficulty was the right one.

He supposed it was proof. He did not have the gift for thinking about these matters. He could often see things very clearly when they happened: that was his gift and he had been told to treasure it. But when he began to think he became confused. Even to the point where, thinking about a thing some time after it had happened, he sometimes wondered if he had seen it aright. He was, he knew, apt to make blunders. Then again, often one did not see the meaning of an event until a long time afterwards. But in that case, what was there to trust?

Why have you left me?

'I need water', he said.

A metal mug was pressed to his lips. He swallowed. The water was warm and stale. He remembered drinking from a mountain stream near his home: the sweet, clean coldness.

'Thank you', he said.

The soldier moved heavily back to the table and sat down.

Chink.

Click, click, click.

'You dice', said Kepha, 'as if the world had a thousand years still to run.'

Clatter.

'Dog again'.

Chink.

Perhaps he had not spoken aloud, although he could hear the words clearly in his head. Sitting in the half darkness day after day, not knowing even if it was day, he found his head much visited by voices, and sometimes did not know whether they came from inside or outside. The voice for which he hungered rarely spoke: he had to conjure it with memories.

The voices passed the time, and were better company than his thoughts. Time: for years he had longed for time. Now he had it, and no one could take it away: his own time in which to confront his own life in the light of his own approaching death. It was a fine gift: kingly in all senses.

He could not use it. He surveyed his life, and it was a winding road marked by ciphers. He played host gladly to the voices; even when loudest among them, cutting across his mind like a whip, was the voice he least wished to hear.

'I demand to be listened to.'

'Saul, I am listening.'

'If you are, you're the first person who has. I've been cold-shouldered ever since I arrived here. Are your people afraid of me?'

'Of course they are', said Kepha. 'Last time your face was seen here you were hunting them like a wolf. What do you expect?'

'But can't they see I'm sincere?'

Sincerity burned in the man with an intensity that could be felt. It was not likely to endear him to the lukewarm or reassure the fainthearted. The small community of which Kepha was supposed to be the head contained numbers of both.

'They're ordinary people, and they remember the past', said Kepha.

Saul snorted.

'What about my work, then? Does that count for nothing?'

'It could be a trick.'

'God send me patience!' Saul banged his fist on the table. 'They were going to kill me in Damascus! I had to escape over the walls at night. That's going rather far for a trick, isn't it?'

'I heard about it', said Kepha. 'You hid in a basket, didn't you?'

Saul flushed. Kepha had noticed that he was sensitive about his size.

'It swayed like the devil', he said, 'and I hate heights.'

He grinned unexpectedly, with self-derision. Kepha studied him. He could not make up his mind whether he liked this man or detested him.

'We're none of us heroes, Saul', he said gently.

'I would prefer you didn't call me that. I've changed my name.'

'I know', said Kepha. 'I don't see what was wrong with your first one.'

'You would if you knew Greek.'

'Oh? What does it mean in Greek?'

'Never mind. It's unsuitable. My appearance is hardly likely to impress as it is.'

Kepha was not sure of that. Certainly the body had something dwarfish about it, but the shoulders were wide and powerful, the eyes fierce, and the forehead massive, its height accentuated by the prematurely thinning hair.

'Well,' he said lightly, 'if you will live among heathens ...'

'Do *you* believe I'm sincere?' demanded Saul.

'Oh yes.'

'Then if you believe me, why won't you listen to me?'

'Listen to you? But ...' Kepha stopped. Obviously he had not grasped what was being required of him. 'What is it you want?' he said.

'Equality', said Saul.

'Equality?' Kepha frowned. 'With whom?'

117

'With you. With John and Jacob. I want to be one of you.'

It seemed to Kepha that only yesterday he had heard another urgent voice demanding the same thing. It was strange that people always wanted what they were unfitted for, and disdained what they were given.

'You can never have it', said Kepha simply. 'You never knew Joshua.'

He saw the flash of anger in Saul's eyes, and the internal struggle that followed it. After a while Saul said, 'That is what I expected.'

'Be reasonable', said Kepha. 'It's not a question of merit. If it were ...' He tapped the table thoughtfully with his finger and left the sentence unfinished. 'However sincere you are, whatever work you do, however many times your life is threatened, you must see that you cannot ever have the same authority as the people who actually *knew* him.'

'Why not?' said Saul.

Kepha stared. 'Are you serious?'

'Perfectly.'

'Because ... because we know what he was like', said Kepha helplessly. Why did it sound so childish? 'We heard him teach, we talked to him, we ... we were *with* him.'

'And did you', asked Saul, 'understand him?'

Kepha raised his eyes and met Saul's gaze. There was no mercy in it.

'A faulty understanding', said Kepha, 'is better than no understanding at all.'

'Your intolerable complacency!' Saul brought both fists down on the table with a violence that shook the room. 'You were given the most extraordinary privilege that has ever been granted to anyone, and what you have done with it is turn it into a strong-room which no one else is allowed to enter. How did you benefit from being with him? Two years in his company, and when the day of reckoning came you all ran away!'

Kepha clenched his hands. 'There was a reason ... It was necessary ...'

'Of course it was *necessary*. The point I'm making is that you behaved no better than anyone else would have done. Probably rather worse, in fact. It didn't help then that you knew him, did it. Everything you'd ever learnt from being with him was suddenly irrelevant. And it still is. The touching little stories of his life which you all retail are irrelevant. The only thing that's relevant is *wha*

118

happened after he died. But for that, none of you would be here. Would you?'

Kepha took a deep breath. 'No', he said.

'Very well. What happened after he died, what happened to *you*, happened also to me.'

Kepha stared at him.

'That experience', said Saul, 'that experience which makes impossible things possible, that experience from which you date whatever understanding you have and from which you derive whatever authority you possess, was also granted to me.'

Saul's language had a way of swinging from brutal directness to passionate abstraction. It was very disorienting. Kepha with some difficulty worked out what he meant.

'Oh yes', he said. 'Your vision.'

'Vision be damned! Any fool can have a vision.' Saul leaned across the table and pointed a thick forefinger at Kepha. 'When he appeared to you, after his resurrection, would you call that a *vision*?'

'No', said Kepha shortly. It was a subject he avoided discussing.

'What, then?'

'Are you questioning me?' Kepha fought down a vicious surge of anger. 'I prefer not to speak about it', he said.

'That's understandable', said Saul. 'I prefer not to speak of my own experience. But it is important.'

There was a pause. Kepha realised he would have to talk about it. Whenever he was obliged to talk about it there was something soft and unpleasant at the back of his mind, like a worm turning in earth.

'It wasn't a vision', he said. 'Visions are quite different in quality ...' His voice trailed off. 'He *appeared* to me,' he said.

'Just so', said Saul. 'And he appeared to me.'

'This was on your journey?'

'Yes. And I repeat that it was not a vision. It was an Appearance.'

Kepha closed his eyes for a moment. 'Then you too have been given a great privilege.'

'Yes.' The terse word was eloquent.

'What ... happened?' murmured Kepha.

'It was a terrible shock', said Saul. 'I was blind. It took away my sight.'

'Blind?'

'For three days. In the circumstances it was a great ... mercy.'

The room was suddenly very still. In the silence an insect whined.

Saul spoke again.

'There is more, which I have not told anyone.'

The voice trembled slightly, and stopped, as if afraid to follow the thought. With a visible effort Saul forced it.

'I have seen Heaven', he said.

Kepha wiped sweat from the back of his neck.

'Go on', he said.

'No', said Saul. 'I should not have mentioned it. But you doubt me, and you don't accept my work. So what else can I do, but allow you to trap me into boasting of my ... credentials?'

Credentials?

If anyone is to boast ...

'No', said Kepha involuntarily, as if something had hurt him. The guards glanced at him curiously, then returned to their game.

Saul was right, of course: it was an extraordinary privilege that had been bestowed on everyone who had been close to Joshua. How much more extraordinary, then, the privilege that had been bestowed on him? Boast of it he could not: the words would choke him.

All the same it was hard not to cry out, as he had longed to cry out at Saul, 'I was the first to be chosen. I was the first to see who he was. The Key is in my keeping.'

It could not be said. But it could be thought about. There was comfort in the past, and in this place he needed comfort. Resting his head against the wall with half-closed eyes, he allowed himself to take it.

In the past lay privileges beyond Saul's reach.

Light, unearthly light, flooded the form of the master.

Kepha, his knees numb from the vigil, his mind dazed, watched a mystery.

It was broad day, but the brightness seemed to have gone out of things. It was as if all the light in the sky were being drawn into the seated figure before them, there intensifying while everything around it grew darker, until there would come an impossible moment when the frail body contained all the light in the world.

Kepha tried to shift his position but could not move. His head seemed to be occupying a different kind of space from his body. He

120

wanted to look at the bar Zabdai brothers a few feet away to see if they saw what he saw, but he could not take his eyes from what was happening in front of him.

Joshua sat motionless on one of the three curious platforms of rock that crowned the hill, while light hung round him like a tent.

The air around Kepha was growing darker, and the figure on the rock seemed to recede, so that there was a gulf between him and it. Kepha, afraid, stifled a cry. Then he saw that a new thing had happened. Joshua was no longer alone. On each platform of rock now sat a shining figure. In the space between them shivered something like moonlight on water. They were talking.

He needed desperately to know what his friends saw. He looked for them in the half-gloom, and his heart froze. They were not there.

He realised at that moment that the vision was for him, and that if he did not understand it it would be lost for ever. He must speak at once, to affirm it.

His tongue was like a stone. He forced words out, and heard them tumble, uncouth, into the silence.

The darkness seemed to fold in on itself, like a net as it is withdrawn from the water. The veil of light around each seated figure swayed and distorted as if caught in a wind. There was a rushing sound like the sea, and then for a moment of utter terror there was only the rushing and the darkness.

His eyes opened into daylight. Joshua sat smiling and alone on a rock. A short distance away the brothers bar Zabdai stared and rubbed their eyes.

Making their way down the hillside, they were silent almost until they reached the foot. Then, as if something had been breached, they all three began talking at once.

Joshua, walking apart, turned to stop them.

'Now now', he said. 'Let it rest. None of you knows when to talk and when to be silent.'

The door clanged back on its hinges. Kepha, jolted out of his reverie, saw the guards at the table stand up and throw their cloaks round their shoulders. They strode in step from the cell.

Two new guards came in. The door clanged shut. The new guards took off their cloaks, settled themselves at the table and, without even a glance in Kepha's direction, started dicing.

Click, click, click, clatter.

'Pay on sixes?'

Chink.

'Double.'

Day after day, night after night. Not that it was easy, in this gloom, to tell which was which. The only ways he had of measuring time were the arrival of his food and the change-over of the guard.

There were four sets of guards. One of them, a young Syrian, was friendly, and sometimes exchanged a few words with him. He came from a village near Kepha's home, and had been conscripted into the king's militia. He was unhappy in the army, and occasionally passed on to Kepha a subversive piece of news — disturbances in the city, guardroom gossip about the king's latest excess.

Kepha's dish of bread and beans arrived just after the friendly guard had gone off duty. Kepha assumed that he was given one meal a day, and deduced that the guard changed every six hours. He calculated that he had been in the dungeon for nearly two weeks. Perhaps it was longer: he did not know how much he slept, and it was difficult to keep count of the plates of bread and beans when there was nothing to distinguish one from another. Except that once they had given him a raw onion with his meal, which was kind of them but upset his stomach.

It was a mistake to try to count the days. It attributed a meaning to this stretch of time which it did not possess. Its duration did not matter: it was simply the last part of his life.

It seemed best to assume that he would be killed. Jacob bar Zabdai had been killed, and Kepha's arrest had followed almost immediately after. The king had waited a bare three days to gauge public response to the execution. He need not have worried. It was exactly what the priests had wanted.

It was strange, mused Kepha, that the preaching of love should arouse such hate. But of course it was not what they preached that earned them enemies, it was what they did not preach. Faced with the careful structure of good deeds, charitable works and observance of the Law behind which people hid their emptiness they did not say the one thing they were required to say — 'Well done'.

And the king, unsure who his friends were, would use their deaths to buy friends where he needed. He would try to kill them all. He would not know that in doing so he was fulfilling th prophecies. Before the Kingdom must come the Tribulation. The Tribulation, indeed, would bring about the Kingdom.

Therefore, though they might pray to be spared the suffering, they might not seek to avoid it.

Kepha remembered, with a pain still fresh, the time when they had all hoped to avoid it.

'I must take the burden on myself.'

They had been shocked, they had dared to argue with him. They were afraid. Buried deep beneath their fear and misery had been a small, shameful relief. They did not have to do anything themselves. It would be done for them. One man's blood, shed for God, would suffice.

Later they had realised that that could not have been what he meant. They had taken too literally his mysterious, muttered allusion to a ransom, and with the short-sightedness that had cursed all their thinking at the time they had applied it solely to themselves. He would die instead of them. Only when it became clear how long a time might elapse before the coming of the Kingdom had they seen that he could not have been referring to so limited an act. If he had been, what then had been the meaning of his death, since the Kingdom had not come? There must be a deeper meaning; and after months of discussion and prayer and study of the Writings they had found it. They were ransomed, not from death, but from the holy anger. They were forgiven.

Kepha had not been sure about it at first, although there seemed no other explanation. The murder of Jacob bar Zabdai now confirmed it. They could not have been ransomed from death if one of them had died.

Kepha shifted uncomfortably on his straw. He did not like, and had never liked, the confused area in which his thoughts were wandering.

Confusion distressed him. It was a kind of failure. Once, everything had been so clear that confusion did not seem possible. But then, of course, he had not thought the world would last long enough for him to get confused again.

It was the Feast of Weeks, fifty days after Joshua's death, forty-eight after the first Appearance. They had gathered, with a few friends, in the room where he had appeared. In the minds of all of them was a hope they dared not speak. Instead, they prayed.

'May the Kingdom come.'

123

They had begun their vigil of prayer at evening. As the hours wore on, so did the distance between them, their separateness, diminish, so that they spoke with one voice, and the voice was the prayer it uttered, and the room was the prayer that filled it.

'Father in Heaven, whose Name is holy, may the Kingdom come. May earth, like Heaven, be subject to thy will.'

Space had ceased. Soon time would cease.

'Give us today the bread of Tomorrow. Forgive us as we forgive others. Do not test us in the Tribulation, but protect us from the Evil One.'

Heads bent, bodies swaying, they drew the future towards them on a chain of words.

'Father in Heaven, whose Name is holy, may the Kingdom come.'

Chanting towards them the last days, the final and terrible purification.

'May earth, like Heaven, be subject to thy will. Give us today the bread of Tomorrow ...'

The voices faltered, caught in an irresistible stillness. Then there was a roar which seemed to come from the very fabric of the building. A tearing wind ripped the door from its hinges and sucked the air out of the room so that they struggled like netted fish. The air rushed in again and struck the walls with a clap, and the room shuddered as if shaken by a giant. They lay gasping under an enormous hand that forced the breath out of their lungs and sharp tears from their eyes. The pressure was suddenly withdrawn and they drew in air that burned. Through tears of pain they saw that the room was filling with fire. A golden glory blazed in the middle of the air, and they were being lifted to their feet, with infinite gentleness, so that their heads were touched by it, and the fire did not burn, but settled about them, and hung there, and faded.

They floated in a silence as deep as the sea.

In the depths of that silence there then evolved little threats of sound. Then strange words like knots.

Then bursting over them, a torrent of alien speech. An ecstatic babble, rending and weaving the air.

Kepha, the language of Heaven spilling like pearls from his tongue, strode to the door where a gaping crowd had gathered.

'They're drunk', he heard someone say.

Love for them in their blindness welled up and for a moment he could not speak. Then the words came, the meagre human words that had to serve.

124

'The Kingdom has come!' he cried, and the tears gushed from his eyes like the first torrents of autumn. 'Thanks be to God, the Kingdom has come, and this is the sign!'

The sign. Kepha straightened his back and moved his shoulders to ease the stiffness. The chains, which were not quite long enough to enable him to stretch his arms fully, pulled at his wrists. A sign was a mystery, containing more than it said. A sign could mean almost anything. Sometimes you did not see the meaning until a long time later. Signs were to be read backwards.

When a dead man came to life, what kind of sign was that?

Reading forwards, it meant an end. An end of history, of the predictable birth and dying. Effects would no longer follow causes. A man would reap where he had not sown. God had lifted the inescapable ban, and the dead would walk the earth.

But it was ten years, and the sun had not darkened.

Reading backwards, then, a beginning. A beginning of waiting? No, more than that. They had been given time. They were expected to use it.

How, exactly, were they to use it?

Why, in building up communities of converts. It could not be clearer.

The only trouble was that Joshua had never said anything about it. He had expected the world to end with his resurrection.

But it had not.

Therefore ...

Kepha shook his head impatiently. The thoughts dragged him round and round in a circle.

To break the circle, all he had to do was believe something he had not seen. It was the hardest thing that had ever been asked of him. To believe, and not to say that he had not seen it. It was fitting that his burden should be silence: he had always talked too much.

'No throw.'

'Dog!'

'Five, two threes and an ace.'

'Two aces. You threw the Dog!'

'It was a no throw, I tell you.'

Kepha opened his eyes from a fitful sleep. The guards were staring at each other across the table. One of them had risen and had his hand on his dagger.

'Don't be a fool. Put your money in.'

'Are you calling me a liar?'

'Oh, sit down. Throw again.'

Grudgingly the guard sat down and stretched out his hand for the dice.

'I won't be called a liar.'

'And I won't lose three years' service for you.'

Click, click, click.

Pause.

Clatter.

Kepha tried to sleep again, but sleep would not come. Words and images jostled disjointedly in his brain. He wondered if he had caught a fever.

There had been a time when everything was clear. How had he lost it, that visionary simplicity? It had not been suddenly withdrawn. It had leaked away, imperceptibly, through the cracks in his nature.

At the beginning, when Joshua was with them, all they had needed to know was that they were in possession of an enormous truth, and must spread it as far and as quickly as possible. The truth was the truth of the relationship between God and man. It was not a new truth: on the contrary, it had been said so many times that people had ceased to hear it. Into the familiar words, become dead and empty, Joshua infused shocking life. The words became a revelation, a challenge. 'You are God's children.'

It changed the world. It meant an end of placating and pleading of the anxious counting of faults and the unending rituals to earn favour, and the desperate certainty that no effort would ever be enough. Everything was free, there was no earning. All that was needed was to ask. It meant an end of calculation for the future God would give. It meant an end of fear: God was the father. It effaced every doubt and cancelled every debt: and it abolished the need for the Law.

It had taken them a long time to understand all this: the roots of the old ways grew deep. But when, at last, they understood, they knew from where he drew his strength. It was in them too.

And then had come the first bad thing: the first inkling that God's mind was not so easily read. Before they had time to visit all the towns of Judaea, he had promised, the Kingdom would come. It was a long, exhausting journey; there was power in their hands but as many as they healed cursed them, and most were indifferent with that cold indifference that was worse than hate. They struggled on until the task was completed. Completed, when it should not have been. The Kingdom had not come.

They had returned to find him wandering in the hills, his face drawn. He had misled them.

Everything that had ever disturbed and perplexed Kepha seemed contained for him in the paradox of that completed, and therefore futile, mission. Later, he had even attempted to trace what subsequently happened to its failure. That had been stupid of him, but it was undeniable that Joshua's behaviour afterwards had changed. He was withdrawn, subject to moods, and melancholy. He was convinced that someone would betray him.

And yet, Kepha reflected, it was at that time, that gradually darkening time, that the brightest light had shone. For it was then that he had grasped the mighty secret of Joshua's identity, and as reward for that leap of understanding, he had been entrusted with the Key.

It had come strangely, this strangest of all revelations. Joshua had asked, quite unexpectedly, a question which none of them knew how to answer. Fumbling and embarrassed, Kepha had suddenly heard, quite clearly, the answer in his head. It was the shrill voice of a demoniac, one of the dozens Joshua had cleansed. The wild words rang again in his ears, and rang cold and true.

'The One Who Is To Come.'

He had been terrified. But he had said it.

And Joshua ...

Joshua's initial reaction had been as strange as everything else.

'You have said something that should never have been said, and here will be a heavy price to pay.'

'Is it true?'

'It should never have been said.'

'But why not, if it is true?'

'*Because* it is true, son of an idiot. Have you listened to me all this ime and you still don't understand? Things must not be said.'

'I don't see why.'

'If you throw pearls to pigs they will attack you, because what hey wanted was scraps; and then what happens to the pearls? And or another reason, which you must never tell to anyone. There is a ind of truth which, when it is said, becomes untrue. Do you nderstand?'

Kepha stared, numb with bewilderment.

127

'Round and round the well you all go, and no one goes down into it to get the water. But now that you know this, I have given you the Key to the Kingdom. Do you see?'

Kepha moved his head, his enormously heavy head, in a gesture of hopelessness. Then with sudden alarm he said, 'What key have you given me?' and his hands travelled fearfully in the folds of his tunic.

Joshua began to laugh. It was a terrible laugh, high, sharp and mirthless.

Kepha put his head in his hands and wept.

Pearls.

Made in the darkness at the bottom of the sea.

Towards the end, much that Joshua said had baffled him. He had felt, often, that the words were not addressed to him: it was as if the master were conducting a long and urgent dialogue with himself which Kepha was at times allowed to hear.

He had sought, in prayer and meditation over the years, the nature of the Key. It was not, of course, a real key: he had quickly got over his stupid mistake about that. Nevertheless he believed that one day, in a day beyond time, he would see it shining in his hand.

But it was not simply a promise for the future. He was already in possession of it. Joshua had said so, plainly. And since he already possessed it, it must have meaning in the present. And what meaning could it have, the key to a kingdom that had not come?

A key was for locking and unlocking, for barring out and letting in. The Kingdom had not come, but those who were to fill it were now on earth. From this, Kepha had taken the clue to his earthly task. It must be a foreshadow of his heavenly one: gatekeeper of the brotherhood, watchful that none crept in who were unfitted, that none were left out who belonged inside.

He had tried to discharge it to the best of his ability. He had visited as many of the communities as he could, talking to the members, testing their belief, observing their way of life. In most places he had found much that pleased him. In a few, notably one of Philip's in Samaria, he had had to expel unwholesome influences. But he had become aware, in the past few years, that the task, taken so literally, was beyond him or any man. The communities were spreading, seeding into regions beyond the mountains and the eastern desert, along the coasts of the Great Sea. Saul . . .

Kepha groaned inwardly. Saul presumably would take no steps without consulting them. But the man was utterly unpredictable, and nothing had been heard from him since his departure from Jerusalem. What, by now, might Saul be doing?

'The whole world, Kepha!'

'The message is for us only. He said so.'

'Oh, "he said, he said". Do you do all the things he said and nothing he didn't say? The situation has changed: there are new perspectives. *You* said so.'

Kepha glared at him.

'This is *life*, Kepha', said Saul urgently. 'Life, truth, freedom. How can we keep it to ourselves?'

'Look', said Kepha. His patience rode above his irritation like foam on a swell. 'Our race is a priesthood. How can a message be given to the world before all the priests have heard it? It makes no sense.'

'A lot of things do not appear to make sense', said Saul. 'To me, at any rate. But perhaps you understand the mind of God?'

Kepha was silent.

'Put it another way', said Saul. 'Are you having much success with your ... priests?'

'There will be time. The truth cannot be withstood.'

'It seems to me', said Saul, 'that they are withstanding the truth remarkably well. How are your scars healing?'

'Surely you aren't contemplating a mission to the heathen because you're afraid of your own people?'

Saul's eyes blazed. 'At present I'm contemplating nothing. I'm merely putting an idea before you. As you'd know if you listened properly. And never tell me that *I'm* afraid.'

The stress on the 'I' was unmistakable. Kepha felt his cheeks flush.

'I apologise', he said.

There was a pause. They smiled at each other warily. In several days of conversation they had established almost nothing except that they might one day be friends, and that in the meantime it was going to be very difficult. They circled like stags. They could not come to grips either with each other, or with the subject that lay between them, for long enough to settle anything.

The conversation began another circle.

'You say that it's just an idea', said Kepha. 'You've no intention at the moment of extending your preaching?'

'I'm not ready for it. I'm simply asking for your reaction to the principle.'

'Have you mentioned it to anyone else?'

'No.'

'Then don't', said Kepha. 'There are other priorities. After all, we don't have much time.'

'Time?' Saul laughed harshly. 'Just now you said there would be time.'

'For the Jews, yes. There must be. That is the priority. But it does *take* time. Not just the preaching, baptising, the initial mission work ... in a sense that's the easiest part.'

Saul's thick eyebrows rose a fraction.

'The administration', explained Kepha. 'These groups have to be held together. Have you any idea how much of my time administrative work takes up?'

'Then give it up', said Saul. 'You obviously aren't suited to it.'

There was another pause.

'What I mean', said Kepha, 'is that first things must come first.'

'The first shall be last.'

'You try my patience, Saul'.

'And you mine, Kepha. You talk about priorities, but whose priorities are they? Are they yours or God's? They sound to me like the priorities of a small group of frightened men afraid to move outside their own back door. You're afraid, all of you. Little minds. God preserve me from little minds.'

Kepha waited for his blood to subside. Saul sat, fists clenched, on the other side of the table. After a while he rested his forehead on his knuckles in a gesture of despair.

'I'm sorry', he muttered. 'I should not have said that.'

He looked up at Kepha with eyes full of pain. 'How can I make you see it?' he said.

He was like a child sometimes. Kepha said gently, 'You don' look to me like a man who needs anyone else's consent.'

'That is not true', said Saul. 'I can't do without your approval You know it. Unfortunately I'm not very good at asking.'

They smiled at each other. There was a pleasant silence for a time.

Kepha mused. Saul's idea was mad, of course. It was also unnecessary. Yet it was magnificent. He allowed himself to dwel on it for a moment, and saw its grandeur. A world united in faith, awaiting the return ...

He stopped short, baffled, as he saw also its complete impossibility. In such a world, what would be the significance of a Return to deliver an oppressed people? In such a world, there could be no Tribulation. And what would the Kingdom be, if nobody was outside it?

He shook his head briskly, to dispel a kind of vertigo.

'Well, as long as you don't intend rushing off to convert the empire straight away, I don't think the question of approval arises', he said. 'Talk to me again when you've given it more thought.'

'Oh, I will', said Saul. His eyes were far away. 'I will indeed.'

Saul had gone home shortly after that. His stay was brief, but in the course of it he had managed to antagonise most of the population of the city. In the end Kepha and Jacob the Pious had done the only thing possible. They had invented a plot against Saul's life and shipped him off home for his own safety. Since then there had been peace.

For how long, Kepha wondered, would the peace continue? Saul was not a man to abandon ideas because they were difficult. Sooner or later he would attempt his impossible venture, and the reverberations of it – Saul being Saul – would reach all the way to Jerusalem. It could, one way and another, cause a great deal of trouble.

He should have stamped on the idea at the outset. But there was a boldness about it which compelled his admiration. And in any case, Saul would not have listened.

Well, there was no point in worrying about it: there was nothing he could do. Jacob the Pious was in control now, and he would have to deal with Saul. No doubt he would deal with him efficiently. He had been scathing in his contempt when Kepha told him of Saul's dream.

Jacob the Pious. Kepha sighed. Piety was a cold thing. Of the two, he would have preferred Saul's fire. One could not always choose.

But Jacob. No one had chosen Jacob. He had simply appeared. He had stepped in, boarding in mid-voyage, confident of the value of his contribution. And he had been right. Within a few weeks his flat voice, expounding, analysing and quibbling with a lawyer's precision, had become a regular feature of their meetings. Before long it dominated them.

And by what authority? It was implicit in the first statement he made when he walked into their meeting-room. A statement quite unnecessary in the literal sense, since they knew well enough who he was.

'I am Jacob,' he had said, 'Joshua's brother.'

Brother? Had he not been told that the master had renounced him? 'I have no brothers. These' – the arm swept in a circle to indicate his friends – 'are my brothers.'

Brother? What kind of brother was it who mocked, and said of his brother, 'He has a demon', and sided openly with his enemies, and did not lift a finger to help when he could have helped, being a friend of the priests? Brother?

Where had Jacob been in the days when they tramped the roads and begged their bread and were driven from unfriendly towns? Where had Jacob been when Joshua talked to them of the King-dom? On the dreadful last night when everything lay broken, where had Jacob been? On his knees, praying to be made still more righteous.

But when the Appearances began, the miracles, the prophesying, the signs of the Spirit – then, suddenly, Jacob was there. 'I am by birth one of you', his manner said. 'You cannot reject me. I am his brother.'

And of course they had not rejected him. No recruit was unwel-come, but Jacob was a prize. He had influential friends. He was versed in the Law and his knowledge was widely respected. He had an inexhaustible memory and a clear, orderly mind. He was a good organiser. He lived a life of the sternest rectitude, the most striking manifestation of which was that he had never been known to take a bath. He was pious, capable, dirty, and cold.

He was now head of the brotherhood in Jerusalem. And he was better at it than Kepha had ever been.

Click, click, click. Clatter.

'See that?'

'Where d'you get these dice?'

'Nothing wrong with the dice. Get on with it.'

Passing the time, the precious dwindling time.

Soon the Syrian guard would come on duty. Kepha looked forward to their brief, furtive exchanges. The previous day, the soldier had told him that the king was sick. But the same thing, and worse, had been rumoured for months. Some people said he was possessed. His extravagances, and his cruelties, grew by the week

132

The country was worse ruled by a native prince than by foreign governors.

It was all the same thing. The Kingdom would come.

Kepha leant his head against the wall, and slept.

He knew, without being able to see it, that the door of the cell was open. He also knew that it had not opened in the normal way, swung slowly back on its hinges, but that it had, as it were, simply been changed from a door that was shut to a door that was open.

He knew he was expected to get up and walk out of the door.

For some reason he could not do it. Puzzling over this, he realised it was because he was chained. But when he turned his wrists to confirm that he was chained, he found that his arms moved freely. The chains swung loose and struck the wall, making no sound.

He was in total darkness.

He stood up. He was unsteady: his feet seemed at the same time very heavy, so that he could not move them, and very light, so that if he stepped forward the foot would disintegrate under his weight. He shuffled, and felt straw drag at his ankles.

He was suddenly sure that the guards would see him and he would be killed. He gave a sob of fear, but heard no sound.

A moment later he understood that the guards were asleep and would not wake. All he had to do was walk out.

But he could not see.

He forced himself to move towards where he sensed the door of the cell to be. The door did not come nearer. Or rather, if it appeared to come nearer it then retreated again. At moments he seemed to be almost level with the sleeping guards, but then he would feel them still five paces beyond him.

He sobbed again. This time he heard the sob, and it had turned into a prayer. 'Lord', he had said.

The realisation that he should pray seemed to unlock something in his mind, and he understood that the reason why he could not see was not that the cell was too dark but that it was too light. And at once he could feel the light all round him, beating against his eyelids.

'Lord?'

'Come, Kepha.'

He moved forward, borne up by his joy. He moved over the flagstones without feeling them, past the slumped guards, and through the doorway. He was in a labyrinth of passages. He realised that he could now see. The passage was illuminated by a pale golden light, like moonlight, but warm. He walked over the stones, not touching them. Someone walked beside him. He tried several times to look at this figure but found he could not turn his eyes.

They mounted steps and passed through another doorway and were in a cobbled courtyard. Soldiers stood about, leaning on their weapons, motionless and blank-eyed. They passed the soldiers and came to an iron gate in the middle of a high wall. The figure touched the gate and it swung open, and they walked through. The gate shut soundlessly behind them.

All at once he was alone. Looking round, in grief, for his companion, he saw that he was in a street of houses and shuttered shops. He paused, then sensed it to his right: a house with friends. He moved towards it, gliding over the stones and between high walled buildings. Now he was at the door, gazing at the metal studs in the thick wood.

He knocked. The sound was cavernous. There were running footsteps, a girl's voice, and laughter. He knocked again. He heard the footsteps run away from him, and more laughter, far away in the house. He knocked again, and then again, the sound travelling through all the rooms of his head.

Terror struck him suddenly.

The door opened.

Clang.

Kepha jerked awake, opened his eyes and at once screwed them tight again in the dazzle of a swinging lantern. The guard had changed. The friendly one was on duty.

Kepha heard the bench scraped back, the dicing start.

He moved his shoulders and the chains pulled at his wrists. What did a dream mean? Was it a sign; or was it to test his patience? What use was a sign, when you had to read it backwards?

Huddled on his straw staring at the soldiers in their pool of light, he saw how much he had lost.

It had been clear once. But looking back, now, at the time when it had been clear was like looking from a shady doorway at a group of friends caught in bright sunlight. The longer he looked, the more the shadow in which he stood seemed to deepen.

He did not, he realised, understand anything. He could not

134

interpret any of his experiences. He did not know the meaning of his vision on the hilltop, or of his vision much later at Joppa, or indeed of any vision he had received; and the one experience that would have made everything else clear had, through his own fault, been denied him.

He did not even know any longer what he was supposed to do.

In the early days it had seemed simple. As chief disciple, spokesman, and repository of Joshua's teachings, he must be head of the brotherhood.

But the brotherhood grew. His duties grew, consuming his time in tasks which seemed to have nothing to do with the real work Joshua had laid on him. He had been glad when Jacob the Pious showed an interest in the administration. Little by little he had ceded the work to Jacob, until one day he had realised that it was Jacob's hand, not his, that guided the community.

Well, it was a capable hand, and he was still consulted on all matters of importance. With a relief that carried about it a tinge of unease, Kepha had gone back to preaching. It was exhilarating at first to see the road again stretching before him, the new faces, the ever new challenge. He had thrown himself into it joyfully. It was several years before he became aware of a lessening of his purpose, aware that the clarity of the message was clouding. Something was wrong. Probing it, he found that where there had been solidity there was now unsteadiness, as if an underground shifting had taken place.

For what did he preach?

Eyes closed, he saw again Joshua's lean figure in the midst of the crowds, heard the quiet assurance of the voice. Forgive. Trust. Submit. Love. Do not make plans for the future. Do not accumulate possessions. Do not care what people say about you. Do not say what you do not mean.

Was it this he told them?

He told them what he could. It was difficult, these days, to tell people not to make provision for the future when the future had already lasted ten years longer than they had expected it to; and it was difficult to tell a rich and influential businessman, sympathetic to the community, to abandon his possessions. So he told them what he could.

And even what he told them had taken second place. The ideas Joshua had exhausted himself in spreading, and on account of which he had been murdered, had taken second place. The central

135

position was now taken by the master himself, and in such a guise as Kepha had never known him. Was this glorious figure, this avenging Judge of the Last Days, sacrificed at the end of his earthly career to provide unearned forgiveness for thousands of people of whose existence he had never dreamt, the man with whom Kepha had gone fishing, shared jokes and broken bread?

Kepha rebuked himself, as he had done many times. It was a form of pride. Saul had been right: he wanted to keep Joshua to himself. There was nothing to recommend his opinion apart from the fact that it was *his* opinion. Often not even that, for often he was so confused that he did not know what his opinion was.

Well, there was not much longer. He was going to die. And then presumably it would all be made clear.

It came to him suddenly that if he were to die it would mean that his task was finished. He would have accomplished it. Without ever knowing what it was.

He laughed aloud. The sound echoed strangely from the stone walls, and one of the soldiers snarled at him to be quiet.

It was, he recalled, at about the time when the doubts began to trouble him that he received his vision at Joppa.

It had helped him greatly. For months he had brought new energy to his work. But as for what it meant ...

A maritime town. Every other face had a foreign cast, and walking round the waterfront you could hear a dozen different languages spoken in the space of an hour. He had intended to be there only a few days, but he stayed on, attracted by the diversity of the place. The bustle of the harbour reminded him of home. He spent a lot of time on the quayside, watching the sailors and the fishermen, and the sea lifting to the horizon.

His thoughts turned frequently to Saul.

One day he went up to the rooftop of the house where he was lodging to pray. It was an odd place to choose in the full glare of the noonday sun, and he did not know what drew him there. He had not eaten since the previous evening, and as the sun beat down on him he began to feel faint. The roofs of the surrounding houses seemed to float and merge to form a series of huge steps that led down towards the sea, and he felt that he was being drawn along them, so that in time he would come to the end of the steps and have to walk across the sea. He knew that he would fail.

Even as he thought this he found himself at the water's edge, gazing down not into shallows but a transparent immensity as deep as the sky. He begged to be allowed to remain where he was, and a voice which seemed to speak from the very heart of the depths said, 'Why do you doubt?'

Then, gazing into the vastness which was now both sea and sky, he saw that it was being cleft by a great chasm that widened and deepened until it filled his vision and began itself to be filled with every kind of thing on earth. He watched as an unimaginable order unfolded itself: creeping insects, fish and long-legged sea things, plants and bearded grasses, darting birds and snakes, bright butterflies, deer and leopard and slinking jackals ... and, dwelling among them, every race of man. He gazed, filled with a profound sense of peace.

'I am the Giver', said the voice. 'Trust me.'

He had not known what it meant, but he had trusted. Bathed in the peace of it, he had confided the vision to Jacob the Pious, who had reported it to the committee, who had discussed it for weeks and decided there was no meaning in it at all.

And now there was no time left to understand it. There was no time left, and there was still everything to be understood.

What had Joshua said, when, a few days before the end, Kepha questioned him about the Key?

'You have it. Don't you know that you have it? Perhaps you really don't.' He had paused, with a faint smile that seemed only to grave deeper the strain in his face. 'Well, it's too late now. If you still don't understand, you'll never understand. Perhaps it's better so.'

In ten years the words had not lost their chill.

Kepha gazed bleakly at the damp stones glistening in the lamplight.

Once he had admitted the doubts, they could not be sent away again. Here, in this dismal place, they crowded from their corners like rats.

The Kingdom had begun, with Joshua's resurrection. But in what sense, since it was still awaited? It was dawning, soon it would burst on them like day. But how soon, how long, why was the sun so late in rising? The Kingdom was for the outcast, the desperate and self-despising, who were given life because they did not believe they had deserved it; and its earthly affairs were administered by Jacob, on whose heart was engraved the principle of just desert. The Kingdom abolished the Law; and daily, hourly, in every prescribed particular, they continued to observe it.

And what of the new interpretation, that 'ransom' they proclaimed, the forgiveness through which they gained entry to the Kingdom? It was essential to the preaching. Without it they could make no converts, for the first thing people asked was the meaning of Joshua's shameful death, and without the new interpretation there was no meaning, since the Kingdom had not come. And the interpretation worked: its fruits were seen. The converts, as they stepped bright-eyed from the baptismal waters, *were* transformed and freed from sin.

But Joshua had never said anything about it.

What he had said, and its implications, pointed in another direction entirely. He had taught them to pray, 'Forgive us as we forgive others.' No mention there of atonement or sacrifice: forgiveness was dependent solely on one's readiness to do the same. And was it not just? What you do, shall be done to you. Was it not natural? What you sow, you shall reap a hundredfold. Was it not in keeping with everything else he said? God is your father, he wants to forgive.

And a father who exacted blood-payment for faults, a father who *could not* forgive without it: was that not . . .

Kepha moved restlessly in his chains. Twist and turn the idea as he might, it presented itself to him each time afresh with the same horror. Forgiveness through death-agony, blood-ransom from a father's vengeance . . . This was no revelation of the Spirit, no holy mystery he must pray for the grace to fathom. It was an idea conceived in the lawyer's brain of Jacob the Pious, and it was the most monstrous, disgusting and blasphemous idea Kepha had ever heard.

And he preached it because the alternative was to accept that Joshua's death *had* been meaningless. That it could have been avoided. That there had been a hideous mistake.

Whose mistake?

Not mine, Lord.

'You have said something that should never have been said, and there will be a heavy price to pay.'

But not that price?

'None of you knows when to talk and when to be silent.'

What did it matter that he had told others? It would soon have been on everyone's lips anyway.

138

'Things must not be said.'

He had grasped that eventually: just in time to save himself.

'I don't know him. I've never seen him before.'

And, saving himself, he had lost himself, and everything he had done since had been a further step into the darkness.

'Day after tomorrow.'

'What?' Kepha looked up, startled.

The young Syrian guard stood looking down at him.

'You go to Caesarea under escort the day after tomorrow. I heard it in the guardroom.'

'Ah', said Kepha. The king was at Caesarea. It meant the end.

'Thank you', he said.

The soldier stood there awkwardly.

'D'you want anything?' he said. 'The bucket?'

'No thank you', said Kepha. The stench from the bucket at close quarters was sickening. He used it as little as possible. 'But I would like some water.'

The soldier brought the mug and put it into his hand. As Kepha drank – clumsily, because of the chains – he murmured, 'The king is dying.'

Kepha glanced at him in astonishment. The soldier's eyes were expressionless. He waited for Kepha to finish drinking, then went back to the table and picked up the dice.

Kepha's heart was racing. He tried in vain to slow it down.

Almost certainly the king was not dying. Rumours had circulated before. And even if he was dying, it would make no difference. Kepha had enemies enough to ensure that he stayed in prison. Jacob bar Zabdai had been killed: they would all be killed. 'When I go, you will be like sheep among wolves.'

Sheep among wolves could not, in the nature of things, expect to last long.

It dismayed Kepha that his body should persist in its blind will to live when his spirit was ready for death. But he supposed that to embrace the thought of death was also a kind of cowardice. He could not escape his nature.

Yet he was the doorkeeper. The promise had been given, and could not be retracted. He, so flawed, so unfit, so cursed by doubt, would stand at the gate ...

He drew in his breath as a chill like the grave struck into him.

The doorkeeper *stood at the gate*.

Was that what was meant? That he should open the door for others but not go in himself? Like Moses, dying within sight of the Promised Land?

If it is your will.

But Lord, let it not be your will. I cannot bear it.

'The first shall be last. The last, first.'

Help me.

'I have come to give sight to the blind.'

Yes, Lord.

'And to blind those who can see.'

I do not understand anything.

'You will have to be clever. As wily as snakes.'

But we are not clever people . . .

'You must be like children.'

Children?

'The Kingdom belongs to children.'

But, master . . .

'I have given you the Key.'

Kepha closed his eyes. He was utterly weary.

'I am a simple man', he said. 'Could you not have given it to someone else?'

Mary.

The face, contorted hideously, was sometimes that of a child and sometimes that of an old woman. The mouth screamed obscenities, then hung slack and drooled saliva. The eyes were pits of nothingness. She rocked and writhed, intermittently clasping her arms around herself with a whiplike movement, humming snatches of a song.

'Name yourself', said Joshua coldly.

She backed away. After a few paces she stopped and flung out an arm at him, pointing.

'I know you', she hissed.

'Name yourself.'

'I know who *you* are', she jeered in a singsong.

'Hold your tongue!'

He moved towards her threateningly. She wailed in fear and thrashed her arms.

He raised his arm also, and held it towards her, the palm facing downward, fingers extended.

'Thou mockery, shadow of nothing, I adjure thee by the God that made thee to confess thy name.'

140

'No-o-o.' The cry seemed torn from her, and her hands flew to her throat as if to choke it.

'Thy name.'

She howled, and threw herself prostrate on the ground, clawing at his feet. He did not move.

She lay still for a moment, then broke into passionate weeping. 'I'll be good', she sobbed. It was a frightened child's voice. 'I'll be good. Don't beat me. Take me out of this place.'

'Stand up', ordered Joshua.

The weeping stopped. She flung herself with incredible rapidity into a crouch and rocked back on her heels, humming. Then, body rigid, she moved her head in a series of little sideways jerks as if trying to locate a sound. She seemed to find it, and listen. Her expression became sly and knowing. Slowly she raised her arm again and pointed at him.

'Speak thy name!' he thundered.

She howled, leapt to her feet and ran from him, still pointing. Words poured wildly from her.

'I am wickedness, I am corruption. I am Shibbeta, I am Kuda, I am Eshshata, I am Shabriri.' Pause, then a shriek of triumph. 'I am Ruah Zenunim.'

In the abrupt silence that followed she watched them, mocking. She began to move her shoulders and hips in a slow gyration, then thrust her hand downward in a gesture so lewd that the watching men turned their heads away and shuffled with shame.

'You know me', she whispered, 'oh you know me. Even he' – she flung out her hand again, pointing, and her voice rose to a yell of derision – 'even *he* knows *me*.'

Joshua strode forward.

'By the power of God I command you. Be silent and come out of this child. You have no place in her, for the child is of God. By the Hand that made you, I constrain you to depart.'

A silence. Then a slow shuddering passed through her, starting at the feet and gradually convulsing the entire body. Her head dropped forward. A low moaning arose from somewhere in her chest, and, rising in pitch, burst out of her in a dreadful wrenching cry.

The cry stopped, as if cut off. She stood for a moment swaying, then collapsed to the ground.

Joshua walked over to where she lay and bent down. Cautiously the spectators gathered round and looked at her. A young woman of about seventeen years, thin, fine-featured, deathly pale.

Joshua straightened up, unsmiling.

'Give her food', he said. 'And be kind to her, for once.'

Mary. After the exorcism she had joined them, attaching herself to their little company as if it were her right. She was never far from Joshua and her eyes followed him constantly. She spoke to him only when he addressed her, which he would do in a tone of exceptional gentleness as if speaking to a child.

But he did not treat her like a child. Several times Kepha had come across them in private conversation and been shocked at what he heard, for the master was talking to Mary of things which he seldom mentioned even to Kepha. They were mysteries about the Kingdom.

'The sky will pass away, and so will the sky above it; but the dead will not live, nor the living die.'

'If the Kingdom is in Heaven, it is a Kingdom for birds.'

'It is here, and no one sees it.'

Strange, difficult sayings over which Kepha puzzled, trying them this way and that against his stock of knowledge, looking for the space into which they must fit. They fitted nowhere. It was almost as if only by forgetting what he knew, and accepting in its place something quite different, could he grasp their meaning. But he did not know how to forget what he knew, or what it was he was required to know in its stead.

In that dark language the master talked to Mary, and she understood him, and answered.

It caused Kepha more pain that he could admit. Eventually he asked Joshua to send her away, or at least to take more care to observe the proprieties. It was improper for them to have a woman in their company at all, he said; and it was also unsuitable. Women had a lesser aptitude for spiritual things than men. Joshua said curtly that he would be the judge of Mary's spiritual aptitude. Kepha, wounded, pointed out that it was enough to give rise to scandal merely that Joshua talked with Mary in private. Joshua laughed and said that if that was the greatest scandal he'd caused he had done a poor job so far. Kepha retreated, baffled. Later Joshua said, 'Mary sees things which you don't, Kepha, and therefore needs things which you don't. Leave her alone: she will be going away soon in any case.'

And two days later she had gone, no one knew where. Afterward they had seen her again, at intervals, before they went to Jeru salem. She would appear unexpectedly, keep company with them for a few days and then go away again. Neither she nor Joshua gave any explanation for these visits, or why they ended so abruptly, or how she knew where to find them. It was like an animal coming to water when it needed and then going about its business, Kepha thought. There was in fact something wild about her, something which could not be approached. The master had cast seven demons out of her, but there had been an eighth.

And it was true that Mary saw things Kepha did not see. She had seen the greatest thing of all: she, first and alone. They had not believed her, of course. They had not believed until they saw him themselves; and then, in their joy and incomprehension and the necessity to think out everything entirely afresh, the order of events, and who had seen what and in what circumstances, had become confused, and seemed, in face of the fact itself, unimportant, so that in the end a story had become current which seemed to embody both the essential truth and the best way of looking at the truth.

Only with great difficulty and some pain did Kepha take in, years later, the distance that had grown between the jumble of events and the story that represented them; and by then, when Mary's story came to the ears of Jacob the Pious, it was too late.

'I *saw* him, I tell you. I saw him in the garden, before anyone else knew of it.'

'Nonsense', snapped Jacob.

'I did! Ask Kepha. He was in the room when I told them.'

'I remember you saying something,' said Kepha, 'but I don't remember exactly what it was ...'

'I said – oh, I don't know what I said. I was so upset and excited and confused, I probably didn't know what I was saying at the time. Finding the grave empty ... and then there was someone standing beside me and I thought – I don't know, I think I thought it was the gardener.'

'It was the gardener', said Jacob.

'It wasn't! I was talking to him and something happened, I mean something happened inside me, and suddenly I knew it was him.'

'Remarkable', said Jacob. 'The Kingdom of Heaven appears in such equivocal guise that it can be mistaken for the gardener. The ways of God are indeed strange.'

Mary's eyes filled with tears.

'Jacob', said Kepha uneasily. Jacob rounded on him.

'Don't be a fool, Kepha. The woman wants attention, it's always been the same. Look how she trailed around all that time with you as if she were a man – it was nothing short of scandalous. Now she's making up this ridiculous story that she was the first to see him when he came back from the dead. Well, we shan't tolerate it. He appeared first to *you*, as was only right, since you were the leader. Then he appeared to all of you together. Subsequently –' Jacob's face softened briefly into an approximation of modesty – 'he appeared to me. That was the order of it, and the necessary order, and to invent any other order is preposterous.'

Kepha cleared his throat. 'Well, as a matter of fact', he said, 'He appeared to two other friends of ours before he appeared to us, and perhaps even before I ...'

'What?' said Jacob sharply. 'It's the first I've heard of this. Who were these people?'

'You don't know them. They used to come and listen to him sometimes. They were on their way to a village near here and he joined them. They said it took them a long time to realise who he was.'

'Exactly', said Mary.

'Be quiet!' snapped Jacob. He turned back to Kepha. 'You mean well, Kepha, but you don't understand. He could not have appeared to these two completely unimportant people before he appeared to the rest of you because it would have been totally inappropriate. The uncertainty surrounding this so-called Appearance is proof that it was not genuine. When he appeared to me there was no room for doubt at all, and the same will have been true of your own revelation. Things are ordained, Kepha, in a fitting manner. These poor friends of yours were misled by an imagination already burdened with grief, and then excited by Mary's report – which was, fortunately, verifiable – that the tomb was empty. If they hadn't heard that, they would certainly not have fancied that they saw him.'

'You might say the same of all of us', said Kepha tightly. There was a feeling of nausea in his stomach.

Jacob stared at him. 'Don't be absurd', he said.

'I was just pointing out a weakness in your argument', said Kepha.

'Thank you. I shall be further indebted to you, we shall all be indebted, if you will keep silly remarks like that to yourself. We are not dealing with sophisticated people, Kepha, we are dealing with

144

people who take every word literally and are easily confused. We must keep things simple, and that is not a difficult task since the truth is simple. It is simple because it is necessary and orderly. All we have to do is stick to it.' He turned to Mary. 'And *you* will invent no more stories to confuse it.'

'I have never told a lie in my life', said Mary, 'since he cured me of my madness. And even when I was mad, it seemed to me that I was telling the truth.'

'Of course', said Kepha. He had an overpowering need to get out of the room. He laid his hand lightly on Mary's shoulder. 'My dear, no one is accusing you of lying. You have always . . . In any case, the truth . . . ' Something was rising in his chest, choking the words. 'He loved you greatly', he said, and, turning, met Jacob's angry stare for a moment before he walked away.

He stopped in the shadow of the house and prayed, his nails dug hard into his palms with anguish. He prayed for forgiveness and for help. He prayed that one day the burden of his punishment would be removed and that the lie he had once told would be wiped out by the lie he was forced to endure. He prayed that one day he too might see the risen master.

He had been dimly conscious of the noise for some time, but only now, with the creak and slam of the heavy bolt slid back, did it present itself to his attention. Shouting. At first far away, beyond the maze of stone corridors; now nearer, accompanied by a tramp of feet.

The guards at the table had stopped dicing. They sat tensed, trying to read the meaning of the sounds. One of them ran his thumb along his sword-belt and rested his hand on the hilt.

Kepha shivered.

The feet tramped nearer, the sound reverberating along the stone. Further up the corridor they stopped, there was a metallic grating noise and a door clanged open. There were more shouts.

The guards at the table sat motionless, staring at each other.

Feet now approached Kepha's cell. They halted outside. A pause, then the door was unlocked and flung wide. Light from the lanterns blinded him momentarily. Three soldiers crowded into the doorway, shouting and gesticulating. The guards sprang up. There was a quick exchange of question and answer. Kepha strained to make out what was happening, but it was all military jargon and the only words he could understand were 'the king' and 'no reprisals'.

The two soldiers who had been guarding him flung their cloaks around their shoulders and made to leave the cell. The friendly one jerked his head in Kepha's direction and said something. The other soldier spat contemptuously. All five left the cell, the young Syrian last. As he went through the doorway he lifted his hand with a casual movement to a key hanging on a nail in the wall, unhooked it and tossed it on to Kepha's pile of straw. He walked out, not looking behind him.

The sound of feet died away down the echoing passage. The bright rectangle of light in the open doorway faded, leaving only a phantom glow which fuddled his eyes.

The key had fallen out of reach of his hands. His eyes, which had been fixed on the doorway, could not see anything in the darkness. He felt for the key with his foot, cautiously, lest he push it down into the straw and lose it.

His toe touched metal. He tried to scoop it towards him but it was awkwardly placed and he could not twist his foot to the necessary angle. He tried to push the key with his heel, but it fell further into the straw. Struggling against the chains to get himself into a better position, he found he could burrow into the straw with his toes. But now he had lost the place where the key had fallen.

There was cold sweat on the back of his neck. He closed his eyes and leaned his head against the wall, steadying his breathing. He opened his eyes and resumed the careful exploration with his toes.

Then he felt it, cold and heavy, against the edge of his instep. Gently he moved his foot along it and grasped it between his toes. He brought his foot up and, grunting with the effort, transferred the key from foot to hand.

The lock on the fetters was on the inside of the wrist, and the chain linking them was too short for him to locate the key in one lock with the opposite hand. He fumbled with the key and nearly dropped it. He placed it between his teeth, and, bringing his left wrist to his mouth, located the lock. He tried to turn the key, but it hurt his mouth. He rested. He found that he could hold the key between the base of his middle and third fingers. Holding it, he turned his hand. The resisting metal bit hard into his flesh, then yielded with a sudden click.

He eased the iron from the wrist, and stretched and clenched the fingers. He unlocked the fetter from his right wrist. The chains swung back against the wall and struck it with a clatter that sent his heart pounding. The noise died away into silence.

The door was open.

He took a step forward and was suddenly afraid. It was safe in the cell. He did not have to do anything. He did not have to make decisions. As long as he was in the cell he could not be anywhere else.

He took another step forward. He could not see.

As long as he was in the cell he was asked no questions that he could not answer. As long as he was in the cell he could not make mistakes. As long as he was in the cell he could fail nobody but himself.

He forced himself forward.

As long as he was in the cell he was not asked who he was, because everybody knew who he was. In this place they called him by his real name.

'Lord', he whispered.

In front of him, cut out of the blackness, was a rectangle of less impenetrable blackness. He walked towards it.

He was in the passageway. He turned right, then paused, listening for sounds. He could hear nothing but his own heart. There was a faint greyish light, enough for him to distinguish the walls. It must be early dawn. He began to walk along the passage. He realised he had forgotten his sandals.

The passageway wound and forked, with smaller passages leading off it. He could not remember which way he had come, but his feet seemed to know what direction to follow. He passed cells with their doors standing open. He passed a larger room with a painted door, and saw inside, by the light of a forgotten lantern, a disorder of cloaks and upturned cups on a table and an obscene drawing scrawled on the wall. The guardroom. Had all the soldiers deserted, then? He listened again. Still there was no sound, only his heartbeat and the faint hiss of the candle in the lantern. It was like a dream.

He walked on, through his dream, and came to a flight of steps. He went up it, keeping to the wall, and found himself facing a large door. There was a line of grey light at the bottom of the door, and a cold fresh draught blew in on his toes.

His heart was pounding, and his hands shook as he felt for the bolts. They were already drawn back. Resting his weight against the door so that the iron would not scrape, he lifted the latch, then stepped back. The door swung free. He stepped outside.

The air was like wild honey: he drank it in with his lungs, his blood, his skin. The sky was light, a few clouds hung in it, rose-fringed. The courtyard was empty. It came to him that the whole palace was empty and perhaps the whole city, the whole world, were empty. The Kingdom had come, and its doorkeeper was late. He began to laugh.

He walked across the courtyard to the iron gate, and opened it. As he stood with his hand on the gate a soldier came out of a side door and stopped, staring at the sight of a barefoot madman laughing in the dawn. Kepha gazed at him for a moment, then went through the gate and shut it behind him. He walked straight ahead down the shuttered street, and on through other streets and alleyways until he came to a small paved square. He was near the centre of the city. There was a stirring in the houses, and the clop of a donkey's hooves.

The house was to his right. He stood for a while looking in its direction. Then he turned left.

V

SALVATION

The full moon hung like a whore's belly over the graveyard. By its light, a man with a hump shoulder and a deformed right foot was skinning a kid.

A few paces away, three more figures sat round a gradually dimming fire. One of them was barely more than a child, but the grotesqueness of his appearance made judgement of his age difficult. He had almost no forehead: the scalp began only a finger's breadth above the eyebrows and was flattened, as if it had been crushed against a rock. Next to him sat a large, well-muscled man whose straggling hair could even by moonlight only partly conceal the fact that he had no ears. The third man, sitting a few feet away, was cadaverously thin, shivered constantly, and picked at the livid scabs which covered his legs.

At either side of the fire a pair of stout sticks had been thrust into the ground slantwise so that they crossed near the top. Nearby was a pile of smaller sticks. These were for firewood but, although the fire was fading every moment to a paler red, no one moved to put any of the sticks on to it.

Some distance from the fire a fifth figure sat with his back against a tomb. His clothes were ragged and filthy like a beggar's, but he had no evident deformity. He was looking at the men around the fire.

With a flick of the knife the man with the hump shoulder finished skinning the kid and tossed away the hide. He opened the stomach with a quick downward sweep, reached in and pulled out the entrails, which he flung away in a bloody heap on the ground. He rummaged in his girdle and brought out a piece of twine with which he tied the kid's feet together. He inserted a long stick between the body and the feet so that the kid was suspended upside down, and limped, carrying it, to the fire.

He stopped a few feet away in disbelief.

'Why have you let it go out?'

The three men raised their heads, as if from an absorbing contemplation, and regarded the fire as if they had not noticed it before. The hump-shouldered man dumped the kid in the lap of the man with no ears, stirred the ashes until they glowed bright again, and threw on an armful of sticks. The fire dimmed for a moment, flared, and blazed.

'It wasn't out', said the cadaver morosely.

'No thanks to you.'

The hump-shouldered man limped away, and came back in a

few minutes with some small flat-topped stones which he threw into the hottest part of the fire. Then he picked up the kid again, carried it over to the nearest tomb, laid it on the covering slab and began cutting it into sections.

'Argh gar gar', said the man who had no ears, with evident anxiety.

'He says you shouldn't do that, it's unclean', interpreted the boy without a forehead.

'Tell him to keep his imbecile mouth shut.'

The knife flicked expertly, dividing and slicing.

'What are you doing?' asked the boy.

'Well it'll never cook whole, will it? Not after you let the fire go down like that. Parasites, all of you. I have to do everything.'

As if reminded of something, he turned his head and stared at where the solitary figure sat in the shadows, his back against a tomb. The men around the fire followed his gaze, then looked away again. The hump-shouldered man spat, in the ancient gesture of one averting a curse.

'Gar ... argh ... argh', said the man with no ears.

'He says it was us that caught the kid', explained the boy with no forehead.

'And who told you where to find it? Name of God, if I had the right use of my legs ...'

Limping, the hump-shouldered man carried a handful of sliced meat to the fire. The flames had died down and the stones were covered with a layer of glowing ash. He blew the ash away and spat on one of the stones. It sizzled. He laid a piece of meat on top of each stone, then limped back to continue cutting up the kid.

The man with no ears, the boy with no forehead and the cadaver stared hungrily at the cooking meat. The fire began to hiss as the exuding fat dripped into the hot embers. A delicious smell arose. Three heads drew gradually closer to the fire.

Dreamily, the man with no ears picked up a twig, lifted a slice of meat from its stone and carried it to his mouth. He removed it instantly, howling, and waved the meat in the air to cool it. It was snatched away by the hump-shouldered man, who had returned with another handful of meat for the fire.

'Greedy pig! Want more than your share, do you?'

'Haargh ... gar ...'

The hump-shouldered man swung his fist at the man with no ears, who rocked with the blow but seemed too puzzled to defend himself. The boy tugged anxiously at the hump-shouldered man's sleeve, was kicked aside and turned instead to the cadaver, who shoved him away and went on picking his scabs.

The boy fell awkwardly, at the edge of the fire, and screamed.

The man with no ears pulled the boy out of the fire and stood up ponderously.

The solitary figure sitting against the tomb leaned forward to watch.

The hump-shouldered man and the man with no ears grappled by the edge of the fire. Teeth bared, grunting, they struggled to force each other back into the flames. Eventually, feet braced on the very edge of the embers, the man with no ears flung his opponent away and ran to the tomb where the severed remains of the kid lay. He turned with the knife in his hand as the hump-shouldered man lumbered at him.

The knife went in at the neck. The hump-shouldered man gurgled and fell across the tomb, clutching at the kid's carcass. His hands slipped down and he fell to the ground. He lay in a widening pool of blood, clutching a skinned foreleg in his right hand.

The man with no ears dropped the knife, ran to the boy and pulled him by the hand. Together the two of them disappeared into the darkness.

The watcher who had been sitting against the tomb stood up. He passed his hand, with a habitual gesture, over the girdle at his waist, as if to check something, then walked to the fire. He crouched down and lifted one of the slices of meat from its stone: it was agreeably browned on one side and moist with juices on the other. The cadaver, who throughout the fight had continued picking his scabs, stared at him and edged away.

The stranger held the piece of meat out to him. The cadaver, after some hesitation, took it.

The stranger helped himself to two slices of meat, and threw more sticks on the fire.

He had been on the road a year, mingling with beggars, lepers, outcasts, thieves. He sought, in each community he encountered, the lowest level to which the sediment of humanity could sink.

Because degradation was his object, he avoided the small, close communities of the countryside and frequented the larger towns and cities. There he found much to his purpose: the maimed beggars picking their lice under the arches of the aqueduct, the

153

shrivelled whores in the doorways of mean alleys, the waterfront taverns where, after the brawling sailors had departed, the rats came out in the dark to nibble the vomit on the cobbles.

These things gave him no pleasure – though pleasure, ultimately, was the goal he strove towards – but they brought a peculiar satisfaction to his mind. By constant exposure to what offended him, he had trained himself to overcome the revolt of his senses. He had almost ceased to see ugliness as ugly. But if ever he was on the point of losing that discrimination, he was brought back to it by the consciousness that he was still in a sense privileged in that he had chosen his surroundings. Once he had joined a band of lepers and tried to live with them, but they had driven him away because he was whole. The maimed resented him, the thieves distrusted him, and the poor eyed him with anger and suspicion. He regretted his isolation, because he liked the society of his fellow men, but he preferred it to a forced hospitality.

From the beginning he had done his travelling alone, abandoning house, possessions and slave at dead of night and slipping out unnoticed while the city slept. He could not, in the despair that then enveloped him, have tolerated curious eyes. It was months before he could meet a stranger's gaze without fear of recognition and the consequent questions, but then one day, seeing his reflection in a pool, he realised that he had become unrecognisable and, at the same moment, that it had ceased to matter. He had so thoroughly abandoned his old identity that the memory of it could no longer hurt him; and in retrospect his flight from Sebaste assumed the nature not of defeat, but of a strategic withdrawal from a position that could not be defended.

His purpose now was to define a position that was immune to assault. Such a position must rest on a true apprehension of the world, and after a year of sojourning in its vilest places he had found that truth.

It was, quite simply, that God was evil.

The province was experiencing one of its periodic upsurges of religious zeal. The immediate cause was yet another change in administration.

The country, after the initial period of chaos which had preceded and followed its annexation, was ruled for nearly forty years, under imperial protection, by Herod of Idumea. This capable tyrant having obtained the throne by craft and kept it by murder, died

154

insane after a lifetime of bloodshed, intrigue and municipal improvements. On his death the kingdom was divided up, and for thirty-five years its most turbulent region, the religious heartland, was administered directly, with a mixture of savagery, good intentions and stupidity, by a series of military governors.

The old tyrant's territories were reunited under his debt-ridden grandson, but the arrangement was short lived. The new king died strangely and suddenly at Caesarea after a brief reign. While parading before his subjects in a silver robe and allowing his flatterers to acclaim him as a god, he was taken ill, and, retiring to his palace, died a few days later. Struck down for impiety, murmured an approving populace. The emperor sighed, and placed the province under direct rule again.

The king had been at least nominally of the national faith. So much could not be said for the governors. With cold eyes the people watched the paraphernalia of imperialism return uncloaked to their streets. The governors, for their part, simply did not understand the people they had to deal with. Nothing in their experience had prepared them.

Hence the incident of the High Priest's Robe.

When Fadus the governor arrived in Judaea following the sudden death of its king, he found the Jews of a northern border area engaged in a private war with their neighbours. He dealt with the situation with commendable efficiency, and proceeded to Jerusalem. There, believing that an immediate show of authority was needed to prevent further trouble, he ordered the citizens to hand over to him the ceremonial robe of the high priest. For generations this sacred vestment had been kept in the Temple. Fadus demanded that it be placed for safe keeping in the fort where the occupying troops were garrisoned.

It was a disastrous miscalculation. There was uproar. So threatening was the situation that the Legate of Syria himself arrived at the head of an army. The citizens appealed to the emperor, but were forced to hand over their sons as hostages before sending a deputation to Rome.

It is doubtful whether the emperor, any more than the governor, would have understood the emotion aroused by a ceremonial vestment. Fortunately for the peace of the province, the late king's son was at the imperial court, serving his apprenticeship in diplomacy and hoping for his father's throne. He put his skills to use, and the priests were allowed to keep their robe.

To the official mind it was an inexplicable crisis, one of those outbursts over nothing for which the province was notorious. But the religious mind perceived no difference between small matters and great ones. Life was seamless, and significance was woven into every part of it.

A dangerous perception.

A blind beggar squatted in the paltry shade of a shop awning at one side of the square. From a hook beneath the awning swung the freshly-skinned carcass of a sheep, already attracting flies. Other flies buzzed around the face of the beggar, from whose eyes issued a yellowish substance thinly streaked with red. The flies moved indecisively from the eyes to the carcass, and back again.

'Look over there,' said Simon, 'and tell me whether that is the work of a benevolent deity, or of a perverted mind.'

He had been talking for an hour without denting their complacency. He appealed now to their observation. The heads turned.

'Oh, that's old Mordecai', said a man whose arms were stained purple from the dye-works. 'He's been sitting there for years.'

'Waiting for the Deliverer', said another. There was laughter.

'It doesn't matter who he is,' said Simon irritably. 'The point is –'

'It matters to him', objected the dyer. 'That's his pitch. He doesn't half get angry if someone else sits there.'

'Idiots!' shouted Simon. 'You're blinder than he is!'

'Who are you calling an idiot?'

'Everyone who refuses to see what's in front of his eyes. Look around you. Waste. Sickness, disease. Old age, poverty. All of it needless. Death, death everywhere, all of it needless. A blind man and a dead sheep. Look at them. Why is he blind? Why was the sheep killed?'

'So we can eat it', yelled a delighted heckler.

'Precisely', Simon yelled back. 'We can only live by killing. What kind of world is that?'

'But it's got to be like that', laughed someone.

'Why?'

'Well ... it always has been. I mean ... what else can we eat?'

'I don't know', retorted Simon, 'but someone knows. Whoever put us here, knows. Whoever had the filthy idea of a world which feeds on filth, knows. He knows because if he had the power to create this system, he had the power to create a better one. And if he didn't, he isn't worthy of our respect.'

156

They stared at him doubtfully.

'You are better than your Maker', said Simon. 'Honour yourselves. You, *you* are the gods.'

There was blank amazement. Then a few grins appeared.

'Gods, eh?' said the dyer. 'Wait till I tell the wife.'

'But that can't be right', protested a large man at the back. 'How can we be better than the god who made us?'

'What's your trade?' Simon asked him.

'I'm a shipwright.'

'Would you use poor timber if you could get the best? Would you deliberately make a boat that leaked?'

'Of course not.'

'Of course not. Who would make a thing flawed, if he could make it perfect? Look at your own work, and then look' – Simon extended his arm to point at the beggar under the awning – 'at *that*.'

'Yes, but wait a minute', said a serious-looking young man. 'If there's any goodness in us, and the god who made us is wicked, as you say, then where does the goodness come from?'

'Goodness is an illusion', said Simon. 'An idea planted in our minds to confuse us ...'

'Who's confused?' said the dyer. 'I'm not.'

'Yes, but if you say we're *better*', persisted the young man, 'that implies ...'

As a point of logic it was exceedingly inopportune.

'Don't bother me with linguistics', roared Simon. 'Use your eyes!' He jabbed his finger in the direction of the beggar. 'The god you worship is a fly, a monstrous, overblown fly. He feeds on the suppuration of the world.'

'Hey, that's a bit strong', said the dyer.

'And you', said Simon, 'are truly his creation. He is welcome to you.'

He climbed down with dignity from his fish barrel and walked away.

In those days there were many teachers. It was an age in which politics had made nonsense of morality and intellect had outstripped religion. Familiar values had become untrustworthy, or dangerous, or had simply disappeared; the gods had died, or changed their names. At the rotting heart of the empire insanity had so corrupted judgement that the very foundations of society – dis-

157

tinctions of class, of sex, of merit – were most imperilled by the emperors themselves. Nothing, in short, made sense.

And since sense could not be found it was feverishly sought: in religious cults which promised a better life, or at any rate survival, beyond this one; in metaphysical speculations which assured the hopeless that although life was dreadful it was at least unimportant; in astrology, which said that however dreadful life was there was no point in worrying about it, because everything was predetermined. These panaceas travelled the great routes of the empire, carried by wandering sages many of whom gained, on the tongues of their disciples, reputations for great sanctity and – inevitably – miraculous powers.

Disdaining sanctity and abandoned by his power, the man once known as Simon Magus joined the ranks of these vagabond sages. He travelled the roads of Judaea and Samaria, the land God claimed as peculiarly his own, preaching. He took with him no companion, and no possessions other than a sum of money sewn into his girdle which he did not allow himself to use. He begged, and sometimes stole, his food, and slept under the open sky. Wherever he stopped to preach a small crowd would gather, and listen with a strange mixture of emotions. Recognition, even sympathy, would give place quickly to bewilderment, unease and often anger. He left some places under a hail of stones. For what he told his audience was too wicked to be listened to, too dangerous to be contemplated, and in any case too difficult to be tried.

What Simon preached was this.

Man is the dupe of a divinity that hates him. Brought up to believe ourselves the glory of creation, we are blind to our helplessness and to the nature of that creation of which we are a part. For the world, which might have been made perfect, is a running sore. The nature of the world, the real and hidden nature, is not life but death.

Death is the matrix, the corpse on which life feeds. For each birth there are a thousand dyings. For each new thing there are a thousand destructions. For each note of music there is the huge unhearing silence. Each life must nourish itself on murder, each beauty take its little light from ugliness. Our bodies, corruptible, feeding on and producing corruption, are themselves corrupted before their time by sickness, deformity, unsoundness of mind. The fortunate, preserved whole into age, stumble bereft of all dignity towards their dissolution.

Of a wracked creation is man the palsied king.

No reason has ever been given why this must be so. Job, daring to question, was answered by the whirlwind. The reason is clear and terrible. We are the playthings of a devil, and we are made for pain.

The God who fashioned us to torture us keeps his creatures in subjection by a twofold trick. Firstly he proclaims that his actions are beyond human understanding and we cannot judge him. Secondly he distracts and fools us with a code of moral laws, promising that if we obey them we will obtain deliverance from our plight. Not only is this promise false, for lawbreakers flourish while the guiltless suffer, but the Lawgiver himself does not respect these laws. They are in fact meaningless, set up only in order that man may be forced to break them, and that in attempting not to break them he may so confuse and entangle his mind that he can never act freely.

For of the intricate web in which the Creator keeps us prisoner, the most cunning strand is the idea of right and wrong. It paralyses the will, and perverts thought constantly from its goal of truth. It is also fruitful of unending anguish, as the baffled mind cringes in fear of punishment, despairs in its manufactured sense of sin, and grovels in self-abasement to appease its Judge. And all these things are nourishment to the Maker and Mocker of the world.

Although defiance is hopeless, such a God, omnipotent and vengeful, may yet be defied. He may be defied by breaking every law whose observance he has commanded, and inverting every value he has given his creatures to live by. The sins he prohibits must be committed, not once or several times, but again and again until the consciousness of the act is lost; ugliness and misery must be embraced and gloried in; the deformed must be worshipped as if it were the beautiful; the obscene must be made holy.

And in time perhaps it will prove not to be hopeless. For time, the Creator's great weapon, may be turned against him. In time, the daily, hourly committing of sin may exhaust the idea of sinfulness; in time the love of the loathsome may transform its loathsomeness and the whore be made pure by the excesses of lust. Thus may man in time burst the walls of his prison and redeem Creation from its servitude.

So preached Simon of Gitta, saviour and outcast, to sullen ears.

Contemptuous, angry, and with a grim satisfaction in failure,

Simon walked through the streets of Tyre. He walked briskly because he was angry, but he walked without aim. One place was the same as another.

He had not intended to enter a brothel, but his feet, as he came to the gatepost with its carved priapic emblem, turned inside. It was, after all, appropriate.

He had forgotten that it was impracticable.

The woman who met him at the door took in his filthy clothes, the ingrained dirt of his skin, in a long, cold glance.

'We don't cater for your sort', she said. 'This is a respectable establishment.'

'The great charm of a brothel', observed Simon, 'is that one does not hear the truth spoken in it.'

He had become aware that he had no money.

'Get out', she said, 'or I'll call the proprietor.'

Simon left.

He walked on a little way, considering. It was getting dark.

He stationed himself in a courtyard doorway near a tavern from which a great deal of noise was emanating. When, after a time, a sailor came out, swaying, to urinate, Simon dragged him into the doorway, banged him against the wall so that he slid to his knees, and relieved him of his tunic, purse and sandals. On the way to the public baths he saw a cloak lying folded on the ground while its owner discoursed to friends, and took it.

Two hours later he returned to the brothel, and was not recognised.

He chose a whore who did not please his eye. She was dark of complexion and well-fleshed, rather short in stature, with a broad, wide-nostrilled nose and a slightly jutting chin. Her hair, incongrously, was pale, almost gold. Her eyebrows were thick and the lids heavy; a sign of wantonness. But the eyes, as she looked at him, were distant.

He followed her upstairs.

It was a bare room, containing nothing that was not entirely functional: a bed, a table with mirror and cosmetics, a small stool and in the corner a bowl and a pitcher of water. A room for business. He took off his clothes.

He saw, when she had undressed and was lying on the bed, that her triangle of hair extended far out towards the hips, and that her legs were unbecomingly muscular.

She smiled at him.

160

'If you don't like me,' she said, 'why did you choose me?'

It was the first time she had spoken. Her voice was unusually deep for a woman. Simon sensed in her a wealth of ambiguities. His organ rose.

He told her to kneel, and took her from behind. She was tight enough for pleasure, and obligingly moist, and he was surprised to feel, as he approached his spasm, a fierce surge of desire.

He rested, listening to the hum of the street outside.

Turning to her at length, he found her watching him with a hint of what could only be amusement. He was irritated, and, forcing himself to smile in response, began with deliberation to explore her body with his hands. He found himself suddenly uncertain what he intended, and glanced up at her face: she was smiling still, still distant.

He plunged his hand into her roughly, wanting to hurt. She drew in her breath, but did not resist.

'Do you have a woman lover?' he asked. 'Most whores do.'

'You prefer boys, don't you?' she said.

He hit her – not for the truth, but for the impertinence. She got up and went to the table, and examined the mark in the mirror.

'It's nothing to me', she said. 'I just do my job. But there's a place round the corner that might be more to your liking.'

'You presume a great deal, for a whore', said Simon.

'It's my business to please the customers. That's what they come here for. At least, that's what most of them come here for.' She put down the mirror and regarded him. 'You came here for something else.'

'You talk too much, too', said Simon. His astonishment was beginning to get the better of his anger.

'Why did you come here?' she asked.

It was ridiculous. After a moment Simon began to laugh. His anger ebbed away, and with it, for the time at least, a bitterness that for twelve months had never left him.

He stretched out his hand to draw her back to the bed.

'Tell me about yourself', he said.

Without surprise, she began to. Her mother had been Greek, her father Spanish. She had been conceived in a ditch in Corinth and born under a bush outside Smyrna. At the age of ten she had been raped by her uncle, and after her mother's death had lived with him as his concubine for two years. Then she had run away to another town, and earned her living for a time selling amulets

161

which she made from seashells. She became, almost without realising it, a prostitute. She took up with a sailor who was killed in a brawl and left her pregnant. The child was stillborn, which was just as well. She had sold herself into slavery because it was better than starving. A brothel-keeper from Tyre had bought her. She was eighteen years old.

Simon lay silent. He had no doubt that she was telling the truth, but even if she was lying it made no difference. It was the story of a whore: a story of perfect and arbitrary degradation. It humbled and exalted him. His phallus hardened insistently.

He made her take him in her mouth, and his pleasure this time was intense.

Afterwards he looked at her as she lay back on the pillow, left hand toying absently with a strand of hair that had fallen across her eyes; and he saw that she was beautiful.

The religious leaders of the province had counselled patience under various oppressors for two hundred years. It seemed to most of their hearers that patience had profited them nothing. It was the oppressor who flourished, blessed by his unreal gods.

When, after the Zealots and the revolutionary preachers, the visionaries appeared, it was an expression of a people's rage and despair. Despair, because what these men promised was by definition impossible. They were not political agitators: they had no plan. They were not guerilla leaders: they did not intend to fight. Neither planning nor war would be necessary, because God would deliver their enemies into their hand. A sign would be given that the divine intervention had begun. The sign was to be sought, most often, in the desert.

Thousands flocked to them: the poor, the desperate, the dreamers, the impatient young. A rabble, in other words. It was a convenient term. Every public servant knew what to do with a rabble.

Among the visionaries thrown up by these troubled times was the prophet Theudas. His name, and his tragic boast, are all that is known about him. Shadowy, without origin, his life compressed, as it were, into the moment of his death, he seems as if history, or a people's longing, had invented him.

Theudas gathered a throng of followers and led them down the mountain slopes, through wilderness and swamp, to the river Jordan, hallowed in tradition as the nation's frontier. At his command, he promised, the waters would part and they would cross on dry land.

The cleaving of waters was an act fraught with meaning for those who listened to his words. It had been performed twice in the remote past: first by the man who led their race out of subjection to a foreign power, then by his successor when he led them into the land that was their inheritance.

The political significance of Theudas's promise could not be mistaken.

'Never mind,' she said, 'it's all the preaching. It takes it out of you. I'm sure you'll be able to do it tomorrow.'

When she spoke softly her voice was as mellow and rich as a Jericho fig. It stimulated Simon's imagination to a delicious pitch. Unfortunately it had on this occasion stimulated nothing else. His organ, despite all encouragement, lay like a roll of wet pastry in her capable hand. He wished he could dissociate himself from it.

'I don't know what's the matter with me', he muttered. 'I'm not usually ...'

He stopped, conscious that every whore in the world had heard the same lament.

'Don't worry', she said, and bending down, nibbled the tip of his penis. It stirred, pulsed, and sagged again.

Simon stared gloomily at the bare walls. His cheeks were hot. He felt he ought to leave, but did not want to. As the silence progressed he felt increasingly he ought to break it before he drowned in intimations of defeat, but it became increasingly difficult to find the right thing to say.

Then he recalled her remark, and registered it for the first time.

'How do you know I preach?' he said.

'Oh, they told me'. She waved her hand vaguely in the direction of the street. 'They say you're a philosopher.'

'Do they?' said Simon. 'What else do they say?'

'That you're wicked.'

'Well, that's something. Did they tell you what I preach?'

'Something about God, and we ought to break all the laws.'

'I am encouraged', said Simon. 'I didn't think they were listening.'

She smiled. 'Oh yes, everybody heard the bit about the laws.'

163

'It doesn't seem to have made much impression.'

'People break the law anyway', she said. 'You don't have to encourage them.'

'Ah, but they break the law for personal advantage. I am telling them to break the law because it is the law', said Simon.

'Oh', she said doubtfully. She took his penis in her hand and toyed with it absent-mindedly. It did not respond.

'Why?' she said.

For a moment Simon was on the verge of telling her. He caught himself irritably. 'You wouldn't understand', he said.

'Being a whore', she said.

He decided that he would leave, at once.

Before he could get up she said, 'I don't see the point. If people don't obey the law they'll have to do something else, and whatever they do, that'll become the law.'

There was a short silence.

'I told you you wouldn't understand', said Simon.

She got up and went to the little toilet-table, picked up an ivory comb and began to comb her hair. It was lustrous, falling to her shoulders, framing her face so that the features stood out strongly. A bold, mobile face, with grey intelligent eyes. The features coarse, at times to the point of ugliness, at other moments lit with a disturbing beauty. The change depended on the expression of the eyes. The mouth changed little: it was wide, soft and generous. It occurred to him that a whore should have a hint of meanness in the mouth. She conformed to nothing he was entitled to expect.

She put down the comb, picked up a small wooden stick and started to apply green eye-paint with long deft strokes to her eyelids.

'Have you broken all the laws?' she asked.

'Of course not', said Simon. 'It's a lifetime's work.'

'Mmm, it would be. Perhaps you should just concentrate on one.'

He pretended to consider it. 'Which one?'

'I suppose it would have to be murder.'

She was logical enough for a man.

'No', said Simon. 'Death is what's wrong with the world.'

She thought about this, eye-paint poised.

'But you can't get rid of death', she objected.

'It will take a long time, certainly', Simon agreed.

She glanced at him to see if he was serious, then laughed.

164

'You men and your ideas', she said. 'And none of you can make a loaf of bread.'

'Bread!' snorted Simon. 'I should think not. That's women's work.'

'Of course it is', she said. 'That's one of the laws, isn't it?'

He stared at her. Exasperation, resentment and an unwilling admiration swirled in his brain. His phallus stirred, confusing him further.

She smiled at him. The light in the grey eyes was like the gleam on a distant sea. Yes, she was beautiful; yet she was ugly. She was remote, but he had bought her. She was a whore; and somehow, in the most vital region of her being, she had not been corrupted.

He felt himself growing angry.

'How can you do this?' he said. 'Day after day, night after night, selling yourself to any man who comes through the door?'

'What else can I do?' she said.

'Doesn't it make you feel – unclean?'

'No', she said. 'I feel nothing. It has nothing to do with me. Whatever people do to my body, I am still myself.'

'Nonsense', snapped Simon. 'Your body *is* you: what else can it be? And what is it? A plate scraped and licked by a thousand men. A bit of waste earth for every passer-by to jerk his unused seed into.'

His phallus throbbed and grew.

'Still yourself!' he repeated bitterly. 'You're anybody and anything. You're whatever men make of you. You're nothing. You're an animal.'

She watched him.

'The proof that you're an animal', said Simon, cradling his monstrous purple engine against his thigh, 'is that you'll do whatever I tell you. Won't you?'

She nodded, expressionless.

'Lie on your stomach', he ordered.

It was unfortunate that at that moment he could not think of anything more humiliating than to take her *per anum*, as he would a boy, roughly and ignoring her initial gasp of pain, and then, when he had brought himself to just short of the threshold, to withdraw, thrust her on to her back, and, kneeling astride her, pump his burning torrent into her mouth.

She lay with her eyes closed, and after a moment wiped the corner of her lips with one hand.

165

'Whore', said Simon.

She opened her eyes and looked at him. Her gaze was cool and clear. It contained something he did not want to recognise. It forced itself on his recognition. It was pity.

The river wound like a snake. Stumbling down the parched hillsides in the pitiless sun of the previous day, they had seen its green coiling furrow below them in the narrow plain, and it had promised refreshment. Now that they were near it, they saw that the dense greenery which clothed the banks on either side was rank and tangled jungle, swampy and treacherous, steaming in a heat which brought the sweat drenching on their bodies.

Demetrius walked mechanically, eyes fixed on the group ahead of him. He had almost forgotten why he was there.

The front of the crowd was turning right, skirting the shallow gorge that was the floor of the forest, and continuing south, through groves of thorn-bush, poplars, the clumps of bamboo that flourished wherever there was a stream, and the increasingly frequent arid patches where the soil seemed crusted and discoloured and no plants grew. Occasionally they traversed ridges of a greasy yellowish clay, or passed an isolated boulder of the same material. On the barren stretches the boulders afforded the only shade there was. It seemed to Demetrius that he was wandering through the landscape of a nightmare.

They came, after another hour's walking – the crowd moved slowly in this heat, and there were women carrying children – to a place where the plain sloped directly to the river. Demetrius, his energy reviving at the nearness of the goal, forced himself onward to the bank, but saw, as he approached, nothing like the clear and majestic waters of his imagination, but a swirling, muddy torrent, foaming white around the uprooted tree-trunks that littered it.

A vague, unlocated dread began to take hold of him. He turned away from the river and gazed back at the city in the foothills. The City of Palms: they had passed within a few miles of it, and looked with longing at its gardens and glistening streams. At this distance, green and shimmering in the haze, it seemed a place of safety and familiar comforts. He turned again towards the river, and saw beyond it an arid stretch identical to the one they had crossed, and beyond that the mountains of the Overside. To what paradise, then, was this brown and angry water supposed to be the gateway? He looked at his fellow pilgrims, tired, anxious, clutching their bundles of food and their children, the weakest of them half-fainting from the heat, but all of them having in their eyes a light, a hope, a treasure. He realised that he did not understand, that it was not his business. He should not be here.

Their leader had climbed on to a boulder and was addressing them. The pilgrims crowded closer, following his words with eager eyes.

'... And shall not the Holy One, blessed be He, that brought our forefathers out of the land of the oppressor, and smote the hosts of Midian, and laid low the pride of Assyria, shall He not hear the cry of his people? Day and night it goes up to Him, carried to His throne by the holy angels, and shall He not hear it?'

'Hear us, O Lord', sighed the crowd.

'Every tear shed by the just is a pearl before the Lord. Shall the Lord not see the suffering of His people? Shall He not bring them home?'

'Bring us home, Lord', yearned the crowd.

'Every one of you is wholesome grain in the granary of the Lord. Shall the Lord suffer His fields to be overrun by weeds, that thieve the soil's goodness and the light from the crop ...'

The crowd were rapt, nodding at the speaker's every phrase. There was an atmosphere of wonder, as if the miracle were already taking place. Perhaps it was, thought Demetrius. Perhaps the imparting of hope to these people was in itself a miracle. But suppose the miracle did not work? Would they turn on their prophet, as a crowd had once turned on the man he served? Demetrius wondered, for the thousandth time, where Simon was. It was difficult to believe that he was dead.

He glanced at the people near him. One man was moving his lips in prayer. Demetrius was conscious again of the gulf that divided him from them. They tolerated him, as people always tolerated him, but he could not be one of them. He had come to see a wonder: they had come to see their God. He heard the same words as they heard, but the words did not mean the same. His gaze roamed restlessly through the crowd, over the emaciated, gesturing figure of the prophet, and away into the distance. Far off in the foothills where the city was he saw something gleam. He blinked, and it had gone. He returned his attention to the words.

'When the abomination that is written of was set up in the sanctuary, did not the Holy One hear, and drive the blasphemer from the land? When, in our own time, the prince of the *Kittim*

– that madman, who called himself a god and made his horse a dignitary – when he too wished his image to be set up in the holy place, lest he be thought inferior to the Most High, did not the hand of the Almighty strike him down?'

Demetrius's head was swimming with the heat. The sermon went on and on; exhortations, denunciations, lists of names and places and long-ago battles that meant nothing to him. He dozed a little on his feet, and jerked awake in time to stop himself falling forward. He took a drink from his waterbottle and ate a couple of dates, which made him feel thirsty again.

Suddenly he became aware that the oration had finished. The prophet stood, arms and face uplifted to heaven, the focus of the crowd's stillness. Faintly then Demetrius heard it: the drumming. It was so small a sound he thought at first he had imagined it. Then it came to him that it was the noise of the river, which he had not noticed before.

The prophet descended from his rock and walked to the bank, where he stood a long time in prayer. The people murmured and shifted. Many of them too were praying. A few children ran about and played in the sandy soil, mildly rebuked by their elders.

The noise of the river had risen.

The prophet turned again to face them, and his gaunt features were alight with a vision. He called out once, in a loud voice, on his God. Then slowly, under a sky that now burned and reverberated like brass with the noise of the maddened river, he stretched out his hand over the waters.

The horses burst on them like thunder. It seemed to Demetrius that there was one moment of utter silence, when all might yet be averted, when it was still possible that there had been a mistake, because surely they could not ride into a defenceless crowd . . . and then the screams began. For a long time there was only the screaming, and the dazzle of armour too bright to look at in the sun, and the horses wheeling, and the chop, slash, chop of the swords. Demetrius flung himself on the ground and lay there. Around him the horses trampled. There was blood, not his blood, on his clothes.

The screaming died away and was replaced by worse sounds. These too, in time, became fainter or were extinguished in a sudden, surprised gasp. Finally it was very quiet. Some distance away he heard weeping. Nearer, the horses trod and whinnied.

A foot kicked him hard in the ribs. He grunted, opened his eyes and retched violently. Above him the prophet's head moved in a

168

slow arc against the sky. It ended at the neck. Below the red pulp was the shaft of a lance, down which drained gobbets of blood.

The foot landed in his ribs again, harder. He fought back tears.

'Pretty boy', said the legionary who was kicking him. 'Lost your way, did you?'

He looked up into a face of savage contempt.

There was no God, Demetrius understood.

Simon ran his finger over the broad, fleshy nose and the unduly prominent chin. 'You have no business', he said, 'to be anything you are.'

It was an admission of defeat. This was his fourth visit, and after every visit he had intended not to return. He went back each time to rectify the mistakes of the previous visit. This time he would direct the conversation, control the course of events, make of her – and himself – what he wanted. Each time the reins somehow slipped from him. The encounter proved nothing, and was in some way hazardous.

But another whore, more amenable, would not have served. He could not define the quality in her that attracted him – perhaps it was her very unexpectedness – but once he had admitted its existence he felt its hold on him increased. For the moment he did not resist it. He allowed her, at last, to please him. And he found that she knew how to please very well.

Her body was ever-changing, a country which constantly renewed itself in differences. At each entry he found the contours unfamiliar, and had to set himself again to learn its ways. Sometimes as he plunged into her he found himself in a seemingly endless landscape, and the further he pursued his pleasure across its plains and hills the further it receded, until suddenly he would be on the very edge of it and it would require all his will to hold himself there, waiting while the pleasure grew and grew and drew him into it, until he could hold himself no longer but yielded, and lay emptied, complete, and drowning. Sometimes it was a garden in which he found himself, secret with arbours, and he would dally in its paths and hidden places until he felt the pathways shrinking and the start of the slow pulsation that would draw him inward, with quickening urgency, deeper and deeper until he reached in a rush the garden's still heart. Afterwards he would linger, exploring with his hands her soft recesses and the swelling nub of her pleasure, while his eyes rested on her, puzzled.

He realised that he was in the presence of a mystery.

Jacob the Pious studied the letter before him with a concentration undiminished by his left hand's pursuit of a louse in his armpit. Jacob was at home with his parasites and exterminated them only when they became over-populous. This tolerance was not compassionate but an ingredient of his discipline. His nails were long and dirty in spite of frequent hand-washing, his beard had been untrimmed since youth, and his matted hair fell almost to his waist. These things were because of a vow. Because of the vow, he did not drink wine, eat meat, or take baths. The lice were not part of the vow, but it would have been inconsistent to resent them.

The letter was long and he read it carefully. He was reading it for the second time. He wished no detail or nuance of it to escape his attention. When he had finished, he looked across at the man who sat on the floor facing him.

'Saul has declared himself', he said. 'He has deserted.'

John bar Zabdai did not look surprised. Since his brother's death he had manifested no emotion except a mild and invariable patience.

'What does it say?' he asked.

'He has been travelling. He took it into his head to go to Pisidia. On the way he caused two riots, was stoned, antagonised the Jewish population of three towns, and was taken to be an incarnation of the god Mercury.' Jacob tapped the letter with a black fingernail. 'What is more to the point, he is preaching to the heathen. He is actually preaching to the heathen *in preference* to his own people, if you can believe it.'

'Why?' asked John bar Zabdai.

'Presumably because the heathen don't stone him.'

John pursed his lips judiciously. 'Saul does not have the reputation of a coward'.

'Saul has the reputation of a clever man', said Jacob, 'but I have never seen evidence of it.'

He was clearly disturbed by the contents of the letter. His eye returned to it again and again.

'Rank irresponsibility', he muttered. 'No advice sought, no permission. The man just rushes in and creates havoc.'

'But you must have expected this', said John. 'After what Kepha told you ...'

The name produced a slight change in the atmosphere of the

room. Kepha was not spoken of these days unless it was unavoid-
able.

'I didn't expect it so soon', said Jacob brusquely. 'I hoped he'd
forget about it, as a matter of fact. It isn't as if there's nothing else
to get on with.' He scowled again at the letter. 'It will bring us into
disrepute. Goodness knows how many people he's alienated who
otherwise would have been well disposed towards us. And causing
trouble between our people and the civil authorities! What is the
madman trying to do?'

'Convert the world', suggested John with a smile.

'Ludicrous', snapped Jacob. 'And unnecessary.'

'Who can tell? I wish I still had that energy. But I do not see',
said John, 'how it can work.'

'It can't work. Of course it can't. The moment he steps outside
the circle of people who've received instruction, they won't know
what he's talking about.'

'I suppose', mused John, 'he is not ... distorting the message?
But then, there is Barnabas.'

'Barnabas', said Jacob, 'will do what Saul tells him.' He frowned
with worry. 'Perhaps we ought to send someone to find out.'

'Where is Saul now?' asked John.

'At Antioch.'

'Well, that should not be too difficult.'

They sat in a thoughtful silence for a while. Jacob pursued,
trapped and despatched two lice. His brow furrowed. He seemed to
be containing a mounting wave of irritation. It burst out of him
finally.

'It really is too much', he said. 'Kepha should be here.'

John said carefully, 'Have you any news of Kepha?'

'He was seen two months ago at Ashdod.'

'Ashdod? What on earth was he doing down there?'

'Fishing', said Jacob.

Demetrius was put in a cell with four others. For the first day he
stared at the wall in front of him and saw on it blood and the
wheeling of horses. On the second day he became conscious of his
surroundings.

The cell was dark, and stank. The only ventilation was a small
grilled window at just above eye-level, which gave on to the courtyard. The dungeon was below ground, and most of the time all
that could be seen through the window was the booted feet of

171

soldiers. Rain and muck blew in through the window, and occasionally one of the soldiers urinated through the opening: whether as a
sign of contempt or because it was conveniently situated, Demetrius did not know.

After a few days he was hardly aware of the stench. It had
become indistinguishable from everything else: the half-darkness,
the mutterings of the other men in the cell, the blood and filth on
his clothing.

Two of the men were robbers. They had been captured by an
infantry patrol in the hills. The new governor had announced his
intention of ridding the country of bandits, and there were cruci-
fixions almost every day. These men had probably a week to live.
They looked so villainous that Demetrius at first could not feel
anything but relief at the prospect of their departure. One of them
was a powerful-looking man with the muscles of a wrestler; he had
a demon, which would not let him speak except in grunts and
gurgles, and where his ears ought to be there were just two holes
surrounded by a curved ridge of gristle. The other robber was very
small and had no forehead. Demetrius studied them with half-
averted eyes for a long time before he realised that the small one
was a boy, probably no more than his own age.

Demetrius would have liked to talk to the boy, but could not
bring himself to. Bodily deformity frightened him. He felt it was
purely by chance that his own body was strong, healthy and
perfect, and that if he engaged in too close a contact with the
imperfect he might somehow catch the imperfection.

Of the other two prisoners in the cell, one was old and a religious
fanatic. He lay on his straw in the corner all day long, gazing with
watery aged eyes at something no one else could see. Often he
muttered to himself – scraps of what sounded like poetry, prayers,
fragments from the holy writings. Occasionally his voice would rise
to a shout and he would declaim, propped on the bony elbow of his
good arm, hurling denunciations until he tired or until a guard
came in to kick him into silence. He had been tortured. His right
arm had been broken and hung useless, and the thumb ended in a
nailless, suppurating stump. The authorities obviously believed
him to be a Zealot.

The last prisoner was a half-wit and thought he was living in
Babylon.

Talking in the circumstances was almost impossible. After a
nervous approach to the Zealot, which was received in stony

172

silence, and a bewildering conversation with the half-wit, Demetrius gave up and retreated into his thoughts. It occurred to him that the coming together of these five people in a dungeon, while it might have been significant, was utterly meaningless. It was a short step from this observation to the idea that the world, while it might have been significant, was utterly meaningless. He was pleased with this idea. It seemed to him to fit all the facts of his experience.

He was in the presence of a mystery. He had bought a thing and he could not possess it. He could not even name it. It was not even the same thing, when he tried to find it. The pursuit of it engrossed him to the exclusion of all else. If he could grasp it, he would be free of her.

He took her in as many ways as he could devise. Prone or sideways, from the front or rear, her body propped with cushions, or crouched or kneeling, or standing, her feet braced against the wall, his hands supporting her, her orifice wide and velvet drawing him in, he plunged inside her. He mounted campaigns of conquest and discovery. He called in all the resources of his culture and imagination, and performed with her a bestiary of acts: the Hare, the Bull, the Monkey, the Hyena, the Crab, the Weasel. Reversing nature, he made her ride him. He pierced her with phallus, tongue and hand or sheathed himself in ivory. Day after day he drove himself into her in a fury to find and possess. He found, at the end of each annihilating spasm, only himself.

He changed his tactics and tried to lure the secret out. Gently he would tease her into pleasure, stirring the rhythms of her body, his fingers straying from the moisture of her open lips to roam among the forest of hair and the silky valleys, returning again to stroke and press and crush the little hardening berry. Once he poured wine into her entrances and licked and sucked out the salty sweetness, but then she laughed, and he realised that it was no more than a diversion. Always in the end his own need mastered him. And coming to himself after the violent surge of relief, he knew that again he had spent himself for nothing.

'You've put a spell on me', he accused her. It was only half in jest.

She was lying face down among the pillows, the lamplight glinting on the smooth, slightly oily skin of her back. He wondered if the strangeness he found in her was just his fantasy.

Perhaps the garden held no secrets, and there was no such thing as an uncorrupted whore.

She turned over, exposing to his gaze the well-learned, still elusive harmonies of her supple flesh: hills, plains and shadowed valleys.

She smiled. 'I've only been doing my job', she said.

On leaving the brothel, Simon walked for a while through the streets, then turned on impulse in the direction of the waterfront. It was a mild evening with an inshore breeze, and the smell of shellfish from the dyeworks hung strongly over the harbour. He stood watching the boats bobbing on the water, and he knew that he must leave.

He set out at dawn the following day, before he could change his mind.

He travelled, as he always did, without baggage and on foot. The road he had chosen left the plain and wound east into the hills. It was shortly after noon when the robbers ambushed him.

He did not resist, merely turned his head aside from the dagger pointed at it.

'Money', said the man with the dagger.

There were four of them. Simon calculated the distance without moving his eyes. There had been a time ...

'I am not a rich man', he said.

The man with the dagger thrust his left hand into Simon's girdle and fingered the material. With a flick of the blade he cut it in two. A gold coin spun into the dust. The man with the dagger weighed the girdle in his hand, grinning, and returned the blade to Simon's neck.

'Not any more', he observed.

'Take it by all means', said Simon. 'Or rather, since you have taken it, keep it. But there is a curse on it.'

After a moment's surprise, three of the robbers laughed raucously. The fourth, a shambling bear of a man with a looted legionary sword stuck in his belt, said nervously, 'What sort of curse?'

'Poison, perversity and damnation', said Simon. 'A most satisfying trinity.'

The man with the dagger pressed the blade against Simon's neck so that it made a small nick just below the ear.

'Don't make fools of us', he said.

'I don't like this', said the bear.

'Take off his clothes', said the man with the dagger.

Simon's clothes were removed. They left him his loincloth. The clothes were examined carefully for hidden pockets, then, when it became obvious that nothing more was concealed in them, tossed aside. The man with the dagger, who had been watching, turned the clothes over with his foot, then stared at Simon. Something had made him uneasy.

'Why are you alone?' he demanded.

'I prefer it', said Simon.

'Rubbish. No one travels alone in these parts without a good reason. Who are you?'

Simon did not reply.

'Ratface, nip up the crest and see if there's anyone else.'

The smallest robber scrambled off, and returned to say that no one was in sight.

The man with the dagger removed it from Simon's neck and fingered it thoughtfully. It was very sharp.

'All that money and you travel alone', he said. 'No servant, no baggage, no donkey. Nothing. Why? What's the game?'

'The money has no value for me', said Simon.

Two of the robbers roared with laughter and hit each other in delight. The man with the dagger told them to shut up. The bear pulled at his lip. 'I don't like it', he said.

'I'll ask you once more', said the man with the dagger. 'Who are you?'

'I'm a preacher', said Simon.

The knife returned to its place below his ear. 'I'm not stupid. I've seen you before somewhere. And wherever it was, you certainly weren't preaching.'

The other three robbers had become very attentive.

Ratface said, 'What's a preacher want with all that money, anyway?'

'I've told you', said Simon. 'The money has a curse on it. It can't be used.'

He saw their eyes widen and begin to cloud, like the eyes of children who have become aware that the game they are playing might be dangerous.

The man with the dagger laughed without conviction. 'Why do you carry it then? Why don't you give it away?'

'I can't give it away', said Simon. 'It's *mine*, because the curse is mine. The money is the sign of the curse. I cannot give away a curse.'

'What's he talking about?' muttered the ratfaced robber irritably.

'Is the curse passed on with the money?' asked the man with the dagger.

'Of course', said Simon. 'Only two people can remove it. The man who uttered the curse, and me.'

The knife moved fractionally upward and nicked his ear.

'Then remove it.'

'It's not as simple as that', said Simon. 'I could only remove it by finding the right use for it. If there is a right use.'

The fourth robber, a pudgy, baby-faced creature, had been following the conversation with deepening perplexity. His features cleared at last with the emergence of thought.

'When are we going to kill him?' he said.

'Why', persisted the man with the dagger, 'is it cursed?'

Simon was beginning to like him. He discerned in him a potential taste for theology.

'I imagine the version that got about', he said, 'was that I attempted to use it to buy the Holy Spirit.'

No one said anything for a while.

The man with the dagger spat suddenly on the ground. 'I know who you are. You're Simon the magician.'

'No, I am not.'

'Yes, you are. I recognise you. I never forget a face. I saw you in Sebaste, doing illusions in the market place. People talked about it for weeks. They said' – he paused – 'you could fly.'

'I have given up magic', said Simon.

'The devil you have', said the man with the dagger.

There was again silence, but of a different kind.

The bear-man moaned. 'Give him his damned money and let him go', he begged.

The man with the dagger had stepped back a pace. He was tense and angry. 'You've been laughing at us, haven't you?' he said.

'You don't understand', said Simon. 'I'm a preacher now. I devote myself to the truth, not illusions.'

'Oh yes? What do you preach?'

'Well, as a matter of fact', said Simon, 'I tell people they must break the law, but there isn't much point in telling you that as you're already breaking it.' He surveyed their blank faces. 'Perhaps you'd like to be my disciples?'

The girdle of money landed at his feet. He picked it up.

'Get on your way', snarled the man with the dagger.

The bear threw him his clothes. Simon picked them up.

'Now go.'

The robber with the baby face had been watching with an expression of bewilderment. He could contain himself no longer.

'You're going to let him go? You're giving him back the money?'

'He's a sorcerer.'

'But the money!'

The baby-faced robber moved towards Simon. The man with the dagger blocked his way.

'He's dangerous, you fool.'

'He doesn't look very dangerous to me.'

'Nor to me', said Ratface. 'He looks to me as if a knife could go through him as easy as cheese.'

'Idiots!' shouted the bear in anguish. 'Don't you understand who he is? He could turn us all into – '

He clapped his hand to his belt and spun round, too late. Ratface had tugged out the sword and launched himself like a wildcat at Simon, who, hands encumbered with clothes and money, was able to do no more than bring his arms across his chest in an instinctive movement of defence. At least, that was how it seemed to Simon. But it was clear that something quite different seemed to his assailant to be happening. After an initial, unaccountably misdirected, thrust, Ratface swung the sword in increasingly wild strokes that cleft nothing but air. After a few of these ridiculous antics he stepped back, his face ashen, and dropped the sword. Step by step, as if entranced, the four robbers moved backwards, staring. Then with a strange sound that was less like a yell than a squawk, they turned as one man and fled.

Simon watched them until they were out of sight. Thoughtfully he began to put on his clothes. When he was dressed he sat for a while in the shade of a rock and rested. Then he stood up and began walking back in the direction he had come.

The brothel-keeper was a mountain of fat with small suspicious eyes. He reacted to Simon's question with instant hostility.

'Why should I want to sell her? She's a good girl. Gets a lot of customers.'

'I bet they don't come back, though.'

'What's that?'

'She talks out of turn, doesn't she? Has a mind of her own. Don't tell me your customers come here for that.'

'Maybe they do, maybe they don't.'

'She gave me a lecture on my inability to cook, one afternoon.'

'She what?'

'In addition to which', said Simon, 'she has the ugliest face I've ever seen on a whore.'

'Distinctive, I call it', said the brothel-keeper. 'And we don't use that word in this establishment.'

Simon drew from inside his tunic a small heavy cloth bag which clinked as he placed it on the table. The brothel-keeper sniffed round it with his eyes.

'What d'you want her for then, if she's no good? I look after my girls here, you know. Don't want them getting into the wrong hands.'

'I am offering to redeem her', said Simon. 'What she does when she's free is her own business.'

The brothel-keeper studied him for a moment, then returned his attention to the cloth bag. He opened it, tipped out a pile of coins and counted them. He arranged them neatly in three little stacks, and ran his thumbnail up the edge of each.

'Well', he said, 'money being what it is these days, and her being pure-bred Grecian of good family and not long since a virgin ...'

'I'm not a fool, and virginity is to the best of my knowledge not a matter of degree', said Simon. 'Understand me. This is the money I am offering for the woman's redemption. Not one drachma more, and for reasons of my own, not one drachma less. I shall not bargain.'

He and the brothel-keeper regarded each other over the three little pillars of gold. The brothel-keeper sighed. 'I shall regret it', he said.

He waddled to the foot of the stairs, hoisted his chin fractionally out of its supporting cushions, and bellowed 'Helen!'

'Helen?' murmured Simon. 'Queen, concubine and whore of Troy. And is that her name? I never thought to ask.'

Kepha mended his nets.

They were not really his nets, of course, but after the passage of two seasons he knew them like a familiar landscape: every knot, every weakness, every patch faded paler than its neighbours by the sun, every tough enduring fibre. His hands moved over them, deft and loving.

In a while it would be time for the evening meal. He ate and lodged with Malachi, who owned the boat. Malachi had been ill, but he was getting better. Kepha's arrival had enabled him to keep the boat in business while he could not fish himself: otherwise he would have had to sell her. She was a good boat, but not as ready to the tiller as Kepha's own had been. It was always difficult to part with a good boat.

The pomegranate-seller passed him, baskets slung on a long pole, and called out a greeting. Kepha called back. The people were friendly here, and they did not ask questions. In a coastal town there were always strange faces. If a man did not wish to talk about himself, he was not pressed to do so.

The sun was setting crimson behind bars of cloud, turning the sea to silver. It would be fine tomorrow. But in a few weeks the weather would worsen. It was a dangerous coast. Squalls could come up from nowhere. Kepha had learnt his seamanship in the squalls that blew up without warning on the Lake: but on the Lake you could run for a lee shore. Here for a score of miles there was only exposed rock and cliff and nothing to stop the pounding sea.

He would not return to the Lake. He had considered it, and knew it was the wrong thing to do. Chance – it seemed at the time – had brought him to this small town, and as soon as he arrived he had known it was the right place. For a while.

The year was dying into winter. There would be little fishing, and in any case Malachi was getting better. It was nearly time for him to leave. He would know the day when it came.

He smiled with content. There was a simplicity in his life now which nourished him. Everything needed was given. And there was time: yes, there was time.

He finished the torn patch of net he had been working on and laid aside his needle. He would make no plans. Something was moving towards him; as yet it was distant. He would know it, and that it was for him, when it came.

'This time', said Simon.

She moved expertly under him, occasionally pricking him to quickness but never for so long that he broke into ungovernable speed, always by a relaxation of her muscles forcing him to rest. It was of the utmost importance not to lose control. It was his need which each time plunged him into the annihilation from which he had to start afresh.

'A little more', he said, and then had to rein himself as she

179

gripped him. To perform the motions of desire without yielding to desire: it was a rite.

Nearer. But he had glimpsed the goal, and as soon as he glimpsed it he felt its tug on him and his leap of response. He must surrender just so far ... use the onward thrust to carry him ...

Too fast again. Deliberately he lost the rhythm and made his mind drift, until he felt his pleasure becoming distant and lazy, and he roused it again with violence and thrust, and at once was lost, in the pulsing tunnels.

Oh the divine and dangerous urgency, drawing him on. Dangerous to follow, impossible not to follow now that he was sucked, pulled and driven, neither in control nor out of control but one with the driving pulse and the sucking current. On and on, deeper and deeper, plunging in the dark current ... too dangerously now, and he pulled himself back with a groan. Then the sharp and perilous equilibrium, the longing to yield and the not yielding, the holding in check by the taut will that even now wavered and weakened –

He fought desperately to master himself, but with each moment the towering peak of his need hardened, tightened, was a mountain filled with fire that must split and spill –

He cried out with the pain of it: it was like dying. But he forced himself away, beyond, out of the madness. The refusal drained all his strength. As he surrendered to exhaustion he knew he had failed. His body was poisoned. His mind drifted in a desolation.

Time passed.

It began slowly. He became conscious first of a lightening. His veins stirred: he was flesh, not marble. A tingling, which extended to his feet and hands but seemed to have its seat somewhere in the lower part of his spine. The tingling, almost as soon as he felt it, was followed by a strange coldness that was like the thin coldness of mountain air. The thinness seemed to draw the substance out of the surrounding areas of his body, as if he was being drawn through a sieve from which the gross elements would be discarded. The coldness combed along his limbs until he could not feel them. Then the cold centre in his spine began to spread. He felt the pulses of his loins and belly, and the prickling of the hair-roots, cool and become quiescent. The still coolness climbed his spine. At the moment when it reached his neck he thought he would stop breathing. But his breath came slow, shallow, yet sure.

He was a ghost. Nothing of him remained except the brain in its cage of bone. He felt the weight of his skull bearing him down into the earth.

He tried the hinge of his jaw, but the sinews had dissolved. The coldness spread into his skull.

There was nothing but light.

There was nothing but light.

But the light became aware of itself, and as soon as it became aware of itself there was also darkness. If there had been no darkness the light would not have known that it was light.

So there were both light and darkness.

The light created the darkness in order that it might know itself.

But there were then not two things, but three. One was the light, and another the darkness, and the third was Thought. For it was the Thought emanating from the light which caused the darkness to come into being.

Thought was therefore the first creator. Everything which was afterwards created was created by Thought.

Thought emanated from the light and was pulled towards the darkness she had made. She longed for the light because she came from the light, and she longed for the darkness because she had made it. In the ceaseless swing of these desires, time was born, and from time worlds were born, and Thought peopled the worlds with forms.

Thought saw all these things and loved them because she had created them, and she drew back from them because they were not of the light.

Because she loved them she wished to look more closely at them. She travelled to the furthest edge of the light to gaze at the things she had made.

She travelled to the very edge and reached towards them.

They saw her, far above them, and were filled with longing for her beauty. They reached towards her.

She fell into the darkness.

She struggled to return to the light, but the dense dark air held her down and the forms thronged round and prevented her escape. They imprisoned her in a body like their own, a clammy cell subject to time, change and decay. Because they could not grasp her beauty, but only the form in which it was contained, they abused that form and made it suffer. She passed from one form to

181

another, always persecuted, always humiliated, until she had almost forgotten her nature. She was subject at last to the grossest degradation of all.

In the body of a harlot the Spirit of God awaits her redeemer.

The man who could only speak in grunts and gurgles and the boy who had no forehead were fond of each other, Demetrius noticed. So far as they were able, they seemed to look after each other. When the food was brought – a lukewarm greyish mess of beans and barley – the boy would often finish his first, and the man would give him some of his. The boy seemed to understand the sounds the man made, and would talk to him. Once, when a jailer kicked his companion, the boy sprang ferociously to his defence. The jailer was so surprised that he did not retaliate.

Demetrius wondered if they were father and son, but dismissed the idea with a shudder.

Sitting or lying in a stinking dungeon, in the company of the maimed, the deformed and the lunatic, Demetrius occupied himself in trying to make sense of his life. It seemed to him that an obscure and vicious joke had been played on him. He had never been in control of his destiny in the way in which even the two monstrosities who shared the cell with him had been in control of theirs. It was because he had been born a slave.

That single fact had determined everything that happened to him. Yet it seemed that another force had been at work as well. For from time to time a kind of freedom had been placed before him – and then, when he reached for it, been snatched away. What he had reached for, without clearly knowing it, was a liberty which would not actually end his servitude – there was no mercy for a slave who ran away – but would make it not important. He had dared to dream that he possessed something that did not belong to his master. But his attempt to locate it, this mysterious thing, and to find the use to which it should be put, had always failed. His fate mocked him. He was a slave, and should have known his place.

There was no escaping one's identity, he realised. Every attempt to do so trapped one tighter in its meshes. If he had remembered who he was, and not joined a pilgrimage to see a miracle that had nothing to do with him . . .

'You should never have been there', said the boy with no forehead.

Demetrius jerked his head up in amazement. The boy was looking at him with bright, animal eyes.

182

'Should never have been where?' asked Demetrius appre-
hensively.

'Wherever you were when they caught you.'

'How did you know I was thinking that?'

The boy frowned, which made him look like a demon.

'Sometimes I can see the words in people's minds, if the feeling is
strong enough', he said.

Demetrius sat back against the wall and thought. After a while
he decided he understood it. Indicating the big robber, he asked,
'Is that how you can tell what he's saying?'

'Yes. And because he's my friend.' The boy smiled painfully.
'They stoned me out of my village for seeing the words in people's
minds. They thought I was possessed.'

Of course, thought Demetrius: they would. He realised for the
first time in his life that the only thing that mattered was being
kind. He brooded on this, and wondered why it was that people
who were kind ended up in prison and people who were not ended
up governing provinces.

'It's a reasonable assumption', said the Zealot, staring at the
ceiling, 'that none of us should have been where we were when we
were arrested, otherwise we would not have been arrested.'

It was the first interest he had shown in any of the other occu-
pants of the cell. Demetrius turned to him gratefully.

'Do you think', he said, hoping to make a game of it, 'that life is a
matter of being in the right place?'

'The hand of God will find you wherever you are', replied the
Zealot solemnly. Then, perhaps sensing Demetrius's disappointment, he added, 'Life is more a matter of knowing where you are.'

'Or what you are', murmured Demetrius.

'I know where I am', said the half-wit unexpectedly.

The big robber started laughing – at least, Demetrius supposed
that was what it was. His shoulders shook and a choking sound
came from him. The boy put his arm around his shoulders and
laughed too.

Demetrius watched them and felt a dull pain inside him. They
weren't meant to be robbers, he thought. They didn't know what
they were meant to be, any more than he knew what he was meant
to be. People were born, wandered around for a while, and died.

He thought how grotesque they would look crucified.

Simon Magus travelled the roads of Judaea and Samaria, and up the Phoenician coast. He took with him one companion, a woman called Helen, who he said was the Holy Spirit. Others said she was a prostitute.

In all the towns, he preached. Where he preached, crowds would gather, and listen with amazement and some ribaldry. But in nearly every gathering there were a few who followed his words with serious attention. Some of these people would afterwards question him, invite him and his companion into their homes, and, after his departure, attempt to put into practice what he told them.

What Simon preached was this.

Man is a spark of fire caught in a web of darkness. How this came about is a mystery not known even to the Ruler of this world, who, blind with an unending age of power, now supposes that no other God exists. We may imagine the primordial existence of two realms: those of light and darkness, or of spirit and matter; and a catastrophic fall, in which the seeds of light became prisoners of the dark.

Thus man is a two-fold creature, part darkness and part light. For the darkness, seeing the beauty of its captive, would not let it go. The world is wholly under the dominion of the powers of darkness, chief of whom is the insane arch-demon worshipped by the Jews. This tyrant hates and fears his captives and has devised a labyrinth of lies to keep us ignorant of our plight. The greatest lie is that he is our Creator and that to him we owe obedience. But we do not belong to him except as hostages, and the world is not our home. We owe him nothing but the betraying and corruptible flesh in which he clothes us, the flesh which is the spirit's fetter and goad.

That which is restless in us, that which seeks, and feels itself in an alien land, and cannot be comforted, is the living spark of a far distant fire. To that source we yearn to return – as it yearns for us, for, lacking us, it is incomplete. There is no easy road of return, for we are trapped and tricked on every side by the walls of matter and the snares of false hope. There is but one way out, and it is for the few who have the courage.

The redemption of the spirit can only be achieved by using that principle which is the nature of spirit and the enemy of darkness: fire. The web cannot be untangled: it must be burnt away. And because the spirit, being immaterial, cannot combat the flesh, it must seek as ally against the flesh that element of the flesh which is most akin to itself. The world of matter is combated and overcome by the bodily burning of desire.

184

The sexual act, invented by the powers of darkness for men's confusion, can be turned against them only if it is used not as an indulgence but as a discipline. It must be freed from all the constraints they have imposed upon it, or it becomes another stone in the spirit's prison. Thus it must be performed in every manner, with every partner, and on every occasion that has ever been forbidden. Only in this way can it be purified and made fit for its purpose. This purpose is nothing less than the redemption of Creation: it is the restoration of Spirit, the whore and holy one, to her source in God.

VI

THE SAVED

The window had been shuttered and covered with drapes to exclude all light and the smallest possibility of being spied on. The only source of illumination in the room was a glowing brazier at the far end. It was a large room, normally furnished with some opulence, but on this occasion bare except for a number of couches set along the walls. A sweet and cloying smoke came from the brazier, making the air rich and heavy and the head light.

There were thirty people in the room. In the centre stood the man known as the Master, and beside him a young woman. Both were robed in white. Around them in a circle stood fourteen men and fourteen women, all naked.

The Master spoke.

'May our rite be holy, may it find favour.'

In unison, the men and women in the circle responded, 'May it find favour.'

There was a pause. The people in the circle linked hands. The Master faced the brazier and extended his hands towards it, then moved in a slow rotation to face each member of the circle in turn, his hands still stretched before him. As he turned, he spoke again.

'A sower went out to sow. He scattered the seed and it fell into many kinds of earth. It grew, and its seed brought forth new seed. Now the name of the seed is light, and the name of earth is darkness. Let them who have understanding, understand.'

As he completed his circle, the twenty-eight men and women stood for a moment, silent, with linked hands, then separated into pairs, each man with the woman to his left. In pairs they walked to the couches at the sides of the room. Each man kissed his partner lightly on the lips, laid her on the couch, and without further preliminary began sexual intercourse.

The Master took the hand of the young woman beside him and led her to a couch which had been placed near the brazier. Slowly he removed her robe, and then his own. He knelt before her, made a gesture of reverence, then parted her thighs with his hand. When, after a moment, he withdrew his hand, there was blood on it.

The young woman lay down on the couch, and he entered her at once with a thrust of his penis.

The air was growing denser. The glow from the coals in the brazier glinted dully on patches of sweating skin.

One by one the couples reached the climax of the first stage of the rite, and rested side by side on the couches. After some time had

189

passed, the circle was re-formed and the Master and his partner again took their places in the centre.

'This is the perfect love', said the Master.

'This is the perfect love', responded the disciples.

'The name of the seed is light', said the Master, 'and the name of the flesh is darkness. The name of the spirit is light.'

'The name of Law is darkness', responded the disciples.

'As the law dispenses death, so does the breaking of law dispense life. In bodies male and female are we bound as long as the world endures, but the spirit knows no distinction of male and female, for the spirit is life.'

'The name of the spirit is life', said the disciples.

Another pause, those in the circle standing silently with linked hands. Then, at a gesture from the Master, the circle was broken and each man turned to one of the two men nearest him and each woman to one of the nearest women. In pairs then, man with man and woman with woman, they walked to the couches and began to couple sexually in whatever way pleased them, but not proceeding to the fulfilment of the act.

The Master, who had remained where he was, took his organ in his hands and manipulated it to full erection.

Eventually, at a word from the Master, the couples rose from the couches and formed two lines facing each other. The men, each grasping his penis, brought themselves in a few moments to ejaculation and caught the semen in their hands. Slowly and with solemnity they raised their hands towards the ceiling.

'This is the sacrament of the perfect Son', said the Master.

'This is the body of the Spirit', responded the disciples.

'Father, we offer it to Thee.'

The men stepped forward and each offered his cupped hands to the woman opposite him, who took some of the liquid into her mouth and swallowed it. The man then swallowed what was left.

'Corruption is of the flesh alone', said the Master.

'The spirit knows no corruption', responded the disciples.

The Master knelt again before the young woman, and inserted one finger of his right hand into her vagina. He withdrew it covered in dark blood. With the tip of his tongue he tasted the blood.

'This is the sacrament of the Mother', he said.

'This is the body of the Spirit', replied the disciples.

'Father, we offer it to Thee.'

The Master walked to each disciple in turn, and each with the ti of the tongue tasted the blood. When all had partaken of the sacrament, he returned to his place.

'We have partaken of the fire of the male and the fire of the female', said the Master. 'All fire is one fire. Let them who have understanding, understand.'

'Increase our understanding, Lord', prayed the disciples.

A long pause now marked the transition to the final stage of the rite. Then the Master crossed to the couch where his white robe lay and put it on. He turned towards the fire in the brazier and the disciples formed a semicircle behind him.

'I thank thee, Lord,' he began, and the disciples joined in the prayer.

'I thank thee, Lord, who hast removed me from corruption and sown in me life, who hast shown thyself to me and hast shown me mine own nature; who hast redeemed me from the transient and found me worthy of the incorruptible; who hast shown me how to seek myself and to know who I was and what I now am, so that I may again become what I was: whom I did not know, but thou hast sought me out like a lost sheep; whom having known I cannot now forget.'

The Master stepped back a pace, and, raising his arms, cried, 'Come, Most High and Most Compassionate. Come, Mother of Life, thou who art mystery. Come, Holy Spirit, thou who revealest mysteries. With the fire of thy burning redeem us. By thy suffering in the flesh redeem us. Redeem us as in this our rite we have redeemed thee.'

For a time there was a silence. The disciples stood with bowed head. Then the Master took a candle and lit it from the brazier. Shadows danced fantastically on the wall.

'Fire is One and Light is One', he said.

'May all be One', responded the disciples.

Each person in the room lit a candle from the brazier, and with each lighting the dancing shadows retreated.

The Master turned to face the disciples. His voice thrilled.

'I am thou and thou art I, saith the Spirit. In all am I scattered, and wheresoever thou gatherest thou gatherest Me; and gathering Me thou gatherest Thyself.'

He paused.

'Let them who have understanding, understand this mystery.'

The smoke from the brazier formed drifting films of purple in the light of the thirty candles.

*

The procurator Fadus, having rid the country of most of its robbers and some of its visionaries, was replaced. The new governor doubtless seemed to the emperor an excellent choice for the job, for, although of expatriate family, he was of the same race as the people he was sent to rule. To the inhabitants of the province, however, the choice could not have been more insulting. Tiberius Alexander was an apostate. He had abandoned his forefathers' religion when he took service with the government.

Only one action of this governor is recorded. To understand it, it is necessary to go back some forty years to the time when the kingdom established under Herod the Tyrant had been broken up and part of it placed under direct rule. One of the first acts of the central administration at that time was to order a census.

Now it happened that the people of the province were strongly averse to being counted. Their sacred books contained an account of a major calamity befalling precisely because such a thing had been done. That the disaster had occurred thirty generations ago would not seem to them important: in that haunted country the past was as real as the present and considerably easier to understand. Their unease turned to indignation when it was pointed out to them by a wandering teacher of the Law that a census was almost certainly the prelude to an increase in taxes.

No one likes to be taxed. But to the people of that province, occupied by a foreign power and unable, for many reasons, to distinguish between their country and their God, taxes paid to the oppressor were far more than a burden on the purse. The teacher of the Law began to preach revolt, and his words fell at first on receptive ears.

In the event the rising came to nothing. The would-be insurgents were dissuaded from their purpose by the high priest. What happened to the teacher is not clear, although one account has it that he was murdered.

But although it came to nothing, it was not forgotten. It was the first small blaze of anger to be directed, not at the swindling puppet-kings, but at the real masters behind them. In sixty years the smouldering ashes of that blaze would burst into a conflagration.

Tiberius Alexander saw the ashes smouldering and thought that he would put them out. Two sons of the wandering teacher were still alive. He had them crucified.

*

192

There was a high sea running and the currents around the reefs would be treacherous. Kepha watched as a single small fishing boat came in under sail. The sky was leaden and the wind, which had veered all day between west and north-west, was gusting stronger. He himself would not have put to sea in such weather, not on this coast. But then, he did not know the channels; perhaps the reefs were not as dangerous as they looked.

He was not sure why he had come to Joppa, except that a farmer at Ashdod, travelling that way with produce, had offered him a lift in the cart. Kepha nearly always accepted unexpected offers of help: any one of them might be a sign. But, strolling through the streets, he had felt nothing that called to him. He felt, in fact, slightly uneasy. There were people he knew in this town and he did not want to see them.

That was putting it too strongly. He felt a great warmth for them, the little scattering of families and individuals he had preached and talked to, and the quiet and thoughtful man with whom he had stayed, whose name he had forgotten although he remembered his trade – a leather-worker. If it had not been for the distance that had grown in his mind between the person he knew himself to be and the person they thought him to be, he would have enjoyed their company. But they would expect something from him that he could not give. They would expect certain words, and he could not say them.

The boat tacked in, skirting perilously close to the patches of white foam. It was low in the water: there was a good catch on board. It was a risk deliberately taken, thought Kepha. A little longer, another hour before the nets were hauled in, and the risk would not have been worth it. But then who was to say, ever, whether a risk was worth it? Risks were to be measured backwards.

The boat was in the channel between the nearest reefs. It was still too distant for Kepha to see the boatman's face, but in his mind he visualised it, still with concentration, the eyes moving constantly over the angry water to the cliffs and the broken shoreline, judging the distance, judging the current, with a kind of detachment. So had he seen his friends, so had he been himself, at moments of great danger when skill had been stretched to its limit and there was nothing left to do but wait. A feeling of brotherhood for the unknown fisherman flooded over him and he felt as if he were himself drawing the boat to safety with the intensity of his love.

A freak wave crashed broadside against the hull and lifted the

193

craft, tilting crazily, towards the rocks. Kepha groaned a prayer. If she did not smash as she dropped down she would surely capsize. He closed his eyes.

When he opened them a few moments later the boat was through the channel and in unbroken water. He gazed at it until it had nearly reached the shore, then turned away and walked back into the town.

He lingered in the thronged bazaar, trying to decide what he should do. He must find somewhere to stay. He had money for a lodging, but there seemed something distasteful in paying for a night's shelter when in the past he had always stayed with friends. In the past there had always been, somewhere, a friendly house. He had turned his back on that comforting, familial network. And although he was free to reverse his decision, to walk up to the door and announce himself, yet he was not free, because it was a stranger he would be announcing.

Perhaps he did not have any friends.

He caught sight, at that moment, of the leather-worker in whose house he had lodged before. The man, haggling over the price of a set of knives, raised his eyes and met Kepha's. Kepha saw, first, startled recognition, and then – to his surprise – deep dismay. In obvious embarrassment, the man put down the knives and hurried off through the crowd.

Kepha stared after him.

The Zealot was declaiming again.

'Then I saw a deep valley, and wide was its entrance. And I beheld the angels of punishment who were dwelling there, and preparing every instrument of the Adversary.

'Then I enquired of the angel of peace who accompanied me, for whom these devilish instruments were prepared.

'And he said, "They are being made ready for the kings and rulers of the earth, who by these means shall be destroyed."'

His voice had risen to a shout. It was extraordinary what strength he still possessed.

'If you go on like that', said Demetrius, 'you'll be tortured again.

The Zealot had been tortured twice since the execution of the robbers and the release of the half-wit had left them alone in the cell. On the first occasion the soldiers had flogged him with thongs to the end of which were attached pieces of metal. On the second occasion they had held his feet over a brazier. They wanted the

194

names of his fellow-conspirators, and every time they asked him he recited the names of the angels. The last time, he had got as far as Galgaliel before collapsing.

The Zealot shifted his weight carefully to his elbow. He was forced to spend most of the time lying on his side.

'My son, I shall be tortured again in any case. They don't need an excuse.'

'But it's horrible!' Demetrius said. The thought of any more pieces being gouged, burnt or torn from that tormented body made him feel ill with pity and revulsion.

The Zealot studied him. 'A very Greek remark', he said. Demetrius flushed.

'Well', said the Zealot, 'you could not be expected to understand.'

True, thought Demetrius. He did not and never would understand. There were things that could not be understood by thinking about them. It was a question of where you belonged. He did not hear what the Zealot heard – the land's lament in his blood.

He said irritably, 'You people don't want to be understood.'

'You're quite right', said the Zealot. 'We want to be left alone. We have our own task to do. And since we have God, why should we need other people?'

'But you could have peace as well', objected Demetrius.

'Ah, not in these times. The price is too high.'

Demetrius sighed. Heroism was another of the things that could not be understood unless you felt them.

'So you prefer to die?' he said.

'If you weren't young enough to be my grandson, I would find that question an insult.'

'But it's pointless!' protested Demetrius. 'What can you achieve? How can you fight the empire? You'll be crushed like ... like ...'

'Grapes in a winepress', suggested the Zealot, and smiled.

Demetrius recognised that smile: he had seen it on many faces, but it was always the same. It was utterly private, it implied the possession of some treasure beyond the comprehension of ordinary men, and it meant that there was no point in pursuing the argument further.

He said nothing. The silence extended and took on a quality of peacefulness, and he saw that the Zealot was asleep.

The town of Ptolemais was pleasantly situated at the northern

195

end of the long, shallowly scooped bay that bit into the otherwise unyielding coastline. The natural shelter thus afforded to vessels had been increased by the building of two moles, extending south and east from the shore, to form a good deep-water harbour. Ptolemais was the port for Rome, and the trading centre for the fertile plain behind it. A forgotten king of Egypt had given it its name, and a vividly remembered king of Judaea endowed it with a fine gymnasium. Simon Magus brought to it his new religion, and – bent to new purposes – his ancient magic.

Strolling along the harbour wall one morning a few days after his arrival, he noticed at the shoreward end of one of the two moles a strange circular tower. It was about thirty feet high and ten in diameter, built of large limestone blocks interrupted by a series of rectangular openings set in an ascending spiral. There was an open doorway at the bottom. Curious, Simon went closer. The lintel above the doorway bore a carved inscription in Latin to the goddess of fortune, and the single cognomen 'Felix'. Inside, a circular stone stairway ran round the circumference to the top, which was open to the sky.

He stepped back and studied it. It was badly sited for defence, and the embrasures were definitely windows and not arrow-slits, being much too wide for safety. The tower could have no military purpose. Nor could he see what other purpose it might serve.

He enquired about it in the town, and was told that it had been built by a prosperous citizen, now deceased, as a monument to himself and in honour of the fortune which he said had blessed him without his doing anything to deserve it. He had bequeathed the tower in his will to his fellow-citizens, with a prophecy that anyone who could find an appropriate use for it would be the cleverest man in the town and would, as an inevitable result of his cleverness, meet with a bad end. The citizens, nonplussed, had held a few not very successful parties in it, but in general, not wanting to come to a bad end, left it alone. The stonework, lacking any protection at the top, was beginning to bulge, and in time the whole thing would fall down as a vindication of Felix's belief in the meaninglessness of life.

Simon chuckled. He went back to the tower and looked at it again. A pointless building, a shell enclosing nothing, dedicated to the injustice of chance, yet many-windowed, open to the sky ... It touched his imagination. He looked long at it, and he saw in it a meaning.

196

He put it about that if the citizens would assemble outside the tower the following evening an hour after dusk they would be shown the answer to Felix's riddle, and a mystery greater than all riddles.

The next evening the shopkeepers locked up their shops early, the theatre was deserted and the taverns were empty. A gossiping, expectant crowd spilled along the harbour front. A party of young wits had installed themselves on the top of the tower with a flagon of wine. Simon invited them to stay if they wished to be the subject of a magical experiment, and they came down quickly.

It took some time to persuade the onlookers to arrange themselves in a ring around the tower: most of them were convinced that something was going to happen in front of the doorway, and at first refused to take their eyes from it. When, finally, he had his circle of spectators, each having full view of at least two windows, Simon beckoned Helen out of the crowd. She was veiled, and wearing a dark cloak. She accompanied him into the tower and up the staircase, Simon carrying a large torch which he had borrowed from someone in the crowd.

Where the staircase ended in a small platform just below the top of the tower, Simon removed Helen's veil so that her long hair tumbled free. He lifted the cloak from her shoulders, and the crowd murmured at a robe of gauzy, silvery fabric glinting almost white in the torchlight.

'You are about to witness a miracle', Simon called down to them. 'You will see an impossible thing. Keep your eyes on the windows, and do not move from where you are.'

Both he and Helen disappeared from view. What happened next was violently disputed in the town for years to come. For each person in that crowd saw, at the same moment, at every window, the same thing. A woman with long hair that gleamed palely in the moonlight, a woman holding a torch that cast its rays on the decaying stonework and the astonished faces of the onlookers, leaned, at the same moment, out of twelve windows of a circular tower.

After the initial bewildered silence there was a buzz of excitement.

'What's happening? I can see her at three windows!'

'She's over there as well.'

'There's a mirror inside the tower.'

'One mirror? More like ten.'

'How can it be a mirror, you fool, when we can see her face?'

Simon appeared again, alone, at the top of the tower, and the multiple apparition vanished. He raised his hand in a vain attempt to silence the crowd.

'What you have seen', he shouted, 'was not a trick with mirrors. There are no mirrors. Come inside and look. What you have seen is an illusion and also a truth. If you want to hear the explanation of this mystery, of how a single light can be dispersed in many places, come to the waterfront tomorrow morning. I will tell you the meaning of what you have seen, and I will tell you what you are.'

It was a day and half's journey on foot from Joppa to Caesarea. Since the donkey Kepha was riding had to keep pace with the man who was walking beside the camel, the journey took a day and a half, and was probably more tiring than a journey on foot would have been. The donkey was bony, and Kepha's muscles, accustomed to bracing themselves to the rise and fall of a boat, adjusted badly to a rhythm which seemed to consist mainly of an irregular series of jolts administered to the base of the spine. The camel resented the presence of the donkey and periodically attempted to savage it. At these moments the donkey, displaying a nimbleness not otherwise apparent, would spring sideways, dart in a semicircle and try to nip the camel's rear. The camel-driver would bring his whip down in quick succession on the camel's flank and the donkey's muzzle, and the journey would resume.

Kepha, when this happened for the fifth time, began to doubt the wisdom of volunteering for the trip. He had imagined he would be doing the camel-driver a service: the man maintained that he could not, single-handed, drive two such ill-matched animals the thirty miles to Caesarea. Moreover the heated conversation on the subject which Kepha had overheard in the bazaar had come with such strange clarity to his ears, had been at the same time so discordant with his thoughts and so close to them, that he had taken it as something meant for him. Well, there were signs and there were mistakes. And as for helping the camel-driver, he was sure that his only contribution had been to increase the donkey's bad temper.

By the time they arrived at the city Kepha was too tired to feel anything but profound gratitude that the jolting, jumping and nipping were about to end. They delivered the camel with its load of rugs to a warehouse, and the camel-driver, with a curt word of thanks, took charge of the donkey. Kepha wandered off down the street, stretching his aching limbs, automatically taking the direction in which he sensed the sea to lie. He walked for about half a mile, then, turning a corner, stopped in amazement.

He had heard of the great harbour of Caesarea, of course; who had not? But he had believed the stories to be exaggeration. There had been no exaggeration. From where he stood he could see, curving out into the sea beyond the masts of the anchored ships, a wide breakwater from which rose a series of massive defensive towers, and, at either side of the harbour mouth itself, a group of gigantic figures carved in stone.

His eye, following the curve of the sea wall, came back to the line of houses which interrupted his view of the northern end of the harbour, and he became aware of the huge building that stood on rising ground a short distance to his right. He stared at it for some time, awed by its size, dazzled by the sunlight glancing off the polished blocks of stone and the bronze panels, before he realised what it was. The temple of the emperor-made-god, the great profanity. It contained, they said, two of the largest statues in the world: one of the emperor himself, the other of a woman representing Rome. Sited so that it would be visible many miles offshore, it proclaimed to land and sea and to all races its message of pagan superstition and temporal obedience; and it had been built by a man who called himself a Jew.

Kepha walked back slowly in the direction he had come. He did not want to look at the harbour, or the temple, or any of the other wonders of the city. This was no place for him. A great weariness possessed him, and a desolate certainty that he had done everything wrong for so long that he no longer had any chance of getting anything right.

He passed the warehouse and walked on, with no idea where he was going. Eventually he saw in the distance the familiar outlines of a synagogue, and quickened his step. There was home, of a kind, in a pagan city. There were ancient rituals which comforted, and a God who had no need of statues.

But when he reached the place he found a violent altercation going on outside. Kepha heard the words 'depravity', 'filth' and 'hypocrite' hurled back and forth in the small crowd, but before he had a chance to discover what the argument was about he saw a face he recognised – young Marcus, once a regular attender of their meetings in Jerusalem, whose family, he now remembered, lived here.

Kepha had no time to decide whether he wanted to see Marcus or not. Marcus threw himself at him.

'Kepha, Kepha! Thank God you've come!'

'Now look', said Kepha, 'there's something ...'

'Thank God, thank God. I have been *praying* ... Kepha, something absolutely dreadful is happening in this town.'

'The man is in the grip of Satan', said Jacob the Pious. 'I have always suspected it. He aims at nothing less than the overthrow of religion.'

'Perhaps', suggested John bar Zabdai, 'his idea of religion is not the same as yours.'

Jacob threw him a sharp look.

'As ours', amended John bar Zabdai.

'The principles of religion', said Jacob the Pious, 'are very simple, and anyone who has *ideas* about them is a heretic.'

'You're a harsh man, Jacob.'

'So is a farmer when he weeds his crop.'

'I seem to remember', mused John, 'that Joshua said something about that. He told us to let them grow together, the crop and the weeds, until the harvest.'

'Joshua', said Jacob, 'never grew a row of beans in his life.'

There was a pause, broken by the click of Jacob's fingernails in pursuit of lice. The lice had had a thin time lately: Jacob had taken to killing them in moments of preoccupation, and in the past weeks he had been increasingly preoccupied.

He glanced up at John irritably. 'Well, what do you suggest? That we let him carry on like it?'

'It's too late. The men you sent to Antioch have already spoken to Saul's converts.'

'The men *we* sent to Antioch. Really, John, do you refuse to take any responsibility at all? Perhaps you'd like to go off and join Kepha.'

John shifted his position and reached for the bowl of ñuts in the middle of the floor. He chewed thoughtfully.

'I'm sorry', he said at last. 'I don't mean to leave you with all the responsibility. But I'm afraid I don't regard the matter in such a serious light as you.'

'Circumcision was a commandment given to Abraham and has been carried out on every Jewish male and every male convert ever since, and you do not regard it as *serious*?'

John stared at the floor. 'Of course it's serious', he said. 'But I can't believe that it's more important than a man's soul'.

'You aren't required to believe anything so nonsensical. All you're required to believe is that it's necessary to salvation.'

John chewed another mouthful of nuts. He said nothing.

'You surely *do* believe that?' demanded Jacob.

'I don't know', said John.

'You don't *know?*'

'Joshua always warned us against attaching a lot of importance to the external observance of the Law.'

'Joshua – ' Jacob's face contorted and he bit back the rest of the sentence. John wondered what Jacob had been about to say and realised he would never know. It crossed his mind sometimes that Jacob still hated his brother. He pushed the idea away, shocked that he was capable of thinking it.

'Joshua', resumed Jacob evenly, 'was quite right to assert that the spirit of the Law is more important than the letter. He cannot possibly have meant that the Law should be broken.' He fixed John with a stare. 'Can he?'

'No', said John.

'And Saul, by omitting to circumcise his heathen converts, is in breach of the Law.'

'Of course he is', said John, 'but if he insisted on them being circumcised they probably wouldn't become converts.'

'Then if they're as frivolous as that, he has no business talking to them in the first place.'

Jacob's verdict was delivered with finality. John realised that the subject was closed. He looked at Jacob, toying absently with the fringes of his matted beard, and saw that the furrow between his eyebrows had become deeply etched. It came to him that Jacob was a lonely man.

John pushed the bowl of nuts towards him in mute sympathy.

'No thank you', said Jacob. 'They get into the holes in my teeth. I have constant trouble with toothache as it is.'

'It's not my concern', said Kepha.

He had been saying it at intervals for the past twenty-four hours, mostly to Marcus. He now said it to himself, as Marcus had declined to accompany him beyond the corner where he had pointed out the centurion's house. 'I'm sure you understand', Marcus had excused himself. 'I have to live here.'

'And I should never have come here', growled Kepha to the absent Marcus.

After all, it was *not* his concern. The officer was a heathen. Admittedly he was or had been a sympathiser, giving money to the synagogue and receiving instruction in the faith. But he had not been received into it. He was a heathen, and if he got up to heathen practices that was only to be expected.

But Marcus had said that what went on in the house was far worse than the usual heathen idolatry. 'Terrible things', Marcus had said, averting his eyes. 'I can't tell you. *Orgies*. They eat ...' He had shuddered, and left the sentence unfinished.

What, wondered Kepha as he approached the house, could they possibly eat? What they normally ate was bad enough. Pig's flesh, squirming things out of the sea ... He was going to have to walk into that place of uncleanness, from whose imagined sights and smells his senses already revolted ... And for what? An excitable boy who thought he had discovered a plot to corrupt the world. Well, let it be corrupted. The innocent were safe.

Kepha stood with his hand on the gate, and there flashed into his mind a remembered face, linked with a forgotten name. Were the innocent safe? Why had the leather-worker in Joppa been so dismayed to see him?

He knocked on the gate. There was no sound of life. He raised the latch and went into the courtyard.

A large house, the courtyard elegantly laid out with seats, shrubs and fountains. The centurion had private means besides his army pay. No lights in the house although it was growing dark. Yet standing there, motionless, his scalp prickling, Kepha heard voices. The voices seemed to come from a shuttered window to his left. He moved towards it, trying to make no noise on the stone paving, and, examining the shutters, saw that where he would expect to see a line of faint light between them, there was blackness. Something had been hung on the inside of the shutters to ensure that no one could see anything that went on within.

He listened. The voices had now ceased, but he could hear movement in the room.

He became conscious, first, of the ridiculousness of his position, and then of its danger. If he were discovered he would be hauled straight to prison without even the formality of questions. Or the servants would simply beat him to a pulp.

But where were the servants? The house seemed deserted except for the shuttered room where presumably one of Marcus's orgies was in progress. Did servants take part in orgies? Surely not. The more likely explanation was that whatever was going on in the room was so appalling that the servants had been sent out for the evening. In which case the house would be locked.

Kepha took off his sandals and walked to the front door. He tried it. It was locked.

'It is not my business', hissed Kepha angrily through his teeth.

He walked round the house until he found a small window in an inconspicuous corner shaded by a bush. It was shuttered, but the gap between the shutters was wide enough for the insertion of a knife blade. Kepha took his gutting knife out of his belt. The latch holding the shutters lifted easily and almost silently. He pushed the shutters back and heaved himself on to the window-sill.

'I'm getting too old for this', he muttered.

He wriggled through, dropped down on the other side and found himself in the kitchen. Chicken carcases, mollusc shells and gnawed bones to which scraps of pale flesh still adhered lay in a mound on the table. Fighting down his nausea he walked through to a passageway. As he paused to orient himself he heard the voices start again, in what seemed to be a chant. He followed the sound along the passageway past several rooms, and came to a door through which he could hear the voices distinctly.

He stood there for a time, not with the intention of listening, because what came to his ears made no sense. He realised afterwards that he must have been praying, but the clearest thought in his mind as he opened the door was that he had left his sandals outside.

He opened the door, and went into the room.

Dark. Heavy with some unnatural smell. A brazier at the far end. Couches round the walls, and on the couches . . .

'Lord God', cried Kepha, 'didst Thou smite Sodom, and dost Thou permit this?'

The writhing on the couches ceased abruptly. Thirty pairs of eyes stared at him in petrified astonishment.

'Come Satan', roared Kepha, 'and claim your own. Truly the kingdom of Hell is established on the earth. Oh, that the heavens might fall and wipe this sight from my eyes. Lord God, if Thou seest, send forth Thy thunder – '

'What on earth do you think you're doing here?' demanded the man at the far end of the room.

' – crush this place of abomination into the ground, burn it utterly with the fire of Thy wrath. Let not one stone remain upon another, nor spare from Thy holy indignation the last of these children of iniquity.'

Kepha stopped for breath. In the silence no one moved. Nothing happened.

'Your god', observed the man at the end of the room, 'seems to be the only person who has not heard you. You have interrupted a religious rite, and I presume that you have broken into the house. I suggest you get out of here before we kill you.'

'Kill me', said Kepha.

There was a pause.

'Kill him', said the man at the end of the room.

Half a dozen young men – so young, Kepha thought sadly, they could be his sons – leapt from their couches and rushed at him. They grabbed him clumsily. Their clumsiness, Kepha thought, had something to do with the fact that they were naked and he was not. Having grabbed him, they seemed uncertain what to do next.

'Tie him up', said one.

There was a hunt for something to tie him with. Eventually a silk girdle was produced and used to tie his hands behind his back. It was the most expensive article of clothing he had ever worn.

Having tied his hands, they looked at each other doubtfully. Since he was not resisting there seemed no point in tying his feet, and in any case to tie his feet they would have had to look for another girdle and also sit him on the floor, which, since he was not resisting and they were going to kill him anyway, would have seemed silly.

'What do we do now?' muttered one of them.

'Kill him,' muttered another.

'What with?' muttered a third.

They looked over their shoulders uneasily, as if expecting to see a sword stuck in the wall.

'In my belt you will find a knife', said Kepha. 'But be careful, it's very sharp. I use it for gutting fish.'

The grip on his shoulders relaxed a little, as if weakened by incredulity. No one attempted to take the knife out of his belt.

'Who are you?' asked the man at the end of the room.

'I am known as Kepha', said Kepha, 'and I am the guardian of the Key of the Kingdom of Heaven.'

It was as if he had dropped a stone into a deep well, and while the ripples spread out sideways and the sound rose to the ears of those above, the stone itself continued downward on its invisible, disturbing journey.

'He's mad', said someone at last.

'Bring him here', said the man at the end of the room.

Kepha was brought. He looked into intelligent, angry eyes that were clouded with confusion.

'Are you the centurion Cornelius?' he enquired.

'I ask the questions, not you. Why have you illegally entered this house?'

'I apologise for that', said Kepha. 'It seemed the right thing to do at the time. I got in through the kitchen window, it was badly secured. You ought to do something about it. You *are* Cornelius?'

The centurion seemed to be wrestling inwardly with some gigantic mental obstacle. He gave up finally. 'Yes', he said, 'I am Cornelius.'

'Good. I came to see you.'

'I don't know you. And I don't normally talk to madmen.'

'I'm not mad', said Kepha. 'Just hasty, so they tell me.'

'You are in your right mind? And you have the key to the kingdom of heaven?'

'I do.'

'You don't look as if you have the key to your own front door.'

'Quite true', said Kepha. 'I have no possessions except my clothes and my fishing knife.'

'I *could* have you killed, you know.'

'Of course you could', said Kepha. 'It would solve nothing at all, except possibly for me. They say in the town that you used to be a good man, a religious man. What happened?'

'There is no such thing as goodness, there is only truth,' said the centurion impatiently. 'And I am still a religious man.'

'You call *this* religion?'

'If you can give me a single reason why I should answer your questions, I will answer them.'

'I will give you a reason', said Kepha, 'but you must allow me to talk for a few minutes first. And it would help if you would be so kind as to untie my hands.'

The centurion hesitated. Then he shrugged. A man came forward and untied Kepha's hands.

'Thank you', said Kepha. 'It's dark in here, isn't it? Do you mind if I ...?'

He lit several candles from the brazier and set them in holders. Thirty pairs of eyes watched him, bemused. Thirty pairs of hands moved automatically to cover private parts from the suddenly increased light.

'There are things that should be done in darkness and things that should be done in the light', said Kepha, 'and I can see that you know which is which. And there are things which should not be done at all, which you also know, but someone has bewitched you. God has sent me here. I do not know what god you worship, but the God I worship lives in light, and light was the first thing He made. I want to tell you about Him.'

He had never felt surer. He preached for an hour, the eyes fixed on him, and he saw their expression change gradually from suspicion to guarded interest, and in one or two he saw even the flash of eagerness that always made his heart leap, because it meant that another soul had begun its stumbling path along the Way. Sensing that they were ready, he began then to speak to them of Joshua, and as he spoke he felt as though his heart would burst with pity for them and love for his master and grief for his own dereliction. Tears gathered in his eyes and fell like rain, and there were tears in the eyes that watched him.

He raised his arms and began a passionate prayer for those around him, and as he stood thus, arms outstretched and face turned to Heaven, he felt the grace, the love, the illimitable power streaming into him, renewing and transforming, streaming in and in until he was full and overflowing and the power streamed from him outwards, outwards, to fill every corner of the room and lift on its gigantic wave all those souls to God.

He was not aware at first of what was taking place. It was a series of ecstatic screams that recalled him to himself. He saw then that the room was in tumult. His attentive audience was weeping, howling, laughing, jerking in uncontrollable bodily spasms, babbling and screaming and shouting in unintelligible tongues, in the wildest manifestation of the Spirit Kepha had ever witnessed. He stared around him, momentarily paralysed with shock.

The Spirit had come.

And these people were not even ...

There was only one thing he could do. He went to the kitchen, found a pitcher of water, and baptised them.

'How long do you think we've been here?' asked the Zealot.

206

'I don't know', said Demetrius. He had long ago lost track of the days. From time to time he made an effort and started again, breaking the straw of his bedding into short pieces and laying one piece aside every morning, but after a while he would forget to do it, or the jailer would kick the little pile of straw pieces back into the bed, and in any case the days he had not counted now far outnumbered the days he had, and in the end he gave up altogether.

'Six months?' he suggested. 'A year? Ten years?'

It was a poor enough joke, but the Zealot smiled. 'In the reckoning of the Holy One, a thousand years are but a day', he said.

'I don't find that very helpful', said Demetrius.

'No? Well, you're young.'

Demetrius had grown used to having most of what he said dismissed on the grounds either that he was Greek or that he was young. He had decided not to resent it, since there was no point in resenting it. In any case, he and the Zealot did not often talk. The Zealot spent most of his time sleeping, praying, staring into space or declaiming, and disliked being interrupted in any of these activities. Demetrius had discovered in himself unsuspected talents for sleeping and staring into space. He did not pray. He had made a stony resolution that he would never pray again.

The Zealot astonished him by his next remark.

'I have a feeling that I shan't be here much longer. If you're going to tell me about yourself you'd better start now.'

Demetrius blinked. 'Why . . .?'

'Never mind', said the Zealot. 'Talk to me.'

Demetrius pushed the straw around with his foot and found his mind utterly blank.

'Well,' prompted the Zealot, 'where were you born?'

'I don't know', said Demetrius. 'My mother was a slave. She died when I was two years old. I was brought up with the children of the other slaves. That was in Cilicia, but I think my mother came from Thrace. I don't know where I was born. I don't even know what my mother's name was.'

The Zealot was looking at him as if seeing him for the first time. 'I suppose', he said, 'it would be silly to enquire what your father's name was?'

'Very silly', said Demetrius.

'How old are you?'

'I was just sixteen when I was arrested.'

'Sixteen? And for sixteen years you haven't known who you are

207

or where you come from? To me that is . . .' the Zealot searched for a word, 'unimaginable.'

'Yes,' said Demetrius. 'It must be very comforting to know where you come from.'

'And how did you leave Cilicia?'

'The master of the house died and everything was sold up. We were all bought by a trader. He took us down to Berytus and sold us in the market. I was bought by' – Demetrius smiled wanly – 'a magician'.

'A magician! What was his name?'

'Simon of Gitta.'

'Never heard of him', said the Zealot with finality.

'He was very famous. He could fly.'

'Nobody can fly.'

'Simon could. He could do all sorts of things. I used to help him sometimes.' There was a faint note of pride in Demetrius's voice. He began to describe his years with Simon, the marvellous and terrifying sights he had seen, the strange places, the noble patrons . . . It became, as he elaborated it, a good story. He added a few touches of his own, and left out the things which were disagreeable, or discreditable, or which he had simply not understood.

'I don't believe a word of it', said the Zealot eventually. 'But you tell it well. You must have been fond of him, your mad master. Why did you run away?'

'I didn't run away.'

'He sold you? He was a fool.'

'No', said Demetrius. '*He* ran away.'

'What?'

'He disappeared one night. Took some money and just vanished.'

The Zealot yawned. 'Why? Were the authorities after him?'

'No more so than usual', said Demetrius. 'No, it was something else. Something strange happened. I could never work it out. I went back to them afterwards to try and find out, but all they would say was that he was a wicked man and I was better off without him.' He paused thoughtfully. 'He wasn't wicked really. They were just different sorts of people.'

'Who were?' asked the Zealot sleepily.

Demetrius fiddled with the straw, winding it in spirals round his finger. It was two years ago, perhaps more, but he had never made up his mind what he thought about the episode.

'Have you ever heard', he asked, 'of a sect who call themselves the People of the Way?'

There was a long, meditative silence, and then the Zealot snored convulsively.

'Sidon is much pleasanter than Tyre', observed Simon as they watched the·crowd gather in the adjacent square. 'You were quite right not to want to go back there.'

'It was you who didn't want to go back to Tyre', objected Helen.

'Nonsense', said Simon. 'You distinctly said – '

'Ah well', sighed Helen, 'I suppose I may have forgotten saying it.'

Simon nodded, with a satisfaction that was general. His preaching was finding many hearers. He was not sure that they entirely understood it, but that was to be expected; a message so radical would take time to grasp. Meanwhile, they practised it with alacrity. In half a dozen towns he had left vigorous, well-instructed cells of converts. The groups were small, but they would grow, attracting and absorbing selected members of the community. Selection was important: it was not a creed for the dull-witted or frivolous. The groups would grow, spreading their tentacles of subversion among the influential and the rich, the businessmen and the teachers, the philosophers and politicians, the men who ran the army and thence, creeping upward, the men who . . .

'No, no', Simon rebuked himself, on the edge of a dizzying dream. The world would not be turned upside down in a day.

Nevertheless he was beginning to think that a work which he had believed would take many lifetimes might be accomplished in his own.

The square was filling up steadily. He had promised to perform a miracle. They listened to his preaching, but they came to see his magic. It was human nature. His fame had preceded him along the coast, and as soon as he set foot in a place he was besieged by requests for signs and wonders. What had begun as a flight into obscurity had turned into a triumphal progress.

He would not let it turn his head, as fame had turned it once before. But he made certain concessions to his celebrity. He now wore, for public occasions, a robe of white linen richly embroidered with gold thread. Helen's robe was similar, but with silver. Each of them wore a thin circlet round the temples: his of gold, Helen's of silver. 'Symbolic of the twin lights, the sun and moon', he explained to wide-eyed followers.

The crowd milled and murmured, colourful in the bright after-noon sun.

'Shall we go down?' he said.

'This is a crisis', pronounced Jacob the Pious.

'You must have expected it', said John bar Zabdai.

'I wish you'd stop saying that', snapped Jacob. He stroked his beard to soothe himself, and, when it failed to soothe him, caught and despatched a louse instead. In a calmer voice, he said, 'Of course I expected it. Not only did I expect it, but I welcome it.'

'Ah', said John bar Zabdai.

'It is a blessing in disguise. It will be a great opportunity. It will strengthen us. It will clear the air.'

'It will be extremely difficult', said John bar Zabdai.

'Yes', said Jacob. He killed another louse.

'When is he coming?' enquired John.

'I don't know. With Saul, one never knows anything. If he stops to see all his friends on the way he won't be here for a year. On the other hand he might arrive tomorrow.'

'That *would* be a blessing in disguise', murmured John. He had not met Saul, he had only heard the stories. He discounted two-thirds of what he was told as being gossip inspired by envy, fear or malice. The remaining third still presented a character not far removed from the demonic. John looked forward to making the acquaintance of a man who at a distance of three hundred miles was capable of making Jacob nervous, but he deemed it unwise to say so.

'Well', said Jacob with unconvincing breeziness, 'we shall be ready for him.'

'Yes', said John.

'He will say that we interfered with his community, which is quite untrue. All our people did was to point out that his converts were not members of the brotherhood until they'd been circum-cised. No one can argue with that. I shall tell him – '

'Why be so defensive?' asked John. 'Surely you, as acting head of the Jerusalem community, should be asking *him* to account for his actions?'

'And I shall. Make no mistake. I shall.'

There was a slightly uneasy silence. The unease was Jacob's. His eyes shifted around the room as if looking for something.

'"Acting" head?' he repeated.

210

'No offence meant', said John.

'You are a subtle man', said Jacob, 'although one wouldn't think it. You would have made a good lawyer.'

'Thank you.'

'You're right, I suppose. He may not be much more than a figurehead, but we need Kepha.'

'He might be anywhere', John pointed out. 'For all we know he might be dead.'

'He isn't dead. I shall know when Kepha is dead. And wherever he is, he'll have to come back. We'll just have to find him,' said Jacob.

Kepha stood on the plain with the sea at his back and looked at the hills where he was born. They were green hills, not the bare stony highlands of the south: hills forested with oak and sycamore and fresh with flowers, hills where even in the height of summer you could find a stream to slake your thirst. He knew them with the same unthinking intimacy as he knew his own body. He could have gone straight to the spot where as a boy he had robbed a bird's nest and then, remorseful, returned the eggs, and found them months later rotten, the nest abandoned. He had not looked at these hills for fifteen years.

He felt a perverse sadness that they did not move him as he had expected. He had been almost afraid to return to this landscape, and if it had not been for the search that brought him here he would not have returned. But the past, instead of surging upon him, held aloof. He had no desire to climb the ridge in the distance and look down on the Lake. He had no wish to see his village. And after fifteen years, it was scarcely reasonable even to think of seeing his wife.

Elizabeth. Sharp-tongued and generous-hearted, and always worried about money. He had given her little of what she was entitled to expect from a husband. There had not been time. And now, again, there was not time. Perhaps one day there would be time, and he would go back.

He turned to continue his journey. The town was a few miles ahead. As he walked – it was strange that since he had known his destination there had been no more offers of help, and he had been walking for days – his eyes dwelt on the great sweep of the bay and the little harbour jutting into the northern end of it. It looked tiny from this distance, dwarfed by the horizon, but no doubt it would do well enough when a storm blew up from the west.

It was to the harbour he went first when he reached the town. A waterfront was one of the best places to pick up gossip. He sat thankfully on a bollard near the breakwater, and, after a few minutes, found his gaze constantly attracted to a curious stone tower to his left. Something about it perplexed him. He wondered what it was for.

He had intended, as soon as he found a likely person to question, to come straight to the point. But to his surprise he found himself asking about the tower instead.

'Interesting you should say that', said the carpenter, laying down his hammer without reluctance. 'If you'd come a while back I'd have said it was just a bit of nonsense, waste of good stone. But last month there was something so peculiar happen in that tower – I saw it with my own eyes, so don't think I'm spinning you a yarn – '

'It doesn't really matter', said Kepha. 'I don't want to take up your time ...'

'Time? Bless you, this is the off season. Last month, in that tower –it was night, mind, but still I saw what I saw, and there's plenty of others saw it too – there was a woman, holding a torch, long golden hair she had, not braided, it looked beautiful, and she leaned out of that window – '

'Which window?' asked Kepha.

'That's the *point*, don't you see? She leaned out of *all* of them!'

'What's so extraordinary about that?'

'She leaned out of twelve windows', explained the carpenter with great patience, 'at exactly the same moment!'

'It's very kind of you to stop work on my account', said Kepha, 'but I really must ...'

'And the man who was with her, he said if we'd all come to the same place the next morning he'd tell us what it was all about. Something about light, he said, in different places. I didn't bother to – '

'What was his name?' asked Kepha sharply.

'Well, as I say, I didn't go in the morning, so I never found out any more about it, but I gather he was some sort of magician. Mind you, I reckon it was done with mirrors.'

'Where can I find him?' demanded Kepha.

'Oh, bless you, they aren't here now. Only stayed a few days. Went on up the coast, I heard. Tyre or Sidon you'll probably find them. Friend of yours, is he?'

*

'When they come for you', said the Zealot, 'don't tell them that your master ran away.'

It was a strange utterance with which to break nearly a day of silence. Demetrius tried unsuccessfully to imagine in what regions the Zealot's mind had been wandering before it came to rest at this point.

'Why not?' he asked.

'They won't believe you. They'll think you're being insolent. If there's one thing the *Kittim* can't bear, it's insolence. Secretly they believe they're inferior.' He smiled. 'They are, of course.'

'Will they come for me?' murmured Demetrius. He had been here so long that he had begun to believe he would always be here. Why should they remember him? He was not important.

'They never forget anything', said the Zealot.

Demetrius's stomach went cold.

'They will come for me quite soon', said the Zealot. He propped himself on his elbow. His back was healing, but the soles of his feet still suppurated. He had to crawl on his knees and his good arm to use the bucket in the corner. He refused Demetrius's help.

'How do you know?' said Demetrius.

'I've had a dream.'

Demetrius waited, but the Zealot did not elaborate.

'It doesn't matter', said the Zealot. 'I have five sons.'

That quiet statement, with its pride, its certainty and its huge unspoken assumptions, plunged Demetrius into a sea of self-pity. His eyes smarted. He blinked, hoping the Zealot had not seen.

'It must be very hard to have no family', remarked the Zealot.

Demetrius bit his lip.

'Oh, come on', said the Zealot roughly. 'You're a man.'

'I've never belonged anywhere,' sniffed Demetrius.

'All the better. You belong everywhere.'

'Not here.'

The Zealot glanced round the filthy cell.

'In your country', explained Demetrius.

'Ah. Well, that's a different matter. You couldn't expect to belong *here*. Unless, of course ... But then, why should you want to convert? People do from time to time, but I've never seen the point. It can't be the same.'

'I thought about it once', said Demetrius.

'You did? You never told me.'

'I tried to,' said Demetrius, 'but you went to sleep.'

213

'Sorry. Age, my boy.'

'It was in Sebaste', said Demetrius.

'Sebaste? Those half-caste, idolatrous ...'

'No, no. They were good people, they lived very simply. There was a man called Philip, who healed cripples. Well, he couldn't heal all of them, but he healed a lot. And he talked ... I used to like to listen to him. Simon came too, but that was before ... They were very kind,' said Demetrius. 'Most of the time, anyway. They said love was the most important thing. They called it The Way.'

It was hardly less of a jumble than it had been at the time.

'I've heard of them', said the Zealot. 'Their leader was executed, and they've been tying themselves in knots trying to explain it ever since.'

'Well yes, it was rather a muddle actually', said Demetrius.

'Is that why you didn't join them? Or wouldn't your master let you?'

'Yes. No. I mean, he was going to join them himself. But then he disappeared, and I went back to them for a time', said Demetrius, confused again.

'You went back?'

'For a few months. I lived with them. Then I left.'

'Why?'

'Because ...' What could he say? The real reason was impossible to divulge. 'It wasn't for me', he said. 'I didn't fit in.'

'What you mean', said the Zealot, 'is you didn't want to be circumcised.'

Demetrius flushed. The Zealot laughed. As Demetrius's discomfort grew, the Zealot threw back his head and laughed and laughed with merriment. Demetrius sat, crimson-faced, his fists clenched with anger.

'Oh, my boy,' said the Zealot eventually. 'I'm sorry. But it is such a small operation.'

'I know', said Demetrius sullenly. He pushed the straw around with his foot. He became conscious of the silence, and of the Zealot watching him. He smelt suddenly the stench of the cell, and his own stench. It was the smell of futility.

'I'm a coward', he said.

There was a pause, and then the Zealot said, 'No, you are not.'

Demetrius heard the words with incredulity.

'You simply haven't found your courage, that's all,' said the Zealot.

'Found it? How do I find it?' Demetrius was bitter. '*Where* can I find it?'

'I don't know. In this place, perhaps.'

Demetrius looked around him. Nothing on which his eye rested inspired him with the smallest spark of defiance.

'Where do you get your courage from?' he whispered.

'From God.' The Zealot paused. 'And sometimes from despair. When everything has gone, there comes ... a kind of anger. Like a wind in the desert. It is strong, very strong. But it cannot be bidden. It is a wind, a spirit.'

Demetrius was silent for a while. He stared at his feet. But his feet, as he stared at them, became the scorched and suppurating feet of the Zealot. He covered his face with his hands.

'But it may be for nothing!' he cried.

'Nothing! Oh, my son, lift up your eyes!' The Zealot's face was alight with a strange joy. He began to recite again, his voice rising in a slow crescendo.

'Where were you when I laid the foundations of the earth? Tell me, if you can. Who arranged its dimensions and measured it? On what do its pillars rest? Do you know who laid its cornerstone, when the stars of the morning sang in chorus and the sons of God shouted for joy?

'Have you called up the dawn, or shown the morning its place? Have you taught the day to grasp the fringes of the earth and bring up the horizon like clay under a seal when the light of the Dog Star dims? Have you gone down to the springs of the sea or walked in the deep?

'Have you seen the gates of death and the doorkeepers of the House of Darkness? Have you understood how vast is the world?'

His eyes burned into Demetrius. 'We are so small, my son. So small. And with our tiny measuring rod we try to parcel out the purposes of God. We cannot know anything. We can only endure. And that endurance is part of a purpose. You cannot believe that. Then you must believe that endurance, long and steadfastly continued, will create a purpose. A purpose out of nothing. There is a heroism for you: Greek enough, I think.'

He smiled. His smile did not falter as the door was flung open and two soldiers entered. They picked him up, become somehow small and rag-like in their arms, and carried him to the doorway. As he was taken through it he turned his head and looked back for a moment.

'May God go with you', said Demetrius.

'Tripolis', murmured Simon. 'A pleasant-sounding name. Meaning 'The Three Towns', of course.'

'I do know Greek', said Helen.

Simon glanced at her sideways as she stood with him on the rostrum. He sometimes detected in the manifestation of the Holy Spirit a very unspiritual tetchiness.

'Excuse my presumption', he said. 'It comes of always having known more than anyone else around me. Are you getting tired of travelling?'

'Yes', said Helen.

'When we've finished here we'll go up to Antioch and stay for a while. I'm getting a bit tired of it too.'

He was: constant movement from place to place no longer exhilarated him. His progress through the coastal towns was a task, where once it would have been an adventure. Something had gone: perhaps it was danger. Or perhaps he was getting old.

His power, though, did not wane. He was more sure of it than he had ever been. He owed that to her. Or did he, he wondered. Perhaps it would have come back anyway.

He surveyed the crowd below him. Crowds were much the same everywhere. One had turned against him once. This crowd would not.

He stepped forward, and the people stilled. He kept the preliminaries to a minimum. After he had woven his magic, they would let him talk for hours.

'Men and women of Tripolis', he cried, 'I bid you welcome to a feast.'

Faintly on the air came music. Heads turned, seeking the source of it, but finding none. Then a low ripple of wonder spread through the square.

In the roped-off space to which he directed their attention there appeared what seemed at first six moving wisps of smoke. Curling, gyrating, darkening, they took on denseness, became flesh, were six dancing Ethiopians, dark-skinned and turbaned, playing flutes. Simon pointed, and behind the dancers came a line of slaves carrying between them, on long poles, six whole roast oxen steaming from the fire. He waved them to one side and filled the space with tables, which in a moment were burdened with sweetmeats, eggs stuffed with delicacies, pyramids of glistening olives, a huge

216

goose made out of pastry which at a movement of his hand rose to its feet, unfolded its wings and flapped away. Silver dishes piled high with fruit next appeared, grapes and figs and plums and fiery pomegranates, topped with a glittering crust of ice.

'Wine!' cried Simon, and an amphora on the table upended itself and spurted a jet of ruby on to the cobbles.

The citizens gaped, and were silent.

Holding the mirage with his mind, he brought on entertainment for them. Tumblers, jugglers, acrobats, a troupe of child dancers. He invented a flock of flamingoes and made them step and sway to the music of the flutes. He dismissed the flamingoes and brought in a bear which began to eat the food on the tables; the bear-keeper appeared, wildly gesticulating, to shoo the animal away, and a chase around the tables began which had the crowd roaring in delight. The tumblers, the jugglers and the acrobats joined in the chase, leaping over the tables, throwing food at each other, fighting over the wine. The bear jumped on a table, balanced a dish of pomegranates on its head, and began to dance. The crowd were ecstatic.

'Enough!' said Simon. He made a series of abrupt movements with his hand, and the scene vanished.

'Aah', went the crowd, like children.

'What did you expect?' asked Simon. 'Nothing lasts, and nothing is what it seems. I have mocked your senses with an illusion, but your whole lives are a mockery. Any of you might die tomorrow, and what will have been the point of your lives? What do you know? Nothing that can help you. Where are you going? Where have you come from? What are you doing in this sham of a world, where nothing is what you want it to be and which you may be taken from at any moment? Have you never wondered? Of course you've wondered. And the fact that you've wondered is your salvation.'

He spoke until the sun cast long shadows in the quiet square. Among the crowd who listened to his words were two men who had just arrived in the town, in the course of a journey south. One of them looked worried. His companion, a short, ugly man with fierce eyes, listened with great attention and from time to time gave a wry smile.

He had visited the region before, and he didn't like it. There was an arrogance about the people, they smiled at his clothes and were too busy to talk. Even if he found someone who was not too busy, it was probable the man spoke only Greek. Kepha had a few words of Greek, but they served mainly to construct questions to which he did not understand the answers.

He found at last, in a back street, an itinerant knife-sharpener who spoke Aramaic and had no customers.

'I am looking for a man called Simon of Gitta', said Kepha.

'Don't know him.'

'He's a magician. Sometimes he calls himself Simon the Magus.'

'Don't know any magicians', said the knife-sharpener, and studied Kepha suspiciously.

'He travels with a woman called Helen. They preach, and perform tricks and illusions. I was told he might be in Sidon.'

'Well, this is Sidon', said the knife-sharpener.

'I know', said Kepha.

They looked at each other.

'Want your knife sharpened?' asked the knife-sharpener.

'No, thank you', said Kepha, 'it's sharp enough. You don't know of him, then?'

'No. Let's have a look at that knife.'

'It's sharp enough', said Kepha.

'I've never seen the knife that's sharp enough. Give it here.'

Kepha handed him the knife. The knife-sharpener tested it and cut his thumb. He gave the knife back.

Kepha smiled, nodded, and walked away.

Just as he reached the corner the knife-sharpener called after him.

'Hey! Those people you were talking about. Do they dress fancy, and talk about . . . you know, sex?'

'Shh', said Kepha.

'They were here last month. Caused a proper stir. They went on up to Tripolis.'

Tiberius Alexander was succeeded by the procurator Cumanus. The new governor's period of office did not begin auspiciously.

At the great spring festival, when pilgrims from all over the empire traditionally gathered in Jerusalem, Cumanus, following precedent, stationed troops in the outer courtyard of the Temple to discourage demonstrations. The festival lasted seven days. It was hot. The troops were bored. On the fourth day a soldier, yielding to his resentment, pulled up his tunic and, bending over, exposed his

218

naked buttocks to the crowd in the universal peasant gesture of contempt.

There was tumult. The enraged worshippers demanded the soldier's immediate punishment. Cumanus, instead of giving them satisfaction, ordered them to be quiet and proceed with the festival. For answer he received a hail of stones.

Riot seeming inevitable, the governor called in reinforcements from the fort which overlooked the Temple to the north. From this fort a flight of steps ran down into the colonnade that ringed the outer courtyard, the only part of the Temple precincts to which heathens were admitted. (The proximity of the occupying garrison to their holiest place of worship was in itself a long-standing grievance among the Jews.) The Temple and the adjoining fort and royal palace were the most ambitious of Herod's architectural projects and covered a huge area; nevertheless, into this area were now crowded many thousand men, women and children and a tense cohort of troops.

The fresh troops began to march down the steps into the outer courtyard. The people lost their heads. Fleeing, they collided with each other in the narrow colonnades and fought and trampled in their desperate attempt to get out into the streets. But the streets around the Temple, when they reached them, were just as narrow, and were steep and winding. The soldiers did not have to draw sword. Hundreds of people were crushed to death or suffocated in the panic.

It was not long after this that a government official was attacked and robbed on a mountain road outside the city. Cumanus sent soldiers into the surrounding villages to carry out reprisals. One of the soldiers went too far. Finding a scroll containing part of the book of the Law, he tore it up and threw it on the fire.

A furious mob confronted Cumanus at his comfortable residence in Caesarea. This time he had learned his lesson. The offending soldier was beheaded.

Cumanus never took the measure of the people he was sent to rule. He did not grasp their passion for justice, or its cause – their sense of the huge injustice of history. This failure of imagination brought about his downfall.

Towards the end of his period of office, a pilgrim travelling to the Holy City for the festival was murdered as he passed through Samaria. Cumanus did nothing. It is said that he was bribed by the Samaritans. The murdered man's friends took matters into their own hands and, under the leadership of some Zealots, carried out a punitive raid on Samaritan villages. Cumanus crushed the raiders with his cavalry.

The Samaritans went to the Legate of Syria, Cumanus's superior officer, and demanded restitution for the ravaging of their countryside. At the same time a Jewish deputation arrived to complain about the murder of the pilgrim and the fact that it had gone unpunished. The Legate ordered the crucifixion of the Zealot prisoners captured by Cumanus, and sent the leaders of both parties, and the governor himself, to Rome. The emperor sentenced to death the Samaritans who had begun the trouble, and banished Cumanus in disgrace.

There were several consequences to the governor's mishandling of this fratricidal flare-up. One was that Cumanus was replaced by a procurator even more ill-fitted for the post than any of his predecessors. Another was that religion and war had, for a heady moment, run unchecked hand in hand. The exultation of that moment was not forgotten. Of the Zealot-led raiders scattered by Cumanus's cavalry, some did not return to their homes. They stayed in the hills, in that barren, labyrinthine land of crags and precipices which for centuries had been their nation's stronghold. Little by little they made it theirs again. It was bandit country and it was holy land. It was also perfect terrain for guerillas.

The young man had been watching Kepha attentively as he ate his meal. Kepha, uncomfortable under the stare, told himself that it was probably normal behaviour in these parts. The people had no reticence.

He chewed the last olive, spat out the stone, wiped his plate with the last morsel of bread, popped the bread in his mouth, and sat back contentedly, reaching for the wine. It was his first proper meal for five days.

The young man rose from the bench he had been sitting on, walked over with easy grace, and seated himself at the table opposite Kepha. His eyes were a lustrous brown, his hair was curled, oiled and perfumed, and his fingers were slender and manicured.

Kepha edged back in his chair.

'You are a stranger here?' the young man asked in careful Aramaic.

'Yes', said Kepha.

'Welcome to Tripolis.'

220

'Thank you.'

'You like our city?'

'I've only been here two hours', said Kepha irritably.

'Then you have seen nothing. I will show you.'

'It's kind of you, but I'm here on business', said Kepha.

'Please. You have time. You are my guest.'

'I don't have time', said Kepha. 'My business is urgent.'

'What kind of business cannot wait for an afternoon?'

'I'm looking for someone', said Kepha.

'Ah, then I can help you. I know everyone in Tripolis.'

That, thought Kepha, was probably true. He wished the perfumed young Greek would go away, but it was stupid to pass up an opportunity.

'I am looking for a man called Simon of Gitta, or Simon the Magus', he said.

Something flickered in the bright brown eyes, and they clouded. Perhaps it was just disappointment.

'Where is Gitta?' asked the young man.

'In Samaria.'

'Ah. A long way.'

'Never mind where Gitta is', said Kepha. 'I want to know where Simon is. I was told he had come to Tripolis.'

'This is Tripolis.'

'I know', said Kepha between his teeth.

The young man gazed at the table, then raised his brown eyes to Kepha's and smiled expansively.

'I do not know him', he said. He stood up. 'Now I will show you the city.'

From time to time, dating from his first encounter with Joshua on the Lake, Kepha had experienced moments of startling mental clarity. They came quite unexpectedly, cutting like shafts of light into the muddle of his thoughts, clean like a breeze on a sultry day. At such moments he understood all sorts of things which normally baffled him. At such moments he knew exactly what he must do and was able to do it. At such moments he could often read people's minds.

Kepha looked at the young man and knew that he was lying.

'Sit down', he said.

He called for more wine. When it was brought, Kepha poured two cups.

'Later you will show me the city', he said. 'I shall be very

221

pleased to have your company. But first you must drink with me.'

They toasted each other. The young man's smile was uneasy.

'Please excuse me if I was rude earlier,' said Kepha.

'You were not at all rude.'

'I've been travelling for a long time, and I'm tired. If I can't find my friend, my journey will have been wasted, and he may be in great danger.'

'Danger?'

'He has enemies. There are people who would like to kill him. One of them' – Kepha suppressed an urge to giggle – 'is looking for him at this very moment.'

'Really?' The Greek's eyes gleamed with excitement. 'You must be a great friend of his, to go to such trouble.'

'Oh yes', lied Kepha with a fluency which appalled him, 'Simon and I have been friends since boyhood. We're almost brothers.'

'It is extraordinary, but you do look alike.'

There was the sort of silence which follows on the fall of a heavy object to the ground.

Kepha pulled himself together. 'So you do know him.'

The Greek smiled shamefacedly. 'You don't look – forgive me, you don't *dress* – as if you were a friend of his. He doesn't like everyone knowing where he stays, you understand.'

'Can you tell me where he's staying?'

'No. But I can take you to someone who can. He and Helen are a few miles up the coast, staying with the brother-in-law of a friend of mine.'

Kepha forced himself to sit still. He poured some more wine.

'How fortunate that I met you,' he said. 'Why did you come over and talk to me?'

'My cousin owns a brothel. I introduce new customers when I can.'

Kepha kept his eyes fixed on the wine jug.

The young Greek said suddenly, 'How do I know you're a friend of his?'

'Fire is One and light is One', Kepha quoted softly.

The young man bowed his head. 'May all be One.'

'Amen', said Kepha. They smiled at each other.

'Let's go and find this friend of yours', said Kepha.

'Ah. This afternoon he will not be here. He is visiting his mother. Tomorrow morning I will take you to him.'

'But . . .' said Kepha.

'There is no problem. Listen. This afternoon I show you the city. We need not go to my cousin's brothel unless you wish. Tomorrow morning you meet my friend, and he will take you to his brother-in-law's house and you will see Simon.'

'There's no need – really . . . '

'It is nothing. My friend will be pleased to go. You cannot find the place alone. So this afternoon you can enjoy yourself, and this evening . . . ' He paused impressively. 'You could not have come on a better day. This evening we perform the Rite. You will be our guest.'

Kepha's stomach contracted into a ball and rose towards his mouth. He commanded it desperately to return to its place. The young man was watching him.

'The fish I've just eaten', muttered Kepha, 'I don't think it was very fresh.'

'Oh, how disgraceful!' The Greek sped into the inn and berated everyone inside it for the shameful standard of the cooking. He emerged triumphant, and Kepha allowed himself to be led off for a tour of the city.

The tour took three hours and involved the consumption of several more jugs of wine with his guide's numerous acquaintances. Kepha, pleading tiredness, escaped for a short rest, and was at the pre-arranged meeting-place – a public garden in the city centre – just as it began to get dark. His head was throbbing.

The Greek appeared, accompanied by another man and two young women. The women carried garlands of flowers, and draped them round Kepha's neck. He protested feebly.

'Yes, yes', insisted the young Greek. 'You are an honoured guest. It is the custom.'

They linked arms and, with Kepha in the middle, began to walk down the road. Two figures approached them from the opposite direction.

When they drew level, one of the figures stopped dead and exclaimed in a shocked voice, 'Lord Almighty, there he is!'

Kepha's legs turned into tree-trunks and would not move.

'Kepha!' screamed Marcus. 'What are you *doing*?'

Kepha's four companions unlinked their arms and stared from Kepha to the two strangers and back to Kepha.

'Ah . . . friends of mine', said Kepha to anyone who would listen.

The man who had recognised him fixed him with a stare like a winter's morning. Kepha remembered him well: a distant cousin of Jacob the Pious. A counter of small coins, who never smiled.

223

'Twenty people who have better things to do have been looking for you all over the country', said Jacob's cousin. 'I have a message for you from Jacob. It's a matter of extreme urgency. You must go back to Jerusalem at once.'

'Now listen ...' said Kepha.

'At once.'

The man in the purple-edged toga was short and thickset with a brutish face. You couldn't always tell by faces, of course. Demetrius had met some very alarming faces which had turned out to harbour surprisingly mild sentiments. He tried to concentrate on the hopeful aspects of the situation and ignore the pall of cold which enveloped him.

'Stand forward!' barked the man in the toga. His eyes bit into Demetrius like pincers. Demetrius realised that the face was the truth.

The guards pushed him forward on the tiled floor. It was a huge rectangular mosaic of nymphs and sea-gods. One of them, sitting astride a dolphin, was tilting a wineskin to his lips: the wine ran down his beard and splashed on to the dolphin's back – like blood, Demetrius thought. He blinked to clear his vision. He could see some things with unusual clarity, while others seemed to have a mist around them.

The governor's voice was wrapped in mist. He had asked the same question twice: Demetrius had heard it but did not know what it was.

The governor was shouting.

'Answer me! What are your political opinions?'

Demetrius concentrated. He said carefully, holding on to his voice as if it might fly away, 'I don't have any political opinions.'

There was a pause, as though something else was expected. Oh yes. But he did not know what was the correct form of address. After a moment's frantic thought he mumbled, 'My lord.'

The guards smirked. The governor lounged back contemptuously in his large carved chair.

'You have no political opinions? No sympathy with rebels? No interest in religious movements directed at the overthrow of authority?'

'No', said Demetrius. 'No, my lord. None at all.'

'If you have no political interests', said the governor, 'how did you come to be in the company of people whose avowed aim was the overthrow of the State?'

224

Demetrius stared dully at him.

'According to the records before me', said the governor, 'you were captured by a cavalry detachment sent out to quell a religious riot on the banks of the Jordan. What were you doing there?'

Demetrius's head swam. He saw the crowds, the flashing swords, himself younger – much younger. How old was he now?

'I don't know', he muttered.

'What were you doing in an illegal religious procession?' roared the governor.

Demetrius shook his head. The question was wrong. If the question was wrong, how could he give the right answer?

'You don't understand,' he said.

The governor leaned forward and peered at him as if unsure he had heard correctly.

'I wasn't there because . . . It was a mistake', said Demetrius.

'Indeed it was.'

The guards started to smirk again. The governor glared at them, and they stopped.

'There was a prophet who had promised to part the waters and lead people across', explained Demetrius. 'I went to see it.'

'Have you ever seen a river stop flowing when someone tells it to?'

'No, my lord.'

'Do you believe such a thing is likely to happen?'

Demetrius tried to think, but his brain was jammed, like a rusty lock.

'No, my lord.'

'How long did it take you to walk to the river?'

That was not so difficult. 'Almost two days, my lord.'

'In the heat? Without water? You slept in the open?'

'Yes.'

'You walked two days in the heat, in difficult country, just to see a so-called miracle which you did not believe would take place?'

Silence. Cold sweat bathed Demetrius from head to foot. He nodded.

'What were you doing there?' shouted the governor.

God, prayed Demetrius. God, help me.

'Are you a Jew?'

'No, my lord.'

'Have you ever taken instruction with a view to becoming a Jew?'

'No, my lord.'

'When you joined the procession, were you aware that it was a Jewish religious procession?'

'Yes, my lord.'

The governor beckoned to a clerk who stood at the side of the room and took a document from his hands. He scanned it briefly.

'In the statement you made to the commanding officer when you were captured, you said that your last settled place of residence had been Sebaste, where you lived with a Jewish community calling themselves the People of the Way.'

'I never became a full member of the community, my lord.'

'No, you merely lived with them, ate with them and listened to them. Are you aware that the founder of this sect to which you attached yourself was executed on a political charge? And that his followers are awaiting some sort of worldwide catastrophe which will involve the downfall of the Empire?'

'I never understood that part of it', said Demetrius.

The governor stared at him with a contempt so profound that Demetrius felt it curdle his bones.

'A boy who walks for two days to see something which he knows is impossible. A boy who mixes with revolutionaries and doesn't know they're revolutionaries. A boy who hears talk about the end of the Empire and doesn't understand what it means. A boy who eats with Jews and does not intend to become one. What are you, an imbecile or a lying little Jew-loving rat?'

Something stirred deep inside Demetrius. It made his skin tingle and his breath come sharp. It was anger. He felt as if he were being lifted very slightly off the ground.

'In this document,' said the governor, consulting it once more, 'you gave your status as "slave". Is that correct?'

Demetrius knew that he was going to die.

'Yes, my lord.'

'Where is your master?'

'I don't know, my lord.'

'Did you run away?'

'No, my lord.'

'Then how did you come to be living with this subversive group in Sebaste?'

How did I, thought Demetrius. How did I come to do anything that I did? There has been no reason in anything.

'My master disappeared', he said.

'Disappeared? You expect me to believe that? Why should he disappear?'

No reason. No purpose.

Demetrius's gaze travelled over the mosaic floor. The god drinking from a wineskin looked like Simon.

'I suppose he disappeared because he was a magician', Demetrius said softly. There was no purpose. But it might be possible to create a purpose out of nothing.

The trial was taking place somewhere else. From an immeasurable distance, he was aware of the governor's face staring at him in a passion of fury. Demetrius looked at the face and saw that this man too would one day die. He looked deep into the furious eyes, and far away at the back of them he saw fear.

He felt the corners of his lips lift in a faint smile.

'... deceit, insolence and contempt for authority', mouthed the face. And then, with sudden distinctness, 'Case proved on both counts. Sentence is execution by the usual method and will be carried out the day after tomorrow by a detachment from the ninth cohort. Bring in the next prisoner.'

Demetrius was led out.

The leavings of a feast littered the table. Simon put down the pheasant bone he had been gnawing and dabbled his fingers in the silver water-bowl.

'Excellent', he said, and belched genially.

So large a meal was not really advisable immediately before the Rite, but it was impossible to persuade people to be moderate in their hospitality. He wondered if he ought to make a rule about it.

On the next couch was a boy of sixteen or seventeen who had been glancing at him for some time as if he wanted to say something but was too shy to say it. Simon discouraged serious conversation when eating: it was not possible to do justice either to the subject or the food. The boy, he knew, would ask serious questions. He was waiting to be initiated. He looked like Demetrius.

'What's on your mind?' asked Simon.

The boy blushed gratefully. 'Something's been worrying me', he confided. He leaned over so that the other diners would not hear. 'They won't tell me what the rules are.'

'What?' said Simon.

'I expected to be told the rules of conduct. I mean, in any other religion it's the first thing you learn.'

'I see', said Simon.

'When will I be told? When I'm initiated? I don't want to do anything wrong, you see. It would be dreadful to start off ...'

'You misunderstand', said Simon gently. 'There are no rules.'

The boy looked startled. 'No rules?'

'None.'

'But ...'

'What we are doing', explained Simon, 'is trying to break down a prison. There are no rules for that: you use whatever comes to hand.'

'But surely there are certain prescriptions to be followed, certain prohibitions ...'

'The trouble with you', said Simon with a smile, 'is that you want to be told what to do. That is exactly what we are trying to put an end to: the multiplying of laws, the obedience to authority.'

More wine was brought in. Simon, testing it against his palate, detected a faint, elusive bitterness. He raised his eyebrows. He had not given his permission for an aphrodisiac.

The boy was pondering, curly head lowered on to his arms, showing the lean curve of his neck.

'I can accept that there are no rules', he said, 'but surely there must be *something* – some fundamental principle – '

Damn the boy, who reminded him so forcibly of Demetrius.

'Well, as a matter of fact there is', said Simon, 'but I do not normally divulge it, especially to non-initiates, on the grounds that it is extremely dangerous.' He twinkled. 'I don't think you're old enough.'

'Oh. Oh, that's unfair.'

'It's a secret. I leave people to find it out for themselves.'

'Why is it dangerous?'

'If misused it is the quickest road to extinction.'

'I'll take the risk.'

'No you won't', said Simon. He stood up. 'It is time', he said to the other diners.

They followed their host out of the dining room into the adjoining room, which was in darkness except for a fire burning in a brazier at the far end. The light of the fire dimly illuminated a kind of shrine set against the wall, on which the smoke of incense rose to wreathe the heads of two carved figures.

Simon, taken by surprise, stopped, then walked to the shrine and stared at the images. He picked one up and turned it in his hands, frowning.

The persistent boy was at his elbow. 'Please tell me,' he begged, 'what is the principle which is so dangerous?'

Simon set the image back in its place and regarded him thoughtfully.

'If you know what you're doing, you can do what you like', he said.

Simon took off his gold circlet and threw it across the room. He took off his golden robe and kicked it into a corner. He turned on Helen.

'What on earth are we doing?'

'If you don't know, I'm sure I don't', said Helen. She lay down on the bed and removed her circlet. 'This thing gives me a headache.'

'Are you aware', stormed Simon, 'that in the room where we performed the Rite there was a little shrine with our images in it?'

'Really? How thoughtful.'

'You stupid woman!' raged Simon. 'Don't you understand? They are worshipping us as deities!'

'Well of course they are', said Helen. 'What do you expect? People need something to worship. All you've given them so far is a distant fire. They can't worship that.'

'They aren't supposed to worship anything. That's the *point*. We *all* contain the Spirit, we are *all* gods.'

'People don't want to be gods', said Helen. 'It's too much of a responsibility.'

Simon sat down. He buried his head in his hands. He raised his head after a time and looked at the golden robe in the corner.

'Gold and silver', he said. 'Falernian wine and stuffed pheasant. Know what you're doing, and do what you like. The trouble is that if you know what you're doing when you start, you've forgotten six months later. We are supposed to be trying to escape from the material world.'

'You're a success', said Helen. 'Didn't you want to be? These are the fruits of success.'

'Do you think they understand a word I'm saying?' asked Simon.

'I doubt it', said Helen. 'How can you expect them to, when you don't practise it yourself?'

Simon stared at her. She held his gaze without a smile.

'What's gone wrong?' he said.

Only now did he see how hopelessly, completely wrong every-

229

thing was. And he knew that it had been wrong for months, and that part of his mind had been telling him so, with moods of boredom and irritability and ridiculous imaginings, such as that someone was following him.

'I have to start again', he said.

That, too, he only fully grasped as he said it. Then he knew what he had to do.

'I'm going away', he said. 'Alone.'

She drew in her breath slightly. He saw that she had expected it.

'Back to the wilderness?' she mocked.

'No', said Simon. 'It's perfectly easy to deal with the world when you don't live in it. I have to resolve this problem. I shall resolve it by going to the heart of it, not running away from it.'

'And how do you propose to do that, philosopher?'

'I shall go to Rome', he said.

Demetrius was not conscious, on the last day, that it was day. He was surprised when the soldiers came to fetch him, and thought they had made a mistake.

He was taken to a place outside the walls. There were three others. He noticed the silky roundness of the cobbles underfoot, and the way the sweat collected in the furrows of the soldiers' foreheads before running down.

They stopped before he expected it. There was a line of high wooden posts. He was roped to something by his wrists.

He told himself that perhaps it would be quick, it would not be so painful. They would give him a drug to help the pain.

They gave him no drug, because supplies were short and he was a slave. It was painful beyond any pain he had imagined. And it was many hours before the sun began to go out.

'I have no quarrel with Kepha, and why you should ask me to address my complaints to him I do not know, since you are obviously the one in the saddle', said Saul.

Kepha kept his gaze directed at the window, where there was nothing to be seen but a line of washing on the roof opposite.

Jacob the Pious said, 'I ask you to believe that I did not send anyone to interfere with your work.'

'They came from Jerusalem, and they said they had your authority. How do you explain that?'

Jacob ran his long black nails over his beard. To run them

230

through it would have been impossible. The room was stuffy, and there arose, in the still warm air, a faint odour from Jacob's undergarments. A louse crawled across his forehead. He ignored it.

'Perhaps', said Jacob, 'it is we who should demand an explanation of you, for trying to make life easy for yourself.'

'Easy!' The room rang with Saul's harsh laugh. 'Let me tell you, Jacob. I have been in prison, I have been physically attacked, I have been slandered – '

'So have we all', murmured Kepha.

'And for the past six months I have been ill. All that time I carried on working, in the face of quite unbelievable difficulties. There have even been plots against my life. In two years I have travelled nearly three thousand miles, on foot, and in ships that aren't fit to cross a harbour let alone the sea; and all the time with an intermittent fever.' He jerked his head towards his companion. 'Ask Barnabas.'

Barnabas looked surprised that he should be asked anything. Before he could reply, Saul swept on.

'And when I stay in a place, I do not impose on the hospitality of friends, unlike some I could mention. I *earn* my keep.'

'I have only once or twice – ' began Kepha.

Barnabas said, 'I think we should remember that we are all workers in the same cause ... '

'Oh, for heaven's sake,' snapped Saul.

John bar Zabdai, at the end of the table, remarked quietly, 'Saul has a grievance. No one has attempted to answer it.'

There was a pause. Jacob inclined his head in acceptance of the rebuke.

'I'm sorry your work has been disturbed', he said to Saul. 'I authorised no interference in your community at Antioch. If any responsibility does rest with me, I apologise.'

Saul relaxed a little. Kepha wondered if Jacob was speaking the truth. Not that Jacob would ever lie; but he was a student of the Law, and he did not always define the truth in the same way as other people.

'Do you accept,' John asked, 'that our intention was not to interfere?'

'If you tell me so, I must accept it.'

'We do. But surely the issue over which the trouble arose ought to be discussed. Why *don't* you insist on your Greek converts being circumcised?'

231

'Why?' Saul jerked his head back as if cold water had been thrown on it. 'Don't you know how the Greeks regard circumcision?'

'How do they regard it, Saul?' murmured Jacob.

'As a barbaric mutilation.'

'And is that how you regard it?' smiled Jacob.

Saul flushed. 'I am proud to be a Jew.'

'I am glad to hear it.'

'But if', said Saul, jabbing his finger at Jacob, 'I ask a Greek to submit to something which he regards as – '

'How he regards it is not the point', broke in Kepha impatiently.

'It is!' Saul banged the table. 'It will deter him from joining us. He'll throw away his chance – '

'The Way can't be made easy', said Kepha.

'But for the sake of something so stupid, so petty, so unnecessary – '

'So that's how you regard it', said Jacob.

Another pause.

'Yes', said Saul. 'I do.'

'I think we should remember . . .' began Barnabas.

'Remember?' Saul was on his feet. 'We do nothing but remember. What we ought to do is forget. We carry the past around with us like a ball and chain.'

'The past?' John enquired sadly.

'The past. The Law.'

'Ah', said Jacob. 'Now we come to it. The Law.' His eyes had sharpened. He appeared composed, but his pallid face carried a flush of excitement.

'Yes, the Law', said Saul. 'The cutting of the foreskin. The manner of killing the meat. The washing of the hands. The precise distance one may walk on the Day of Rest. All the nonsense for which Joshua had such contempt, and you have such reverence.'

Kepha held his breath.

'My brother always observed the Law', said Jacob icily.

'He did not observe it, he abolished it, and he was not your brother!' shouted Saul.

There was an astonished silence.

Jacob, gripping the edge of the table, hissed furiously, 'How dare you dredge up that disgraceful slander!'

Saul plunged his head into his hands as if about to weep. Into the small cavern of his hands he muttered, 'You stupid, stupid man.' It was not clear whom he was addressing.

Barnabas, after a moment, took Saul by the elbow and made him sit down. Saul uncovered his face. 'I apologise', he said.

Jacob nodded coldly.

In the uncomfortable pause that followed, John went to the door and called for some wine. It was brought in, with a jug of water for Jacob.

The atmosphere relaxed slightly. Saul, visibly controlling himself, returned to his argument.

'There are two reasons why I do not require my converts to be circumcised. One is that some of them will find the idea so offensive that they'll never come back. The other is that, if they do submit to circumcision, they're likely to misunderstand what it means.'

We need this man, thought Kepha. Why can't Jacob see it?

'The Kingdom', said Saul, 'is not attained by following the Law alone. You must agree with that?'

Three of them agreed. Jacob scowled.

'Since', continued Saul, 'there is no salvation in the Law, it is vital that we do not give anyone the impression that there is. People find it much easier to *do* something than to *be* something, and if they think they can enter the Kingdom by being circumcised and eating the right kind of food, that's all they'll do.'

Jacob said testily, 'The outward act signifies a spiritual state. There is nothing wrong with it.'

'Yes there is', said Saul. 'The Law is a trap. It fools people into thinking it's their salvation, and it can never be. The Law is a labyrinth no human being can ever find his way through.' He fixed Jacob with a cold stare. 'People spend their whole lives wrestling with it, and have nothing but a handful of ashes at the end.'

'The Law God gave to our fathers', exploded Jacob, 'the Law by which this nation has been guided and nurtured – '

'Sometimes it seems to me that the Law was not given by God at all, but by some malign spirit who wanted to mock us', said Saul.

Kepha stared at him. Jacob was speechless.

'If salvation is by love, the Law is irrelevant', said Saul. 'And if it is irrelevant it is a threat. And it is a deadly threat. It dispenses, not life, but death.'

Kepha leaned forward to stare into Saul's eyes as if he would draw secrets out of them.

Saul smiled at him. 'I believe that that is what Joshua came to show us.'

'Look here', began Kepha hoarsely.

Jacob cut in. 'This is blasphemy, or a hair's breadth from it!' He turned to Saul as if about to savage him. 'Do you preach this?'

'Of course not', said Saul.

'Why not?'

'There are a lot of things I don't preach. They're not for everyone's ears, and in any case they aren't yet clear enough in my mind.'

'They're clear enough in mine', said Jacob.

'What exactly', asked Kepha, 'do you preach?'

Saul leaned back with a tired smile. 'Ask Barnabas', he said. 'Or ask your spies.'

'We preach exactly the same message as you', said Barnabas. 'Nothing has been added.'

'That is considerate of you', said Jacob. 'In view of the fact that Saul did not trouble to seek our permission in the first place before starting to preach, I suppose we should be grateful – '

'Permission?' Saul's face contorted. 'Jacob, you delude yourself. I have all the permission I need. I was *entrusted* with this work.'

'No you were not', said Jacob. 'You usurped it.'

Kepha stiffened with surprise.

'The mission to the heathen which you are carrying out was entrusted to Kepha', said Jacob.

Saul sat like stone. After a long time he turned his head, with exaggerated slowness, and stared at Kepha as if looking at a strange and unnecessary species of animal. He turned back to Jacob.

'Kepha?'

'To Kepha.'

It seemed to the owner of the name that the more it was repeated the less it had to do with him. He wondered if years of praying had unbalanced Jacob.

'How was it entrusted to Kepha?'

'In a vision at Joppa.'

Kepha's eyes widened. He took it in gradually. Saul was staring at him again.

'I did have a vision at Joppa', said Kepha, 'many years ago ... '

'What did it say?'

'It was not easily interpreted.'

'Not at first', said Jacob. 'Like all great revelations, it was difficult to grasp. We discussed it many times. But in the light of what happened subsequently, the meaning became clear.'

234

'What did happen subsequently?' demanded Saul.

'Kepha received an unmistakable sign that he must baptise a heathen household in Caesarea. And, of course, he did so.'

John made a small noise of astonishment. Jacob sat back with a look of triumph he did not trouble to conceal. Kepha sat quite still.

'Why was I not told of this?' whispered Saul.

'My dear Saul, you are never long enough in our company to be told anything.' Jacob smoothed his beard.

The air in the room had become stifling. Saul, motionless, gazed at the rough wooden table. Then he said, 'Why should I believe you?'

'You surely don't believe we're lying?' murmured Jacob.

'Why not? You'd do anything to discredit me. You never have accepted me as an equal.'

Another silence. The accusation was either too monstrous to be refuted, or too true.

Barnabas cleared his throat. 'I think we should remember – ' he began.

'Very well', said Saul. 'So Kepha had a vision. I had a vision, but we won't go into that. Kepha baptised a household. I've baptised hundreds, but we won't go into that either. The question is' – he rounded on Kepha – '*why* didn't you continue with it?'

'I was called back – ' said Kepha.

'The precise circumstances are irrelevant', said Jacob. 'As I say, we discussed it. And we decided that the vision might well have been granted to Kepha as the head of the brotherhood rather than as an individual; in other words, it might be that the mission was a corporate work. Furthermore, by the time we had been able to consult everyone who should be consulted, you were three hundred miles away and pleasing yourself. In the end, we did not feel it particularly important' – he smiled kindly at Saul – 'who carried the message to the heathen, as long as it was carried. Kepha is happy to extend his privilege to you.'

Saul stared at the wall. He would not look at any of them. Kepha, trying to read the expression in his eyes, flinched away from the intensity of bitterness he saw.

Saul stood up. 'You did not consider it important', he said with contempt. Still without looking at them, he began to walk towards the door.

Jacob said, 'Saul.'

Saul turned, his face stony.

'We have not resolved the matter you came here to resolve.'

'I no longer have any wish to resolve it', said Saul.

'I think you do.'

'I don't need your approval.'

'What is your work, cut off from its roots?'

'More than you can imagine, clearly', said Saul.

'Never mind what we imagine. What do *they* imagine – your people? They believe they are part of a brotherhood which has its heart and its meaning here.'

'That may change', said Saul.

'How can it change? It would no longer be the same religion. Where do you preach, Saul, where do you find your Greek converts? They are friends of the synagogue. They are people who have already sickened of heathen gods and turned towards the one place where they see the light shining. You build on us, Saul. You are bound to us. You feed off us.'

'The food is tainted', said Saul.

'You may think so. But you cannot do without it. Without it, your work can't exist.'

Saul said nothing.

'I offer you a bargain', said Jacob.

'I will not bargain with you.'

'The bargain is this. We will give our consent to your work. And as a great concession, which I am not at all sure we should make, we will not require you to circumcise your converts, since you insist that that would make your work impossible. In return we require certain undertakings from you. The first is that your converts should observe the Law in so far as it relates to the killing and eating of meat. The second is that they refrain from sexual impropriety.'

'Don't insult me', growled Saul.

'The third requirement', pursued Jacob calmly, 'is that you give us some measure of financial support.'

'Financial – ' Saul's face took on an expression of contemptuous disbelief. 'You are asking me for money?'

Jacob folded his hands over his beard. 'The community here is very poor. There have been shortages of food. Your community at Antioch is very prosperous. It is surely not too much to ask.'

'Indeed it would not be too much to ask, were it not for the fact that it's payment!'

'Payment?' Jacob appeared puzzled.

236

'Payment for the right to carry out my mission. Payment for equality with you. I already have those things. Do you expect me to *buy* the gift of God?'

Kepha held his head as if the wine had fuddled him.

'Those are the terms', said Jacob.

Saul walked from the room.

As the door closed, Barnabas said nervously, 'I'm so sorry about all this. I never imagined ... After all, I was responsible for introducing him ...'

'For pity's sake,' said Kepha, 'go after him and bring him back. Or at least stay with him. Or if you can't manage to do either, at any rate try to say something sensible.'

Barnabas hesitated, gnawing his lip.

'Come on', said John. 'I'll go with you.'

They went out together.

Jacob and Kepha sat in silence for a while. Jacob trapped lice.

Kepha said at length, 'Next time you intend to give a public interpretation of one of my visions, perhaps you will let me know first.'

'My dear Kepha, I couldn't: it only came to me as Saul was talking. A pure inspiration of the Spirit.'

'Odd that it came to you and not to me.'

'Not at all. Visions seldom are understood by the people who had them. Consider Daniel. But you need not reproach yourself. You may not have understood, but you did act correctly when you baptised those people.'

'That wasn't what you said when I told you about it.'

'Admittedly. But at the time I was not enlightened by the Spirit.'

'I see', said Kepha.

'Anyway', continued Jacob comfortably, 'it turned out to be a very satisfactory meeting. I don't think we need worry about Saul. His ideas are so wild, and his way of expressing them so offensive, that they can carry no weight. We will keep him on a loose rein, and he will do no harm.'

'You think so?' said Kepha.

'Oh yes. He will shout himself into oblivion. Believe me, in a few years no one will remember Saul and his malign angels.'

'But in that case, the mission ...' said Kepha.

'Is it important, really? Your vision was hardly a command, as I interpret it. More like permission, wouldn't you say? In the light of that permission, you ... acted as you acted in Caesarea.'

237

Kepha grunted. 'I intend to go back', he said.

Jacob frowned. 'Must you?'

'Yes. I have found my mission.'

'Saul will have your blood.'

'I am not in competition with Saul.'

Jacob sighed. 'Oh well, if you really think it's your duty to go running about after foreigners ... ' He stood up. 'I am going to the Temple. Perhaps you'd like to accompany me?'

They walked out into the cool evening streets. Through a gap at the end of a steeply-descending alleyway Kepha saw that a new row of crosses had appeared on the skyline.

Jacob was saying, 'For some reason I have never seen an angel. I suppose there was never any need for one to appear to me. Tell me, what do they look like, Kepha?'

'What?' said Kepha.

'Angels. The angel that released you from prison, what did it look like?'

A shaft of late sunlight between buildings struck Kepha's eyes painfully. He frowned, and said nothing.

'You're very reticent about your experiences, aren't you?' observed Jacob. 'You shouldn't be, you know. Too much humility is a fault, Kepha.'

'Perhaps.' They walked on a little further in silence. Something occurred to Kepha. 'What does "Saul" mean in Greek?' he asked.

'You know I don't know Greek', said Jacob.

They turned into the Temple courtyard.

VII

EMPIRE

It was, observers commented, a sign of the decadence into which the imperial court had fallen that the man next appointed to the procuratorship of Judaea was a freed slave.

Felix owed his elevation to the emperor's favour and the recommendation of the Jewish high priest, who was in Rome at the time of Cumanus's disgrace. He was unscrupulous, ambitious and resourceful. Each of his three marriages connected him with a family of royal descent, although it was rumoured that he had needed the help of a sorcerer to contract the third. On arriving in the province he applied himself with energy to the problem of the Zealot bandits who were infesting the hills. He began by inviting their chief to a meeting under guarantee of safe-conduct and then sending him in chains to Rome.

Felix's lack of scruple initially paid off. He was successful in his first ferocious drive against the bandits. Thousands of the nationalist outlaws, together with their supporters in the countryside, were rounded up and killed. The hill roads were safe again, for a time, for the friends of the government.

But the city was not. Under the very noses of the occupying troops, a new breed of resistance fighter brought a new threat into the religious capital: political assassination. The *Sicarii*, or Dagger-men, struck usually at festival time. They would mingle with the crowds, carrying under their clothes the small curved knife which was their characteristic weapon, stab their victim and melt again into the crowd. One of their first victims was the high priest who had recommended Felix's appointment. He was murdered, it seems, on Felix's instructions. The assassins hated the priest for his moderate views; Felix hated him because he had dared to criticise the way in which the governor carried out his duties. An arrangement was come to. Not surprisingly, Felix was unable, after this, to rid Jerusalem of assassins.

He was on easier ground with the visionaries. The preaching of these God-haunted seers was increasingly to be heard. Whipping the credulous into a frenzy of faith, they would lead them out into the wild places of the countryside, promising them supernatural signs of the approaching end of oppression. The sign they unfailingly saw was the approaching dust of Felix's cavalry. The most imaginative of these prophets was an Egyptian who led a huge crowd to the Mount of Olives just outside Jerusalem, telling them that at his word the city walls would collapse and the garrison would surrender. Most of the crowd were slaughtered out of hand; the Egyptian escaped.

241

But the time had passed when the province could be cowed by ruthlessness. It had now precisely the opposite effect. Religious and political fanatics – never, in that country, easily distinguished – sank their remaining differences and joined forces in a campaign to rouse the people to revolt. Intimidation of collaborators began. Prominent citizens were murdered and their homes looted. The smoke went up from burning villages which had preferred to settle for an emperor they knew rather than a God they feared they might not.

As the history of the province moved towards its bloody resolution, in the heart of the empire another step into anarchy was taken. The empire had been ruled for thirteen years by a man who had not sought the throne: a stuttering, scholarly liberal whose vices were private ones. Two years after he had sent the freedman Felix to govern Judaea, the scholarly emperor died, naming his adoptive son as successor. For the second time in seventeen years, a young man whose nature utterly unfitted him for supreme power ascended the imperial throne.

The city loved novelties.

Every day a crowd of rich young idlers, out-of-work entertainers, pensioned-off veterans, women of rank who had nothing to do, and youths playing truant from their tutors, gathered in a corner of the Roman Forum to listen to the latest thing from the East.

It was a new philosophy. Or perhaps it was a new religion. At first they could not quite make up their minds what it was. In the end they decided it was a sort of religion in reverse. The gods were still there, if you wanted them to be, but they were not to be worshipped. On the contrary, they were to be treated with contempt. They were tyrants, enemies of the human race.

The crowd drew in its breath sharply and looked skyward the first time this was said; but there were no thunderbolts. The preacher was still there the next day. Indeed he had been saying the same thing for years, he told them, and no harm had ever befallen him. The gods, once one turned to face them, were cowards. Perhaps they did not exist at all. Perhaps they were just shadows in the mind. It did not really matter. What mattered was the power which the *idea* of gods held over the mind. The fear, the obedience to precepts, the observance of rituals designed to please and placate. All these things were chains. Human beings, whatever their grand illusions, were no more than convicts in a vast prison. And he had come to show them the way out.

Freedom, said the preacher, that was what he offered them. Freedom, and the regaining of their birthright. For they did not belong in this world, and all of them, with one small part of their minds that had not been enslaved, knew it. They came from a better place. They had been tricked; and every religion that had ever spawned its priests and acolytes on the face of the earth perpetuated the deception. It was time for the truth to be told. The gods were phantasms. The Creator was a murderous despot. The divinities, the true divinities, were men and women.

Nothing he said shocked the crowd as much as this last statement. Its first utterance was greeted with silence, then with nervous laughter. They were accustomed to emperors becoming gods, but even an emperor had to die before he could safely be made immortal. That they themselves were gods was surely a presumption inviting immediate punishment.

'You have been taught to fear that idea more than anything else', said the preacher. 'That is why you cannot think it.'

He told them a story which was current in his own country. The first man and the first woman were placed in a beautiful garden, and were given one prohibition by their Creator: they must not eat the fruit of a certain tree. They ate it, and were punished. The tree was the tree of knowledge. The reason they must not eat the fruit was that if they did they would know what they were: they would know that they were gods. Their punishment was that they were banished from the garden and from that moment became mortal: prey to sickness, destined to old age and death, and condemned to live in a world which had become, with their disobedience, hostile in its gross materiality.

Everything they had had was taken from them, said the preacher, except the knowledge they had stolen; that the Creator could not take away. But as generation succeeded generation in toil and uncertainty he saw to it that the knowledge became buried, crushed out of mind by a weight of cares, confused utterly by the lies he told them and the endless, meaningless rules he gave them to live by. In the end they were so confused they believed everything that had happened to them was their own fault, and they regarded knowledge, and any desire to understand their situation, with fear and suspicion.

The story was a fable, explained the preacher, but its meaning was true. It was an indication of the stupidity of the priests in his country that they did not understand its meaning and so had not

243

suppressed the story. He offered this story now to them, his audience, as a fable for their own predicament. For they too were
confused, and frightened, and had lost something, and did not
know what it was.

It seemed to the men and women who heard these words that
something touched them, very lightly, in an obscure and sensitive
region of themselves. They were reminded of something, they could
not say what, something they had once known. A power possessed?
A place inhabited? An identity enjoyed? All and none of these
things, but something ... And they felt for it a sharp, bewildering
stab of nostalgia.

Perplexed, oddly excited, joking among themselves but thoughtful nonetheless, they went back day after day to hear him. They
listened docilely when he told them a strange myth about sparks of
light descending into webs of matter. They listened with smiles,
which slowly faded, as he told them that a whore was the symbol of
the Great Mystery. They listened with incredulity, and questioned
him, and went away silent, when he said that to be free all they
needed was to know that they were free, and to accept no laws of
conscience, and to turn the instinct that most enslaved them into a
weapon of liberation.

They listened, thought, argued, and went back. Once he astonished them by a miracle. A customer had dropped a ring into a
pavement brazier in the arcade at the side of the Forum: the
preacher thrust his hand into the coals. The ring was blackened
when he brought it out, but there was no mark on his skin.

They asked him to show them more miracles, but he refused. He
said he had done it only to prove to them that the flesh could be
overcome. He was not there to entertain them, he said.

They went back, and took their friends. Daily the crowd in the
Roman Forum became larger. He became a minor celebrity, this
strange Jew (or whatever he was) who said things that no one had
ever dared to say before, and could touch fire with his bare hands,
and made them feel a painful regret for something – a freedom? a
power? a place belonged to? – that they had never known.

Only once or twice did the audience become restive. That was
when a covered litter, borne by four slaves, its occupant quite
invisible, made its appearance at the edge of the crowd. On these
occasions people would stand aside to make way, but the litter
never advanced into the crowd, remaining always on the edge.
After its departure the audience would relax, but it was noticeable

244

that they did not for some time afterwards give the preacher their full attention.

He did not comment on the litter or ask about its occupant. They did not volunteer the information. The preacher had not been long in the city, and there existed a tacit understanding that about some things they knew more than he did.

The sea was a sheet of gold in the setting sun. There was land to starboard but they would not put into harbour. They could sail all night under clear stars: the sky was cloudless. The masts creaked under a strong southeasterly wind. They would make Rhodes by the following evening. So far the voyage, apart from Marcus's seasickness, had been uneventful, even pleasant.

Kepha sat in the stern and glowered at the horizon.

He should never have gone to Antioch. What had he hoped to do there? Heal the breach between Saul and Jacob? It was not possible to heal a breach which neither of the two parties wanted healed. All he had done, by his bungling, was to make things worse.

And invite Saul to confide in him things which he would give a great deal not to have heard.

Saul had been pleased to see him. More than pleased: he had been delighted. The other side of the man's fiery temper was a warmth in its way almost as consuming. There was no meanness in Saul, no holding back or calculation: he gave of himself completely. Kepha valued that: it was rare, the ability to sink oneself, as it were, to offer without reservation and without counting the risk. Yet it was at war, in Saul, with a pride that would allow not the slightest diminution of his position. The combination of these two qualities, the wholeheartedness and the pride, when added to an intelligence which Kepha found alarming, made Saul a character who should not be underestimated. And they had underestimated him, Jacob most of all. 'I don't think we need worry about Saul. He will do no harm.'

So might the Philistines have said of the blinded Samson, as he stretched out his arms to pull the roof down on their heads.

Well, he could not deal with the problem Saul had presented him with. It was too big for him. Jacob would not be able to deal with it. God would have to deal with it. Which was just as well, because there was no one else Saul would listen to.

He heard the straining of the sails, and turned to look at them.

245

They rode, huge and ghostly, against the sky. A ship was a beautiful thing. Even an old tub like this one, which wallowed in the slightest sea and would no doubt go round like a bucket in heavy weather. Still, she was sturdy. A no-nonsense cargo boat. He had enquired what they were carrying. Timber for Rhodes, where they would pick up a new cargo, and salted fish for Rome. He had smiled about the salted fish. He knew where it came from. He could probably name at least half the people who had caught it, salted it, packed it and made the barrels. It was the only thought in a week which had given him any satisfaction.

Kepha sighed, in a depression of spirit which boded ill for the mission he was embarked on. He should not have gone to Antioch: but he had been sure at the time that it was the right thing to do. Perhaps he should not be going to Rome?

He pushed the thought aside. It was his most persistent fault, this proneness to self-doubt.

That, and cowardice.

He should have stuck to his principles, irrespective of whatever else was happening. It had been difficult enough working out what his principles ought to be: once he had decided, he should at least have had the backbone to stand by them.

But Saul had made everything so confusing.

'I see you're not making them observe the dietary laws', Kepha had remarked after a couple of days with Saul's converts, during which meat had been eaten which everybody knew had been bought in the market and not from a Jewish butcher.

'Of course I'm not', said Saul. 'It's nonsense. What does it matter how you kill a sheep? Anyway, Jacob isn't keeping to his part of the bargain. He's still sending people to poke around. Two of his spies were here just a few weeks ago.'

'I hope you don't think I've come to poke around', said Kepha.

'I know you haven't', Saul said.

It had caused Kepha a certain amount of mental anguish, but he had done it. He had made himself do it because he believed that Saul was right. He had forced himself to eat with them. The food at first threatened to rise in his throat, but he persevered and in the end it was easier.

And then, just as he was congratulating himself on an advance made both in his own mind and in his relations with Saul, two things had happened in quick succession.

The first was that Saul had confided in him certain ideas on which he had been working which would make the Way more accessible, he said, to the Greeks.

'You must understand', Saul had explained, 'I am not talking about making it *easier*. I'm talking about putting it into a shape, so to speak, which they can immediately identify. You can't, for instance, expect Greeks to get excited about the prophecies. They've never even heard of the prophecies.'

Kepha nodded slowly. The prophecies were the proof. But what Saul said was reasonable.

'A lot of things have to be dispensed with', said Saul. 'But in their place ...' His eyes took on a strange expression which Kepha saw with surprise and a tingle of alarm: it was a kind of awe. Awe at his own creation. 'It is extraordinary', continued Saul, 'but I started this as a sort of mental exercise, and the more I pursue it, the more I realise ...'

'Come to the point', said Kepha.

Saul had come to the point. With digressions, explanations, illustrations, and references to heathen philosophy which Kepha did not pretend to follow. Even an excursion into the peculiarities of the Aramaic language. He had talked for three hours by the sand clock in the corner. Nevertheless he had come to the point, and he had made the point so brutally clear that even Kepha, who at one stage had covered his ears (Saul did not notice), was left with no excuse for not understanding what he said.

He had given Saul a last chance to unsay it.

'In order to make more converts', he said, trying to keep out of his voice an emotion which, if he expressed it, would choke him, 'you are proposing to tell them that a man whom I know beyond any doubt to have been a human being, and whom you never knew at all, was not a man, but a god.'

'Not a god', said Saul. 'God.'

Consequently, when another group of well-wishers from Jacob arrived on the doorstep the very next morning, Kepha had reacted, not from his head, or even from his heart, but from his stomach. He had turned his back on Saul and the converts and eaten apart with the guests.

Saul's contemptuous 'Hypocrite!' rang in his ears like a verdict on a lifetime of compromises.

The emperor of the world lay on his back with a sheet of lead on his chest.

247

He opened one eye as Simon, flanked by guards, approached. He shut it again.

The guards clattered to a halt, saluted, and did something noisy with their spears. The emperor opened both eyes and removed the sheet of lead. He sat up and made a finicky gesture with his fingers, as if he had discovered a fly in his drink, and the guards marched back to line the walls with a noise like ships colliding.

Simon was looking at a girlish youth of about eighteen years, with small, curiously pale blue eyes that looked as if they might enjoy seeing things other people would not much enjoy.

The pale eyes focused on him without interest.

'What are you doing here?' said the emperor.

'Great Caesar summoned me.'

'Did I?' said Caesar. 'I wonder why.'

The eyes travelled down to Simon's feet and up again. The emperor's face cleared suddenly.

'Do you like music?'

'Yes, Caesar.'

'Tell me what you think of this.'

The emperor rose from his couch and moved, with an extraordinary gait compounded of a mince and a strut, to a small inlaid table on which reposed a lyre. He picked it up, touched the strings, then, with a soulful expression, began to sing in a thin, wavery voice to his own accompaniment.

Simon composed his features.

The song finished. The emperor stood for a long moment in what appeared to be enraptured contemplation of his own performance, then laid the lyre aside.

'Well?'

His tone expressed a satisfaction amounting to triumph. His eyes betrayed anxiety.

'Caesar's artistry upon the lyre is the talk of the empire', replied Simon, 'but if I had not heard this performance I should not have believed it possible.'

'Ah. Good, was it? I intend to go in for competitions when I have time. They hold musical contests, you know, in Greece. Do you like Greece?'

'Yes, Caesar. A delightful country.'

'You think so, do you? Yes. I think so, too. I would like to live there, you know, but it's quite impossible. Oh, quite impossible.' He leaned forward and whispered, '*Affairs of State.*'

'Really?' said Simon, controlling an urge to step back. 'Caesar carries a great burden', he murmured.

'Oh, I do. I do.' The emperor turned away and flung his hand in a despairing gesture towards the lyre. 'And to be an artist! Do you understand what that means? To be an *artist*?'

'It is vouchsafed to few, Caesar.' A flicker in the pale eyes warned him. 'And artistry such as I have just heard, to perhaps one in a generation.'

'As often as that?'

'Caesar must pardon me', stammered Simon. 'I can only make comparisons with what I know. I have never heard the lyre played with such ... poetic feeling.'

'The middle passage, you didn't think it was a little too expressive, that I should have given more of an impression of, well, holding back?'

'Oh no, Caesar. No indeed. The passage was played with perfect discretion.'

'And the voice? What did you think of the voice?'

'Superbly melodic, Caesar. The control, the ... sensitivity ... astounded me.'

'Did it really? That's very gratifying. I have had doubts, you know, about the voice. I spend an hour every day with a weight on my chest to strengthen the lungs. I think it's wise, don't you?'

'Art is an exacting mistress, as Caesar understands.'

'Or do you think it's a waste of time? The voice is good enough?'

'In my judgement, Caesar's voice cannot be improved', said Simon desperately. 'But Caesar's own judgement in the matter is of course far better than mine.'

The pale blue eyes fixed on him with complete lucidity. 'Nobody tells me the truth', said Nero, 'because I'm emperor.'

For a moment the eyes stared into his own, then their expression changed. The emperor threw up his hands in a theatrical gesture of recollection.

'You are the Jew! The man who preaches in the Forum!'

'Yes, Caesar.'

'Why didn't you say so? I didn't bring you here to talk about music. Well, never mind. Let's get down to business straight away. Tell me, all these things you preach, are they true?'

'I believe so, Caesar.'

'All that business about breaking the law? True, is it? All the

249

stuff about authority? About the gods? There are no gods? True, is it? People should do whatever they like?'

He peered at Simon sharply.

Simon felt sweat drench his clothes.

'I believe so, Caesar.'

The emperor stepped back and studied him, head on one side. Then he walked away, towards the end of the room, making a gesture like someone summoning a dog.

Simon followed him.

The emperor stopped in front of a window which led on to a balcony. Simon joined him at a respectful distance. Nero motioned him closer, and jerked his head in the direction of the guards.

'Away from *them*', he hissed.

'Er . . . yes', said Simon.

'What would you say,' whispered the emperor, 'if I told you that I killed a man last night?'

Simon swallowed. The voice whispered on.

'Stabbed him. Took his purse. Dumped the body down a sewer. What would you say to that? Eh? Eh?'

Simon took a deep, careful breath.

'I would say that it was an inspired example of lawlessness, Caesar.'

'I thought you'd be pleased. What would you say if I told you that I'd done the same thing no less than fourteen times?'

Simon shut his eyes.

'Speechless, eh? I thought you would be. Yes, I thought that would surprise you. Mind you, it wasn't you that gave me the idea. I thought of it all by myself. To go out alone into the streets at night – the dark is so exciting, isn't it? – and to do . . . what I don't need to do. Art, you see. The freedom of it. And the danger. I am quite unprotected, you know: anything might happen to me. It's really very brave.'

'Yes', said Simon.

'Do you see that it is art?'

'Yes', said Simon, 'I see.'

'I wear a wig usually', said Caesar. 'For disguise.'

Simon gazed out of the window. Before him, in marble and mosaic, lined with guards and statues, stretched the precincts of the palace. Beyond it, the ordinary citizens of Rome went about their ordinary business.

'You don't think I'm mad, do you?' sniggered the boy beside him

250

'Caesar has the most logical mind I have encountered in many years', said Simon.

'I was always good at logic', said Nero, 'but my tutors never realised it. I had a terrible childhood.'

He wandered back to the lyre table again. He seemed to have lost interest in the conversation. He picked up the instrument and tried a few notes.

'Tell me what you think of this', he said.

The music went on and on.

Someone had crucified a bat upside-down to a window-sill for luck. It fluttered feebly as Kepha passed.

'Babylon', he muttered.

The city made him ill. The air seemed already used by the time it reached him. It was worst by the river, which was filthy and stank. The clatter of carts down the street kept him awake half the night. He saw poverty of an abjectness which his own people would not allow, existing side by side with a luxury which sickened him. He saw columns and temples and palaces, and squads of gigantic blond-haired soldiers, and men who looked like women and women who looked half-naked, and whores who looked like children, and he could not make sense of any of it and he did not understand a word that was said to him.

He caught up, with some difficulty, with Marcus, who was striding ahead.

'Have some consideration for my age', he grumbled.

'Sorry', said Marcus. 'I can't seem to slow down. It's something about the place.'

'You *like* it here?'

Marcus blushed. 'It's ... well, it *is* rather exciting, isn't it?'

There were times when Kepha despaired of the young.

They walked on through the commercial quarter at a pace which was too fast for Kepha and too slow for Marcus. They were going to the Roman Forum. Kepha had insisted. They had been in Rome two days and not begun the business they had come for. Marcus had wanted to 'look around'; Marcus's uncle, with whom they were staying, had said they should rest.

Rest? Who could possibly rest in this monstrous place?

'Today', Kepha had said firmly at breakfast, 'we are going to the Forum.'

He did not know what he would do when he got there. It was a

251

mistake to make plans. He would listen to what was being said, and take his direction from that. Or rather he would have to listen to Marcus's translation of it, since Simon would presumably be talking in Greek.

Kepha chewed his lip crossly. There were certain advantages to an education.

Well, Marcus would translate, and he, Kepha, would then know exactly what it was he had to contend with. Far better to confront the man himself, the source of these filthy doctrines, in public and in front of his followers, than to waste time trying to repair the damage while the one who had caused it went unchallenged. Yes, he had been right to ignore the flock and pursue the shepherd. He would listen carefully, and if necessary, at the right moment, with all the authority at his command, he would interrupt.

Or rather, he would interrupt and Marcus would translate his interruption.

Kepha groaned.

The thing to do was to challenge Simon to a public debate. Each of them would present his case. It would be clear and orderly, like a law-court. The people would decide.

Simon's people, under Simon's eye, listening to Kepha's words translated by Marcus.

Well, there was no other way. All the boy had to do was give a faithful rendering of what Kepha said. It should not be too difficult. His Greek seemed fluent enough.

He thought of Saul. Saul would have none of these problems. Ideally, he should be able to leave it to Saul. But how could he when every time Saul opened his mouth he sounded more like Simon?

Marcus was racing ahead again. Kepha caught up.

'Sorry', said Marcus.

'Can you tell me', asked Kepha as they crossed the road and missed a cart by inches, 'what "Saul" means in Greek?'

'Afraid not', said Marcus. 'My Greek isn't perfect, you know.'

'You can begin', said Kepha.

'No, no', demurred Simon. '*You* begin. You're the guest. Would you like me to introduce you?'

Kepha's mouth tightened. Simon smiled. He was going to enjoy himself.

Kepha had brought a boy to translate for him. The boy wa

252

clearly nervous. Even in Kepha's eyes Simon detected a hint of anxiety. The seamed, serious face had changed, he thought. It was age, of course, but there was something else; not exactly a softening, more a resignation. Kepha had grown smaller. Simon found it difficult to believe that the man sitting beside him had been strong enough to rob him of his power, and strong enough to curse him with a curse that had sent him into a year of darkness.

But productive darkness. Really, he should be grateful.

And Kepha was still a man to be reckoned with. That was shown by his arrival here. He had no friends in Rome, he spoke neither Greek nor Latin, he was a peasant from the provinces and wholly out of his depth. Kepha was not a particularly clever man, but he was not so stupid as to be unaware of his crippling disadvantages. He was, in a way, almost to be admired.

'Is the boy's Greek good enough?' asked Simon on impulse. 'If you like, I can translate for you.'

The offer was quite genuine. The more accurately Kepha's words were translated, the better.

Kepha fixed him with a stare like a basilisk.

'Oh, very well', said Simon. He cast an eye over the crowd. There were a number of new faces – drawn, presumably, by the promise of free entertainment. There was no sign of the covered litter. Nero would not be interested in a theological wrangle.

'Better start before they get bored', he said to Kepha. 'You can do anything with a Roman audience except bore them.'

Kepha disdained to look at him. 'I shall not bore them', he said.

Somewhat to Simon's surprise, he did not. The crowd were intrigued by the spectacle of a strangely-garbed peasant addressing them with evident passion in a language totally unintelligible. They watched him as they might watch a new freak of nature imported for the Circus. When Kepha stopped to allow Marcus to translate, they gazed from the boy to the man and back to the boy, clearly amazed that the sounds they had heard could yield sense and that the extraordinarily unfashionable creature before them was capable of formulating it.

Kepha began, as Simon had expected, with an attack on Simon's doctrines. Sensibly, in the circumstances, he moderated his language and described them only as perverse, mistaken, and contrary to reason and human dignity. He reproached those who embraced these doctrines with having so far yielded to Simon's persuasion as to forget their natural and wholesome instinct that God was good.

All they had to do to realise how wrong Simon was, said Kepha, was reflect on their manifold blessings – the security of their homes, the happiness of family life, the satisfaction of their work, the unfailing fertility of nature that nourished them.

The faces of the crowd remained blank. Simon stroked his beard. Kepha did not know he was speaking to an audience of city-dwellers most of whom had never seen a cow in a field, a quarter of whom were unemployed and probably a third divorced, and whom their emperor crept out at night to murder.

Kepha said he would not linger on Simon's doctrines, since their falsity was best exposed by comparison with the truth. He then presented his own belief. One God, omnipotent, omniscient, bene-volent; creator and giver, judge and lawmaker, father and friend. This, he said, was the belief of his race, and it had endured for a thousand years.

This drew a murmur of approval. They would have preferred something that had only just been thought of, but something a thousand years old was almost as good.

Kepha misinterpreted the murmur of approval and launched into the history of his people. It was a mistake. The crowd, per-plexed as to the relevance of the conquest, in the remote past, of a small territory which now formed one of the third-class provinces of the empire, grew restive. Kepha noticed belatedly, and tried to recapture their interest.

'Through all those centuries', he said, 'the hand of God guided and defended his people. The wicked were punished, the virtuous rewarded, the innocent protected. Never has a faith been so trium-phantly vindicated.'

'Never have I heard such rubbish', remarked Simon. Kepha glared at him. Simon promised not to interrupt again.

The last part of the address concerned Joshua. Simon felt almost sorry for his adversary as he led into the subject. Kepha was attempting an impossibility. A belief of its nature narrowly racial linked to historical events in which his hearers could have no conceivable interest, culminating in a promise of deliverance which did not apply to them. Did he really think he could sell these sophisticated people such a product?

Plainly he did.

'I want to talk to you now', said Kepha, 'about a man I knew personally. In his earthly life I was privileged to be his friend. I say "his earthly life" because he is now in Heaven. He has survived

254

death. And he has left us a promise: that those who believe, shall survive death too.'

Ah, that was good. Whatever else they hadn't understood, they understood that. The capital was full of cults that promised some kind of life after death. In pure ignorance, Kepha had struck the right note at last.

But he could not hold it. He talked about Joshua's teachings and his healing and his miracle-working, and the occasion when he had appeared in transfigured form, streaming light like an angel. He talked about Joshua's boldness in facing the country's leaders who, out of jealousy, had put him to death. He talked about the reason for that death, in terms which obviously bewildered them. He talked about the expectation of Joshua's return in supernatural glory to rescue his followers, which perplexed them further as they did not know what they were to be rescued from. Only very briefly, and with curious reticence, did he talk about the one thing they wanted to hear — that astonishing, unprecedented return from the dead.

When Kepha finished and sat down, the crowd shifted with a restlessness that Simon read easily. They wanted to be entertained.

He stood up. There was little he needed to say. Kepha had done nearly all the work for him.

'We are grateful to the speaker who has travelled all this way to tell us about the history and beliefs of his people', he said. The quicker-witted among the audience grinned. 'I should like to put a few questions to him', said Simon. 'Of necessity, they will be questions about particular details of his faith. I hope you will bear with me in these rather obscure matters. However, as he has spent an hour on the religion of the Jews, I hope I may be allowed to spend a few minutes on it.'

The crowd chuckled. Marcus translated Simon's remarks for Kepha. Kepha scowled.

'I shall make reference to certain Writings which are the holy books of the speaker's religion,' said Simon. 'These Writings are an account of the dealings of the speaker's God with his people, and everything in them is believed to be true. The speaker will confirm this.'

Marcus translated. Kepha nodded.

'The speaker contends that God is good', said Simon. 'I shall now ask him why, if God is good, it is recorded in the Writings that he caused the entire human race, except for one family, to die by drowning.'

255

The crowd stiffened with interest. Kepha, when the question was translated, scowled again.

'The human race was wicked and deserved to drown', he said.

Simon smiled. 'It seems to me that a God who drowns almost the whole human race is neither good, nor loving, nor a father', he remarked. 'Most of this God's supposed qualities are very strangely at odds with his actions. He is, for instance, said to be omniscient. He knows the future. You would have thought, wouldn't you, that if he knew he was going to have to drown everyone he wouldn't bother to create them in the first place?'

Laughter. Kepha fiddled angrily with his beard.

'A similar lack of foresight', continued Simon, 'is shown by the story I told you some time ago about the first man and woman. If you remember, they disobeyed God by eating the fruit of knowledge. But if he knew everything, he must have known they would eat it, so why did he put it there? So that he could punish them?'

Nods from the crowd.

'There's an even odder story in the Writings', went on Simon, 'about a city called Sodom. It came to the ears of this omniscient God that there were bad things going on there, so he went down himself to have a look. He wouldn't have been sure otherwise, you see.' He paused for the chuckles. 'There were in fact *very* bad things going on there. Believe it or not, there were men indulging in homosexual practices. God was absolutely livid. He sent down fire and burnt up the whole place.'

Roars of ribald laughter. Kepha was white.

'Well, I suppose you can concede him an enthusiasm for justice', said Simon, 'although it's justice of rather a primitive order by our standards. But even by his own peculiar standards he is impossible to please. For instance, he told his people that on no account were they to hold a census. Perhaps he thought it would be a bad idea if they learnt to count. Then one day he apparently changed his mind and ordered the king to hold a census. The king held a census. God punished him by killing a sizeable part of the population. I mean, it's very difficult to do the right thing in those circumstances, isn't it?'

Snorts of merriment.

'It was Satan who told David to hold a census', snapped Kepha when this was translated.

'You haven't studied the books', retorted Simon. 'The story is given twice. In the original version, it was God.'

The crowd wanted to know who Satan was.

'The other god', said Simon blandly.

Kepha's protest was drowned in renewed hoots of laughter.

'Well, let's consider for a moment this business of God being the only god', said Simon. 'If there is only one God, then he combines all qualities within himself. That is possible. But this is not the speaker's God. The speaker's God has some qualities and not others. He is good and just. Where then do evil and injustice come from? Perhaps they simply exist and God is unable to do anything about them. But the speaker's God is all-powerful. We are presented with a logical absurdity. It is so absurd that even God himself doesn't believe it. When he decides to create the human race – I refer again to the Writings – he makes the remarkable proposal, "Let *us* make man in *our* image." Well, perhaps, being God, he feels entitled to use the plural. But a little later, when the couple he has created have disobeyed him and eaten the fruit of knowledge, he says, "The man has become *like one of us*, knowing good and evil." Like one of whom? And to whom is he speaking?'

Simon spread out his hands in a gesture of comic appeal. 'If someone tells you the same thing over and over again, and demands that you believe it, and flies into a furious temper if you deny it, do you not begin to suspect something? This God has visited terrible punishments on his worshippers for acknowledging the existence of other gods. He's as jealous as a dotard who has married a young wife. He *insists* that he is the only deity in the universe. Is the reason not obvious? He is *lying*.'

With a quick glance he took in their reactions. They were ready for the steel.

'Now we come', said Simon, 'to the most extraordinary part of all. For nowhere are the vicious characteristics of this lying God more in evidence than in the story you have just heard about the death of the speaker's friend Joshua. The speaker has told you that his death was necessary as an "atonement". You may not be familiar with that word. What it means is offering a sacrifice to induce God to forgive some wrong you have committed. In this case we are asked to believe that the sacrifice offered for the forgiveness of sins was the sacrifice of a human being. Mark that. A human sacrifice. And not just any human being: the man God had singled out for his special favour. And we are asked to believe that the sacrifice was *required*, was found to be absolutely essential, by a God who is supposed to be *fatherly* and *loving*.'

257

He turned to Kepha. 'Is this a fair rendering of what you preach?'

Kepha made a small, oddly rigid motion of assent. The crowd murmured.

'I think I have said enough about the habits of this disgusting God', said Simon. 'I should just like to say one or two things more about Joshua's death, things which the speaker has omitted to tell you. *How* did he die, this wise and good man? Was he assassinated, stabbed in the dark by a coward, like Agamemnon? No, he was not. Did he die honourably in a battle or fray? No, he did not. Was he forced to drink poison, like Socrates, or to open his veins, like many in this city who have taken their politics too far? No, nothing like that. Tell us how he died, Kepha.'

Kepha, in a hoarse voice, told them.

There was an astonished, contemptuous silence. Someone spat.

'Not very noble, is it?' pursued Simon relentlessly. 'But now listen to the most ignoble thing of all. Or the funniest, depending on your point of view. When Joshua, his friend, was captured, when his death was clearly imminent, what did our speaker do? He was there, he saw it all, he was even armed. What did he do? I will tell you.' Simon leaned forward, cupped his hand to his mouth, and said in a stage whisper that carried to every corner of the Forum, '*He ran away.*'

He waited only a moment as the gale of laughter rose around him, then, with a salutation to the crowd and a courteous nod to Kepha and Marcus, he walked home.

Two messengers arrived at his lodging in the course of the afternoon. The first was Marcus. He brought a message from Kepha challenging Simon to a contest of miracle-working. The second messenger wore the purple tunic of the Praetorian Guard. He carried an invitation from the emperor, couched in defective Greek verse, to a party on the Palatine the night following.

There was a wrestling match in progress on the lawn when Simon arrived. He asked if he was late. No, he was told: the emperor had been watching the wrestling all afternoon.

There seemed to be about a hundred people in the garden and adjoining shrubbery. Simon recognised a popular charioteer, at least three gladiators, a ballet dancer, two pantomime actors, and most of the staff of a high-class brothel reputed to cater for unusual tastes. Interspersed with these guests like mourners at a picnic were

258

a number of middle-aged men wearing the purple-striped toga of the senator. Slaves came and went, bearing trays of little delicacies.

Nero lolled on a couch in front of the wrestlers, fondling a pretty young woman.

Simon presented himself.

'So glad you could come', said the emperor. He was wearing a green silk dressing-gown embroidered with peacocks. His left hand toyed absently with the girl's breasts, while his eyes watched the wrestlers. 'Do you like wrestling?'

'Oh yes, Caesar.'

'I intend to take it up myself one day. It combines the mental and the physical in a way which is particularly interesting. It's an under-rated art form. But the Greeks understand these things.' He parted the lower folds of his dressing-gown and placed the girl's hand inside it. 'Do you like poetry?'

'Very much, Caesar.'

'I shall read some of my own later. You must tell me what you think of it.'

He nodded his dismissal.

Simon wandered away, and was intercepted by a slave who escorted him to a couch. Another slave filled his wine cup, and a third brought him a plate of roast goose. He ate, drank, and watched the wrestling.

The contestants were well matched, but the smaller one was faster. Recovering himself from a perilously off-balance position he twisted in an unexpected movement under cover of which he jabbed his thumb into his opponent's eye. As the other wrestler staggered, the small one caught, swung, lifted him and crashed him to the ground.

The cup in Simon's hand stayed half-way to his mouth. It was clearly a foul.

The emperor applauded enthusiastically. So, after a moment, did everyone else.

Simon turned to the man on the next couch. A purple stripe, sunk in some comfortless contemplation of his own.

'Did you see that?' he asked.

The senator raised his head and looked at him. 'No', he said. 'And neither did you.'

'You aren't serious.'

'That is one of the emperor's favourites', said the senator.

'I see', said Simon, and addressed himself thoughtfully to the goose.

Two more wrestlers came on. The emperor watched them with less interest than the first pair. When Simon looked at him again he had uncovered one of the girl's breasts and was drawing concentric circles round the nipple in eye-paint.

'Pretty girl', remarked Simon to his neighbour after a time. Whatever Nero had invited the man for it was evidently not his conversation.

The senator made no reply.

'Do you know her?' pursued Simon. 'Presumably she's from one of the ...'

'That', said the senator, 'is my wife.'

After a few more bouts the wrestling finished and a trio of musicians began to play under the trees. Nero had disappeared. Simon strolled off to look at the gardens. They contained an impressive collection of Greek statuary and bronzes and some rare plants, including, high up in a wall, a small undistinguished-looking herb which Simon noticed with a start of surprise. It was not native to Italy and it had only one use. He wondered if Nero knew about it, and realised that Nero had probably put it there.

The flower beds were laid out in neat rectangles bordered by paths of tesselated stone. One path, separating at an angle from the main design, led between rose bushes to an ornamental iron gate. Simon followed it, and found his way suddenly barred by the largest soldier he had ever seen. He stopped with a murmured apology, and glimpsed, just before the guard moved to block his view, a strange scene: in the small courtyard beyond the gate a woman, not at all young, reclining, eating grapes, her head turned aside in an attitude of studied indifference to the green-robed emperor who in a frenzy of supplication was kissing her ankles.

Simon walked away quickly. At the point where the paths forked he turned and looked back. The soldier had moved away from the gate and was relieving himself against a copy of Praxiteles' Aphrodite.

The party had become livelier when Simon returned. A heated dispute had broken out between the gladiators over one of the girls from the brothel; several of the other girls had begun to dance, to the visible annoyance of the musicians, who were playing an instrumental arrangement of the Death of Ajax; and the ballet dancer was being sick into a fountain.

260

In a corner of the shrubbery Simon found the taciturn senator. 'I would have thought you'd gone home by now', he remarked.

'No one leaves until Nero's read his poetry', said the senator in a tone of sepulchral gloom.

'I see', said Simon. 'And when will he read his poetry?'

'Oh, not for hours. We've got the comedy, the Fall of Troy and the surprise first.'

'What?'

'You'll find out.'

'But what's the surprise?'

'We shall all find out', said the senator.

Simon left him to his introspection and wandered back to join the main group of guests. On the way he was accosted by Nero, hanging on the neck of the wrestler who had jabbed his opponent in the eye.

'This is Jason', said the emperor. 'Isn't he sweet? Say hello, Jason.'

'Hello', said Jason.

'He's *incredibly* strong', said the emperor. 'Did you see the way he just picked up that man and *flung* him to the ground? Wasn't it wonderful?'

'An education, Caesar.'

'An education. Oh, I like that. It's very apt.' He considered it, head on one side, then dug the wrestler sharply in the ribs and leered. 'Now, Jason is *very* educated, aren't you, Jason? He knows *all sorts* of things. At times he gets quite above himself. Naughty boy. I keep telling him' – the emperor's face became feline with cunning – 'I shall have to do something about it. I'm thinking of having him castrated. Would you like that, Jason?'

Jason smiled without his eyes.

'Then, you see, I could marry him, couldn't I, and there would be no doubt about who was boss. Do you think that would be amusing?'

'Most original, Caesar'.

'Original. Is it? Yes, I suppose it is. You mean it's never been done before?'

'Not to my knowledge, Caesar.'

'But how wonderful!' The emperor's eyes lit with pleasure. 'Would you say it was art?'

'Art of a kind, Caesar.'

'Art of a kind. So it is. We must do it!' He moved away, arm round Jason's muscular neck, murmuring, 'How exciting!'

Simon found a couch and told the slave to mix his wine with water.

The comedy was a bawdy sketch about a crooked lawyer, an abducted ward, a philandering husband and a case of mistaken identity. The plot contrived to be at the same time feeble and incomprehensible. The audience applauded wildly, on the principle that it had probably been written by Nero.

After the comedy there was more music by a young Greek slave playing the cithara. He played it well. As the sweet, pure notes drifted over the lawns in the growing darkness the noise of conversation slowly died away, and the boy finished his song to an attentive hush.

Nero frowned.

The slave began another song. After a few notes the emperor darted forward, snatched the instrument from his hands and struck him on the head with it. He hit him again across the shoulders, so that the boy fell to the ground. Nero threw the cithara on top of him and kicked him in the side.

'I'll teach you to insult my guests with your rubbish!' he screamed.

The slave dragged himself away, clutching a deep gash on his forehead. Nero smashed the cithara with his foot.

The next entertainment was a torchlit spectacle with chariots. A large area was cleared, then, from opposite ends of the garden, two charioteers, masked and wearing light armour, drove at each other as if to do battle. One swerved at the last moment and turned tail, pursued by the other in a chase which took them several times round the improvised arena. It was apparent that while the charioteer in flight was a skilled driver, the one giving chase did not know what he was doing. He nearly lost his balance twice, and on one occasion narrowly missed running into the spectators.

The leading chariot finally allowed the other to draw level. They slowed, then halted, and a mock sword fight ensued. After prolonged feinting and parrying of a distinctly theatrical nature, the second charioteer with a balletic flourish knocked the sword out of his opponent's hand and mimed the death-thrust. Triumphantly, one foot on his enemy's prostrate body, he removed his mask and revealed himself, to tumultuous applause, as Nero.

After a time the fallen driver was allowed to get up and unmask. He was the professional charioteer who had been among the guests. The applause was a model of discretion.

Simon assumed that that was the end of the spectacle, and was surprised to see the emperor, after a short interval, again mount his chariot and begin a triumphal tour of the arena. This time there was a brief, uneasy lull before the clapping started. Simon, edging forward, saw that Nero was dragging a life-size dummy behind his chariot. It was some moments before he noticed the smear of blood in the torchlight and realised that it was not a dummy.

'One way of dealing with a rival', muttered the man next to him.

'Who is it?' murmured Simon.

'The slave who was playing the cithara.'

Simon left the crowd and walked back to the area where the couches had been arranged. His head was aching.

The gloomy senator passed him.

'I presume that was the surprise', said Simon.

'No', said the senator. 'That was the Fall of Troy.'

It was growing late. At least half the guests were drunk. The quarrel between the gladiators had resumed and developed into a fist-fight in the shrubbery. Quite a number of people had now been sick in the fountain.

The emperor drifted by with his wrestler again. 'Enjoying yourself, are you?' he said to Simon. 'Good. You haven't seen anything yet.' He drifted on.

Some time later a series of crashes and roars assaulted the alarmed ears of the guests. Into the area which had been cleared for the chariots marched four slaves pulling behind them a large wheeled cage. The cage had been completely covered with foliage so that whatever it contained could not be seen. From inside it came a bestial howling.

The cage stopped. Three of the slaves vanished instantly into the shrubbery. The fourth, picking up a long pole, retired to a distance and slowly pulled back the catch.

There was not a sound in the garden as the cage door swung open.

For a moment, before the panic started, there was glimpsed a misshapen, hairy creature with claws and gaping mouth. As people turned and ran, Simon saw the animal rush forward and fling itself on one of the female guests. Something in its movements arrested him, and he stood where he was, behind a bush, and watched.

The animal, with a snarl, half-ripped the girl's clothes off, then left her and bounded after someone else. Failing to catch this victim, it pounced on a struggling knot of guests who had fallen over each other in their haste to get away. It mauled and trampled them – but more playfully, it seemed, than with vicious intent –

then, catching sight of an elderly senator making a desperate and ludicrous attempt to climb a tree, lunged after him, dragged him down and, as he wrenched himself free, pulled off his toga. Roaring with delight, it pursued him as he fled, tunic flapping at his shrivelled thighs, towards the shrubbery.

Simon had been too absorbed in watching the animal to watch the guests. He noticed the gladiator only at the last moment. The man had snatched up a food tray from the tables; holding it in his left hand as a shield, and with a dagger raised in his right, he ran for the animal's back.

Simon opened his mouth to shout.

A guard stepped like lightning out of the shadows and felled the gladiator with a blow to the neck.

The animal stopped, hearing a noise behind it, and turned. It surveyed the scene. It walked on its hind legs, with a strange, mincing gait, back to the centre of the garden, where the guests cowered against the walls, behind couches and under tables.

The game was over. Nero took off his bear skin.

A longish interval now passed before the final entertainment of the evening – less, Simon surmised, to allow the guests to recover their composure than to allow the emperor to recuperate his voice. After about an hour the seating was rearranged and a small rostrum was carried in.

Simon found his gloomy senator again.

'That was the surprise?'

'Dear gods, I hope so', said the senator.

Occupying a couch set slightly away from the rest, with a guard stationed immediately behind it, was the woman to whose ankles Nero had been paying such devoted attention in the courtyard.

'Who is that?' murmured Simon, indicating with his eyes.

'That? Goodness, you don't know much, do you? That's Messalina. The emperor's mother.'

Nero began to read his poetry.

'I don't know what you think this will prove', said Simon, as they stood together in the Forum surveying the assembled crowd. 'Or is it a matter of what they think it proves?'

Kepha appeared not to grasp the implied insult. 'It will show them which of us is speaking the truth', he said.

'If you believe that, you're a fool', retorted Simon. The emperor's

264

party had badly affected his spirits. He was not in a mood for courtesies, even ironic ones. 'They're fools too', he said.

'You despise your flock?'

'At least I know them.'

'Even the simplest mind', pronounced Kepha, 'can perceive the truth.'

'The trouble with you', said Simon, 'is that you define the truth in such a way that only the simplest mind *can* perceive it.'

Kepha said nothing. He seemed remarkably confident this morning. Simon shrugged. The contest was childish. He should not have accepted the challenge. But if he had not, Kepha would have said he was afraid. More to the point, Kepha would himself have begun performing miracles, and he, Simon, would have been forced into a position where he had to challenge Kepha. It was all ridiculous. The only difference between them, as they stood there, was that he knew it was ridiculous and Kepha did not.

But then, that was a profound difference.

'All right', he said, 'let's get it over with.'

'You start', said Kepha.

'No. It's your challenge.'

'I started first last time.'

'For heaven's sake', said Simon.

He considered the earthquake illusion: that would clear the Forum in no time and Kepha would have no audience to perform to. However, it wouldn't do. The farce had to be played out.

The crowd was large, filling about a third of the Forum, and extending back some way beyond the fountain that stood at its nearer end. Simon studied the fountain, then instructed the crowd to turn so that they were all facing it.

The water began to change colour. It gushed pink, crimson, deepening to purple, shading to blue. Finally it was a soft, iridescent greenish-pearl. It was, Simon thought, one of his prettiest effects. To complete it he made the central statue – a rather clumsy Neptune – move on its pedestal and raise its trident in salute.

The crowd roared its appreciation.

Simon glanced at Kepha. His face was frozen in astonishment. It dawned on Simon that Kepha had never seen an act of magic performed except by his master or in his master's name. He had not believed Simon could do it.

Kepha recovered himself. 'I'm sure I can do something more useful than that', he grunted.

He spoke to Marcus and gave him a coin from his purse. The boy darted off to one of the shops in the arcade, and came back holding something between his thumb and forefinger. Something brown and mummified. Simon peered at it in disbelief. It was a kipper.

'Didn't you have time for breakfast?' he muttered.

Kepha took the kipper and held it up before the crowd like a trophy. The crowd stared, and tittered.

'Tell them it's a kipper', ordered Kepha.

Marcus told them it was a kipper. The audience began to laugh. It was not friendly laughter.

'Do something with it before they start throwing things', hissed Simon.

Kepha walked down from the steps and moved into the crowd. They parted, reluctantly and a little scornfully, to let him through. He walked to the fountain and threw the kipper in.

'The man's obsessed with fish', explained Simon to the people nearest him.

But the spectators by the fountain were crowding round it, jostling to get a look. A murmur of amazement arose.

Simon, frowning, left the steps and walked to the fountain. The kipper was swimming in the water. He stared at it.

Kepha smiled.

'Peasant', said Simon.

He stepped up on the rim of the lowest bowl of the fountain to face the audience. 'You've heard our friend talk about the resurrection of the dead', he said. 'Well, so far they've only tried it with fish. But they're working on it . . .'

Kepha climbed up beside him.

'Whose God is the true God?' he shouted.

Silence.

Marcus hastily translated.

'Simon's!' boomed a voice behind them. It came from the statue. Kepha jumped.

Simon giggled. 'Your turn', he said.

Kepha searched the crowd with his eyes. Simon realised he was looking for someone to heal. As luck would have it, there was no one with any visible affliction. It was predominantly a middle-class crowd, and could afford doctors.

'Another kipper?' he suggested.

Kepha ignored him.

On the ground at the base of the fountain lay an injured pigeon;

266

it seemed to have a broken leg. It had been struggling for some time to get to its feet, and had received several kicks from the spectators. It now lay still, its breast heaving. Kepha made Marcus bring it to him.

He held it in his hands for a moment, then passed one hand over the injured leg. The bird stirred and opened its eyes. Then, with an ungainly movement, it got to its feet and stood. Kepha tossed his hands and it flew away.

'A pigeon!' sneered Simon.

Kepha appealed to the crowd again to say whose God was the greater. The crowd's reply was that there were too many pigeons in Rome as it was.

'You haven't quite got the pulse of the audience, have you?' observed Simon.

Since Kepha had given them a pigeon, he gave them an eagle. A Roman eagle, splendid of plumage, bright of eye, cruel of beak and claw. It perched on the topmost bowl of the fountain and blinked its golden eyes in the sun. Then slowly, in a movement of superb disdain, it spread its wings and rose. It circled in a magnificent sweep around the perimeter of the Forum, and disappeared over the rooftops in the direction of the Capitol.

The crowd watched it go in respectful silence. Then there was a deep growl of approval.

'I would advise you to be very careful', said Simon, 'what you do next.'

Kepha did not know what to do next. He glanced about him uncertainly. Chance, or something, came to his aid.

One of the shopkeepers in the arcade – a pottery merchant – had erected outside his premises, partly from political expediency and partly to advertise his wares, a large terracotta bust of Caesar on a plinth. Being not only expensive but remarkably ugly, it had attracted no buyers, and had been there so long that it was now a feature of the Forum. Young men arranged to meet their girl-friends by it.

The shopkeeper's son had climbed a pillar to get a better view of the proceedings. Leaning far out to watch the eagle, he lost his hold and fell, bringing the terracotta bust and half a dozen pots down with him in a crash of broken earthenware. Heads turned. The initial burst of merriment among the bystanders stilled abruptly. The boy was shaken but unhurt. The features of Nero lay in a hundred pieces.

The shopkeeper, who was standing in the crowd, began to wail. Someone attempted to comfort him. 'No one will know. Sweep it up quickly and put up another one.'

'I haven't got another one!' howled the shopkeeper.

A numb silence spread through the crowd as the awfulness of what had happened dawned on everyone.

'What's the matter?' whispered Kepha to Simon. 'Was it valuable?'

Simon explained to him.

'But it's a *statue*', said Kepha. 'It was an *accident*.'

'We live under an emperor', said Simon, 'who will drag a man behind a chariot for being a better musician than he is. The word "accident" is not in his vocabulary.'

'But what will he do to them, the man and his son?'

'From my knowledge of the emperor', said Simon, 'he will probably dress them in bear skins, put them in an arena and make them kill each other.'

Kepha stared at him. In his eyes Simon saw a darkening. Kepha was beginning to learn.

'Marcus', said Kepha quietly, 'fetch me a bowl.'

'A bowl? What –?'

'Fetch it.'

Marcus went off, shoving his way through the crowd. He came back shortly with a little pewter basin. 'Borrowed it from the barber', he said. 'We have to take it back.'

Kepha stooped down and filled the basin with water from the fountain. He made a sign over it. Then he began to push through the crowd, holding the basin carefully so the water would not spill. Marcus and Simon followed him.

They arrived at the spot where the bust had fallen. The shopkeeper and his son were clutching each other, weeping. A small group of would-be comforters stood around, offering useless advice. Fragments of pottery lay scattered for yards.

'Tell them to pick up all the pieces and put them in a heap', said Kepha to Simon.

Simon raised his eyebrows, but did so.

Grudgingly and with sarcastic asides, the bystanders began to collect the fragments. Kepha made them hunt around to make sure no piece had been overlooked. When the pile had been assembled, he turned to Simon.

'This I do for them', he said. 'I ask you not to impede it.'

'Impede it? What on earth are you talking about?' said Simon.

Kepha raised his head and seemed to be praying. Then, taking a little water from the basin in his right hand, he sprinkled it on the pile of broken pottery.

There was a sort of movement of the air, too quick to be seen. Simon blinked.

On the ground stood four earthenware cooking pots, a flower vase, a jug with a frieze of Bacchus and Ariadne, and a large bust of Nero. The nose was slightly chipped.

Simon's scalp prickled.

Behind him the crowd began to shout. '*Cephas! Cephas! Cephas!*'

Kepha smiled. His Greek was good enough for that.

'Your turn, I think', he said.

Simon studied him thoughtfully. 'How did you do that?'

'I did nothing', said Kepha. 'God works through me.'

'If you were not such an obstinate prig', said Simon, 'we could be friends, you and I.'

'Like fire and water. It's your turn.'

They went back to the fountain. Simon saw to his disgust that the kipper was still swimming about in it.

The crowd were continuing to chant Kepha's name. Simon searched his repertoire. Something sensational would be needed after the last demonstration.

Kepha was watching him.

'Can you raise the dead?' asked Kepha casually.

'There is no point in raising the dead', said Simon. 'They'll only die again later. Besides which, it's socially disruptive.'

'Can you do it?'

'No', said Simon, 'and neither can you.'

'That remains to be seen.'

'Then do it', snapped Simon.

'Oh no. It's your turn.'

'What is more, I think you will agree with me that there is nobody dead in the Forum at the moment.'

'Then kill somebody', said Kepha.

Simon looked at him. The eyes were a shade harder. Yes, he had said it.

'You are proposing that I kill somebody?'

'I've heard that it is possible for a magician to kill with a word.'

'It is.'

'Then do it.'

'It would be interesting to be tried by Nero on a charge of murder,' said Simon, 'but it is an amusement I do not propose for myself.'

'You may be quite sure', said Kepha, 'that if you have the power to kill a man with a word, I shall have the power to raise him with a word.'

'You'd better', said Simon angrily. He felt cornered. It was bluff and he could not afford to call it. 'It's all very well', he said. 'All you can do is put things together. You rely on other people to break them in the first place.'

'The crowd is getting impatient', said Kepha. 'Are you going to do it?'

Simon's eye fell at that moment on Marcus. Bluff, was it?

'We'll use the boy', he said.

'Oh no, we will not', said Kepha.

'Oh?' said Simon.

They looked at each other. Kepha, reluctantly, nodded.

Simon beckoned Marcus over.

'This won't hurt', he said.'Close your eyes and think of your mother.'

He held the boy's head firmly between the palms of his hands for the space of a dozen heartbeats. Then he bent and spoke softly into his ear a many-syllabled word. Very slowly, as he released his hands, very slowly and very gracefully, the boy began to go down, like a doll crumpling under an invisible weight. He sank to his knees and fell forward to lie in the dust at the base of the fountain.

For a moment Kepha stood rigid. Then he leapt to Marcus and turned him over on his back. The face was drained of colour and peaceful. Angrily Kepha pushed back the people who were crowding round.

'Stand back', called Simon. 'Give him room.'

Kepha prayed. Simon could see the sweat on his face. Tears, too. Kepha prayed as if his heart would break. Then he bent down and lifted the boy's right hand.

'Marcus!' he called loudly, and there was something in his voice at which Simon's eyes widened.

A pause. Then a flush like dawn crept into the white cheeks. The boy yawned. He opened his eyes, blushed crimson with embarrassment, and scrambled to his feet.

The crowd buzzed with excitement. Simon remembered, too late, that no one had explained to them what was happening.

270

He and Kepha stood looking at each other. Simon experienced an absurd impulse to grasp Kepha by the hand.

'Well', he said briskly, 'what shall we do next?'

'Surely', said Kepha, 'that is the end of it. I have just restored a boy to life, which you have admitted you could not do.'

'He wasn't dead', said Simon impatiently. 'Do you think I'm a fool?'

'I think you are a liar, a mocker, a cheat and a fake', burst out Kepha bitterly.

'You'd rather I was a murderer? That would suit your purposes better, wouldn't it? You need me, Kepha. Why don't you admit it, and then we can both go home?'

'You're mad', said Kepha.

The crowd, not understanding the conversation and uncertain what they had seen, were demanding to know if the boy had really been dead.

'Neither dead nor alive', answered Simon.

'What's that supposed to mean?' growled someone.

'There was a man died in the night in a house round the corner', volunteered a helpful youth. 'They should be getting ready to carry him out now. Shall I tell them to bring him here?'

'No', groaned Simon.

'Yes', roared twenty voices. The helpful youth sped off.

'What was that about?' asked Kepha.

'You're going to have to do it again', said Simon.

It was a long wait. Simon felt tired. He was also hungry. So, obviously, was Kepha. He sent Marcus off on another errand and the boy came back with something wrapped in a piece of bread. It was pickled fish.

A small procession appeared at last: mourners, bearers and bier. A respectful path was cleared, and the bier was put down in the space in front of the fountain. Simon saw a man in early middle age: no sign of wasting in the face. An intelligent face, so probably a conscientious civil servant who had been to one of Nero's parties and died of heartbreak. He looked very dead indeed.

'Well?' said Kepha to Simon.

'Yours', said Simon.

Kepha approached the bier. He enquired, through Marcus, the dead man's name, and asked everyone to move back. He prayed for a long time. Then, taking the hand of the corpse in his own, he called loudly on the name he had been given.

271

Nothing happened.

Kepha tried again. Simon, watching and listening, knew it was no use. The thing that had been in the voice before was not there now.

Kepha tried three times, under the sombre gaze of the crowd. Nothing happened.

He came back and sat down, clearly distressed.

'Never mind', consoled Simon. 'It's only to be expected. You've exhausted your power.'

'It's not mine', said Kepha with dull obstinacy.

'Oh, very well.'

'You try', said Kepha.

'I've told you', said Simon. 'I cannot raise the dead.'

'Try anyway.'

'Why?'

'Because this is supposed to be a contest.'

Simon shrugged. He got up and went to the bier. He did not attempt to do what he knew he could not do. Normally he would not have attempted to do anything. But Kepha insisted on a contest, and a contest he should have.

Simon concentrated his mind on the marble features of the corpse. He concentrated, drawing into his will the minds around him, until to the shocked eyes of those standing by the bier the dead man seemed to move his lips and smile, and turn his head.

Incredulous murmurs turned by degrees into shouts of triumph. 'Simon! Simon! Simon!' the crowd began to roar. Kepha had jumped to his feet and was staring.

Simon made a gesture with his hand and walked away. The marble head lay still.

There was a bewildered silence. Then muttering began. It grew louder.

'It was an *illusion*!' shouted Kepha, beside himself with rage.

'Of course it was', yelled Simon in exasperation. 'What's that damned kipper if it isn't an illusion?'

The debate got no further. The crowd's murmur died away as the noise of birds is said to cease before an earthquake. Simon stepped up on the edge of the fountain to see the cause.

In the corner of the Forum stood a covered litter.

A slave in imperial livery was making his way through the hastily parting crowd. He arrived in front of Simon.

'Caesar sends greetings to his honoured friend', he announced.

272

'Caesar's loyal subject returns Caesar's greetings with prayers for Caesar's health', replied Simon.

'Caesar regrets', continued the slave tonelessly, 'that affairs of State prevented him from attending the magical contest held here today. He therefore commands Simon the sage and his adversary to present themselves at the imperial palace tomorrow at noon for his entertainment, and to determine which of them is the greater magician.'

'What *is* going on? asked Kepha.

It was a long afternoon. Simon spent it lying on his bed watching the play of light and shadow on the ceiling.

Evening came, as it had never failed to come. Evening became night.

Simon rose, put on his cloak, and walked through the streets to the house where Kepha lodged.

Kepha opened the door himself. 'Ah', he said, 'you've come. I thought you might. Come inside and have some wine.'

'I came to you once before', said Simon, following Kepha into a plainly furnished room, 'bearing a gift, and you sent me away with a curse.'

'It wasn't a gift, it was a bribe', said Kepha. 'I'm sorry about the curse. I have a quick temper.'

'I hope you won't curse me this time, because this time I'm proposing an exchange of gifts.'

'I know', said Kepha, pouring wine. 'You've come to admit defeat. In return you want me to come to some arrangement about the contest tomorrow.'

Simon sipped the wine. It was surprisingly good.

'You're quite wrong', he said.

Kepha straightened up abruptly and spilt wine on the rug.

'You don't understand anything', said Simon. 'In the first place it's not possible for us to come to an arrangement. Our antagonism is irreconcilable, and it will seek to resolve itself on every level offered. Tomorrow it will seek to resolve itself before the emperor, and there is nothing we can do about it. In the second place, although I acknowledge defeat, it is not you who has defeated me.'

Kepha sat down thoughtfully opposite him.

'Then why have you come?' he asked.

'To talk', said Simon. 'I need to talk. That is your gift to me.

And the things I want to say are things you should hear. That is my gift to you.'

Kepha stared into his wine. 'I don't think I am a proud man,' he said, 'but I cannot believe that you have anything to say to me which I need to hear.'

'I know', said Simon. 'That is precisely why you need to hear it.'

Kepha said nothing.

'We have both been wrong', said Simon. 'We have been wrong in exactly the same way, although, being very different men, we have taken different paths. It happens the path I have taken has shown me I was wrong; that is its nature. But the path you have chosen will never show you you are wrong: that is its nature. So it falls to me to tell you.'

'How kind', said Kepha.

'It will do no good, of course,' added Simon. 'That's in the nature of things as well.'

'Perhaps', suggested Kepha, 'you will tell me what you're talking about.'

'It's not so easy. There are so many places to start from. I could start with anything. Any two things, rather. The two of us here in this room, for instance. There are always two.'

'I know you believe that there are two Gods', said Kepha with a touch of impatience. 'Is that what you're getting at?'

'If you like. But I am also talking about day and night, man and woman, sweet and sour, right and wrong.'

'What?' said Kepha.

'I am talking about substance and shadow', said Simon. 'I am talking about land and sea, sound and silence, cold and heat. I am talking about life and death, salvation and damnation. I am talking about what is and what is not.'

'Oh, pairs of things', said Kepha. 'I follow you.'

'No you do not, because there are no pairs. All there is, in reality, is a twinnedness. Of that twinnedness, every pair of opposites we know is a reflection. Put a light in a room full of differently shaped metal objects, and the light will create on their surfaces different patterns; but when you look at those patterns what you are seeing is a series of distortions – distortions of one light. There is only one duality. Matter expresses it wherever matter comes into being: it cannot help itself. Our minds express it in every thought we produce: we cannot help ourselves. The root of the world grows forked.'

274

Kepha turned his wine cup slowly between his hands. 'High-flown talk', he said. 'I never did understand philosophy. I don't see that it matters.'

'The words "good" and "evil" mean nothing', said Simon. 'They are the words we use when the duality manifests to our minds in a particular way. We could as well use other words – "sweet" and "sour" or "cold" and "hot" – and be saying something as true. The play of light and shadow on a surface: that's all good and evil are. Now do you understand?'

Kepha was silent.

'I saw it long ago', mused Simon. 'I saw the light and the darkness. But I did not understand what it meant. I did not follow it to its conclusion. And now I must. Because of the intelligence of a whore, and the earnestness of a boy, and the madness of an emperor, and the riddles of your master, which you cannot solve.'

Kepha stared at him, and his face in the lamplight seemed to pale.

'To do me justice,' pursued Simon, 'I did understand a great deal. I understood that creation was evil, though I did not understand why. It is evil because creation is a separating, a differentiation; and therefore it brings out whatever it is in things that men call evil, which before was so thoroughly mixed with its opposite that it did not exist. And I understood that the God you worship was the enemy and must be fought against, but although I thought I knew why, I did not know. And I understood that the world was a trap, and that traps must be escaped from, but I did not understand that the escape from the trap is part of the trap. That part was hard.'

He was silent for a while, drawn into his thoughts. Kepha refilled his cup with a hand slightly unsteady. 'Why', he murmured, 'is the God I worship an enemy who must be fought?'

'Because', said Simon with a patient sigh, 'he proclaims himself to be the *only* God. It is the foundation of your faith, is it not? It is the thing on which he most insists. It is a lie, Kepha. Nothing is one. Everything is two. There is no statement which does not create its own denial. But your people have not understood that, and for generation after generation you have worshipped your God as One until he has grown greedy and proclaimed that there is no Other. And this delusion has created a monstrous imbalance in the world that can only be corrected by a worship of the Other.

That is what I set out to do. I thought I was attempting the salvation of mankind, but I was not. I was attempting the salvation of God.'

His words fell into a strange stillness. It was broken by the rattling of a cart down the street.

'Where', said Kepha at last, 'in all this blasphemy and madness, is the gift you bring me?'

'Do you really not see?' asked Simon. 'We have followed different paths, you and I, different and opposed, but we have done the same thing, made the same mistake. We have each believed that we are right and the other is wrong. The truth is that neither of us is right as long as we believe that we are exclusively right. Nothing is one. There is no statement that does not create its own denial, and of which the denial is not the necessary reflection.'

Kepha shut his eyes. He seemed to be struggling painfully with a thought. 'It seems to me', he said slowly, 'that you have just made a statement, and that if the statement is true, it is also untrue.'

Simon laughed without amusement. 'You understand me better than I thought.'

'What?'

'When a truth is spoken it becomes untrue', said Simon. 'Which is why certain things should not be said.'

Kepha went as pale as death. Simon looked at him curiously. However, as Kepha said nothing, he continued.

'What is wrong with your way, and has been wrong with mine, is the insistence on singleness. Any singleness will seek to find its shadow, its other half. And if it is thwarted' – Simon paused, conscious that here he reached the fantastic heart of his impossible discourse – 'if it is thwarted, it will do a strange and terrible thing. It will not simply create its shadow. It will become it.'

He did not know if Kepha had heard him. He was staring at Simon as one might at a man arisen from the grave.

'It has happened to me', said Simon. 'I tried to destroy law, and I found that the destruction of law had become a law, and that I was a lawmaker. I taught that men were gods and should worship nothing, and I found that I was worshipped as a god. I preached the pursuit of freedom, and I found a man who had pursued every kind of freedom to its end, and enslaved himself and a whole city to his nightmares. It will happen to you: you will find yourself in the very place you have spent half your life journeying away from. And you will not be able to bear it, because you believe that God is One.'

Kepha seemed to have recovered from whatever shock Simon's

words had given him. He sat slightly hunched, jaw jutting pugnaciously.

'Do you expect me to pay any attention to these ravings?'

'Then listen to a voice for which you have more respect', said Simon. '"The first last. The last first." "Seek to save your life and you will lose it." "I have come to give sight to the blind, and to blind those who can see."' He smiled at Kepha. 'Paradoxes. Impossible sayings. Can it be that I listened better than you did?'

'You are a clever man', snarled Kepha. He reached for the wine and poured himself another measure, then passed the jug ungraciously to Simon. 'As clever as the Devil your father.'

'I have no such pedigree, I assure you.'

'Like the Devil you twist, you pervert, you play tricks with the truth. Like the Devil you'll fall.'

'No doubt,' agreed Simon. 'The way up and the way down are the same.'

Kepha was not listening. 'Like the Devil you tempt. That's why you came here, isn't it? To tempt me? To tell me that whatever I did I could never manage to be right. That's what lies behind your clever phrases, isn't it? That's the emptiness they really contain, the abyss of madness they lead to. That there is no point in trying to do anything.'

'You are nearly there', said Simon, 'but not quite. The true abyss is one step beyond.'

Kepha stared at him.

'The true abyss', said Simon, 'is that there is no point in trying to do anything and yet we have to try. Our effort is required, although it means nothing and will come to nothing. It is required precisely *because* it will come to nothing. It will be negated, but also it will negate. It will hold the world in balance, and ensure that, for a little longer, nothing happens. For if we stopped acting, the world would end.'

'You are mad', said Kepha.

'In any case we have no choice', continued Simon, 'for if we stopped acting we would die.' He smiled. 'And thus, in another sense, the world would end.'

Kepha took a long pull at his wine. He appeared slightly relieved.

'I see that you did not come to tempt me', he said. 'No man alive could be tempted by such an argument. It leads nowhere but to utter despair.'

'Yes', said Simon.

'You surely can't believe it?'

Simon made no answer. He stood up and fastened his cloak. 'It's late', he said. 'We must both rest.'

'Simon, do you believe what you've been telling me?'

'What does it matter whether I believe it or not?' said Simon wearily. 'All that matters is that I see it, and that it is, at this moment, the opposite of what you see. And as you have taken the burden of your vision, and its impossibility, on yourself, so must I take the burden of this on myself. We don't matter, Kepha, you and I: we are simply used.'

He walked to the door, then turned. 'You need not reproach yourself for Joshua's death', he said. 'None of you had anything to do with it. Nor does that idiotic explanation you peddle. He had to die: it was inevitable.'

He went out, carrying into the dark streets the image of Kepha's white, staring face.

'D'you think he's forgotten us?' asked Marcus hopefully.

They had been waiting in the ante-room since midday. The sun was now casting long shadows across the terrace outside. In the time they had been there, a crowd of at least fifty petitioners, sycophants and exasperated government officials had come and gone – some admitted to the imperial presence, others dismissed without an audience, and quite a few drifting away of their own accord. There remained, apart from Simon, Kepha and Marcus, a landowner with an obscure grievance about his estates, a trader who was hoping to be granted a monopoly, and a fat man who kept telling everyone about his family tree.

'No', said Simon, 'he hasn't forgotten.'

Kepha said nothing. He had appeared sunk in thought for a long time; perhaps he was praying. Perhaps he had simply decided there was nothing to say. If so, thought Simon, he showed uncharacteristic discernment, because there was in fact nothing to say.

'I'm hungry', complained Marcus.

'It is one of the little ironies of life', observed Simon, 'that you should be in the company of two magicians and neither of them can conjure up anything for you to eat.'

'I am not a magician', said Kepha.

'I advise you not to say that to the emperor'.

'I shall say as little as possible to the emperor.'

'I hope you won't make me say anything he doesn't like', worried Marcus.

'If he does, pretend to be overtaken by a fit of coughing', suggested Simon kindly, 'and I'll substitute something suitable.'

Kepha opened his mouth and Simon waited for the blast of righteous scorn.

'What', asked Kepha, 'does "Saul" mean in Greek?'

'What?' said Simon.

A slave came through the doorway of the ante-room.

'What does "Saul" mean in Greek?'

'It means,' said Simon, 'someone who – '

'Simon the Jew!' shouted the slave.

Simon and Kepha stepped forward simultaneously.

'Waddles,' said Simon. Kepha appeared confused. The slave stared at both of them. Then he pointed to Marcus.

'Who is this?'

'My interpreter', said Kepha.

'What did he say?' asked the slave.

'His interpreter', interpreted Simon.

'This is most irregular', said the slave. 'Please come with me. The emperor will receive you in his private apartments.'

They crossed the floor, went through the adjoining room, and began to mount a wide staircase. Six guards lining the stairs fell into step behind them as they went up.

It was the room Simon had been in before: long and spacious, with a large, balconied window from which half the city could be seen.

The emperor was reclining on a couch, toying with something. 'Ah, there you are', he said, as they approached and greeted him. The guards clattered back to stand against the walls.

'What did you think of my poetry?' he enquired of Simon.

He was wearing a purple toga and long gold earrings, and was trying to pull the feathers out of a swallow.

'I think that when Caesar has mastered the hexameter he will write very passable epic verse', said Simon.

The pale eyes fastened on him. The emperor made a small noise like a cat sneezing. It was laughter.

'Very good', he said. 'I like that. Who is this fellow with you? Hasn't he got anything better to wear?'

'He is a religious teacher, Caesar, and believes that a man's apparel is not important. Consequently he has to be very careful what he wears.'

Nero did his cat's sneeze again. 'And what does he teach?'

'With your permission, Caesar, I shall ask him to speak for himself.'

Kepha, through a stammering Marcus, had managed three sentences when the emperor interrupted.

'I can't understand what he's talking about. It's boring. Show me some magic.'

'As Caesar commands.'

'What's going on?' whispered Kepha.

'He wants magic', whispered Marcus.

'I am not a magician', growled Kepha.

'*Shut up*', hissed Simon.

'Don't talk in that barbaric language in my presence', said the emperor. 'It irritates me.' He tossed the swallow into a corner. Later, when its fluttering became obtrusive, one of the guards threw it out of the window. 'Show me some magic', said the emperor to Kepha. 'It might encourage me to listen to you.'

Kepha, when this was translated to him, raised his eyes skyward and prayed. Simon pondered on the indulgence of a Deity who had presumably been listening to Kepha's prayers since dawn.

Kepha fumbled in his purse and brought out something. For a moment Simon thought it was a sardine. It was a scrap of bread. Kepha laid it carefully on a small bronze table, and spread his hands over it.

Something happened, Simon could not see what. Kepha moved his hands away, and on the bronze table lay twelve loaves of bread.

'Jupiter!' said the emperor and sat bolt upright on his couch. 'How extraordinary! Can he do that with money?'

This was translated to Kepha and he said he doubted it.

'What other powers do you have?' the emperor asked Kepha.

Kepha said he had no powers of his own: they came from his God.

'And what else can your god do?'

Kepha replied that He was all-powerful and could do anything.

'Really?' murmured Nero. He fixed Simon with an unfriendly eye. 'What can you do?'

'I can make Caesar laugh', said Simon.

He filled the room with monkeys. He kept them at a respectful distance from the imperial couch. They descended, chattering with glee, on the bronze table, snatched up the loaves, and began alternately cramming their mouths and pelting each other with bits of bread. After a few minutes there was not a crumb left. Caesar laughed.

Kepha muttered something.

The monkeys vanished.

'Very good', said the emperor. 'I liked that. You must do it for my next party. It always worries me terribly, having to think up things to entertain people.'

'Caesar flatters me', said Simon. He was staring at Kepha. Kepha gazed back impassively.

'Show me something else,' the emperor commanded Kepha.

Kepha asked permission to call forward one of the guards. The man had a fresh and nasty-looking cut on his cheek – souvenir, no doubt, of a barrack-room brawl. He stood awkwardly as Kepha laid his hand on the cut and held it there.

Kepha took his hand away. Save for a slight whitening of the flesh, the cheek was unmarked.

'I don't believe it!' said the emperor. He inspected the place where the cut had been. He turned to Kepha. 'Where did you obtain this power of healing?'

Kepha said that none of the things he did were his doing: they were done by his God.

'Oh, do accept some responsibility', snapped Simon.

'And what else', enquired the emperor of Simon, 'can *you* do?'

'Prevention is better than cure, Caesar', said Simon.

He asked permission to borrow the dagger of the soldier who had just been healed. He rolled up his left sleeve, offered the dagger to Nero, and asked him to drive it into the bared arm.

Nero stared at him, then tittered. He took the dagger.

'I shall do it, you know', he said.

'I know', said Simon.

Nero tried four times. The blade, each time driven down with a more vicious determination, each time glanced aside. After the fourth time the emperor flung it impatiently on the floor. Had he not been so impatient he might have noticed a streak of blood near the tip of it.

Simon rolled his sleeve down and looked at Kepha. Kepha returned his gaze evenly.

'I am not sure', said Caesar, 'whether that makes you a very good man to have around, or a very dangerous one.'

Simon bowed with an Oriental flourish. His arm was hurting. 'I am Caesar's loyal servant.'

'Of course. So are they all. Your rival' – he flicked his fingers at

Kepha – 'has perhaps more useful gifts, but you are decidedly more amusing.'

'He will tell you, Caesar, that he has no gifts at all. They come from his god.'

'Oh dear yes, his god.' He turned languidly back to Kepha. 'What sort of god is he, this deity of yours?'

Kepha, through Marcus, said that he was a God of love.

'Oh, a sort of male Aphrodite?' giggled the emperor.

No, said Kepha, it was not that sort of love. It was like the love of a father for his children.

'My father was a doddering old fool', said Nero. 'Show me some more magic.'

'With Caesar's permission', said Simon. There was no point in prolonging the comedy. He walked to the window. The gardens, the fountains and the tiled roofs of Rome lay below him. Above, the blue sky was fading.

'With Caesar's permission,' said Simon, 'I shall perform for his entertainment a feat which has never before been witnessed in Rome.'

'Is it amusing?'

'I think Caesar will find it very amusing.'

'Then you have my permission.'

Simon turned to look at Kepha. 'Do you understand?' he said.

Kepha was pale, but his eyes were expressionless.

Simon stepped through the window on to the balcony. He climbed on to the low balustrade and stood for a moment gazing at the sun. The day was drawing into evening. After evening would come night; and after night, day. He stared into the eternal sun.

He was not conscious of the moment when his feet lifted, or of the three figures first behind and then below him on the balcony, craning upward. He was not conscious of the shouting. He heard the silence. He felt the peace of the drifting air.

He was aware, in the instant when it began to happen, that he was falling. He fell with arms outstretched, motionless in his fall, as if transfixed to an invisible, plummeting cross. He saw, as he fell, the sunlight glance on a pool of water in the palace gardens and break into an infinity of tiny mirrors.

As the body struck the ground, Kepha ceased praying.

Beside him, the emperor laughed like a cat. 'Extraordinary. I shall never understand you people', he said.

*

A hundred and thirty years after its annexation, and fourteen years after the appointment of the procurator Felix, the province of Judaea broke into open revolt. Four years of bitter fighting ensued. When they ended, the holy city lay in rubble and the Temple had been razed to the ground.

The spirit of the people was not crushed. Unrest was still continuing sixty years later when an emperor, hoping thereby to destroy a faith which had caused so much trouble, prohibited circumcision. The response was a second rebellion. It was bloodily suppressed, and followed by exemplary punishment. The religious capital was rebuilt as a pagan city and its own people were denied entry to it. A heathen shrine rose on the site of the Temple. The city, and the province itself, were renamed. The past ceased to exist.

The sect which believed that the end of the world was at hand was in a sense correct. It had simply attached the wrong value to the term 'world'. Thus what happened was the reverse of its expectation. The destruction was confined to the matrix in which the sect was rooted.

The sect had to transplant or die. It did both. The successful transplant bore – many said – no relation to the native growth: it was a devilish impersonation. The voices of these critics soon faded into oblivion. Down the centuries, oblivion overtook most of the enemies of the sect. Occasionally the process had to be helped. There were many methods, of which a tampering with history was the mildest and in the long run the most effective.

The sect justified its defensive measures by the importance of the message it taught. To maintain that message intact, it must survive. When critics enquired into the truth of the message, it pointed to its survival as proof of the veracity of its teaching. The argument was pleasingly economical. If the entire structure rested, as it eventually did, on a mythologising of history, the sect might have remarked with perfect truth that it was quite impossible to know what had really happened and that any version of history is a myth in any case.

It never did say that, for some reason.